The Place We Met

ISABELLE BROOM

PENGUIN BOOKS

PENGUIN BOOKS

UK | USA | Canada | Ireland | Australia
India | New Zealand | South Africa

Penguin Books is part of the Penguin Random House group of companies
whose addresses can be found at global.penguinrandomhouse.com.

First published 2017

001

Copyright © Isabelle Broom, 2017

The moral right of the author has been asserted

Set in 12.5/14.75 pt Garamond MT Std
Typeset by Jouve (UK), Milton Keynes
Printed in Great Britain by Clays Ltd, St Ives plc

A CIP catalogue record for this book is available from the British Library

ISBN: 978–0–718–18668–5

www.greenpenguin.co.uk

MIX
Paper from
responsible sources
FSC® C018179

Penguin Random House is committed to a
sustainable future for our business, our readers
and our planet. This book is made from Forest
Stewardship Council® certified paper.

PENGUIN BOOKS

The Place We Met

Isabelle Broom was born in Cambridge nine days before the 1980s began and studied Media Arts at the University of West London before starting a career first in local newspapers and then as a junior sub-editor at *heat* magazine. She travelled through Europe during her gap year and went to live on the Greek island of Zakynthos for an unforgettable and life-shaping six months after completing her degree. Since then, she has travelled to Canada, Sri Lanka, Sicily, New York, LA, the Canary Islands, Spain and lots more of Greece, but her wanderlust was reined in when she met Max, a fluffy little Bolognese puppy desperate for a home. When she's not writing novels set in far-flung locations, Isabelle spends her time being the Book Reviews Editor at *heat* magazine and walking her beloved dog round the parks of north London.

You can follow her on Twitter @Isabelle_Broom or find her on Facebook under Isabelle Broom Author.

By the same author

My Map of You
A Year and a Day
Then. Now. Always.

For Poppy and Zachary, forever the brightest stars.

I

Taggie

Winter is on its way.

I can feel it creeping through the folds of my scarf, and when I breathe in, the air pooling into my lungs is sharp and cool, bringing with it a clarity and freshness. I feel more awake, more alert, and I allow myself to inhale deeply. There is a faint scent of pine, and something else that I can't distinguish. Perhaps it is coming from the plants that I know are there, but cannot see, behind the high stone walls, or perhaps it is the lake that I can smell, which is just now coming into view below me.

It is silent, as it always is at this early hour, and I wonder if the birds have even woken yet. When I come down here in the afternoons, they're always busy rustling away in the surrounding trees, doing whatever vital job it is that they always seem to be in the midst of completing. It would be nice to be a bird, I think fleetingly. To have the freedom to take off whenever you desired, and soar through the endless blue sky above the water as if you were weightless. Then again, I remind myself, the birds aren't the only things that have escaped.

The gradual downward slope of the stony path ends abruptly in front of me, and ahead sits a narrow strip of beach. Beyond that, the lake sits calm as glass, with barely a ripple interrupting its deep blue canvas. I feel better already.

I stand for a while gazing out towards the horizon, and then my eyes trail west, to where the distant mountain-tops seem to shimmer in the morning light, and I take another breath. Yes, winter is definitely on its way. Soon I will wake to find blankets of frost thrown over the ground, and red berries will burst out amongst the clumps of holly that decorate the outer walls of the hotel. It will be cold and stark, but the sun will still shine. Even when the snow comes, it will be baked into a glistening meringue, and the clouds will be permitted only for a short time each day – perhaps not at all. Such is the desire of good old Mother Nature here in Lake Como, and I would not want it any other way. The beauty here feels like a tonic, the relentless sun like a beaming clown, chasing away sad thoughts, and the rich colours of the contrasting land-scape a palette that soothes and calms me.

And this is the place where it all comes together. This beach, this view, this place. My place.

I bring my hands up to rub some warmth into my upper arms, and lift my shoulders to keep the chill from my throat. My scarf is a helpful barrier, but the thin cotton material is no real match for the cold, and I pull it tighter in a fruitless attempt to cover up more skin. Turning left, I make my way along the narrow corridor of shingle, my hand on the high wall to steady myself, and follow it along until I reach the corner. There's a wide gap where the lake floods in through an underground passage, and then a wider stretch of beach beyond. An abandoned rowing boat sits idle on the shore, and in that moment, I have a sudden urge to reach it, to run my hand across its coarse, rotting surface and watch the paint disintegrate beneath my fingers – but I hesitate. I will have to jump, and from this position on the corner there is no room for a run-up. And what if I make it across, but then have no way back? It's too cold to paddle back through the water, and anyway, my skinny jeans are far too tight to roll up.

'Don't be such a wimp,' I say aloud, scolding myself as I so often used to as a child. The young Taggie would not have deliberated; she would have leapt straight over and already be at the helm of that boat, on course for an imaginary adventure. I smile as I conjure her up in my mind, that fierce and fearless version of me. How I wish I still had her strength.

Mind made up, I take a deep breath and crouch down on my haunches, the plan being to spring up and over the channel in one graceful leap. I pause, my hands on the wet stone walkway, then fling myself up with as much energy as I can muster, letting out a shriek as I go. There's a split second of exhilarating movement, followed by a splash, and then awful, total coldness.

'Wahhhhhh!' I yell, swallowing a good portion of the lake in the process and spluttering in disgust. I have somehow managed to land face down in the water, and my rapidly soaking clothes are pinning me down. I try to shuffle myself up, but my knee connects with the jagged edge of a stone and my leg buckles again beneath me. Now I'm not just angry, but scared, too, and the realisation causes me to thrash about wildly. I'm going to drown in ten centimetres of water, I think hopelessly, and it will be days until I'm found, washed up on the shore in Como, pecked apart by swans.

I'm just about to try and roll over on to my back when I hear a shout, and a few seconds later strong hands reach down under my arms and I'm hauled out of the water, dripping and coughing and shuddering with cold. Taking an instinctive step away from my rescuer, I bang the back of my head against the wall and swear in earnest, my chattering teeth making the words sound ridiculous.

The man, who I realise guiltily is now almost as wet as me, starts laughing gently.

'It's not funny!' I snarl, rubbing the sore spot as I look at him properly for the first time. He's very obviously Italian, with jet-black hair and the remnants of a summer tan, and his eyes are the most extraordinary shade of bright green. He's wearing a red jumper that's been turned part-maroon by the stain of my wet body, and the sleeves are rolled up to reveal thick, muscular forearms.

'Are you OK?' he asks, peering at me in amusement. His English is heavily accented, but he speaks it with an ease that makes me suspect he's fluent.

'I think so,' I reply, my cheeks burning with mortification. 'Thank you for helping me.'

He shrugs. 'Of course.'

I want to ask him what he's doing down here, on my special, secret beach, so early in the morning, but I don't. I simply stand there mutely, wringing out my dripping hair and peeling off my saturated scarf with a grimace.

'You're all wet,' I point out needlessly, and he looks down at himself, again with a wry smile.

'It will dry.'

'Aren't you cold?' I want to know, but he shakes his head.

4

'Not really. I don't really feel the cold too much.'

'What are you, a robot?' I joke weakly, but he frowns in confusion.

'Just a man.'

He's certainly that, I can't help but agree. In fact, this man is the most manly-looking man that I've encountered in a long time. Which makes the whole plucking-me-out-of-the-lake thing all the more humiliating. Why couldn't an old fisherman have found me?

'You are shivering,' he tells me, stepping forwards. 'Can I help to warm you up?'

'No!' I practically yell, stumbling away from his outstretched arms in horror. He's right, I am shaking with cold, but there's no way I'm going to let him hug me. Who the hell does he think he is?

The man folds his arms as he considers my rebuff, his eyes narrowed and his mouth set in a line.

'I do not bite,' he informs me lightly, but his smirk rankles. I can tell exactly what he's thinking – he's looking at me, so small next to him and so apparently helpless, and he's assumed that I'm just another pathetic female that needs looking after. He's doing what so many men do when they meet me – he's making a presumption based on my size and on my sex, and there is literally nothing that annoys me more. OK, so I fell into the lake, but that doesn't mean I'm weak; it just means I'm unlucky.

'I'm going home,' I inform him, giving him as challenging a look as it's possible to do when you're a sodden mess, and turning my back on him before he has a chance to reply. My boots, which have filled with water, make an embarrassing squelching sound as I stomp away, but I hold my head up high regardless. By the time I reach the beach and the opening that leads to the path, my hot head has cooled, and a twinge of guilt makes me glance back the way I came.

He's still standing there, his hands now in the pockets of his jeans and his head on one side. What I should do is mouth a silent apology, or flash him a small smile, hoping it will convey that I'm sorry for overreacting, and that I'm genuinely grateful to him for saving me, but I don't. The humiliation still feels too acute, and I've lost too much face already – so instead I stick my chin defiantly up in the air, and stomp away out of view.

2

Lucy

I was nine years old the first time someone cheated on me.

His name was Johnny, and he had curly brown hair and permanently pink cheeks. We had been officially boyfriend and girlfriend for two whole weeks, which was a record at our primary school, and I had written his name on the back of my hand in purple felt-tip pen and drawn a heart around it. I was so proud to have been singled out by Johnny, because he was the most popular boy in our year – if not the whole school – and so he could have taken his pick of the girls. But no, he'd chosen me, Lucy Dunmore, with the train-track braces and scuffed knees. The girl who wore her older sister's tatty hand-me-downs and still sucked her thumb in her sleep; the quiet one in class who would never raise her hand even if she knew the answer; the nondescript, non-beautiful and non-exciting Lucy. I was as surprised as everyone else.

Every lunchtime, I would make my way to the edge of the fenced-in pitch where all the boys played football, and watch my beloved tearing up and down the grass after the ball. Occasionally he would glance my way and smile, or blow me a sly kiss behind one of his hands, and I would swell with such pleasure that even my fingertips would tingle.

On this day, however, he was nowhere to be seen.

'I saw him with Chloe and her lot,' one of Johnny's minions informed me, abandoning his position between the goalposts and lacing his dirty fingers through the gaps in the mesh fence.

'Oh. Thanks.'

'They said they were going to play kiss chase,' he retorted, failing to keep the glee from leaking into his voice like spilt milk. 'I heard that Chloe always picks a three.'

The version of kiss chase we all played was based on a simple numbered system: one was a cuddle, two a kiss on the cheek, and three, the most daring of all, a kiss on the lips. The fact that Chloe always picked a 'three' if she was caught by the boys was not news to me, but Johnny's friend's words still made my throat tighten up and my tummy twist into knots.

I feigned nonchalance, of course, but as soon as I was a safe distance away from the pitch, I started to panic. If Johnny was playing kiss chase, then it was up to me to find him.

He wasn't up in the makeshift fort or on the swings. There was no sign of him in the cobweb-ridden alley behind the science block or over near the infants' sandpit. I ran around the playground twice, my legs burning and my breath coming faster and harder, but still, nothing. The tears were threatening and other children were starting to look at me with ill-disguised bemusement. I was about to scale the big slide for a better look when I saw him.

And he wasn't alone.

They were a fair distance away from me, but I could still make out the beam of pride on Chloe's face as she followed my boyfriend across the playground. He was looking ahead, rather than at her, but one of his hands was stretched behind him, his fingers entwined with hers.

I took a breath, and followed them.

I knew where Johnny was taking her, because it was the same place he'd led me a fortnight ago, on that magical day when he'd whispered in my ear that he liked me, that he thought it was cool how clever I was, how well I could spell, how I was the only person in the class who could hold Snuffles the guinea pig without him wriggling.

He was taking Chloe to the kissing corner.

I went as far as the cloakroom doors before I stopped and leant against the glass, watching with a mixture of shock and inexplicable fascination as Chloe and Johnny went straight for a three, both shutting their eyes as they rubbed their faces together. She was taller than him and had to bend down a bit, and if it had been anybody else, I would have laughed. But it wasn't – it was my Johnny, my boyfriend – and so instead I turned away and went inside. I washed his name off my hand and glared at myself in the toilet mirror, willing my bottom lip to stop trembling. Nine-year-olds aren't cry-babies.

In that moment, it was myself I hated, not him. Not even Chloe.

I went back into the cloakroom and sat by my peg, waiting for the bell to ring and signal the end of lunch break. There was a faded sticker of Kermit the Frog on the wooden bench seat, and I picked at it absent-mindedly, chewing the inside of my cheeks until I could taste blood.

I never told anyone what I'd seen, or how it upset me. But I never forgot it, either.

'Lucy, are you in there? The patient in cubicle three is back from X-ray.'

'I'll be right there.'

There goes my tea break, I think, tipping the remainder of my brew down the sink and giving the mug a cursory rinse.

Letting the staffroom door swing shut behind me, I almost collide with Doctor Dhillon, who is also on his way to cubicle three.

'Nurse Dunmore.' He nods a greeting.

'Vikram.' I smile back.

'All set for a busy night?' he enquires politely, and I roll my eyes good-naturedly. It's the first Friday in December – AKA the night where all the office Christmas parties begin – and as such the Accident and Emergency department here at All Saints Hospital in North London is undoubtedly going to fill up with revellers as soon as the pubs start to call last orders. As Vikram and I are doing a late shift, we've only been here for a few hours, and both of us know that we have a very long night ahead of us.

'So, what's the poor little duck broken?' I ask as we turn a corner, my rubber-soled shoes squeaking on the laminate floor.

'Ulnar fracture,' the doctor replies, raising a sympathetic eyebrow when I instinctively glance up at him in dismay. 'It's a clean break, though, and she won't need an op.'

'I've got my brave-girl stickers at the ready,' I tell him, tapping my pocket, and the two of us exchange a knowing grin before I reach up and pull aside the curtain.

The little girl in the cubicle is pink-cheeked and subdued, while the woman beside her looks positively terrified. It's a look I'm used to, and as always, I'm relieved that Doctor Dhillon is bringing relatively good news with him.

'Is her arm broken, Doctor?' the mother cries, grabbing Vikram's hands before he's even had time to speak. They're fabulous hands, the colour of burnt caramel with long, slim fingers, and his nails are short, clean and buffed.

'Take a seat, Mrs Davis,' Vikram soothes, easing her slowly into the chair next to the bed. 'It's a nice, neat break, and she'll need a cast, but once that's done she'll bounce back in no time.'

'Am I going to get a new arm?' the little girl asks now, and the three of us turn to her. She looks so tiny and helpless sitting up on the bed, with her cuddly toy dog clutched in her good hand and tear marks streaking through the dirt on her cheeks.

'You don't need one,' Vikram says kindly. 'This one will mend just fine, you'll see.'

The girl doesn't look convinced. I know from her notes that she's only just turned four, but she seems older. There's a knowing look behind those eyes of hers that I'm not sure I had at the same age, and she gazes at me without trepidation.

'My Uncle Max lost his leg in the desert and his doctor gave him a new one,' she informs us. 'He has to plug it in at bedtime, like a phone.'

The woman sighs and pats her daughter's leg.

'She's talking about my husband's brother,' she explains. 'He lost a leg in Afghanistan.'

'I see.' Vikram widens his eyes and looks back towards

the bed. 'It sounds like your Uncle Max is a very brave man indeed.'

I expect the girl to agree, but she shakes her head.

'No. He's scared of spiders. Even I'm not scared of them.'

'You're not?' I exclaim. 'I think they're the scariest thing in the world!'

'Not scarier than sharks!' she cries, adorably indignant. 'And strangers.'

'Yes, Poppy. Strangers are very dangerous and very scary,' her mum says quickly, and Vikram and I nod in obedient agreement. I decide that I like Poppy very much indeed, and while the doctor takes Mrs Davis to one side to explain the course of treatment, I approach the bed and sit down on its edge.

'It sounds to me like you're the bravest one in your family,' I tell her conspiratorially, and she smiles at me for the first time.

'Here at All Saints Hospital, we have special stickers for our bravest patients – would you like to see them?'

Poppy nods her head up and down slowly, her eyes widening as I reach into my pocket and pull out my stash. There's a sheet of red hearts, one of gold stars and another of little cartoon dogs, each with a separate ailment.

'Can I have two?' she asks boldly, peering down at them.

'You can have three!' I whisper back, and again I'm rewarded with a smile. 'Why don't you look after these for me?' I add, giving her the whole sheet of dog stickers. 'Then you can use them to decorate the special cast that I'm going to put on your arm. How does that sound?'

'Good,' she says quietly, her attention now diverted by the different designs. One of the little black-and-white dogs has got a broken arm, just like her, and I point to it with a smile.

'I think this one is a winner.'

Working in A&E can be tough, but it's also the most rewarding role in the world – and the only one I can ever imagine doing. It's my job to care, to provide sympathy, to patch people up and send them on their way with a smile. I spend my days mopping up blood, wiping away vomit, holding hands, making sweet tea and, just occasionally, getting smiles from gorgeous little angels like Poppy – it's moments like this that make the sadder ones worthwhile.

I'm just carefully arranging a blanket over Poppy's legs for her when I feel the vibration of my phone against my leg. I'm not supposed to have my mobile with me during work hours, so I ignore it, but I notice the flicker of bemusement pass across Vikram's face as he hears it, too.

'Take care of yourself now, Poppy,' he says. 'No more climbing trees until you're all better.'

'I promise,' she says sweetly, going back to examining her stickers as he vanishes through the curtain.

'He seems very nice,' Mrs Davis says, rather wistfully, sitting back in her seat and visibly relaxing for the first time since she arrived.

'Oh, he is,' I reply. 'Doctor Dhillon is one of the good guys.'

'Are you and he . . .' she begins, but stops as I shake my head.

'Oh gosh, no.'

'Sorry,' she grins.

'Mummy is very nosy,' Poppy explains, not even bothering to look up, and we both chuckle.

'The truth is,' I say, smiling knowingly at Mrs Davis as I reach the curtain, 'if I didn't already have a lovely boyfriend, then Doctor Dhillon would be at the top of my list.'

It's another two hours until I have time to check my phone, but when I do I find that the text message is from Pete, as I'd hoped it would be.

> Hope you're having a good shift – can't wait to see you tomorrow.

I lean back against the wall of the ladies' toilet where I came to seek refuge and smile indulgently at myself in the mirror.

I knew there was something about Peter Samuels that made him different. It's been five months now since we met, and every time we see each other, I feel closer to him. My stomach still flutters with nerves when I'm on my way to meet him, but I feel as if he's someone that I can really trust, which means everything to me. After what's happened to me in the past, sometimes I find it hard to have faith in people – in men that I'm dating, especially – but Pete is the real deal.

Perhaps it's time to take our fledgling relationship up a notch, I think, tapping out an enthusiastic reply and adding my usual three kisses at the end. What I would like to do is spend more time with him, but real, quality time, not just a few hours here and there. A holiday is what we need – our first trip away as a couple. And I know just the place we should go.

3

Taggie

Oh, great. I'm crying in the toilet again.

Slamming the door of the cubicle behind me and flipping down the seat of the toilet, I bend my knees and stuff my fist into my mouth, managing to muffle the sound of my stupid sobs.

This can't keep happening. I have a job to do. You can't very well coordinate a big, important event if you keep having to run off and cry in corners – and today is the biggest event I've ever done at the Casa Alta Hotel. In fact, it's the biggest one I've ever done anywhere; my chance to prove to myself and everyone else that I can do the job I know I was born to do. But now, thanks to these unhinged emotions of mine, I'm at risk of messing all that up.

Taking a deep breath, I remove my fist from my mouth and reach for some tissue to wipe away my tears. In the beginning, I didn't cry at all. I was simply numb – dumbstruck, even – but lately I'm leaking so many irrational bouts of tears that anyone would think I was a water balloon that had been poked with a needle.

No, this will not do. Taggie Torres is no weakling. The one thing I have never been in my entire life is a wimp, and there's no way I'm letting these weird reactions wear me down. I will beat this; I must.

The sound of the main door opening snaps me out of my melancholy train of thought, and I hold my breath as someone enters the stall next to me and hurriedly locks the door. Looking down, I see a swathe of white material under the partition wall and frown. If my calculations are correct – and I know that they are, because I'm very good at this job when I'm not abandoning it to cry covertly in toilets – then the only bride in this hotel should at this very minute be making her giddy way down the makeshift aisle I had set up in the ballroom to join her beloved.

I pause, unsure of what to do next, and then I hear the unmistakable sound of crying.

'Rachel,' I murmur a few seconds later, leaving my own sanctuary and tapping gently on the wooden door of hers. 'It's Taggie. Is everything OK?'

'No!' comes the tearful reply.

Jittery brides are not that unusual, but I've never had to deal with one before. I only spoke to this one fifteen minutes ago and she was glowing with expectant joy like a lava lamp in a dark room, so heaven knows what could have happened in the interim to send her scuttling in here.

'Is it just nerves?' I ask kindly. 'An upset stomach?'

'No.'

I hesitate, unsure of what to say next.

'Can I fetch anyone for you?'

'No! I mean, please don't. I just . . . I need a few minutes, that's all.'

More sobs.

What I should be doing is telling her that everything will be fine. That the man waiting for her in the dark-blue suit is clearly crazy about her and that they'll be sure to live happily ever after. The words are there, I can almost hear them, but I can't quite bring myself to spit them out.

'You know, you don't have to do anything you don't want to,' I say instead, and I hear a snuffle of interest.

'Seriously. There's a back exit from the hotel that leads straight down to a jetty. I could have you in a boat and on the other side of Lake Como before you can say, "I do".'

I'm rewarded with a small grunt, and I'm just about to try another coaxing method when the main door bangs open yet again and a tall blonde girl appears. The maid of honour.

We exchange a look that tells her all she needs to know, and I quickly stand to one side to let her take over.

'Rach, it's me, Hannah.'

The sobbing begins again.

The blonde turns her eyes to me and rolls them theatrically.

'Whatever is the matter?' she asks her friend.

'I just ... I think. I don't know. This feels wrong,' comes the stuttered reply.

'Please let me in,' soothes the maid of honour, but the door remains stubbornly closed.

'I told her there's an escape route,' I put in, and the blonde girl looks at me with new-found respect. 'You wouldn't have to worry about a thing, either of you. I can deal with all the guests.'

'I wish my dad was here,' mutters the bride, and the crying grows louder.

The blonde leans her head against the door and closes her eyes, bringing one hand up and resting it flat against the wood.

'I wish he was, too,' she says. 'But I'm afraid you're stuck with me.'

'You can't walk me down the aisle, though,' wails the bride.

'Wanna bet?' retorts Hannah, and there's a cough of laughter. We both take a step backwards as the lock clicks open and Rachel emerges. Her eyes are a bit pink and a few tendrils of dark-red hair have attached themselves to her cheeks, but other than that she looks fine. Radiant, in fact. Wedding make-up is an incredible thing.

The two girls embrace and I turn away towards the mirror, studying my own reflection for any traces of my earlier upset. Unlike the bride, I don't have a barrier of foundation three inches thick to save me, but thankfully my eyes look bright behind my thick lashes, my cheeks their usual smooth, light brown, my thick, dark hair pulled neatly up where it won't get in my way. I look like me on the outside. It's the inside that's the problem.

'Do you think I'm making a mistake?' the bride is asking her tall friend now. 'Marrying Paul?'

'What?' The maid of honour is clearly amused. 'Listen here, woman – I haven't spent the best part of two years making friends with your husband-to-be just to have you abandon him at the altar.'

'Do you think he loves me, though? I mean, really loves me?'

Hannah takes a moment to consider this, frowning at her friend in mock concern before poking her in the ribs with a finger.

'Of course he bloody does. He loves you more than I love churros, which is *really* saying something. Now, can we please go and get you married already?'

The bride nods, and I release a deep breath that I didn't even realise I was holding in.

'Thank you,' mouths Hannah over her shoulder as they turn to go, and I smile in return, even though I wasn't much help at all. The only solution I came up with was run, which is just bloody typical of me.

This won't do, I realise, as I make my way out to join the wedding guests. I need to get over this and leave the past where it should be: buried in a very deep hole somewhere remote. What's done is done, isn't that the saying? There can be no going back, so I have no choice but to move forwards.

If it's so simple, though, I wonder, watching from the back of the ballroom-cum-chapel as the bride is finally delivered by her best friend into the waiting arms of her husband-to-be, then why is it so bloody difficult?

It's another nine hours before I sit down again, and when I do, I make the very wise decision to do it on a stool in front of the bar.

'Long day?'

I smile wearily at my friend Shelley and kick off my high heels, bringing each stockinged foot up to rub in turn.

'You could say that.'

'I don't know how you walk around all day in those,' she remarks, and we both look down to where my discarded shoes are lying on the polished wooden floor.

'I have to,' I shrug. 'Not much choice when you're five foot nothing.'

'You're a better woman than me,' she jokes, lifting her

own foot into the air so I can see the black trainers she always wears.

I've only known Shelley since I began working at Casa Alta five months ago, but she's already become my closest companion out here. I love the Italians, I genuinely do, but there's something very comforting about having another English person on the premises. Someone who understands all those quintessentially British cultural references and appreciates sarcasm as humour. Like me, Shelley has been coming over to Lake Como regularly since she was a child, and like me, she's picked up enough of the local language to blag herself a job in one of the hotels. Unlike me, however, she has the freedom that comes with a part-time bar job, while my position as the hotel's resident tour guide is a little more time-consuming. Still, I'm not complaining. I'm lucky to have this job, and I know it. Being a tour guide here is a step closer to my dream role of events manager, and I don't intend to waste any opportunity to illustrate just how great I'd be if my boss here at the hotel did eventually choose to promote me.

The Casa Alta is situated on the west bank of the lake, halfway between the main town of Como at the bottom, and the large alpine village of Cernobbio, which is five kilometres to the north. Casa Alta translates literally as High House, which is appropriate in the case of this hotel, because it's atop a very big hill. Unashamedly grandiose and reeking of history, the imposing yellow villa stands proudly up on its hilltop perch like an overstuffed canary, surrounded by lush gardens full of pine trees, jacarandas, ornate water fountains, statues and flower beds that are currently overflowing with white winter roses. Follow the grounds far enough down the hill, and you'll discover a narrow stone bridge that leads right over the main road and along to the shore of the lake itself.

As well as taking in paying guests, the Casa Alta is also open year-round to the public, who are free to roam the gardens for a small donation, which they leave in a wooden box down by the main gate. I can still remember coming here as a child and moaning to my parents about how bored I was, which seems so ridiculous to me now. These days, I could spend hours just wandering through the rooms and gardens of this place, watching the land-scape change with the seasons and staring through the antique windows at the sunlight sparkling on the surface of the lake far below. It calms me to be here. I feel soothed and safe – cut off from the world but able to dip a toe back into it at will. Once I worked out that I had no choice but to leave England for a while, there was only ever one place on my list, and landing this job just a week after I arrived felt like fate.

'Are any of the wedding guests fit?' Shelley asks me now, easing the cork back into the top of a bottle of Barolo and pushing the full glass of red wine towards me.

'Thanks.' I take a sip. 'Some of them aren't too bad. But I wasn't looking that hard, to be honest. I was too busy keeping an eye on the bride in case she made another run for it.'

Shelley smiles. I told her all about the bathroom inci-dent earlier.

'There's a tall guy with glasses who's cute,' she tells me, leaning over the bar so she can see through the open door into the adjacent room, where the reception is still in full and exuberant swing. 'But I think he's got a girlfriend.'

'Right,' I say, wishing I had it in me to contribute something more fun to the conversation. The truth is, I'm absolutely exhausted, but I won't let myself slope off upstairs to bed until the last guest has tucked themselves in, and this lot aren't showing any signs of slowing down. Because it's December now and many of the hotels in the Como area have closed for the winter, my boss, Sal, is far more relaxed about the noise than he usually would be. The wedding party are pretty much the only guests here, save for a few regulars who visit the lake at this time every year, and Sal wants to encourage them to spend as much money as possible at the bar.

Today's nuptials mark the last big-scale event of the year, which has happily fallen on the very same weekend that Sal's occasional wedding planner chose to go to Paris with her boyfriend, meaning that I, his rather more lowly tour guide, got to take her place. What the Casa Alta really needs is someone to do the job of a proper events manager full-time, but I have yet to convince Sal to hire someone. And by someone, I obviously mean me.

Doing the tours is a lot of fun, though, and despite the fact that it's much quieter in the winter, I still have enough small things happening over the next month or so to keep me occupied – and occupied is exactly what I need to be. Distraction has turned out to be my best friend these past few months. Honestly, without it I dread to think where I would have ended up.

'Are you all right?' Shelley is peering at me. 'You've been staring at that glass of wine for about five solid minutes.'

'Fine.' I shake my head and force a smile. 'Just deeply in awe of my Barolo.'

'It *is* the best wine ever,' she concedes, putting her blonde head on one side. Shelley insists on wearing her long hair in two plaits while she's working, and on anyone else over the age of seven, it would look ridiculous. Luckily for Shelley she has an adorably round little cherub's face, and so the pigtails merely add to her overall appeal. The guy with glasses that she's spotted must indeed have a girlfriend, because if he didn't, I'd put good money on the probability that he'd be sitting where I am right now, trying to chat my friend up.

'Talking of delicious Italians,' Shelley says now, twirling the end of one of her plaits around her finger, 'I met this bloke in town the other day that I think would be perfect for you.'

'Doubt it,' I snort, pulling a face.

'He's tall, dark, handsome,' she begins, but I interrupt.

'Wait – did you say tall?'

She nods.

'Well, then, he can't be Italian.'

It's a running joke between the two of us that Italian men are, for the most part, rather lacking in the height department. It's totally unfair, of course, because as we both know, there are probably plenty of lanky locals mooching around Lake Como – it's just that every time the two of us venture out on a rare night off, all we seem to encounter are the small ones. I can't complain, being the minuscule little imp that I am, but poor Shelley is a much more average five foot five or so, and she only fancies men who are six foot or over.

'He's very exotic-looking,' she continues, her expression going all dreamy. 'And the arms. Oh, the arms . . .'

'Pervert!' I quip, swerving backwards to avoid her indignant swipe.

'Will you come with me to the restaurant he works at next week?' she pleads.

She knows full well that I can never say no to her.

'OK,' I agree. 'But only if you promise not to do anything embarrassing, like attempt to set us up.'

'As if I would,' she replies, but her tone is playful.

'I mean it,' I scold, trying my best to sound firm. 'I'm not looking for a man – not now, and not ever.'

'You say that now,' she retorts, heading over to where the glass washer has just finished a cycle and is beeping incessantly. 'But just you wait till you see him.'

4

Lucy

'Lake Como?'

Pete stares down at the piece of paper in his hands and then back up at me.

'Please say you've never been!' I plead, crossing my fingers behind my back.

'No, I haven't. But this is too much, Lulu – I can't let you pay for a whole holiday.'

'Why not?' I say, reaching for his hands, unable to stop myself from touching him, even for a minute. 'It's a gift to myself as much as you. I used to love it there as a child, and I've always promised myself that I'd go back one day. And who better to go with than you, my most favourite person in the whole world?'

'Most favourite person?' he queries, dimpling.

'Yes,' I concur, kissing his upturned mouth. 'But don't let on to Julia that I said that – she'd never let me hear the end of it.'

'Don't worry,' Pete mutters. 'Your big sister scares the crap out of me.'

'Me too,' I laugh, and he gets to his feet and pulls me against him for another kiss, thanking me over and over again for booking such an amazing trip.

We're standing in the small kitchen of my rented flat in

Finsbury Park, which I share with two other nurses from the hospital. It makes sense for us all to live together, given the erratic hours that we keep, but this evening I'm pleased that neither one of them is at home. Stella, the youngest of the two, is probably out on yet another date. Despite encountering a seemingly never-ending supply of flaky men – so many that one of her friends jokingly wrapped her up a bottle of anti-dandruff shampoo as part of her birthday present a month ago – she continues in her tireless quest to find Mr Right. Luckily for me, I didn't have to go out and search for Pete – he walked right into my life as if placed there by fate.

'This yours?' Pete asks, holding up a part-finished wedge of Stilton. He has this habit of rummaging through the fridge whenever he comes over, and I like it because it means he feels at home here, which in turn must mean that he feels relaxed with me – and relaxed equals happy. I've only been to his place in Finchley twice since we started dating, because he's been in the process of redecorating it for months. Aside from a large double bed, one wardrobe, a beaten-up leather sofa and a few bottles of men's shower gel in the bathroom, everything else is packed away or under a dust sheet.

'Help yourself,' I trill, making a mental note to buy some more from the deli down the road before Gareth, my other flatmate and owner of said smelly delicacy, notices that it's gone.

'It's a good thing you're a cheese fan,' I add, passing him the crackers and a knife from the drawer. 'There'll be plenty of the stuff at Lake Como.'

Pete pauses with the Stilton-laden cracker halfway to

his mouth. He came here straight from his weekly rugby game with the lads, as he refers to them, and his curly ginger hair is still wet from the changing room shower. I've always loved his colouring, the way his pale skin looks almost luminous and his bright blue eyes seem to glow. He's also reassuringly tall and bulky, with strong, muscular thighs and stocky arms. It's nice to be with a man who doesn't make me feel as if my size-fourteen frame is something to be ashamed of. When Pete pulls me down on to his lap, I can relax all my weight against him rather than try to prop myself up awkwardly with one foot. He makes me feel delicate and feminine, which is something I never thought I'd experience, and slowly but surely, I'm even starting to lose my inhibitions and be confident with my clothes off. I'm not quite there yet, but with every encounter that we share, I feel a layer of my self-hate peel away like skin from an onion.

'You're going to have to let me pay half for this trip, at least, Lucy,' he says now, eyeing me over the cracker. 'What will the lads say if they find out I let my girlfriend shell out for my holiday?'

He's never referred to me as his girlfriend before, and I'm forced to quell an excitable squeal.

'I won't tell them if you don't,' I say coyly, wondering if now is a good time to bring up the subject of finally meeting these hallowed 'lads'. As far as I can tell from Pete's casual mentions and the digging I've done on Facebook, there are four of them in the main gang, which includes Sean, the only one I have actually met. In fact, I have him in part to thank for bringing the two of us together.

Pete laughs away my comment and finishes his cracker,

chewing thoughtfully as he raises the knife to attack the lump of smelly cheese for the second time.

'I'd really prefer it if you let me pay my way, Lulu,' he says, looking down at his plate rather than me. 'Please say you agree.'

'Of course I do, you daft ape,' I say, reaching over to pinch a few crumbs. 'If that's what you want.'

Clearly it means a lot to him, because the next second Pete is back up on his feet again and has picked me up in the air.

'Put me down!' I cry, albeit half-heartedly, giggling as he begins to twirl me around in a circle.

'You know what, Lu?' he says, sliding me slowly to the ground.

'What?' I beam at him.

'You're bloody amazing, do you know that?'

'If you say so . . .'

'I mean it.' He fixes me with serious eyes. 'I care about you very much, I really do.'

I swallow the lump that's just formed in my throat and laugh nervously.

'I care about you, too.'

Once Pete has transferred a healthy chunk of cash into my account using just his phone – oh, the wonders of technology – we spend the rest of the evening cuddled up together on the sofa, my laptop balanced on my knees and 'Lake Como' typed into the search engine. Pete seems suitably impressed when I bring up photos of the apartment I've rented for the two of us, which is only a few streets away from the lake. There's a king-sized four-poster bed and a tub big enough for two, and I've emailed the owners already to ask for a chilled bottle of Prosecco to be left out for our arrival. I'm determined that this trip will be as romantic as possible.

We're both thrilled when we discover that Como is hosting a Christmas market this year, complete with ice rink, and that the annual fireworks display will take place as usual on New Year's Eve. It's a big deal that Pete is happy to spend his New Year with me as opposed to his mates, and I had been worried that this detail would put him off the idea of the whole holiday. Now I see that I was being silly. I mean, who wouldn't want to spend their New Year somewhere as beautiful as Como?

Just as we're scouring Trip Advisor for ideas of where to eat, Pete's mobile lights up with a call. Like me, he habitually keeps his phone on silent most of the time because of his job. He works as a radio producer for a sports show that's based over in West London, which is apparently nowhere near as glamorous as it sounds – not according to Pete, anyway.

'Who is it?' I enquire, when it becomes apparent that he isn't going to answer.

'Nobody.' He drops the handset back on the table. 'It can wait.'

I know the names of his closest mates – Sean, Chris, Stuart and Lozza – so I know it wasn't one of them calling.

'Manny's an unusual name,' I probe gently. He knows I saw his phone; there's no point pretending that I didn't.

'I suppose it is,' he says with a shrug, turning back to the laptop and looking steadfastly at the screen. 'This place, Insalateria La Vita é Bella, looks nice – over fifty different salads on the menu, apparently.'

'Yummy,' I manage, but inside my guts are churning with unease. Why didn't he want to talk to this Manny person? Is Manny the name of an ex-girlfriend? Is she unable to move on and was calling to beg him to take her back? Or maybe Manny is a girl he works with, some young intern with a twenty-three-inch waist and boobs up to her chin. Whoever it is, Pete doesn't want me to know, and that means there must be a reason.

'Lulu?'

'What?' I reply, my suspicions souring my tone before I have the chance to rein it in.

Pete looks momentarily miffed, and points to something on the laptop screen.

'George Clooney,' he says, his mouth set in a line. 'Apparently, he has a house on Lake Como.'

'He does,' I reply, smiling with as much enthusiasm as I can muster. 'It's called Villa Oleandra, right?'

'Someone's been reading their copies of *heat* magazine,' he appraises jokingly, but there's an edge to his voice that wasn't there before. I shouldn't have snapped at him like I did just now. I hate that my mind always does this, twists something innocent into a dark tangle of confusion and leaves me on edge. Why can't I just trust that Pete isn't hiding anything from me? Aside from choosing not to take me out to meet the lads, he hasn't done anything to make me doubt him, yet here I go again, jumping to the worst possible conclusions. No wonder my previous relationships ended so catastrophically.

'Perks of working somewhere with a waiting room,' I

say, hoping the extra helping of cheerfulness I've dolloped into the delivery will go some way towards making up for my stroppiness.

Pete is still squinting at the screen, but I can sense that he's starting to relax again. His shoulders are no longer raised and he's tapping his foot on the floor.

'Are you feeling a bit stiff after the rugby?' I ask sweetly, as he stretches both his big arms above his head.

'I am a bit,' he allows, turning to face me. 'Why? Are you offering to play nurse?'

'I was thinking more of a massage to begin with,' I tell him, running a finger slowly along his bicep. 'But I'll get out my stethoscope if you ask really nicely . . .'

And just like that, my silly reaction to the phone call is forgotten and Pete is putty in my hands again. How great it must be, I think to myself as I unbutton his shirt and run my hands expertly across his firm chest, to be able to distract yourself so easily. I know that in just a few hours' time, Pete will be soundly asleep beside me, while I will lie awake for ages, a single question playing over and over in my mind.

Who is Manny?

5

Taggie

'*Vin brulé* for the lady.'

I take the plastic cup from Shelley with grateful fingers, sighing with pleasure as the heat from the hot wine begins to defrost my frozen hands.

'*Grazie,*' I say, smiling at my blonde friend through the steam.

We've decided to stroll through the Christmas Market on our way to the restaurant, and I can feel my spirits leaping with every step we take. I love Como at this time of year, when the days are bright and crisp and the nights festooned with fairy lights. In contrast to the sweltering summer months, when you can barely fight your way along the pavements and across the piazzas due to the volume of tourists, the winter season is calmer and less frenetic. The mood is one of expectant joy, as the locals luxuriate in the relative peace and quiet, content to sit by the water with their dogs by their sides, sipping strong espressos and tossing handfuls of breadcrumbs to the gulls as they jostle for position among the ever-present pigeons. For a few months, everyone gets their town back, and this year, for the first time ever, I feel like a little piece of Como belongs to me, too.

There's been a period of adjustment, of course. After

all, Como could not be more different to London, where people would rather lick the pavement than make eye contact, and you're as likely to get a friendly 'good morning' from a stranger as you are to get a seat on the Tube during rush hour. In Como, everyone takes the time to greet you and ask how you are. Men look you in the eye and aren't afraid to tell you politely and sincerely how nice you look, which is a refreshing change from the catcalling louts hanging off scaffolding or out of the windows of white vans back in London. Car horns here honk, but in a friendly rather than irate way, and nothing is ever too much trouble in a restaurant or café. Service in Como is always with a smile, and that feeling is infectious. Being here has been such a tonic.

'Taggie – look at this!'

Shelley has come to a halt in front of a stall selling alpaca hats, scarves and pashminas, but it's a comedy photo of the creatures that she's pointing at.

'I think I went out with him once,' I joke, gesturing at the toothiest of the three. Alpacas are so odd-looking, but hugely appealing all the same. I vaguely remember a former client of mine in my last PR job had bought two for his farm, only to have them cause all sorts of trouble.

'I'm thinking of getting a cat,' Shelley says as we walk away, and I scoff.

'What? What's wrong with cats?'

'Nothing,' I grin, hunching my shoulders against the cold and sipping my hot wine. It's sweet and delicious, with hints of cinnamon and blackberries. 'Except that they're not dogs.'

I have wanted a dog of my own for as long as I can

remember, but thank God I never got one. Running away to Italy might not have been so easy with a pet in tow.

Shelley is still talking about the breed of cat she wants, telling me that she'd love a Munchkin, so called because of their very short legs.

'I wouldn't wish short legs on anyone,' I say immediately, making her laugh. I'm feeling extra-tiny today because I left my heels back at the hotel in favour of flat boots. Como's pavements are predominantly covered in cobbles, which this evening are coated in a layer of frost, and a broken ankle is not something I can afford to have right now. Or ever, for that matter. I do feel ridiculous, though, and joke to Shelley that she'll have to ask this hot waiter of hers to fetch me a booster seat when we reach the restaurant. I've been referring to him as 'her waiter' ever since she first mentioned him last week, in the hope that she'll forget all about her original plan to hook the two of us up.

No such luck.

'*Ciao, buona sera!*'

Shelley hurries through the door of La Vita é Bella and over to where the tall, dark-haired object of her desire is lounging casually against the bar. He's facing away from the entrance, and from my position by the counter I can see that he is a good head taller than her, but not so lanky as to earn himself giant status. He's dressed in dark-blue jeans, a white shirt and a tatty green apron and, like many of the Italians in Como, it looks as if he's plastered an obscene amount of gel into his thick black hair.

I emit a small cough, already impatient to sit down so we can order some food, but when the two of them turn at the sound and make their way towards me, all I'm aware of is an instant and urgent compulsion to flee. Shelley's companion, who is now peering down at me with what could only be described as ill-disguised amusement, is, in fact, the man I met on the beach. The very same man who, just a couple of months ago, plucked me heroically out of the lake in the manner of some boundless hero in a Jane Austen novel. Oh. Dear. God.

'*Ciao, signorina,*' he says, smiling across at me. It's the accepted custom for the two of us to exchange a kiss on either cheek, but instead I offer him a far more English outstretched hand, which he takes and shakes with good humour.

'Marco, this is Taggie.' Shelley is in her element. 'Taggie, meet Marco.'

'It is nice to meet you,' he says carefully, his Italian accent still apparent despite the fact that he's reverted to English. I remember how easily he slipped into it before, and feel a hot flush start to creep across my cheeks.

'You too,' I reply, forcing myself to look hard at the wall instead of him.

Marco picks up a couple of menus and leads us back through the doorway and into the outside seating area, which is rectangular in shape, with glass walls and a roof. Plants hang down from the ceiling and music plays quietly from a radio in one corner. Thanks to the addition of several fan heaters, it's wonderfully toasty inside, and I've shrugged off my thick coat before we've even sat down.

'It's hot enough to grow lemons in here,' I say, trying not to gawp at Marco's departing bottom. Shelley has ordered us an Aperol Spritz each to drink while we peruse the menu.

'So . . .' she whispers conspiratorially. 'What do you think?'

'Of the restaurant?' I ask, playing deliberately dumb. 'It's really nice.'

Shelley pulls a face. 'Not the restaurant, you wally – Marco!'

'Shhh,' I hiss, as the man himself returns with a middle-aged Italian couple in his wake. I hear the woman mutter something and fan her face in an exaggerated manner, so I can only assume that she's just commented on the temperature in this weird little greenhouse. Marco gestures up at the condensation-covered glass ceiling and pulls a face, and the three of them share a laugh. Italians are always laughing; it's one of the things I like most about them.

'Not even you can deny that he's gorgeous,' Shelley continues, as soon as the coast is clear.

'He's all right,' I allow, my mind unhelpfully reminding me just how strong his arms felt when they were wrapped around my soaking wet body. 'But he clearly knows it.'

'That's just the Italian in him,' she remarks, and I have to agree. Confidence comes as naturally to the men in Como as the requirement to make a cup of tea in a crisis comes to us Brits – it's just bred into them from birth.

'Did you see his eyes, though?' Shelley pesters.

I nod. I can't deny that his green eyes are incredibly striking, even if I do get the impression that he's a bit too pleased with himself.

'They're so exotic,' my friend adds, her voice trailing off dreamily. 'I mean, imagine waking up to those on the pillow next to you.'

'Just the eyes?' I exclaim. 'Gross!'

Shelley tries and fails to give my hand a playful slap.

'Are you ready to order, ladies?'

Marco is back with our Aperol Spritzes, and after depositing them on the table, he takes out a tatty notebook from his apron pocket with one hand and a chewed pencil with the other. Loath to admit that I haven't even so much as glanced at the list of foods on offer, I hurriedly pick a Caprese salad for a starter followed by some simple gnocchi with basil pesto. One of the many good things about eating out in Italy is that the food is going to taste amazing, whatever you happen to choose.

Unlike me, Shelley has no qualms about making Marco wait while she scans the salad selection, and I sense rather than see him staring down at me as she fires questions at him about how the chicken is cooked, whether melon is in season and if she can swap artichoke for extra olives. After changing her mind at least three times only to finally settle on a seafood pizza, Shelley then wants to know which wine Marco recommends.

'The Barolo,' he says without hesitation, and I look up in admiration.

'The Barolo is forty-five euros a bottle!' Shelley shrieks, so loudly that the surrounding diners turn to look.

Marco merely shrugs. 'You ask me what is the best, I tell you what is the best.'

'Cheeky,' Shelley grins, glancing at me. 'What do you think, Tags?'

'I think the house wine will be just fine,' I say. 'Shall we get a carafe or a bottle?'

'A bottle,' interrupts Marco, even though it's very clear

that I was not directing the question at him, and strolls away grinning before I can argue.

'He must like you,' Shelley says excitedly.

'Why do you say that?' I'm mystified.

'Because he wants us to stay longer. Why else would he upgrade us to a bottle?'

'To make money,' I deadpan, laughing as she tuts at me.

The Aperol Spritz is going down far too quickly, and by the time Marco returns with the wine, the nervous energy and burning humiliation coursing through my insides has caused me to chomp my way through all four complimentary breadsticks.

'Hungry?' he enquires, surveying the empty wrappers.

I narrow my eyes at him.

'Taggie works at the Casa Alta, too,' Shelley is now telling him.

'Ah, yes. A good hotel.'

Despite the fact that Shelley is doing all the talking, Marco is focusing all his attention on me, and I wonder when he'll get around to telling her how the two of us actually met. Perhaps he assumes that I've already filled her in – but I haven't. There's only one person who even knows it happened, aside from Marco himself, and that person is definitely not Shelley. I love my friend, I really do, but she is one of the biggest gossips I've ever encountered, and if Sal finds out that I'm the type of woman who goes careering headfirst into lakes, then he might not think me trustworthy enough to become his official events manager – and I'm determined to prove my worth to him, whatever it takes.

Instead of regaling Shelley with tales of my clumsiness,

however, Marco is now telling us that he spent the summer season in Naples, where he was running his friend's restaurant.

'I am used to being the boss,' he explains, looking over his shoulder to check that his own manager isn't within earshot. 'Being told what to do again, you know, it's hard.'

I stifle a yawn.

'Sorry, do you think I am boring?' Marco asks, amused, and I quickly shake my head.

'No, you're not. I was just . . . I'm sorry. Please carry on. I'm just tired, that's all. I had a long day at work and I didn't . . . Well, I haven't been . . .' I trail off as he fixes those bewitching green eyes on me again, and I feel something shift in the pit of my stomach, the echo of a forgotten emotion. It's gone as soon as it appears, though, and so I go back to mutely studying my cutlery.

'I will leave you ladies alone,' he announces, abandoning us to pour our own wine.

'I told you,' Shelley says, her eyes bright. 'Dreamy.'

I manage to get through the rest of the evening without mumbling embarrassingly at Marco again, but I can't help but feel on edge whenever he approaches our table. There's something about him that is drawing me in, but it's the same thing causing me to mildly freak out, and I can't quite work out what is going on. I tell myself that it's simply down to the fact that he's seen me looking like a total idiot, and because he could, at any given moment, land me in it by telling Shelley about the incident at the beach, but even if it is, I can't seem to stop looking at him. My eyes continually seek him out as he delivers food and drinks, only to drop as soon as he glances in my direction.

By the time Shelley and I have finished the wine and are dithering over whether to order a panna cotta to share as dessert, I've decided that perhaps I might just like Marco a tiny bit. Well, like is a strong word, but I am definitely intrigued by him. Just as I'm coming to terms with this fact, the door to the outside seating area opens and a beautiful Italian girl makes her way straight over the threshold and across to where Marco has almost finished taking another order. My Italian isn't good enough to follow exactly what she promptly begins yelling in his face, but the word 'bastardo' is self-explanatory, and she's using it repeatedly.

'Oh dear,' mutters Shelley, as every head in the room turns to stare.

Marco waits patiently while the girl finishes her rant, but when he goes to place a consoling hand on her shoulder, she bats it away.

'She just told him that she hates him,' Shelley whispers with barely concealed delight. 'And that he's a liar. Dear oh dear.'

Eventually the girl runs out of steam and bursts into tears, but instead of following her out of the door and running down the cobbled street after her, Marco merely watches her go, shrugs, then goes back to work. When he arrives to clear away our glasses a good ten minutes later, Shelley is practically foaming at the mouth with unanswered questions.

'What was that all about?' she asks, subtlety and politeness apparently distant memories.

'She was upset that I did not call her,' Marco says, sounding bored. 'But we have been on only two dates, it was nothing.'

'Clearly not nothing to her,' I blurt, only to be left cringing into my wine glass when he looks dismayed.

'I didn't make her any promises,' he argues, clearly nonplussed.

He's making a fair point, I suppose, but the way he's dismissing her when she's so obviously distressed is borderline cruel. I can't believe that I was beginning to like him. He may have hauled me out of the lake, but that doesn't make him an angel.

Shelley, however, is not one to be easily deterred.

'So, you're single, then?' she prompts, although it's not really a question.

Marco looks directly at me before he answers.

'That depends who is asking.'

'Neither of us,' I say briskly, and promptly order myself a huge slab of chocolate amaretti cake before he has time to reply.

6

Lucy

'Pass the sprouts, will you?'

My sister Julia is the only person I've ever met who would put the small, round, green element of a Christmas dinner at the top of her list of preferences – above even pigs in blankets. She's a weirdo, and I tell her so as I lift the overflowing bowl up so she can reach it.

'I'm weird?' she scoffs, tossing her sweep of auburn hair over one shoulder. 'You're the one who's chosen blood and guts as a career.'

'Now, now, Ju. I'm sure there's a lot more to nursing than that, isn't there, Lucy?'

Bless Dad, always coming to my rescue. He's had to do it so many times over the years, the poor man, that it must have become like second nature. Being the younger sister, I've always had to put up with a fair amount of teasing, and it doesn't bother me all that much, but I think that Dad, who is himself the youngest of three brothers, feels as if he should fight my corner a bit. Julia has always been the tougher sibling – small, wiry and no-nonsense – much more like our mum than I am.

'So, where is it Lady Muck's gone this year?' Julia asks then, quickly changing the subject before I can launch into a speech about how vital it is that we save the NHS. She knows me well, my big sister.

Dad frowns at the mention of Mum's nickname, a forkful of roast potato frozen in mid-air on the way to his mouth, and for a moment I think he's going to tell Julia off, but then he manages to swallow whatever remark it was that reared up.

'The Maldives,' I tell her, curling up my nose.

Julia and I might be as different as sprouts and chocolate, in both looks and personality, but one thing we do agree on is that our mum is a complete idiot. Once we'd stopped crying over the fact she'd left Dad for a rich neighbour eight years ago, we came up with the 'Lady Muck' moniker to cheer ourselves up – an attempt to make light of a situation that was anything but. The 'Muck' part is because David, her new husband, is a pig farmer. A very successful pig farmer, but a pig farmer all the same. Dad, who is a far less smelly but not quite as rich dentist, assures the two of us that he's over it all now, but I still notice him wince whenever either of their names comes up in conversation. I haven't spent Christmas with my mum since she walked out, because I refuse to leave Dad by himself, and Julia only did the one time. 'Once was more than enough,' she'd muttered darkly after the event.

Perhaps I had taken the breakdown of their marriage harder because I was a bit younger than Julia when it happened, but then I suppose twenty isn't all that young. The older I get, the more I realise that Mum must have been waiting years for the right time to go. When I finally turned eighteen it must have felt even more exciting to her than it did to me, because it meant that I'd soon be moving away to study, and that she would no longer have any reason to stay. I try not to think about it, but it's always difficult not to at this time of year, especially when I'm witness to Dad rattling around in our big family house on his own. He assures us that he doesn't get lonely, but I'm not convinced.

'The bloody Maldives,' Julia exclaims, stabbing one of the seventeen or so sprouts on her plate with a fork before mashing it aggressively until it turns into mush. I'm holding my tongue, because I'm already feeling tremendously guilty about the fact that I'm abandoning the two of them to fly out to Lake Como in two days with Pete – especially as I missed New Year's Eve completely last year due to work. Dad took the news with his usual good grace and even bought me an Italian phrase book as a last-minute gift, but Julia, predictably, was less impressed. Having met Pete a grand total of twice since we got together, she's decided that he's an 'oaf', and that I could do better. I know she's just being protective, in the misguided and clumsy way she always is, but I wish she'd listen when I tell her that, this time, I've found a good one. Perhaps it's because her girlfriend, Abby, chose to spend their first festive period as a couple with her own family rather than ours, or maybe she's simply miffed that I'm going back to Lake Como without her. Even though I was fourteen and she was twenty the last time we had a holiday there, it's always been our special place, and now I'm sharing it with someone else. I can understand why that might be upsetting.

Dad wisely chooses that moment to fetch the remaining crackers from the box, and we spend a riotous ten minutes retrieving small plastic prizes from where they've been flung mid-crack across the room, and reading out terrible jokes to one another.

'Why was Santa's little helper feeling depressed?' calls out Dad.

Julia rolls her eyes.

'Because he has low elf-esteem!'

I giggle despite the clanging awfulness of the joke, and attempt to get my jumping frog toy to leap into my wine glass. Pete and I haven't done our present exchange yet, and I wonder for the millionth time what he's bought me. His main present from me was supposed to be the holiday, but since he insisted on paying me back for his half, I had to rush out and panic-buy him some other things to open. Now I'm scared that he won't like them. When I'd confessed my fears to Julia, she'd tutted and told me that I should have simply wrapped him up a dirty rugby ball and a pint of ale. She may have a point.

Once we've eaten enough food to render ourselves sleepy, the three of us stack the dishes in the kitchen and retreat to the sofa with a second bottle of wine and a large box of Quality Street.

It's nice to be here, back in the Suffolk village where I grew up, in the house I know so well that I could find my way around it blindfolded. After the noisy A&E department of the hospital and the even noisier London streets, Newton is deliciously peaceful and sleepy – and I felt myself relax as soon as Julia and I boarded the train at Liverpool Street station yesterday. We went for our usual walk around the village before lunch, the three of us, instinctively taking the route that wouldn't lead us past

Mum and David's house. It doesn't bother me now as much as it used to, but a few years ago there was an uncomfortable five minutes when Mum happened to be putting out some rubbish as we wandered by, and Julia had marched off refusing to talk to her. Dad, of course, had tried to apologise on her behalf, but Mum somehow managed to turn that into a row, and I wasn't the only one who ended up in tears. It's a good thing they're not around this year, her and David. I don't know how Dad can stand it, the thought of them living less than ten minutes' walk away. I could never endure such a thing.

Julia was the first to set up home in London, and I followed a few years later. We never discussed our reasons for choosing the big, grubby capital as our base, but I think neither of us liked the idea of moving too far away from Dad. By leaving him, Mum upgraded us from being merely his daughters to his part-time carers, such was his heartbreak at the time. I now know exactly where I get my fragile heart from, but knowing how similar we are makes me love him even more. Plus, I get my bubbliness and warmth from him, too, and it's those two qualities that have helped me to become so good at my job. I see my colleagues struggling sometimes to even reach across and take someone's hand, whereas I'm happy to dish out my affection to whoever needs it. Working at a hospital can be such a complicated business, but if I've learned anything since becoming a nurse, it's that often, a hug is just as good medicine as a syringe full of drugs.

Not long after Mum left all those years ago, Julia insisted that Dad must redecorate the house. 'Paint away any trace of her,' she'd barked, anger making her unreasonable. He'd nodded along, of course, but completely ignored her advice. One thing he did do, though, was unearth a box of our childhood drawings from the loft and create a huge collage, which is now framed and sitting proudly on the wall above the television. Glancing up at it now as the closing credits of the *Doctor Who* Christmas special file up the screen, I find my eyes drawn to the picture in the centre, the one of the secret beach on the shores of Lake Como that I used to pretend was mine. I wonder if I could find it again.

Julia has wrestled the chocolates away from Dad and is selecting all the revolting coffee-flavoured ones for herself. When I look at him, I see that he's smiling at her adoringly, and my heart swells with love for him. I may have had some less-than-brilliant boyfriends over the years, but Dad has always been consistently amazing. He's my hero, and I can't wait to introduce him to Pete. Perhaps this time next year we'll all be sitting here, the five of us. I honestly can't think of a single thing that would make me happier.

As the light outside the living room window turns from slate-grey, to dark violet, to black, I allow myself to picture a future Christmas Day. A tree propped up with presents and decorated with strings of different-coloured lights, Julia and Abby laughing together as they pour the champagne, Dad in his red apron, popping his head around the door to give us an update on lunch, and Pete by my side, our baby bouncing on his lap. All of us smiling, all of us happy.

It's the future I want, and I'm going to do everything in my power to get it.

7

Taggie

The first thing I think when I open my eyes is that Father Christmas must be real after all, because there's definitely something small and solid resting against my feet at the end of the bed. But I'm thirty-two years old, which means I haven't had a stocking on Christmas morning for sixteen years.

'Oh, it's you, is it?'

Bruno returns my gaze, his big eyes conker-brown, and puts his little head on one side.

'Merry Christmas,' I whisper, smiling as he replies by lifting his leg into the air and furiously licking his nether regions. It would be gross if he wasn't so ridiculous, and I tell him so as I extract my warm toes from under him and shuffle them into my slippers. Tiptoeing along the hallway, I pause by the next door along and smile as I make out the sound of three different snores. None of the others are up yet, which means that Bruno and I can enjoy a blissful morning coffee before the madness begins.

Despite Shelley wishing repeatedly for a flurry of festive snow over the past two weeks, it looks like Christmas in Lake Como is going to be another stunner of a cloudless day. The sun is already up and warming my favourite bench in the back garden, and I know that if I walk to the far wall and peer down over the side, I'll see merry twinkles on the surface of the water. The sunshine doesn't mean that it's hot, though, and before I head outside, I wrap a long scarf around my neck and select a woolly hat from the eclectic collection piled up by the front door.

'Come on, Bruno,' I murmur. 'Wee-wee time.'

He does as he's told, albeit in that begrudging way that chihuahuas tend to do most things you ask them to, then promptly demands to be picked up so he can burrow underneath the cosy folds of my dressing gown. It never fails to amuse me how cross chihuahuas get with things over which they have zero control, such as the weather. From the indignant way in which Bruno is now snuffling and grumbling on my lap, you'd think he was giving the light winter breeze a good telling-off. I admire his strident confidence, though, probably because I'm not that dissimilar. When you're small like we are, you have to be extra tough.

I push down the plunger of the cafetière and watch in a half-daze as the coffee grounds dance and spin in the hot water. When did I get to this point? I wonder vaguely. When did I become a person who requires a small vat of caffeine to even function in the mornings? When I was a child, my energy was limitless, but nowadays I feel suffocated with fatigue. I am getting older, but I'm hardly ancient. Maybe the exhaustion is because of what happened, more emotional than physical. Everything always seems to come back to that.

To distract myself away from venturing down that dark train of thought and breaking the promise I've made to myself *not* to cry on Christmas Day, I pour myself a cup of the good stuff and carry it, and Bruno, around the perimeter of the garden, letting the aroma of pine and the sound of the wind soothe me. Similarly to the Casa Alta Hotel, the house here is painted bright yellow, but unlike its vast cousin, this dwelling is a far more modest size. Set over just one level, with three bedrooms, one bathroom, a kitchen and a large living-cum-dining room, it has barely changed at all since I was a child, and for that reason alone, it remains one of my favourite places on the planet.

The sun has been climbing while I've been meandering, and the sky is now a rich azure blue, the lake below it a sparkling sapphire puddle. I cradle my hot mug and hold it close to my face, watching as the steam snakes away into the cold air. Now that I've been here at Lake Como for a while, I can't comprehend that my morning view every day used to be the fume-coated sides of buildings, the sky almost always grey and the pavements below littered with grime and dirt. Everything is clean and bright here, as if the whole area is laundered in the night and spread out fresh as the sun comes up. Colours are more vibrant, the air itself sweet and invigorating, and everywhere there is the throb of life, of nature, of living things flourishing. I don't ever want to go back. I don't think I could ever go back.

'Taggie!'

At the sound of his mistress's voice, Bruno wriggles so violently in my arms that I almost lose what's left of my coffee.

'Idiot dog,' I say affectionately, putting him down carefully on to the grass and raising a hand to wave at Elsie. She's standing by the open back door, Gino and Nico yapping away excitedly by her feet, which are clad in bright green wellies.

'Merry Christmas, darling,' she says as I approach, wrapping a bony hand around the back of my neck and pulling me forwards. She smells of lavender and talc and I kiss each of her soft, lined cheeks before following her back into the warmth of the kitchen.

'It's cold enough to freeze an otter's paws off out there,' she mutters, glaring through the window in the same disgruntled manner as the dogs and shuffling towards the sink.

'Here, let me,' I say, taking the kettle out of her hands a moment later and steering her instead towards a chair.

Elsie sits down without complaint, and the three dogs begin squabbling over which one of them will get to sit on her knee.

'Will you be quiet, boys!' she commands, and Bruno and Nico immediately fall silent. Gino, however, continues to bark insistently.

'Selective hearing,' Elsie mutters, scooping the tiny, angry dog up into her arms. 'Just like his namesake.'

Elsie named each of her three chihuahuas after her three ex-husbands. Bruno, who is long-haired and beautiful, is the soppy one; Nico, who is short-haired and overweight, is the dim-witted one; and Gino, who is dark brown with overlarge ears, is the naughty one. She has always denied having a favourite, but Bruno and I seem to share a bond that I don't have with the others. Funnily enough, Bruno was the only one of her ex-husbands that I got on well with, too. He sadly died a long time ago now, but Elsie often talks about him with great affection.

I put Elsie's green tea down in front of her and she sniffs at it, pulling a face as she realises that it's not her beloved coffee.

'Not even on Christmas Day?' she pleads, and I shake my head.

'You know what the doctor said – it's not good for you.'

'Blah, blah,' she says, waving a vague hand in the air. 'What do doctors know about anything?'

'In this case, I'd say, a lot,' I tell her gently. 'Just be a good girl and drink it all up, will you? For me?'

'Pah,' comes the reply, but I grin as she reaches for the mug.

Elsie was eighty on her last birthday, and aside from a nasty virus last summer that led her to suffer a mild heart attack, she's very fit and strong for her age. Tiny like me and with a shock of bright white hair that she keeps covered in a variety of patterned silk scarves, Elsie is and always has been a real character. Once upon a time a very close friend of my grandmother on my father's side, Elsie and her yellow house here in Bellagio have been an important part of the family Torres since long before I was born. When the idea came to me that I must get away from London – and fast – Elsie was the person I called, and she had welcomed me in with no questions asked. Even now, over five months after I turned up on her doorstep, so obviously in a mess, she still hasn't pushed me to tell her what happened. I hope she knows how grateful I am to her for that.

Elsie has been living in Lake Como since the late 1950s, after coming here on holiday with my grandmother and her family and falling in love not only with the area, but with a local fisherman called Gino at the same time. She never had any of her own children, whether out of choice, I'm not sure, but she certainly lives life to the full, wringing every drop of fun out of any given situation like water out of a cloth. Far from being a doddery old lady who needs help crossing the street, she's a veritable and colourful force to be reckoned with, and there's barely a local in the whole area who she doesn't know. It was Elsie who persuaded my boss Sal to give me a trial at the Casa Alta when he was concerned that my Italian wasn't good enough, and I'm sure he wouldn't have been allowed to say no even if he'd wanted to. Elsie simply would not have stood for it.

I prepare us a simple breakfast of toast, eggs and fruit as Elsie potters around watering her plants and swearing cheerfully at the dogs as they get under her feet. It's a treat for me to be here, as usually I sleep in my allocated room back at the hotel, but there are barely any guests staying over Christmas, and so Sal graciously let me have a few days off. Bellagio is around an hour from Como by road, but only forty minutes if you get one of the high-speed boats from down at the port. Travelling by water is far superior to the bouncy and stuffy buses that trundle hourly along the windy coastal road, and well worth the ten extra euros. It had felt very special indeed to arrive in Bellagio late yesterday afternoon to find Elsie and her pack of boys waiting for me at a café table by the harbour.

In the absence of my parents, who I convinced to stay at home in the UK, Elsie is the closest I have to a family member, and so I'm determined to make today as fun as it can possibly be. Christmas should be like that, full of joy and love; it shouldn't serve as a reminder of all the things you don't have, and of the people you're missing. It shouldn't, but it inevitably does – hence the reason I'm making such a big effort. I *won't* let today dissolve into misery.

'Shall we call your ma and pa?' Elsie asks now, scrunching up her face like a stepped-on doll as she chews a particularly tart chunk of breakfast pineapple.

'Later.' I smile reassuringly. 'After you've opened your presents.'

'But I haven't got a cupboard big enough to hide a nice young Italian man in,' she replies wryly, giving me the benefit of a low chuckle as I widen my eyes.

'Elsie!'

'What?' She shrugs, all innocent. 'I'm old, not dead, my dear. The last time I checked, there was still blood running around these old veins of mine, and a girl can still dream.'

'Is a man really what you want?' I ask, my disbelief glaringly obvious.

'Oh, only for a few hours,' she quips, grinning wickedly. 'I'd put him right back on the shelf when I was done.'

'You're unbelievable,' I tell her affectionately, rubbing the top of Bruno's little head as he settles once again on my lap. 'There's more to life than men, you know.'

'I suppose you're right,' she says, getting up and plodding in her wellies to the fridge, before extracting a large bottle from inside and brandishing it in front of me with a flourish. 'There's bubbly!'

I shake my head again, but I'm laughing.

'Come on, Agatha, just one glass. I promise to go back to drinking the vile tea afterwards.'

For a second I narrow my eyes at her, then let out a big, exasperated sigh.

'Oh, OK then, you win – but just one.'

'You're the boss,' she replies, tearing off the foil, although we both know full well that I'm anything but.

8

Lucy

I snooped. I know I shouldn't have, but I did. And now I wish I hadn't. Why, why, why did I do it?

I'm now sitting on the edge of Pete's bath, trying not to cry, chewing on my bottom lip like it's toffee. If I look up, I'll be able to see my reflection in the cabinet mirror, but I can't do it. I can't even bear to look at myself. Not now I know what *she* looks like, not now I know just how different she is to me.

Of course, it was stupid to think that Pete wouldn't have an ex-girlfriend – that he wouldn't have many ex-girlfriends, for that matter – but I had managed to convince myself that whoever they were, they'd be unremarkable. I was wrong about that. And now I know just how wrong, and there can be no going back. It's this Manny business that's pushed me over the edge and made me revert to the paranoid mess I became when my last relationship disintegrated right in front of me. I've tried so hard to forget about the unanswered phone call and the evasive way Pete behaved straight afterwards, but it's been nibbling away at my confidence like a ladybird on a lettuce leaf. Now, not only do I still have no idea who Manny is, but I have a whole new problem twisting its way around my insides – and this one is way worse.

Pete will be back soon – he's only popped to the local takeaway after managing to persuade me that a Chinese on Boxing Day was a good idea, even though I came armed with leftovers – but now I can't face the idea of food. How can he even stand to be with someone like me after being with her? It doesn't make sense that he would even fancy me, let alone be proud to be seen with me on his arm. He must still care about her, too, otherwise he would have got rid of all those photos, not hidden them away in a shoebox in the back of his wardrobe.

The worst thing is, I can't even say anything. If I do, he'll know I've been going through his things, and I have absolutely no defence. I'm not even sure why I started looking. It just came over me like a compulsion as soon as I heard the front door close behind him, and now I'm convinced that he'll be able to smell the guilt on me, like petrol on an arsonist, and promptly tell me just where I can stick our relationship.

In a panic, I fire off a text to Julia, telling her what I've done and begging for advice. Her reply, when it arrives, is typically unruffled. She always has been the opposite of me.

A few photos don't mean anything. He's with you now –
focus on that.

She's right, of course, but it does little to comfort me.

But she's GORGEOUS and TINY!

I press send and tap my fingers impatiently against my thigh as I wait for her response. 'Typing', my phone informs me helpfully, and I stare at the trail of dots inside the speech bubble, willing them to transform into words of wisdom.

You are GORGEOUS with BOOBS.

I almost laugh. I hadn't considered the boob factor. Now I can't remember if the ex-girlfriend has any or not. All I can picture is her beautiful face, her dark hair, the glow of happiness emanating from the photograph of the two of them.

Another message arrives from Julia.

Abby's ex looks like a supermodel, but she's an evil cow.
Looks can be deceiving, and whoever this girl is, she's in his past. You are the one in his present.

And future!

I respond hastily, and she replies with a thumbs-up emoji, which is very gracious of her, given her thoughts on Pete.

I take a deep breath. Julia's right, just like she always is. Pete's ex-girlfriend may be beautiful and slim enough to slide through the gaps in a drain, but she isn't in his life any more. She's in a box in the back of his wardrobe, buried underneath his rugby socks and a manky old pillowcase. I'm here in his flat, about to share dinner with him, and tomorrow he's coming with me to one of my favourite places in the world. I'm overreacting, just like I always do when I like someone – when my feelings have rendered me vulnerable.

I've just repaired my face when Pete arrives back laden with little white carrier bags, and when I step shyly towards him, he pulls me into such a tight embrace that for a second, I find it hard to breathe.

'I missed you,' he murmurs, and I feel as if my heart has sprouted wings.

I do my best to eat a plateful of sweet and sour chicken and egg-fried rice, but it tastes like old boots after my dad's delicious home cooking. The sooner we get to Italy, which is, of course, the food capital of the universe, the better, although finding those photos has reminded me that I could benefit from losing a few pounds. There was a time when I was slim, but that was when I was ill, and as soon as I started to feel like myself again, the weight returned. I have attempted a few diets over the years, but being a nurse means that my eating pattern is atrocious at best and, more often than not, I'm forced to shovel in something high-calorie just to keep myself going. It's all very well for these health-conscious vloggers to waffle on about 'clean eating' while they sip their kale smoothies – they don't have a job that requires them to be on their feet for eleven hours at a time. Even if I had the energy or the inclination to prepare a packed lunch of quinoa and steamed broccoli, which I don't, I'd barely have the time to sit down and eat it. Nope, give me a sausage roll and a flapjack any day of the week.

'Shall we do our presents?' asks Pete, and we both look over towards his half-hearted attempt at a Christmas tree in the corner. Our gifts to each other are underneath it, and he's been dropping hints about opening them ever since I got here.

'You first,' I tell him, laughing as he leaps up and claps his hands with excitement. He told me earlier that his own family aren't hugely into exchanging gifts. Instead, they all put some money into a kitty, which they use for a big dinner later in the year. It's a nice idea, I suppose, but not a very fun one. My presents are the only ones he's getting to open, and I'm gripped yet again with nerves. What if he doesn't like them?

'Oh wow, these are great!' Pete exclaims, extracting the matching hat and gloves set I bought him and smiling at me with what looks like genuine delight.

'I thought it would be cold in Como,' I explain, mumbling shyly. 'I kept the receipt, if you want to change them.'

'Don't be daft!' He gives me a lopsided look. 'I love them.'

He then proceeds to go into ecstasies over the set of travel-sized toiletries I got him, and punches the air when he uncovers the *Game of Thrones* box set.

'Julia tells me there are lots of tits and dragons,' I inform him, laughing as he widens his eyes. 'That's a direct quote.'

'Can we watch an episode tonight?'

'Of course,' I assure him. He doesn't need to know that I've already seen up to the end of series five.

'Open yours now,' he instructs, handing me my one and only package. It's a small rectangular box.

'I hope you like it,' he blurts as I peel away the Sellotape carefully. I want to keep the paper as a memento, so I make sure I don't tear it.

'It's a bit random, I know,' he says, frowning as I lift the velvet lid to reveal a beautiful brooch. It's been designed to look like a sprig of blossom, and is made from delicate, twisted gold inlaid with tiny blue and white stones. I love it.

'Oh my God, Pete,' I manage, my voice choked. 'It's gorgeous. I hope you didn't spend too much on me, though.'

'I know you like flowers,' he says, as I trail a finger across my new most-favourite thing. 'The guy at the antique shop told me it's a one-off, too, just like you.'

I'm fighting back tears now, and he puts a solid arm around me, telling me not to be silly, and that it makes him happy to treat me. If only he knew the real reason I'm upset. It's not that he bought me something so exquisitely beautiful and thoughtful; it's that I absolutely don't deserve it – especially not since I went rooting through his personal things.

'Sorry,' I mumble, biting my lip until my tears stop. 'I'm not sad. It's just been a long time since someone bought me something so nice.'

'Well, get used to it,' he says, lifting my chin so he can kiss me. 'Because I plan on spoiling you a whole lot more when we get to Italy tomorrow.'

I make myself look at him, at his scatter of freckles and his bright, kind eyes. At the mess of red curls tangled against his forehead and the faint dimples sitting like inverted commas on his cheeks. This man is the real deal, and he does care about me. I know it, I can feel it, so why do I keep doubting him? And, more to the point, why do I keep doubting myself, too?

'How about we both spoil each other?' I ask him now, twisting one of his curls around my finger.

'Sounds like a plan.' Pete kisses the top of my head. 'Now come here, you.'

I begin to relax in his arms. I know I can get past this stupid anxiety and pointless jealousy. The girl in those photos is just a memory, a face from Pete's past. It's not as if we're going to bump into her in the street, is it?

I wait under a blanket on the sofa as Pete dims the lights and fiddles around with the DVD player, and by the time the epic opening credits of *Game of Thrones* are playing and his hand is resting snugly in my own, all I'm feeling is silly for ever getting myself so worked up in the first place.

9

Taggie

'I can't believe I let you talk me into this.'

Shelley pouts at me from under her pink bobble hat.

'You're having fun, admit it!'

'I am not,' I counter. 'Falling over fifteen times in the space of ten minutes is not my idea of fun.'

'I think you'll find it's been sixteen,' she replies, and only just skates out of the way in time to avoid my fist. We're at the ice rink in Piazza Cavour, which has been set up temporarily as part of Como's festive celebrations, along with the Christmas Market and array of lights and decorations. The lake is sitting just across the road, inky black in the darkness, and the sharp, cold air is ripe with the scent of *vin brulé* and roasted chestnuts. Shelley lured me down here with the promise of hot chocolate and pizza, but so far all I've got is a bruised bottom and frozen cheeks.

'You have to let go of the side,' she calls out now. 'It's much easier when you let go.'

Is she insane?

'I'm fine here,' I reply, my teeth chattering as a particularly fiendish gust of wind rushes up from the icy floor. What I don't add is that I've now got a serious cramp in my left foot, which is doing nothing to cheer me along, and that my wet gloves are turning my hands blue with cold. It's a common misconception that small people, such as myself, are automatically nimble and athletic. I am neither of those things – and nowhere has that felt more obvious to me than right here, inside this slippery enclosure of misery.

Shelley, who has just skated backwards – backwards! – past me at speed, is enjoying herself far too much for my liking. If she'd bothered to confess the fact that she was clearly an Olympic figure skater in a previous life, then I never would have agreed to put myself through this ordeal in the first place. How can it be so hard? It's just skating, after all. When I was a teenager, I barely took my roller skates off. Ice skates surely can't be so different?

Momentarily emboldened by the memory of myself hurtling around the youth club roller disco to the buoyant lyrics of the Spice Girls, I finally let go of the side and lurch awkwardly towards the centre of the rink.

'*Attento!*'

I'm aware of a very hard shove in the small of my back, and then I'm face down on the ice. This time, however, it wasn't my fault.

'Who the bloody hell di— Oh.'

Marco the rescuer and lothario waiter is peering down at me, a gloved hand on each of his bent knees and a look of bemused concern on his face. He's covered his jet-black hair with a red hat and has zipped his leather jacket right up over his chin, and I gawp at him as he reaches down towards me.

'Take my hand,' he instructs. 'I will help you up.'

'It's your fault I'm down here,' I grumble, but I let him pull me to my feet for the second time since we met. It's not as if I have much choice in the matter.

'I couldn't help it,' he explains. 'One second you were over there.' He points towards the edge of the rink. 'Then the next second, you were here, right in front of me. I didn't have time to stop.'

He speaks English so well, and looks so annoyingly handsome with his cheeks flushed and his hat askew, that I find myself thawing a bit, despite the new pains I now have on my front, as well as my back.

'I'm terrible at skating,' I admit, letting him lead me slowly back to the infinitely safer edge. 'I honestly had no idea how terrible until tonight.'

He shrugs, finally relinquishing my hands, and folds his arms across his chest.

'You cannot be good at everything,' he says, which is an accurate but weird thing to say, and I hesitate, wondering how the hell to reply.

'What are you good at?' he asks, leaning casually against the very same makeshift wall that I'm clinging on to like a limpet.

'Falling over,' I quip. 'I'm very good at that.'

He frowns at me.

'But what are your passions?'

'My passions?'

He looks back at me and nods, his demeanour deadly serious.

'What is it with Italians and passion?' I ask, trying to make light of his question.

He shrugs again, glancing away towards the lake.

'Do you not think it is important to have passion in your life?'

I consider this for a moment.

'As long as it's for the right reason,' I tell him. 'I think passion can sometimes lead to people taking advantage of you.'

I cast my mind back to the beginning of the month, and the girl Shelley and I saw at Marco's restaurant the night I met him. She had clearly felt passionately about her relationship with him, and that had not worked out well for her at all.

'Do you not want to feel as if you are on fire?' he declares, pushing himself away from the side and skating around in a small arc until he's facing me. I get the sense that he would have grasped my hands in his if he could, but both of mine are still gripping the wooden edge of the rink.

'Right now, I would,' I joke, doing my best to avoid his strangely hypnotic green eyes. 'It's bloody freezing!'

'You are making fun of me,' he states, sliding backwards a fraction and almost colliding with a sprightly old man in the process. It never fails to amaze me just how fit and lithe the over-sixties are in Italy. All that olive oil, cured meat and cheese must be working wonders.

'I'm not,' I argue, but my delivery is feeble. The truth is, I don't find it that easy to talk to Marco. The way he looks at me is too familiar, and it makes me feel on edge. Usually I'm confident with new people and even with total strangers, but in this case, I'm quite the opposite. It's as if Marco, with his heroics at the lake and now here at the rink, has found the one single chink in my stoic armour and wriggled his little finger under the gap.

Just as I'm casting around desperately for something else to say, Shelley skates across to join us, a look of smug satisfaction on her cherubic face.

'*Ciao*, Marco,' she says sweetly, kissing him on either cheek without even so much as a tremble in her skates. 'I thought it was you from all the way over there.'

'He picked me up,' I blurt, realising a second too late that the words I'd chosen could carry more than just their literal meaning. 'I mean, I fell over. Well, he knocked me over. But it wasn't his fault, you see. It was— Oh, never mind.'

They're both looking at me now, Shelley in blatant amusement and Marco in what looks like wry confusion. It must be hard for him to understand what the hell I'm saying when I can barely seem to string a coherent sentence together.

I fall into an embarrassed silence as the two of them begin chatting about their Christmases, mutually bemoaning the fact that they both had to work. Not for the first time that day, I think how strange it is to be here, ice-skating by an Italian lake on Boxing Day rather than sitting under a blanket on my parents' sofa, mainlining wedges of Terry's Chocolate Orange. I feel horribly guilty about the fact that I've left the two of them alone this year, but I just couldn't face the idea of going back to England. Not yet, not even to the family house. Besides, I don't want to be anywhere that I can be easily found.

'I'm sure we'd love to come for a drink,' Shelley is saying now, and I whip my head around to find her and Marco staring at me expectantly.

'Sure,' I say, carefully letting go of the side only to veer off sideways into the path of several American tourists. The sooner I get off this slippery death trap, the better.

*

Once I've thankfully handed over the skates and got my poor, cramped and frozen feet back inside the fur-lined haven of my boots, Marco leads Shelley and me away from Piazza Cavour and across the road, before turning right and heading along the paved stretch of the Lungo Lario Trieste, which runs beside the lake. Trees line either side of the path, and their unruly roots are poking up through cracks in the cobbles. It's as if they're lying deliberately in wait, ready to trip up any unsuspecting tourist whose attention has been diverted by the mass of blue fairy lights tangled amongst the branches above.

The air is still but feels heavy with cold, the lake barely dappling, and the orange glow of lit windows on the hillside ahead of us flickers like merry embers in the gloom. I had assumed Como town would be quiet on Boxing Day, but we encounter a steady stream of both locals and visitors as we make our way towards Marco's friend's bar. I think longingly of my cosy bedroom in Bellagio, and of the small and comforting weight of Bruno asleep on my feet. Perhaps I should have stayed with Elsie for another night, but I'd already made a promise to spend the evening with Shelley. Besides, I have to go back to work in the morning anyway. There's a group of artists arriving first thing who have booked a series of excursions, and I'm excited to get my tour guide cap back on and show off the local area.

We reach a wide junction and come to a halt by the crossing, Marco consulting his phone as a text message flashes up.

'That your friend?' Shelley wants to know, but he shakes his head.

'It's nobody.'

Funny name for a girl, I think, but don't say.

It takes us another few minutes to cross through the Piazza de Orchi and reach the Vista Lago bar on the far side, by which time Marco has ignored two more messages and a call. Why he doesn't simply switch off his phone, or at least put it on silent, I have no idea. The bitter side of me assumes it's because he enjoys the attention, but I must allow for the fact that he simply doesn't care. For all his talk of passion, Marco can be incredibly nonchalant.

As soon as we're over the threshold, he hurries off to greet his friend, leaving Shelley and me to peel off our many outer layers and settle down at a table towards the back. It's dingy and warm in here. The dark-wood furniture has been arranged haphazardly and a series of lamps are casting moon-shaped crescents of golden light over the walls and floorboards. I glance at a framed photo as I drape my coat over a chair – it's of the port here in Como, but taken many years ago, and spots of age have appeared at its edges.

'Wine?' Shelley asks, but I shake my head.

'I might just stick to soft drinks tonight.'

She pulls a predictable face. 'But it's Christmas!'

I pick up the thin, leather-bound menu to have a look at what's on offer, but before I've even found the page listing non-alcoholic beverages, Marco has joined us again, and he's brought a bottle of wine and three glasses with him.

'You read my mind,' Shelley declares, grinning at me with obvious glee. Trust Marco to have taken it upon himself to order for us, without even checking what we wanted. Is it the waiter in him, or the arrogance?

I stand up.

'Where are you going?' Marco asks, his hand instinctively reaching out towards me.

'To the bar,' I say, gesturing to the bottle. 'I don't want wine tonight.'

He considers this for a moment.

'You must,' he says. 'It is Christmas.'

Lord, give me strength.

'Fine.' I sit down again, studiously avoiding Shelley's eye while Marco decants red wine into each glass in turn. I notice that he fills the one closest to me first.

'What shall we toast?' Shelley asks, holding her own glass up above the table.

'Dry January?' I suggest hopefully, and again I feel Marco's green eyes flicker over me.

'I think we should drink to passion,' he says, without a trace of irony, and Shelley beams at him.

'To passion.'

I reluctantly tap my glass against theirs and take a tentative sip. The wine is delicious, of course, but I don't want to let on to Marco just how much I like it. I cannot bear people making my decisions for me, and as I think again of that poor girl he so easily dismissed, and of the one who is no doubt trying to get hold of him on the phone tonight, my resolve hardens. So many men think they can get away with treating women like crap. I may have lost the last battle of this type that I fought, but I don't intend to ever lose another, and it seems to me that Marco is extremely used to getting whatever he wants when it comes to members of the opposite sex. OK, so he's fiercely attractive and unflappably cool, but he's not a god. Underneath all the swagger and charm, he's only another human being, just like the rest of us.

As I have discovered to my detriment in the past, putting a man up on a pedestal only ever ends up with a disastrous topple from grace, and being the person standing on the ground looking up means that you're directly in line to get yourself crushed when the inevitable happens. I suppose I'm being unfair to judge Marco so harshly, but then I don't have the energy to be any other way at the moment. I have an inkling that he may at the very least be intrigued by me – it's clear from the way he keeps glancing over at me while he's talking to Shelley – but I imagine it's purely because I'm one of the few women he's ever encountered who hasn't immediately fallen in lustful awe at his feet. That, and the fact that he's now had to rescue me twice, and so probably sees me as some sort of damsel in distress from a bloody fairy tale. If things were different, if I wasn't still feeling so bruised internally, then maybe I would have been more open to his charms – but I'd put good money on the fact that if I had shown an interest, my light would soon have dimmed for him. He wants the thrill of the chase, not the reality of a relationship.

I shouldn't let my mind stray into this territory, though, not when I'm still so fragile. My random fits of crying are showing no signs of abating, and with every sip of this wine, I can feel my emotions welling up behind my eyes. It's not just sorrow, either; it's rage.

I start as Marco brushes the back of my hand with a finger.

'Are you OK?' he asks, quietly enough that Shelley, who is scrolling through her phone looking for a photo to show him, doesn't hear.

I glance up and look at him, at those bewildering eyes, and all I detect is genuine concern. Pity, however, is one thing I am not prepared to put up with – not even for a second.

'I should go.' I stand up abruptly, my half-full glass of wine wobbling as my handbag bashes against the edge of the table.

'What? Why?' Shelley looks put out.

'I have to read up on Villa Olmo, you know, for the tour tomorrow. I've just remembered. I don't know it that well.'

She makes the same grimace she always does whenever I mention work.

'Yes, you do. You know it better than anyone.'

'Well, it can't hurt to swot up a bit more.'

She sighs in defeat. 'Do you want me to come with you?'

'No!' I say, with far more gusto than is strictly necessary.

I start to pull my coat back on, remembering too late that I need to wind my scarf around my neck first, and then swearing as I'm forced to take it off again, almost sending everything on the table tumbling over as I do so. Marco watches me in silence, his brow knotted and his fingers tapping the stem of his wine glass.

'Thanks for the drink,' I say hastily, then hurry towards the door without a backwards glance and head out into the cold night.

10

Lucy

When I chose Lake Como as the destination for my first romantic trip away with Pete, I pictured the sun setting over the water, his face when he took in the view of the mountains for the first time, and droplets of condensation dribbling down the sides of our Prosecco glasses as we toasted one another on the balcony overlooking the old town. Like the squirrel-brained fool that I am, however, I had forgotten that in order to reach this veritable utopia, you must first run the gauntlet of Milano Centrale railway station.

We're on the second of three long escalators, which we've ridden from the Metro platform all the way up to the concourse, and high above us the glass-domed roof of the aged building gleams white against the winter sunlight. The last time I was here, my dad was in charge of tickets and timetables, and while I can remember trailing up endless flights of stairs after him and my mum – Julia loudly complaining by my side, of course – I don't have any recollection of where the Como train leaves from.

'We need to find the one going to Bellizona,' I tell Pete as we reach the top floor, pointing behind his head to where a vast departure board is hanging up on the ornate stone wall.

'I think I see it,' he says, squinting. 'What's the name of our stop again?'

'Como San Giovanni,' I reply, consulting the printed e-ticket that I booked while we were still in London.

'Platform three.' He raises his arm and I follow the direction of his outstretched finger. 'But not for forty minutes or so. Shall we get a beer?'

Our flight this morning was very early, and it's only just gone ten now, but I nod along in agreement. I want Pete to be happy for every single second of this holiday, and if daytime drinking is what he wants to do, then I'm content to go along with it.

'Happy?' I ask, when the cold bottles of Peroni are in our hands and a dish of mixed nuts has been placed on the table between us.

'Very.' He clinks his beer against mine before taking a long, deep swill.

We ended up watching three episodes of *Game of Thrones* last night, but apparently, no amount of dragons, beheadings, and scenes of an extremely sexual nature were enough to distract my mind away from the photos I'd discovered in the back of Pete's wardrobe, so for once I'd been relieved when he'd dropped off to sleep almost immediately. I'm sure he would have been able to tell something was on my mind if we'd been intimate, because there were far too many dark thoughts whirring around in my silly head to allow me to switch off, and I wouldn't have been able to give myself over to him in the way that I wanted. I did wake up with renewed determination today, though. I know that if I let those photos get to me, then I'll sour things with Pete for sure, and I'll only have myself to blame when he dumps me. I ignore the small voice that keeps whispering to me that I should just talk to him about it. Talking is not an option, because talking would mean confessing to the fact that I've been rummaging through his things. Not cool, Lucy. Not cool at all.

Pete is wearing the dark-blue hat I bought him for Christmas, his matching gloves on the table top in front of him, and one of his ginger curls has escaped from underneath. The more I look at his face, the more I like it. His lips are pale pink and full, his scatter of stubble slivers of spun gold, and his jaw is firm and square. I have never been with someone that I feel so proud to be seen with before, and I tell him so.

'Ditto,' he says easily, giving me a lazy smile, but the one I give him in return doesn't come from a genuine place. How can I be the girlfriend he's been most proud of? I've seen his ex-girlfriend, and I know how beautiful she is. He must have been so smug when he had her on his arm – whereas plain old me? Since seeing those photos, I consider myself to be a poor second at best.

'Hey, why do you look so worried all of a sudden?' Pete asks then, sensing my discomfort and fixing his eye on me. 'We haven't missed the train, have we?'

'Oh no, don't worry.' I shake my head and force myself to smile reassuringly. 'But we should probably start drinking up. We want to make sure we get a seat.'

'Not a problem,' he replies, tipping down the remainder of his Peroni.

'Whoa!' I joke, picking up my own half-empty bottle as Pete uncurls a ten-euro note and slips it under the empty dish. 'Give a girl a chance to catch up!'

Pete takes hold of my hand as we leave the bar and doesn't let go of it again until we're sitting safely side by side on the train. I offer him the window seat, just as I did on the flight over, but he refuses just as he did then, and we chat easily to each other as the Lombardy landscape begins to roll past. There are the usual outer-city landmarks – industrial warehouses, blocks of grotty-looking flats and a few rather splendid churches – and after half an hour or so, more flashes of countryside start to appear. I had forgotten just how gorgeously green this part of Italy is, and how beautifully blue the sky above. This is alpine country, with snow-covered peaks and mountainsides thick with fir and pine trees. There's none of the dust of Spain or the dancing heat of Greece – the air here has a clarity that makes you feel more awake, and more alive. That is something I do remember now that I'm back here again, and it makes me wish I hadn't stayed away for so long.

When I used to holiday here with my family all those years ago, the trains were very different, with creaking wooden seats and windows that you could open all the way down to waist height. Julia and I would split up into different carriages and lean right out until we could see one another, gleefully ignoring the signs warning us of danger. It's even worse these days: everywhere you turn, there seems to be a sign telling you to be careful, to not enter, to not touch. Being a nurse, I should really be supportive of all these extra security measures, but the rebellious ten-year-old me can still remember how exhilarating it felt to have the wind rushing through my hair as I leant out of that train window.

By the time we trundle into Como amid a jangle of

squealing brakes, the few clouds that were dotted around on the journey have dispersed, and the radiant winter sunshine greets us like a warm handshake. We disembark, pulling our suitcases off behind us, and gasp in unison as a gust of cold air blasts past our cheeks. From the Como San Giovanni station, it's only a short walk down the hill, through the park, and into the town centre. I lead Pete out through the small station and down the long flight of stone steps towards the main road. Pete is fascinated by the massive Two Hands sculpture just inside the main entrance of the park, and insists on stopping so that he can pose for a photo stretched out across the lower of the open palms.

'See if you can get me high-fiving it in mid-air,' he says excitedly, handing me his proper camera to use instead of my phone and switching it over to sport mode. I do as I'm told, laughing as an increasing number of people stop to watch what we're doing. Next, he wants a shot of both of us sitting on the bottom hand, and ropes in a nearby German tourist to take it. I do my best to smile engagingly as I snuggle up against him, but I can't help but feel haunted by the other photo, the one from the wardrobe. I stubbornly wish that I was the first girl he'd ever had his picture taken with on holiday, but Pete is thirty-three, not thirteen – of course he's going to have had relationships. He's probably been in love already, had his heart broken or been responsible for breaking someone else's. This is the awful thing about getting older, I think wistfully, as the German tourist snaps away – the people you date come to you damaged and worn down by the callousness of others. If only we could all marry our first love, then none of us would ever have to navigate our way through all the confusion and emotional turmoil that go hand-in-hand with break-ups. I know my dad would agree with me.

We leave the sculpture behind and make our way through Como's wide streets, each of us hushed into silence by the imposing, apricot-coloured buildings stacked tightly together on either side of the road. The sturdy soles of my boots make a pleasant clip-clopping sound against the cobbles, which are stretched like scales across the pavements, and every few yards there is a delicatessen, pizza parlour or grocery store, each one adding a new splash of colour to Como's ever-expanding palette.

There are tasteful Christmas decorations in the windows of all the shops, and more strung up in neat patterns across the pedestrianized lanes snaking through the town centre. As Pete and I stroll, fingers entwined, I point out to him how clean everything is – especially in comparison to the grubby North London streets we drove past this morning on the way to the airport. There is no litter on the ground, no graffiti sprayed on the alleyway walls, and everything from the neatly clipped shrubs to the elegantly draped fairy lights is pristine. It's nice to be in a city so obviously cherished by its inhabitants, and with every step we take, I feel my mood lightening.

Como isn't a sleepy place – far from it – but it does feel a lot quieter than I remember it being in the summer months. There aren't many people on the streets, and – aside from a distant rumble of traffic and the occasional notes of music trailing out from the open door of a bar – there isn't much noise, either. It's only when you leave a big city that you realise how loud they are, and I experience the same awareness every time I go home to Suffolk, too.

I've always been the type of girl to pick a cosy quiet corner over a stadium full of noise, so I suppose it's rather strange that I've chosen to work in such a chaotic environment and base myself in one of the most hectic cities in the world. I must enjoy the madness more than I think I do.

Pete doesn't say much, but his eyes are wide as he takes it all in, his escaped curl still plastered against his forehead. It's becoming increasingly hard to curb the strong urge to tuck it back under his hat, but I clench my fist and resist. Pete doesn't mind me making a fuss of him sometimes, but I know he prefers to be the one doing the spoiling. We have that in common, the two of us, that need to nurture and protect, and so far, it seems to be working out in our favour. When you're both keen to show affection, and receive it in kind, then neither of you ever ends up feeling as if they're lacking – it's only when the balance goes askew that you're in trouble. A fact that I know only too well.

The apartment I've booked is only a few streets away from the large Piazza Cavour square, which looks right out over the lake, and I can see the lights from the Christmas Market in the near-distance as we reach our destination. I sent a text to the owner, Cara, just as we got off the train, and she's waiting for us just inside the building entrance.

'*Ciao, ciao,*' she says, her voice sweetly singsong, and I try not to mind that she gives Pete a kiss of greeting on the cheek as well as me. Being Italian, she's naturally dark, beautiful and effortlessly chic, with her camel coat buttoned up to the neck and the diamond studs in each of her ears making her literally sparkle. Pete would have to be blind not to be wowed. To his credit, however, my boyfriend is merely courteous and polite, smiling along as Cara explains in broken English how to get the shower working and shows us where the extra bedding is stored. I'm gratified to see that she remembered to leave out the bottle of Prosecco as requested, and before she leaves, she presses a business card into my hand, telling the two of us that we must come to her husband's cocktail bar by the lake.

'I thought she was never going to go,' Pete says, as I shut the door behind our glamorous host and turn to face him. He's already picked up the bottle from the ice bucket and is now using his teeth to tear through the foil.

'Me too!' I'm quick to agree, hurrying across to wrap my arms around his muscular middle. 'I can't believe we're finally here. What do you think so far? Do you like it?'

'I love it,' he says, beaming as he struggles with the cork. We both let out a shout of excited delight when it shoots across the room and lands in the kitchen sink.

'Good shot, sir,' I appraise, and he takes a small bow.

'Why thank you, my beloved.'

Beloved? Does he love me? No, he's just being silly. Or is he?

Pete pours two glasses and toasts me with a flourish before putting his down and disappearing into the bathroom. I take a deep breath. Everything is going well. It's all going to plan. Pete is happy, I'm happy. We're going to have the most fun either of us has ever had before; I'm going to make sure of it.

'Lulu?'

I turn around and immediately gasp with laughter.

Pete is standing in the bedroom doorway, a knowing look on his face and a definite glint in his eye. Oh, and he's absolutely, completely, unashamedly and totally naked.

'Wow,' I say, my attention moving swiftly from his face to another part of his body. 'You really are happy to be here, aren't you?'

'Nurse Dunmore,' he says, his head on one side. 'I do believe you're blushing.'

He's right, I am. I may have chosen a profession which inevitably includes regular encounters with naked bodies, but there's still something disarming about seeing the man you're falling in love with standing to attention, so to speak, right in front of you. No matter how familiar I may be with the male form, I'm still a shy girl at heart – and there is emphatically nothing shy at all about the way Pete is looking at me right at this moment. I'm still fully dressed, but I feel completely undressed by his eyes. He wants me, and I want him – I'm just going to have to put that pesky photo to the back of my mind.

'Shall we try out the shower?' he suggests, not taking his eyes off me as I reach for my glass. The Prosecco is cold and tangy, a touch dryer than I usually like, but it does the job, and after a few more sips I feel emboldened enough to remove my cardigan, followed quickly by my knee-high boots. I can feel my cheeks turning pink, and battle to ignore the shyness that has assaulted me. After a few murmurs of encouragement from an increasingly aroused Pete, I roll off my tights and, taking a deep breath, untie my pink wrap dress. I'm too timid to meet his gaze, but a small part of me feels empowered, too, because I know where this is leading, and just how much Pete wants it. When I'm standing still in just my underwear, my undone hair snaking across my bare shoulders and my heart racing with the adrenalin that is coursing through me, Pete moves at last from his position by the door and gathers me into his arms.

'You're so beautiful,' he tells me, his hands roving across my chest and stomach. I instinctively suck in my extra roll of flesh and clench my bottom just as he reaches for it, pulling aside the flimsy material of my knickers as he does so. As he bends his head to kiss me, I slide my own hands across his strong, broad back, all the time stroking, tickling, teasing and squeezing until he's practically panting into my mouth.

We never make it as far as the shower.

Afterwards, we stretch out together on top of the still-made bed, taking it in turns to swig out of the half-empty bottle of Prosecco as we chat aimlessly away about anything and everything. My hair looks like two hens have had a fight in it and I'm sweating so much that even my upper lip is wet, but I don't care. The sex we just had was intense and furious, but more than that, it felt passionate and real, as if I was the only thing that mattered in the whole world to Pete. When we're together in this way, I forget about the wobbles and lumps. Instead, I see myself as he sees me – as he tells me he sees me – which is sexy as hell. The way Pete looked at me had sent shivers of pleasure through me – even more so than what he was doing to me – and I was overwhelmed with wonderful, dizzy and uncomplicated love for him.

This man. My man. The one who is going to be different from all the rest.

11

Taggie

I wake early, before the light, and lie still for a moment in the darkness.

He snuck into my dreams again, in the way that he so often does, and I blink hard to rid myself of his image. It is always the same – he is angry with me and looks at me with disdain, I reach for him and am rebuffed, and then the tears will follow.

Do I *miss* him? My mum thinks that I'm suffering from emotional trauma. She looked it up, found similar cases, then searched for reassurance that it would eventually cease. When I became convinced that I must remove myself from home, from where triggers lurked at every turn, waiting to send me back to the floor, where I had lain and wailed and thumped for weeks, my parents didn't try to stop me. Just like me, they were terrified of anything sending me back to that dark place again. Their strong and capable daughter had disintegrated in front of their eyes, and it was devastating for them to watch.

I no longer cling in desperation to the carpet when the memories or the 'what ifs' assault me, but simply knowing that I was rendered so utterly broken frightens me. It changed me, that pain, and I'm still trying to work out whether I'm now softer or harder as a result. Last night's drink with Marco and Shelley was an eye-opener for me, because my reaction to him, and to the thoughts and feelings he stirred up, told me that it was more likely the latter – I'm as brittle as glass, and quite possibly even more fragile. It's only human nature to protect yourself from being hurt, so it does make sense, but does it also mean that I'm destined to feel closed off and afraid forever? That thought makes me feel very sad indeed.

But this won't do. There's no point lying here in the dark, brooding about things over which I have no control. I've learnt that the best thing to do when I wake up feeling like this is to get up and get out – do something with my limbs to stop them twisting with impotent rage, and take my mind and senses into a new setting.

Throwing aside the heavy maroon blankets with the gold Casa Alta logo stitched into them, I pad barefoot into my en suite bathroom and switch on the shower, waiting until the steam starts to rise before getting in and sliding the glass doors shut behind me. The water is only a few degrees away from scalding, but it invigorates me and helps me to focus on the day ahead. I'm due in the hotel reception to meet the tour group at ten a.m. sharp, which means I have three hours of playtime to myself first – and I know exactly how I'm going to use them.

The kitchen staff greet me with enthusiasm as I slip through the door twenty minutes later to beg for some crusts. Luka – head chef and my self-proclaimed *nonno* – insists that I take the remainder of last night's rye bread, which is still languishing in the little wicker baskets that we put on the tables for dinner. He also lends me his personal thermos flask and fills it with thick, delicious hot chocolate, telling me in no uncertain terms that without it, I will most likely freeze to death on my walk. He may be overreacting a smidgeon, but then that is the Italian way – and I love him for it.

Despite wrapping myself up in a thick cream jumper, heavy coat, chunky scarf and a hat made from alpaca wool, just like those down in the Christmas market, the cold still causes me to gasp as I step outside, and I stamp my feet on the frosty path in a bid to get my circulation going. The grounds of the Casa Alta Hotel look even prettier than usual coated in frost, and now that the sun is beginning to climb, the gravel driveway I'm walking along is sparkling as if it's covered in gem dust. The view of the lake never fails to lift my spirits, but this morning it's part-obscured by a heavy curtain of fog. The bulk of mountains on the opposite shore have all but vanished, but I know that as soon as the morning properly arrives, the sunshine will rapidly burn away any trace of this atmospheric gloom.

Once I reach the pathway that runs alongside the lake, I turn right and head towards Como, enjoying the crunching sound of my boots and the early calls of the gulls that are bobbing on the surface of the water below me. Beauty and nature help, they really do. How can the world be a bad place, when there are sights to behold such as this, and people such as the ones who have taken me in? I think fondly of Elsie, Bruno, Gino and Nico, and irrationally wish that I could reach out across the water and pull them closer to me. Bellagio is just that little bit too far up the coast to make a daily commute worthwhile, but living at the hotel means that I miss the four of them horribly – especially now that it's the festive season. Luckily, however, one of the tours I'm in charge of over the next few days is one that visits Bellagio, so I'm hoping Elsie and the boys will have time to join us for a few hours.

There are barely any cars passing me on the coastal road as I walk, my head dipped so that my nose and mouth are protected from the cold by my scarf. My hands are as deep in my pockets as they can go, but I can still feel the tips of my fingers tingling. This is the coldest it's been since I arrived in Como, but in a strange way I'm enjoying the sensation. Just because I chose to swap England for Italy doesn't mean I don't miss it – and Christmas has always been my favourite time of year back home. I love how everyone pretends not to be excited about it during the build-up, but then still rushes out and picks up a tree as soon as December arrives. I love Secret Santa and work office parties and cheesy festive songs being played on a loop. I adore advent calendars – both the chocolate variety and those ingenious ones stuffed with beauty products – and I'm a firm believer in the fact that most things in life can benefit enormously from a string of fairy lights being draped across them.

The people of Como clearly agree with that last sentiment, because many of the trees that I'm now passing in the lakeside park have been adorned with lights, and the town itself is a veritable grotto at this time of year. As I glance across the water now, towards the cluster of houses emerging through the fog on the eastern shore, I can see more evidence of decoration glowing merrily at windows and along fences. The grey of first light is giving way to greens and browns now, but the lake is still a silent sweep of black below me.

It takes me about fifteen minutes to reach the large white hangar that comprises Como's Aero Club, which is set back from the edge of the water on the opposite side of the road to where I'm now standing. Seaplanes of various sizes and colours are parked both in the water and on the tarmac slope leading into it, and all around them are the reason I walked all the way down here in the first place – the local bird population.

'Steady on!' I say fondly, as a particularly overexcited gosling makes a lunge for my first wedge of rye bread.

My mum and dad used to bring me down to this very spot when I was a child, and we would feed the ducks together with the bread that we'd pilfered either from the hotel buffet or Elsie's kitchen, depending on where we were staying each time. My dad was a keen photographer back in those days, and the evidence of one of his shoots still hangs in his study today. It's of me, aged six, one hand outstretched, my eyes tight shut, and a look of pure terror on my face as an enormous swan waddles over to help itself to my offering of bread. He maintains that it's the best picture he's ever taken. I maintain that he's crazy.

I like birds a lot more these days. I find that the more time I spend down here with them, the braver they become, and I'm even starting to recognise some of them. There's the pigeon with the pure-white face, the young swan who hates the gulls, and a timid little moorhen who's always scuttling around at the back of the flock. I always make sure I save a special handful of crumbs, just for him. I must be going soft in my old age – either that or my dad's fondness for this ritual has finally ingrained itself in me. I wonder if I'll become a crazy old bird lady one day, like the woman in *Home Alone 2*, and the thought makes me chuckle into my scarf. It's nice to know that I haven't lost the ability to laugh at myself, despite all the shit that's happened, and as the thought occurs to me I think immediately of Marco plucking me out of the lake a couple of months ago, and how, back then, I was still too delicate to see the funny side. If I slipped over on a bird poo and the same thing happened again, right here and now, I like to think I'd respond in a less stroppy way. But perhaps Marco wouldn't bother to help me this time – not after I ran out on him and Shelley last night.

Once the bread has run out and the birds have all gone back to their complicated business of washing in the shallows, pecking through the dirt or perching imperially on the floating jetty, I sit on a bench for a while, drinking my delicious hot chocolate and watching the sunlight creep through the trees. I can see my breath in the air and my toes have long since ceased to have any sensation in them at all, but I'm determined to stay put until I feel completely soothed. Last night's dream is receding back into the murky depths of my mind, and I find I can no longer conjure it up, even when I allow myself to try. It's so odd, I think, this yearning for something while at the same time fearing it so acutely. Is it the person that scares me, or the feeling that seeing him will elicit? Perhaps it's both. But hopefully, I conclude, finally getting to my feet and heading back along the western shore towards the hotel, I will never have to find out.

12

Lucy

After a post-coital nap, Pete wakes up ravenous, almost chasing me out of the apartment in his haste to track down some lunch. I deliberately booked us a place with a kitchen, thinking it would be fun if we cooked together while we're here, surrounded by such delicious ingredients, but when I mentioned the idea earlier, he shook his head.

'This is your holiday,' he said, giving me the baby monkey eyes, as I always call them. 'I want you to relax. You work so hard, and you've earned it.'

No matter how many times I tried to tell him that cooking genuinely does relax me, and that it's a treat for me to have the time to prepare a proper meal – something working at the hospital rarely allows – he still talked me out of it by distracting me with kisses. I suspect he plans to treat me to dinner every night, but I don't see why he should pay for all my meals.

It's still a bright and beautiful day outside. The sky is such a flawless blue that it looks almost synthetic, as if someone has selected the whole thing with their mouse and then clicked the tin of paint symbol on their computer. The sun is sitting low, its rays slipping around corners and through windows, leaving everything in its wake brushed with gold. Despite this, however, the cold feels solid and unrelenting, and I snuggle down further into my scarf as Pete locks the door behind us.

It only takes a few minutes to reach the hub of the town, where houses give way to shops and silence is swallowed whole by chatter. Locals greet each other with a merry wave and a shout of '*ciao*', while others sit at the windows of coffee shops, watching the passers-by through the steam rising from their espressos. As well as these cafés, there are all manner of boutiques selling clothes, handbags, shoes and jewellery, and we also pass a bookshop, a tobacconist and even a pet shop. There are designer stores, too, and I point out a silk scarf in the window of one bearing a seven-hundred-euro price tag.

'Unfortunately for you, I'm not George Clooney,' Pete says, and I shake my head and laugh.

'I wouldn't swap you for George even if he offered to buy me all the silk scarves in Italy.'

I mean it, too.

We follow the sound of music and bustle until we find the first few stalls leading into the Christmas Market, and Pete immediately comes to a halt next to one wooden hut that is offering giant pretzels stuffed with Parma ham and melted, stringy cheese.

'Wow!' he exclaims, his eyes widening. 'Shall we get some? They look incredible.'

'Is that drool on your chin?' I joke, smiling at the woman taking the orders as Pete uses his limited knowledge of the Italian language to order us two. She's all wrapped up against the cold in a thick blanket-type coat and hat, but the heat rising off the cheese has turned her cheeks bright pink. I wince a bit at the thought of how many calories I'm about to consume, but it only takes a single bite to convince me that it's well worth the risk. The bread has been toasted just the right amount to keep the cheese warm but not drop too many crumbs, and the chewy, salty ham lifts the flavour up to a whole new level. I know Pete is enjoying his just as much, because he's gone completely silent. The way he's gazing down at his pretzel is almost as ardent as the look he was giving me less than two hours ago in the apartment.

'That was incredible,' he declares, wiping his fingers and lips with a napkin and tossing it into a nearby bin. 'Where to next?'

I don't answer straight away, because my mouth is full, so instead I use my head to direct him forwards, further into the heart of the market. I'm enchanted by the cashmere shawls and delicately made jewellery, while Pete spends a good ten minutes at the cheese hut, charming the stall holder out of free tasters. After the pretzel, I'm stuffed, but I know that Pete could go on grazing all afternoon. I seem to remember it was date three when I first accused him of having hollow legs. This is the man who can go for a Sunday roast at lunchtime, then out for a pizza for dinner, and still have room for half a pint of Häagen-Dazs. It's a wonder he's in such good shape – not to mention blooming unfair.

I'm longing to stroll along by the lake with a *vin brulé* and take in the view from the park on the western shore, but Pete is dragging me excitedly towards the ice rink by the road instead.

'We can look out at the view as we skate around,' he

begs, all bouncy and enthusiastic, and so of course I give in. Ice-skating is not my favourite thing to do – especially given the number of patients I've seen who have suffered everything from a fractured coccyx to a broken jaw whilst partaking. It's unsafe, it's cold and, as we discover when we reach the booth to pay, it's eye-wateringly expensive, too. When Pete tries to pay yet again, I elbow him playfully out of the way, insisting that he has to let me, so that when I inevitably fall over, I'll only have myself to blame.

'Was this ice rink here when you were a kid?' Pete wants to know. He hasn't let go of my hand since we strapped on our skates, and we're now making our circuits at a nice steady pace, while a multitude of daredevil children zoom past us at speed. Being a sporty guy, Pete has a natural flair for this sort of thing, but he tutted at me when I pointed out the fact that I'm slowing him down.

'I can't actually remember,' I tell him honestly. 'We only ever came here for Christmas once, and that time we stayed up in Bellagio.'

'Oh?'

'My dad once knew a guy who had a house there, although I'm not sure if he still does.'

'Maybe we should go and find out?' he suggests, spinning me round in a tentative circle, only to almost lose his balance and burst out laughing.

I cling on to him, willing him not to fall. If he goes down, then I'm going down with him.

'You mean go up to Bellagio?' I ask, when he's regained his composure and we're both on the move again.

'Yeah,' he takes his eyes off his feet to brave a look at me. 'Why not?'

'It *is* gorgeous up there,' I say, picturing the narrow cobbled lanes and the magnificent lakeside villas, not to mention the views of the Swiss Alps in the distance. 'I'm pretty sure we can get a boat up there from just over the road.'

'Let's do it!' He looks excited again, and his eagerness is infectious. I loved Bellagio as a child, with its hidden coves and warren-like streets. Plus, my secret beach is there, and I'd love to show it to him.

We stay on the rink until Pete's finally burned off all his pretzel energy, which unfortunately for me is a good twenty minutes or so after my hands and feet have turned from flesh and blood into solid lumps of ice. Pete tells me a scandalous story about a famous married footballer they had on the radio show recently, who disappeared during what was supposed to be a ten-minute tea break only to emerge from the ladies' toilet a good while later with the station receptionist in tow, her blouse buttons done up wrong and her skirt twisted round to one side. He often regales me with tales from the studio, and promises that he'll take me in one day to show me how everything works. I love that he enjoys his job, just as I adore mine – there's nothing more irritating than someone who complains about their choice of career only to refuse to do anything to change it.

When I can no longer even feel my toes, I steer Pete by the arm to the nearest *vin brulé* stall. I order us a couple and pass one across, blowing steam off the top of mine and smiling as the hot sides of the cup begin to thaw my frozen fingers.

'What's up there?' Pete asks, pointing up to the right,

above the eastern shore of the lake. There are buildings just visible right at the very top of the mountain, and I know from the guidebook rather than experience what it is we're looking at.

'That's Brunate,' I tell him. 'It's only a small village, but the views from up there are supposed to be amazing.'

'How do we get up there?' he asks, scanning the hillside in the middle distance, then spotting the tracks of Como's *funicolare* just as I point them out.

'I reckon we could walk it,' he adds, turning to me.

'Really?' I'm doubtful. It's a very long way up, and it's not as if either of us regularly go hiking. I look down at his trainers, already soggy from the frosty ground, and shake my head.

'It'll be quicker to just catch the *funicolare* up,' I say, putting on my best persuasive-nurse voice, which has served me so well, so many times.

'Yeah,' he allows. 'But imagine how much more fun it will be to walk.'

'Fun?' I deadpan, forcing myself not to react to his ridiculously over-the-top grin. I want to support this foolish scheme of his, I really do, but I know my limits, and I suspect that I know his.

'Come on, Lulu.' He's pleading now. 'Where's your sense of adventure?'

I can't help it, I picture Pete's ex again, the girl in that ruddy photo I wish I'd never found. She looks like exactly the type of girl who would be fabulous at scaling mountains, being all lithe with skinny little arms and a healthy, glowing complexion. The two of them probably legged it up vast, frost-covered hillsides together all the time.

'OK,' I agree, taking a deeper breath than I intend to. 'I'm game if you are.'

'All right!' he whoops, punching the air. Several tourists turn to stare at him in bemusement, but he doesn't even seem to notice, and I can't help but beam at him, besotted as I am.

Pete's so enthusiastic to get cracking that he practically skips along the road next to the lake, pulling me along behind him while I hang back, trying in vain to take in the view. The canopy of branches above the path are playing host to a jumbled nest of blue and white lights, and I make a mental note to walk back along the same route later tonight, so that we might get to appreciate them in the dark.

'I reckon it's this way,' I tell him, coming to a halt as we reach the corner of the lake and a wide junction. We cross the road hand in hand, leaving the water behind us, and take the first road we find leading away from the shore. I've always been pretty good at keeping my bearings, and before long I've managed to locate a steep set of stone steps heading up the side of the mountain.

'Are you one hundred per cent sure about this?' I ask Pete for at least the tenth time since we left the market. 'It's going to take us quite a while to reach the top, and the *funicolare* is just over there.'

'Positive,' he assures me. 'It'll be no bother, Lulu, you'll see.'

'You're the boss,' I reply, rolling my eyes good-naturedly. As I turn and put my boot on the first step, however, I make a silent bet with myself in my head.

13

Taggie

I have had a lot of jobs in my life. Before getting the position of tour guide at the Casa Alta Hotel, I worked in PR, which I liked. Well, I liked the events organising, but all the emailing and chasing journalists was horrendous. Before that, I was a marketing executive in a magazine office for three years, and shortly prior to that, I worked in a museum. I was one of those people who glares at you for stepping too close to the paintings and scurries over to tell you off for taking photos of the artefacts. When I was at university, I had a part-time job in a bar, and once upon a long time ago, before even that, I spent an eventful summer walking my parents' friends' dogs around the local park three times a day.

You could say that my employment history has prepared me for most things, and most people. It had not, however, prepared me for Gladys and Bill.

'Agatha! I say, Aggy, dear. Cooee.'

I grit my teeth.

'I told you already, Gladys – Taggie is fine.'

'Oh, but Agatha is the name your mother gave you, my dear – and it's so much prettier than Taggie. Don't you agree, William?'

'Much prettier,' chirps Bill, who I'm starting to suspect

is more parrot than man. Everything his darling wife Gladys says, Bill – or 'Will-yum', as she insists on calling him – seems more than content to simply repeat.

'Perhaps just Miss Torres, then?' I suggest hopefully, and Gladys's heavily made-up face crumples.

'Oh no, my dear, that's far too much of a mouthful. I'm not sure I could even say it right. Toulouse, is it?'

'Torres,' I say again. 'My father is Mauritian.'

Gladys raises a drawn-on eyebrow. 'I see.'

The three of us are standing on the crunchy gravel beside a large decorative fountain, which sits in pride of place in front of the Villa Olmo. As vast and grand as a palace from a Disney film, and with an immaculate pale-yellow façade complete with tall white pillars, the eighteenth-century villa itself has been predominantly closed to visitors for years now, because it's privately owned, but the extensive grounds have thankfully remained open to the public. An exhibition was hosted inside the main house a few months ago, so I made sure I took full advantage and had a good old snoop around inside. The view from the upstairs window looking out over the lake is one of the most incredible things I've ever seen – and Villa Olmo looks just as majestic and unfor-gettable from the water, too. It's one of the most famous and most visited Como landmarks for good reason, and I love bringing guests here and showing the place off.

Given that Gladys and Bill are here with a group of amateur artists from all over the globe, I chose Villa Olmo as a nice spot for the ten of them to get some inspir-ation and perhaps take some photos. It's far too cold for any of them to set up an easel here on the shore, but these days I find that many of the more creatively minded guests we have staying at the Casa Alta are happy to work from a photo. We even have a room downstairs set aside for painting, which is warm, cosy and filled with natural light. Gladys, however, prefers portraits to landscapes. Well, self-portraits, to be more precise – and it appears that poor old 'Will-yum' is not up to the job of photographer.

'Oh no, you cut my chin off in that one, you funny man!' she shrieked ten minutes ago. I heard her from all the way across the lawn, where I was directing the other eight members of the group to the nearest café, and I couldn't help but cringe. Wherever you go in the world, there always seem to be some British tourists behaving embarrassingly and totally letting the side down. Another English lady named Sue, who has brought her son Tim along on the tour with her, caught my eye just as Gladys was letting rip, and I can tell she feels my pain. Tim, meanwhile, hasn't said much to me at all yet. Looking at him, I'd guess he's in his mid-twenties, but it's hard to tell, because every time I've approached him for a chat, he's mumbled something incoherent, buried his red face into the neck of his coat, and hurried away. Way to give a girl a complex, Tim.

The remaining members of the group – those apparently not afraid or repulsed by the sight of me – wisely agreed that an hour was more than long enough to spend outside in this temperature, but Gladys is refusing to go anywhere until she has the perfect picture.

'Agatha, my dear, will you please have a go? Will-yum is all fingers and thumbs with this camera, aren't you, Will-yum?'

'Fingers and thumbs,' he nods with a helpless grin.

The best way I can think to describe Gladys's ever-patient husband is as a mole. Albeit one with overlarge glasses and a tweed suit, like something out of *The Wind in the Willows*. And while Bill may act like a parrot, it's his wife who dresses like one. I don't think I've seen these many colours on a single person since I went to see Joseph and his technicolour dreamcoat at the theatre aged twelve.

'Are you sure you can lift it?' Bill jokes limply, handing over the weighty camera. 'There's nothing of her, is there, Gladys?'

'Nothing at all!' she trills.

What is it about this particular generation that feels it's acceptable to comment openly on a person's size and shape? Sometimes I wish that I was knocking sixty, too, so I could brazenly warn Gladys against the perils of too much blusher. Clearly the phrase 'a little goes a long way' is not in her vocabulary. Still, I remind myself, lifting the camera up easily and peering through the viewfinder, this quirky pair are exactly the type of client that keeps the Casa Alta in business, and as such I must maintain a polite and professional air around them at all times.

'Oh no, no, no, Agatha. Oh gosh, no.'

Gladys pouts at me as she examines the first batch of pictures.

'Did you want more of the villa in the background?' I guess.

She titters with laughter. 'Quite the opposite, Agatha. I can barely see myself in any of these. Zoom right in on me, if you will. Remember: I'm the subject matter – the rest is merely setting.'

I try again.

'Better. Much better – but I can still see the edge of the fountain there, see? I think let's just focus in on my face this time, OK? Do you think you can do that, Agatha?'

'Taggie,' I mutter, just as Bill says, 'On her face.'

'Focus on the end prize,' I mumble to myself, gritting my teeth as I fiddle with the zoom. 'If you can get through this, then being a proper events manager will feel like a stroll along the lake.'

By the time I manage to bribe Bill and Gladys away from the Villa Olmo and back up to the Casa Alta by promising to point out George Clooney's house on the way up to Bellagio tomorrow, the light is drawing in. In December, the sun falls rapidly from its low position in the sky, and darkness seems to arrive all of a sudden, without warning. The sun sets behind the surrounding mountains rather than on the water, taking its faint but comforting warmth with it, and you can go swiftly from basking on the shores of the lake to shivering there in the pitch dark. It's only just gone five p.m., but losing the light has made me feel instantly tired, and as soon as I've prised myself away from the group, I head into the bar in search of Shelley.

'You look terrible,' is her greeting, as I clamber up on to one of the stools.

'Gee, thanks,' I groan, laying my arms on top of the bar and then resting my head on them. 'You sound like Gladys.'

'Who?' Shelley asks.

'Never mind.'

'You done for the day now?' she enquires, selecting an empty wine glass from the shelf by her waist and holding it up.

'I wish,' I grumble, shaking my head at her offer of a drink. 'I've promised to have dinner with the whole group tonight.'

'That bad, are they?' Shelley remarks sympathetically, putting her blonde head on one side. It's not the first time a member of staff has sat at her bar and bemoaned the guests.

'No,' I say, feeling guilty. 'They're fine. Some of them are, anyway. There's a young guy called Tim who runs away every time I go near him, and a couple who could quite easily have walked straight off the set of a *Carry On* film. No, I'm being unfair now. I'm just tired, I guess.'

'I thought you got an early night yesterday,' Shelley replies. And of course, she would assume that. Hadn't I run out on drinks with her and Marco because I needed to get into bed and do some reading for today's tour? In truth, I had done no such thing. I'd rung Mum back, because I'd been ignoring her all day, then I'd sat with my laptop down here in the deserted bar, looking through old photos. I should know better by now than to pull at the thread of the past, but chatting to my mum brought back things that I'd been doing my best to ignore, and last night the need overcame me. Now I wish I'd been stronger.

'I tried,' I say, sidestepping the ugly truth. 'But I couldn't get to sleep.'

'Too busy thinking about Marco?' she guesses, and I laugh in answer because she's so far from the truth.

'Are you sure?' She peers at me, trying to tell whether or not I'm blushing.

'Very sure. I told you, he's not really my type.'

'Tall, dark, handsome and charming is everyone's type,' Shelley argues. 'And you could do a lot worse.'

'Why don't you go for it if you like him so much?' I ask, genuinely curious. In all the months I've known Shelley, I've never once known her to shy away from what she wants.

'Oh, I would, believe me,' she says, arranging some empty dishes along the bar and reaching for an industrial-sized bag of pistachio nuts. 'But there's no point when it's so obvious that he likes you.'

'He does not,' I counter instantly, but Shelley simply eyes me over the upturned bag of nuts.

'Even if he does, there's no point,' I say adamantly. 'Because I'm not interested in him or any other man. I mean it. He would be wasting his energy.'

Shelley surprises me then by reaching across and lightly squeezing my arm.

'Whatever it is that happened to you,' she says gently, 'it doesn't mean you have to swear off all men for life.'

'Nothing happened to me,' I lie, dropping my eyes before she can fix me with one of her Shelley-knows-best stares. 'I'm just happy as I am, that's all.'

I can't stand the way she's looking at me, as if she feels sorry for me. I may have started leaking water like an incontinent old tortoise lately, but I'm still me; I'm still a tough Torres – and that's the way I intend to stay.

'How do you know for sure that he likes me anyway?' I can't help but ask her then, and she immediately stops filling her dishes so she can rub her hands together with glee.

'Well, he basically told me.'

'What do you mean?'

'As soon as you left last night, he asked me if you were OK. Then he wanted to know if you were seeing anyone, and how long you'd been in Como, and how well you knew the place. It was all he would talk about for the best part of an hour.'

Now I am blushing. I hope Shelley can't tell.

'It's only because he can tell I'm not into him,' I say knowingly. 'He's so used to girls eating out of his hand – finding one who doesn't has intrigued him.'

'It could be that,' she allows. 'But I think he does genuinely like you. It's not so much what he says as the way he says it, and the look he gets on his face when he's talking about you.'

'Now you're being silly,' I chide, but she shakes her head until her pigtails swing.

'No, I mean it. If I was in any doubt, you know I would've gone for it and thrown myself at him. You know as well as I do that I have zero shame.'

I can't argue with that, so I merely smile.

'You should give him a chance to prove himself,' she persists. 'What harm can one date do?'

I think back to all those weeks where I could barely get out of bed in the morning, when my legs would shake with the weight of carrying around my broken heart and I could sit, for hours, staring into the dark recesses of my bedroom back at my parents' house, wishing that the world would curl inwards and swallow me whole.

'A lot,' I say, getting down off the stool and giving Shelley a deflated smile. 'Now, I'd better go and get myself ready for this dinner.'

'Good luck,' she offers, as I turn to go, but I can sense that she's far from finished with the subject of Marco.

14

Lucy

I knew this was a mad idea.

We've been walking uphill for over an hour now, and the small town of Brunate is still nowhere to be seen. What began as a series of concrete steps and steep, but paved, stretches of path, have now merged into a stony and leaf-covered track, which feels as if it's going nowhere at all. On one side, a thick and twisted forest looms above us, clinging to the side of the slope, while on the other is a barely interrupted view of Como, the lake, and the spread of distant mountains beyond. There was one moment about ten minutes ago, just as we came across a rusty old sign with the word 'Brunate' painted across it, when the two of us were jubilant.

'We must be close,' Pete had panted, peering upwards through the dense foliage. 'Just over the next ridge, I reckon.'

He had been wrong. Oh, so wrong.

'Are you OK?' I ask him now, making my way back down the rough, mud-covered steps to where Pete has just collapsed against a fallen log.

'No,' he admits, looking up at me. 'I'm bloody knackered!'

I know this already, and I also know he's very thirsty,

because the adorable fool's been saying it at two-minute intervals ever since we left the safe vicinity of the lake, where there were shops and cafés. Unfortunately for him, there is nothing on this walk up the side of the mountain except trees, parked cars, the odd house and, of course, the continually astounding views. The latter was enough to spur Pete on until he began to feel the effects of the climb, but for the past mile or so his thirst and fatigue has been winning the battle against the local aesthetics.

'Why don't we admit defeat now?' I suggest brightly, in the same voice that I use to chivvy patients into sitting still to have their stitches removed.

'You want to give up?' he replies hopefully, wiping a hand across his hot forehead. 'I mean, I'm sure I can keep going, but if you're tired, then I don't want to make you carry on.'

'I am getting a bit tired,' I agree, forcing myself not to laugh. The both of us know full well that Pete is the one who wants to abandon our climb, but I'm happy to humour him this once.

'It's not like it's been a total waste of time,' I continue lightly, taking a seat beside him on the fallen tree. 'We've taken some amazing photos – and met those nice dogs.'

'Ha!' he states, pulling a disbelieving face. I'm joking, of course, because the dogs we encountered were anything *but* nice. In fact, they barked, snarled and showed their teeth as we made our weary way past their fenced-in garden a few minutes ago.

'What if I'd been a little old lady?' he says now. 'Those monsters would have scared me into having a heart attack.'

Given his slightly beaten-down mood, I decide against pointing out the obvious, which is that no little old lady in her right mind would attempt the hike that we had. Or little young lady, for that matter. I know Pete's only feeling out of sorts because he's desperate for some water, and not because the hill is proving less of a struggle to me than it is to him. I had no idea I was so fit, but I suppose working all those hours on my feet in the Accident and Emergency department has paid off. Pete does play rugby at the weekends and lifts weights in the gym, but the rest of the time he works in a radio studio, sitting on his lovely bottom all day long, whereas I barely get a moment to pause, let alone rest.

'It's probably going to get dark soon,' I add, squeezing his shoulder. The climb has made him so hot that he's removed his waterproof coat and tied it awkwardly around his waist, and his handsome face is the same colour as my dad's rhubarb crumble. This is the first time since we've met that I've known him to be anything but completely affable, but it's actually more amusing than troubling. This is how I know I have it bad.

'You should keep going up,' he says now, like some sort of ridiculous fallen soldier. 'I know you're not really tired – you'd probably be at the top now if it wasn't for me.'

I laugh out loud at that. 'As if!'

'You would be,' he argues. 'You've barely even broken a sweat, woman. Who are you, She-Ra?'

'Trust me, I'm She-Really-Worn-Out,' I joke, fanning my face with my hand. 'Brunate is one thousand six hundred feet above lake level, it says so in the guidebook – that is damn high. And anyway, it's not safe for either of us to carry on without any water. All we've drunk today is beer, Prosecco and *vin brulé* – no wonder you're feeling the effects. That's probably all it is, Pete, just dehydration.'

I hear him take a deep breath as he admits defeat, then he wraps an arm around my shoulder and pulls me closer.

'Thank you,' he mutters.

'For what?'

'For knowing me better than I know myself,' he says, meeting my eyes with his own as I turn to look at him in surprise. 'And for not making me feel bad about being an out-of-shape wimp.'

'You're not a wimp,' I say, holding his gaze. 'You're amazing is what you are – meeting you has been even more exciting than finding the prize in a box of cereal.'

Pete smiles at the childhood metaphor, then shakes his head. 'If you knew the—' He stops abruptly, chewing on his bottom lip and looking back down at the ginger hairs that are beginning to stand up along his bare forearms. I shiver in sympathy, or is it with uninvited trepidation? I can't be sure.

'If I knew what?' I ask gently, leaning aside as he unknots the sleeves of his coat and puts it back on.

'The things I've done,' he says, his voice small. 'Things I'm not very proud of.'

'We've all done things we shouldn't,' I soothe, shamefully picturing the hidden shoebox in his wardrobe, my hands as they lifted the lid, my incriminating fingerprints on the sticky surface of those photos.

'Yes, but . . .' He stops again, and I make myself wait. 'I sometimes feel bad that I met you,' he blunders on, frowning with frustration as if his words are coming out all wrong. 'I mean, I don't feel bad that I met you, of course I don't. But it was . . . Sorry, I'm not making any sense, am I?'

I've started shivering again, but it's nothing to do with the cold. There's an edge to his words, and if I had to describe it, my best guess would be that he's distressed. It's not an obvious, hands-over-face and hair-tearing sorrow, but it is undeniable nonetheless. What is he getting at here? Has he cheated on me already – is that what he meant by doing things he's not proud of? Does he think we're doomed? Is he planning to dump me before we get too serious?

'I'm not going anywhere,' I tell him quickly, my voice sounding far more resolute than I feel. 'I promise you that. I'm yours for as long as you'll have me.'

I know I'm panicking and should instead be playing it cool, but there's no stopping the words now that I've let them out.

Pete looks at me again, his blue eyes shot through with speckles of gold. The sunlight here in Como makes them shine even brighter than usual.

'Do you really mean that, Lulu?' he asks, his voice sounding husky, as if it may crack.

'I do,' I say, nodding to further illustrate the point. 'I don't know what it is you think you've done, but whatever it is, it won't change the way I feel about you. Well, not unless you've murdered someone. You're not secretly a serial killer, are you?'

He laughs at that, clearly relieved.

'No, I'm definitely not a murderer.'

'Well, then,' I say, patting his hand, grateful that we're both wearing gloves, so he won't be able to tell how nervously clammy mine have become. 'You don't have anything to worry about.'

Pete adjusts his position as the cold hurries up with the wind, and wraps his arm further around my shoulders. He is holding on to me tightly, almost as if he's scared that I'll run away. It's the same thing he does when he's asleep, too – reaches out unconsciously and clings to me like a clam to a rock. He's the first boyfriend I've ever had who doesn't turn his back on me once the lights are out, and his need to keep hold of me is such a comfort. What I need to do is remember this feeling when I'm freaking out about a mysterious phone call or a glamorous ex-girlfriend.

This would be a good moment to ask him again about that call from Manny. Or perhaps even probe into the subject of his ex, the girl I can't seem to get out of my head no matter how hard I try. Whether it's the fear of what Pete will say that makes me hesitate, I'm not sure. But just as I'm about to open my mouth and see what comes out, Pete stands up and takes my hand.

'Come on, beautiful – let's get the hell off this hill and find ourselves a drink.'

15

Taggie

I can still remember the first time I ever came to Lake Como, which is quite impressive, really, given that I was only five years old at the time. My parents had debated the choice of location at length, concerned that I would find little to entertain me amongst the narrow cobbled streets or on the stony shores, but they needn't have worried. I adored Como from the very moment we drove around that final mountain corner and I saw the clear blue sky reflected in the water below.

I'm not sure if it's because I'm an only child, but I always was grown-up for my age, and can clearly remember being impatient with the slow passing of time when I was young. I wanted to be old enough to stay up late, to eat off one of the large plates using the adult cutlery, to raise my own glass of wine in a toast at one of my parents' numerous dinner parties. Being deemed 'not old enough' to do things was something I found tremendously frustrating – and being below average height only seemed to exacerbate the problem. There were rides at the fair that I wasn't allowed to go on, clothes I couldn't wear and, a few years later, pubs that kept their doors resolutely closed to me, despite the fact that all my underage college friends seemed to be served alcohol with no questions asked.

'You'll be glad of it when you're older, Taggie,' my mum

would say. 'You'll still look twenty-one when you're forty, unlike me.'

My mum has never tried to hide the fact that she's envious of my darker colouring, being pale, freckled and mousy-haired herself. When we'd visit Como during the summer months, she'd sit defiantly on a deckchair in the full glare of the sun, and I'd wince in sympathy as her skin turned an angry shade of red in protest. This, coupled with an unfortunate fondness for the odd cigarette or twelve, has left the skin on her face and chest lined and coarse as she's reached middle age, whereas my own, in comparison, has remained as smooth and unblemished as the bonnet of a car in a garage showroom. Today, however, I can see a change for the first time, and I squint into the mirror to make sure I'm not imagining things. Nope, that is definitely the beginnings of some frown lines.

Sighing deeply and wrinkling up my nose in disgust, I reach into my make-up bag for a pot of concealer and then think better of it. It's only a few fine lines, after all. And it's not as if there's anyone in Como that I'm trying to impress. I got out of the habit of wearing much make-up during my last relationship. We'd been together for so long that he was more than simply my boyfriend – he was my best mate, the only person on the planet that I would feel comfortable talking to about anything, the one other soul that I trusted with my deepest fears and my secret vulnerabilities. Well, I thought he was.

As an image of him floods into my mind, I catch sight of my expression again and realise that I'm frowning. So, he is the one to blame for these new etchings of weariness on my face, just as he is the one I hold responsible for the bottom no longer being intact in my world, but rather a floating jetty of uncertainty. I drop my eyes from the mirror. That's quite enough dwelling for one morning.

I find my group of budding artists huddled together in the wide tiled hallway at the bottom of the stairs, their cheeks collectively pink after what I know would have been an excellent breakfast, and expressions of expectant joy on most of their faces. It doesn't take me long to spot Gladys and Bill, who today are clad in bright red his-and-hers fleeces, because they are the only two in the group who don't appear to be very happy, and I brace myself as they bustle forwards to greet me.

'Agatha,' cries Gladys, flapping her hands up and down like an agitated bat. 'There you are. We didn't know where you were. I said to Will-yum, "Do you think we scared her off last night?" And he laughed so hard that he choked on his hot chocolate, didn't you, Will-yum?'

Bill nods earnestly in agreement. 'I did – on my hot chocolate.'

'We thought we'd see you at breakfast,' Gladys scolds, giving me the benefit of what I can only assume are her disappointed eyes. I'm starting to feel increasingly like their adopted daughter, and I wonder then if they have any kids of their own. From the manner in which Gladys bosses around anyone in her vicinity, I'd guess that she must be a teacher of some kind – perhaps one of very small children. She definitely seems accustomed to being listened to and obeyed.

'I was hoping to show you some photos of the collection that Will-yum's been working on back in Kent,' she says now.

'Oh?' I manage, before she barrels on with a further flurry of gesticulation.

'Will-yum's calling it Peach Perfection, but I'm not sure if that conjures up the right image.'

'Are they paintings of fruit?' I enquire hopefully, and they both chuckle with mirth.

'Oh gosh, no – that would be so bore-snore,' giggles Gladys, taking Bill's phone out of his skinny hand and flicking through his photos with her finger.

'Ah, here. This is probably the best one.'

I peer down at the screen.

'Wow. I mean, wow. You are so . . .' I pause.

'Resplendent?' offers Gladys, using another finger to zoom in on the painted image of her own – rather untamed, it has to be said – bush.

'Well, yes,' I agree, looking from her, to Bill, to the floor – anywhere but at the image on the phone. 'And, er, naked.'

This admission causes the two of them to shake with laughter yet again, and I take advantage of their momentary loss of speech to make my excuses and scurry across the foyer into the office, shutting the door firmly behind me.

'Something the matter?' enquires Sal, turning from his seat in front of the computer and looking at me curiously.

My boss is nearing sixty now, with a small, neat paunch and almost completely grey hair. But, like a lot of older Italian men, his advancing years don't seem to have dulled either his swagger or his self-confidence. If anything, he struts around his beloved Casa Alta with even more sass than the pigeons down by the lake.

'Gladys just showed me a painting of herself that her husband did,' I tell him, leaning against the wooden door.

One of Sal's perfectly groomed eyebrows twitches with mild interest.

'So?'

'So, it's not really what I wanted to see, first thing in the morning,' I exclaim, checking my watch and grimacing. We need to leave in five minutes if we're going to stand any chance of reaching the harbour in time to catch the first boat up to Bellagio. I don't want the group to miss a minute of what is shaping up to be another stunning day, and there's lots of ground to cover before lunchtime.

'Are you feeling OK today?' Sal asks then. He's appraising me, I can tell, and I curse myself for not applying make-up after all.

'I'm fine,' I assure him, nodding in determination when he raises a disbelieving brow at me.

'You are tired,' he argues. 'Your eyes are red and your skin is crumpled.'

Don't hold back, Sal. Say what you really think.

'I'm fine,' I repeat, turning my back to him as I search through one of the desk drawers for the Bellagio street maps. 'Just traumatised from seeing Gladys and Bill's Peach Perfection.'

'*Che cosa?*' Sal replies, reverting from English to Italian as he's wont to do.

'Trust me, Sal,' I tell him, reaching for the door handle. 'You *really* don't want to know.'

Luckily for me, all thoughts of wrinkles and inappropriate nudity are thankfully swept aside by the beauty of the morning, and as we leave the hotel I pause for a few blissful seconds to drink it all in. The sky is Smurf-skin blue behind the complicated pattern of tree branches, many of which have been stripped of their leaves by the change in season. A mottled frost covers the lawn on either side of the gravel driveway, and its glistening silver surface is polka-dotted with patches of green, where the sun has slipped through gaps and melted the fragile ice.

Oh, how I love this place, I think to myself, as I always do, pushing my gloved hands deep into my pockets. I'm so grateful to have it, to be here, and to feel so cocooned in safety by its familiarity. What would I have done if I hadn't had Como sitting here waiting, ready to shelter me from the misery that had assaulted me with such force? Remaining in London, where it happened, was not an option, and even my childhood home hadn't felt like the sanctuary I'd hoped it might. There were too many memories, even there, of the times I spent with him. The very fittings and furnishings felt like enemies, the photos I knew my mum had hidden away like ticking time bombs. I would have gone mad if I had stayed there any longer.

Our brisk stroll down to Como harbour is sound-tracked by birdsong, the hard, broken earth providing a crunching percussion underfoot. The lake is a deep, murky green today, and the opposite shore is shrouded in the mist left there by night. The group are as entranced by the views as I am, with even Gladys hushed into silence by the emerald sparkle of the sunlight on the water, and the rustling sway of the trees.

The boat is waiting when we arrive, and I'm relieved to see that the upper deck still has plenty of empty seats. It's never as much fun when you're forced to sit downstairs, where the tiny scuffed windows offer barely more than a glimpse of the unfolding landscape. I hand over our pile of tickets and usher the group aboard ahead of me, counting heads as they go. Gladys and Bill seem to have adopted a middle-aged German couple during the walk down from the Casa Alta, and I watch, bemused and sympathetic, as the two of them are beckoned into neighbouring seats. I tried to engage Sue's son Tim in conversation over dinner last night, but he doesn't seem able to look at me without turning redder than a packet of Maltesers. Am I really so terrifying?

Once I'm happy that my ladies and gents are all settled and chatting amongst themselves, I decide to give poor, flustered Tim some breathing space and make my way towards the front of the boat in search of an empty chair, thinking as I do so how nice it will be to grab forty minutes of quiet time before the busiest part of my day begins. I'm in luck, too, because there are two places available – one for me, and the other for my coat and bag.

Using my sleeve to clear a porthole in the condensation covering the window, I arrange myself comfortably on the seat and smile as I feel the boat's engine tremble into life far below me. Just as we begin moving, however, I'm aware of a shadow falling across me, and a deep Italian voice asking, 'Can I sit down?'

Removing my head from where I had already rested it against the glass, I swallow a big sigh, turn around, and immediately feel a rush of heat fill my cheeks. Because standing there, looking unshaven, unrepentant and undeniably bloody attractive, is Marco.

16

Lucy

'Look, there's the boat going up towards Bellagio.'

Pete follows the direction of my outstretched arm and squints into the middle distance.

'It looks busy,' he says. 'I'm glad we decided to get the next one.'

The pair of us are up in Brunate at last, after walking over from the apartment to the *funicolare* straight after breakfast this morning. Luckily Pete saw the funny side when it took us barely ten minutes to complete a journey that yesterday we abandoned after a good hour. Spending all this lovely uninterrupted time with my wonderful man is teaching me lots more about him – on a basic level, I now know that as long as Pete's never too far away from food, beer and plenty of affection, then he's extremely happy. If any one of those things is found to be lacking, his energy level can plummet like a pebble into a pond. But I feel as if I'm seeing new layers to him, too. The conversations we're having are more in-depth, and he's opening up to me about all sorts of things, from his upbringing to why he is and always will be a staunch Labour supporter. It's the first time we've ever really discussed politics, and I'm gratified to know for sure that he sees the world in much the same way as I do, and that he cares for people from all walks of life. It makes me even more sure than I was before that he and my dad will get on well, and I've almost blurted out an invitation for Pete and him to meet as soon as we're back in the UK, only to stop myself at the last minute.

There have also been several occasions where I've caught him simply staring off into space, as if he's lost within his own thoughts, and I have to gently bring him back to the present moment with a kiss or murmur.

It's a flawlessly beautiful day today, even by Como's standards, and for the past ten minutes or so, Pete and I have been content to simply stand by the edge of the road looking down at the view. The sky is clear, the vast lake an ever-changing kaleidoscope of blues, greens and greys, and the brilliant sunlight is making everything below us sing with clarity. Pete has taken off his hat for once, and his ginger curls are clashing adorably with his cold red ears and matching nose. I decided to tie up my hair today, but I've been regretting it ever since we reached the top of the hillside and encountered the wind. Down in Como town, the bulk of the surrounding landscape protects you, but up here the icy draughts seem to work their way through every single layer of clothing, until your very skin is tingling in protest. I'm glad that I have Pete here next to me keeping me warm.

Brunate itself is a strange but beautiful little hamlet, with a handful of gift shops and cafés, a collection of impressive private villas, several churches, and – rather wonderfully – a lighthouse. It's got a vaguely timeless atmosphere, as if nothing has been altered for hundreds of years, and I say as much to Pete.

'Did you never come up here when you were a kid, then?' he asks, keeping his arm wrapped protectively around me as we continue to stroll along the road leading away from the *funicolare*. There are plenty of cars parked up here, but we're yet to see one moving, and I try to imagine how it would feel to live in such a quiet place. London never seems to stop moving – it's like a huge, agitated dragon in comparison to this sleepy hamster of a tiny town – but is that really such a bad thing? Isn't it better to be surrounded by the throb of life than to be marooned in solitude? I can't imagine not having people around me, whether that's family, friends, Pete, or even the patients at the hospital – being alone makes me feel on edge; it always has.

'We didn't, as far as I can remember,' I reply, casting my mind back to the final time I ever came here with Julia and my parents. I was fourteen, so it was half a lifetime ago, and back then I was far more interested in getting a tan and shopping for clothes than I was in sightseeing. Because Julia's a few years older, my mum would persuade my dad to let the two of us spend our days alone, while they took the hire car and went off exploring. Dad never wanted to leave us behind, though, and during that final holiday, it became a huge bone of contention between them. I realise Pete has come to a stop only when my hand snags in his, and I turn to find him looking at me in concern.

'Are you OK, Lulu?' he asks. 'You've gone very quiet.'

I take a deep breath. I haven't divulged any murky details of my parents' break-up to him yet, only the fact that they are no longer together, but I have a sudden urge to tell him, to share something with him.

'Part of the reason I love this place so much,' I begin, gesturing with my hand to show that I mean Como, 'is because for such a long time I associated it with feeling happy. Whenever we came here as a family, it was always so much fun. Well, it was up until the last time.'

'Is that why you haven't been back until now?' he asks me gently, and I think before I reply, momentarily distracted by the rustling sound of a bird fighting its way out of a patch of dense shrubbery.

'It's silly, isn't it, to hold a place to blame for something?' I say, and he frowns.

'I'm not sure I follow.'

'Haven't you ever been reluctant to return to a place where something bad happened?' I ask, and he nods his handsome head up and down a fraction.

'I guess.'

'Well, I suppose that's how I felt about this place. The last summer we all came here, my mum and dad argued almost every single day. It was the first time I'd ever known them to be so cruel to each other, and it was the start of years of rows and fights – the beginning of the end, if you will. I did worry that I'd still be upset by that association, but I haven't been at all, not with you here.'

'Isn't that a good thing?' Pete says, stepping to one side as a tall Dutch couple make their way past us, all blue-eyed, blonde-haired and statuesque.

'It is.' I smile at him. 'I always loved Como so much, and it was sad that my memories of it were tainted. I wanted to come back here with you, partly so I'd be able to create new memories, you see. I wanted to fall in love with the place all over again, like I did before.'

'And are you?' he prompts, his expression thoughtful and his eyes wide. 'Falling in love with it?' Again, I marvel at how easy it is to be mesmerised by him.

'Very much so.' I close my eyes as he leans across to kiss me. What I wanted to say, but didn't dare, was that Como isn't the only thing I've been falling hopelessly in love with since we arrived. Then again, perhaps that is something that deserves more than just words. I'm not convinced there are any phrases in the English language that wouldn't feel inadequate when it comes to describing the way I'm feeling. If only Pete would say those three magical words to me, then perhaps I could find the courage to try.

We spend the next hour meandering aimlessly through the twisting streets of Brunate, taking photos of the decorative metal gates guarding the villas, and the wild flowers that are sitting in colourful sporadic bursts along the edges of the pavements. Pete is attentive and chirpy, chatting happily to the locals we encounter as we stroll along and pointing things out to make me laugh. Before taking the *funicolare* back down the hillside to Como, we stop in one of the cosy cafés for a cup of thick hot chocolate, and he deliberately lets a large blob of cream stick to his nose so that I'll kiss it off. I appreciate the fact that we must look sickeningly soppy to anyone watching, but I couldn't care less. This was exactly what I wanted from this trip: a chance for Pete and me to grow closer, and plenty of new, treasured memories to take home. Aside from the tiny niggles that I brought over with us from London, things could not be more perfect. And anyway, I remind myself, picking up Pete's hand as we take our seats in the *funicolare* carriage, there will be plenty of time to tackle those more difficult questions once we're back on UK soil.

In contrast to the relative quiet of Brunate, Como is bustling with life. Large white gulls sit wing-to-wing along the low wall by the water, their smooth heads twitching to one side as we pass, while pigeons stumble around in circles by our feet, searching for morsels of food. The hum of traffic is interrupted by strains of music filtering out from each of the cafés and restaurants we're passing, and a group of young waiters shout cheerily to each other as they set up tables beneath heat lamps.

'Have we got time to go and pick up one of those giant pretzels for the journey?' Pete asks, and I have to laugh.

'Where do you put it all?' I exclaim.

'My legs are hollow, remember,' he replies, deadpan but grinning.

'Why don't you go and get one while I buy our boat tickets?' I suggest. There's still half an hour to go until anchor-up, but I want to make sure we don't miss this one. If we do, we'll have to put off Bellagio for another day, and I'm positively itching to get up there. That area, perhaps even more so than Como, means a lot to me, and I want to take Pete to the hidden beach I loved so much as a child.

'Right you are,' he says happily, kissing me briefly on the cheek before bounding off across the painted lines of the crossing and disappearing amongst the rows of small wooden huts that make up the Christmas Market. I miss him already, it's pathetic.

I pay the solemn chap in the glass-fronted booth the

rather extortionate twenty-seven euros for two return tickets to Bellagio, before turning and almost walking straight into a blonde girl, who is busy pinning a leaflet to the harbour noticeboard.

'Sorry,' I gasp, leaping backwards out of the way.

The girl shakes her head briskly.

'No need to apologise, honestly. I shouldn't lurk right behind people.'

She's smiling at me with open warmth, and I clock the two blonde plaits sneaking out from under her pink bobble hat.

'Are you here on holiday?' she asks.

I nod. 'Yes, with my boyfriend. He's just gone to get some food for the boat.'

'Ah, you're going up to Bellagio?' the girl guesses, looking over my shoulder to where a short queue has started to assemble beside the water.

'My friend is up there today, leading a tour group around, the poor thing.' She puts her head on one side and considers me for a second. I'm not sure what to say, so I just make what I hope is a sympathetic murmuring sound. I usually find it so easy to talk to people I don't know, but for some reason this girl is making me feel awkward.

'Can I give you one of these?' she asks, holding up her sheaf of posters. I take one and run my eyes over the words.

'I don't know if you and your boyfriend have plans for New Year's Eve already?' she continues. 'But as you can see, we're doing a big event up at the hotel where I work – the Casa Alta. It can be a nightmare booking anywhere for dinner here in town, and we're putting on a really good party. My friend is organising the whole thing, and she really knows her stuff, believe me. After the food, there will be dancing, and you'll be able to watch the fireworks from the grounds, too.'

'It sounds fun,' I enthuse, matching her smile of delight with a polite one of my own. I don't want to admit that I actually have a different restaurant in mind for New Year, and that I was planning to surprise Pete by booking it in secret.

'Let me put my phone number on the back,' she's saying now, taking the leaflet back off me and scribbling on it in biro.

'You're Shelley?' I enquire, peering down at the untidy scrawl. Being a nurse means that I'm accustomed to making sense of illegible scribbles – it's no myth that doctors have some of the worst handwriting in the entire world. Honestly, half the time I feel like 'deciphering hieroglyphics' should have been included in my job description.

'That's me.' The girl beams at me and offers a hand.

'Lucy,' I reply, shaking it.

I can see Pete approaching us now, a brown paper bag in one of his gloved hands and two small cups of what I suspect is *vin brulé* balanced rather precariously in the other, and I hurriedly thank Shelley and start to move away towards him.

'Is this fella your boyfriend?' she guesses, following me, and I'm reluctantly forced to introduce them. Shelley then repeats her spiel about the New Year's Eve party all over again, but with even more gusto than before. I'm more than a little irked when she puts her hand on Pete's arm and squeezes it encouragingly as he takes in the poster, only to glance over wide-eyed and mouth the word 'muscles' to me. I know she's only messing around, but it does grind my gears when women cross the line between friendly and flirty when they know full well that the man in question is most definitely off the market. Not much irritates me, but I'm irritated now.

'She seems fun,' is Pete's predictable comment when Shelley finally bids us farewell, and I take a large gulp of the hot wine to stop myself saying something bitchy. 'Jealousy is a waste of energy,' Julia often lectures. 'Nobody gets hurt by it except you.'

'Shall we get on the boat?' I say sweetly, but Pete's still got his nose in the poster.

'This looks perfect,' he says, all pink-cheeked and excitable. 'I was just thinking about what we should do for New Year, and then this lands in our laps. It feels like fate or something, don't you think?'

In truth, I think absolutely nothing of the sort. I'd much rather go to the fancy restaurant I had picked out, and have Pete all to myself for the evening.

'Maybe,' I reply, looping my arm through his and walking firmly towards where a fair number of people are now boarding the small ferry.

'Don't you fancy it?' he asks, and I can tell he's disappointed. Two lines have appeared in the fleshy part between his eyes and the corners of his mouth are turned down.

'Of course I do,' I tell him, injecting as much enthusiasm as I can into my words. 'If that's what you want to do?'

'I say, bring it on!' he declares, following me along the

wooden gangway. 'The Casa Alta Hotel had better be ready for us.'

My boyfriend, I realise wryly, is a total goof sometimes – but I love making him happy more than anything. And, as we take our seats at the front of the boat and he breaks off a piece of his pretzel to share with me, I decide that this New Year's Eve simply *has* to be the best one he's ever had, even if it's not exactly what I had in mind.

17

Taggie

Of course bloody Marco is here on this boat. Of course he is. On the first day in months that I haven't bothered to wear make-up; a day when, thanks to my flat boots and weary, sleep-deprived skin, I could probably change my name from Taggie Torres to Crumplestiltskin and nobody would even notice. Thanks a lot, sod's law, No, *really*.

'*Ciao*,' is all he says when he realises that it's me, fixing me with those eyes of his.

I lift my coat and bag off the seat.

'*Ciao*.'

Marco unzips his battered leather jacket before folding himself into the seat beside me, and I'm instantly assaulted by the dark, earthy scent of his aftershave. Perfume was the one thing I did bother with this morning, but I doubt he'll be able to pick up the subtle fragrance of violets beneath his own, far muskier tang.

'How are you, Taggie?' he asks, meaning that I have no choice but to turn from the window. Being this close to him has put me immediately on edge yet again, and I glance down to where his large, denim-clad thigh is pressed up against my own.

'I'm fine, thank you,' I say, crossing my leg away from him, and we pass the next few minutes exchanging pleasantries. I tell him about the artist group I'm in charge of, and he reveals that he's heading to Bellagio for a business meeting.

'Long way to go for a meeting,' I remark, even though it's not strictly true. I go up to Bellagio all the time to see Elsie, after all. It's not as if it's the other side of Italy.

Marco takes my comment in good humour, though, dropping his voice an octave before admitting, 'This man I am meeting, he has something that I want.'

'Oh?' I enquire, and he grins at me mischievously.

'But I cannot tell you what it is, I'm afraid.'

'Why not?'

That smile again.

'Because I don't want you to steal my business idea.'

'I very much doubt I would,' I say, hating how prim I sound. What is it about this man that makes me feel so defensive? Perhaps it's just all men at the moment.

'I cannot risk it,' he says, mock-serious. 'I would never forgive myself if I did not get exactly what I want. I'm very good at it most of the time.'

'Good at what?' I reply, biting down on the metaphorical carrot that he's dangled before my brain catches up.

Marco waits until he's sure that he has my full attention.

'At getting exactly what I want.'

'Oh,' I say again, feeling the blood rush into my cheeks. I'm not sure if it's the absence of my trusty high heels or the fact that I'm sitting right next to a man who is easily six foot tall, but I feel very small indeed. Marco is just so confident, relaxed and unashamedly masculine. Being around him stirs something up inside my stomach, but whatever it is, I'd liken it more to a whirring cement mixer than a flock of romance-novel butterflies. I'm not so much turned on as turned up to full alert, and I'm acutely aware of every single part of my body that is currently touching his. And, thanks to his blatant man-spreading, that is quite a high percentage.

'Well, er, good luck, then,' I say at last, refusing to rise to any more of his flirtatious bait. He's only trying to get my attention because he can tell I don't fancy him in the slightest. It's textbook lothario behaviour.

Unprompted, a memory of the first time I met my ex swims into my mind. I was out with the girls from the PR firm where I was working at the time, and he was in the corner of the pub with his mates. They were all shouting loudly and gesticulating at the television screen mounted on the wall, and I looked over to see what all the fuss was about. The England rugby team had missed an important try, apparently, but he hadn't missed the sight of my bemused expression. As soon as our eyes met and he smiled at me, I knew a story had just begun, and that he would be in my life for a long time. I don't know what it was that made me so sure, but I knew at the time that I had never experienced such a strong feeling of pure attraction before.

'I love boats,' Marco says now, calling me back to the present moment. It's quite a change of conversational direction, and it's all I can do not to laugh in surprise.

'Okaaay,' I offer, waiting for him to elaborate.

'Ever since I was a boy, I have wanted to be around boats, to work with them, to be out on the water,' he pauses. 'I feel at home with them.'

'You're lucky to have that,' I reply, the pattern of my

thoughts surprising me. 'To know what it is that makes you happiest. I'm thirty-two now and I still don't know.'

Marco opens his mouth a fraction and shuts it again, and I turn away before my eyes can dwell too long on his lips. We've left Como behind now and are chugging up the lake past Cernobbio. I can see the reflections of the houses and villas in the water, each one streaked and dappled as if painted by hand on to a wet canvas, and the blue sky above us is muddied with a blur of birds in flight.

'It is not about age,' he says after a minute. 'It is simply about following what is in your heart.'

My heart is broken, I think, but don't say.

'What did you want to be when you were a little girl?' he asks now.

I smile with easy affection when I picture myself as I was growing up: stubborn, bossy and fuelled by determination.

'Most of the time, I just wanted to be right about everything,' I admit, and I'm gratified to receive a wry grin in reply.

'I can believe that,' he says, chuckling when I glare at him. 'Taggie, come on, I am not being rude. I am simply saying that you are a strong woman. I can sense that in you.'

If only he knew just how wrong he is. I used to be strong, it's true. But that was before.

'I'm not strong,' I mutter, looking at the view so I don't have to make eye contact.

'You are, believe me,' Marco argues, and I flinch as he shifts slightly, his thigh pressing once more against my own.

'I make you uncomfortable,' he states, making to stand up. 'Sorry. I will leave you alone.'

'No!' I practically yelp, grabbing his leg and pushing it back down towards the seat. 'You don't. I'm in a weird mood today, that's all. Just ignore me.'

For a second I think he's going to get up again and walk away regardless, but then I see him reconsider. While I'm occupied with doing my best not to think about how firm and warm his thigh muscle felt, and how long it's been since I last even touched a man, let alone found myself enjoying it, Marco is removing his jacket and – oh God – stretching his arm around the back of my seat. He's now taking up so much space that I feel even bloody smaller than I usually do. He'll be able to put me in his jeans pocket soon and carry me around like one of those Guatemalan worry dolls. When I said he should stay sitting beside me, I didn't mean it as a green light to him doing the old slide-around.

'What made you move here to Como?' he asks, and I concentrate on the shiny black bob of the Japanese woman sitting in front of me.

'I've been coming here since I was young, and I thought it might be nice to work here,' I tell him.

'That is not the full story,' he says, in that infuriatingly blunt way that I'm learning to associate with him. He doesn't ask questions to get the answers; he merely uses them as tools to express his own opinions.

'Why do you say that?' I retort. I can feel the vibrations from the boat's engine making my plastic chair shake, and I uncross my legs so I can press my feet against the floor.

'In my experience, people do not leave their home and move to another country unless there is a very important reason for doing so.'

He's right, of course, but that doesn't encourage me to come clean.

'Perhaps I'm not like most people,' I say evasively.

'That,' Marco says, lowering his lashes, 'is almost certainly the truth.'

'What about you?' I counter, keen to talk about anything other than myself.

He shrugs and lifts the sleeve of his jacket. The leather is cracked around the fabric of the cuff, and he picks at it absent-mindedly before replying.

'The lake is my home.'

'But you haven't always lived here,' I point out, remembering what he told Shelley and me about his summer in Naples.

'I have lived in many places.' Again, that casual shrug.

'Have you ever lived in England?' I want to know, even though I have already decided that he must have. His command of English is far too good for him not to have at least spent a few months there.

'Of course,' he exclaims, as if I've just asked him something entirely obvious. 'I was in Leeds, for a time.'

'I love Leeds!' I enthuse. 'One of my best friends lives there. When were you there?'

He drops his eyes. 'It was a while ago.'

'Did you like it?'

He gives me the benefit of a lazy smile. 'Not as much as I like it here.'

'I like it here, too,' I tell him. 'Como to me is like boats to you. I feel at home here.'

'Ah,' he says, looking at me properly and appraising me with his green eyes. His lashes are long, too, I notice, but not the thick black colour that I would expect. They look almost chestnut. 'Then you are already halfway there.'

'Halfway to Bellagio?' I say stupidly, looking out through the front window of the boat to see how far up the lake we've come.

'No, Taggie,' he murmurs, placing his hand briefly on top of mine. 'Halfway towards finding happiness.'

I stifle a laugh. Bloody Italians, romanticising everything.

It takes the boat another twenty minutes to reach its destination, during which time I deftly manage to lasso the conversation and drag it back into more comfortable territory – namely, the subject of Elsie, which I could happily talk about for hours. Plus, the lady herself has promised to greet the boat in Bellagio, and if I know Elsie as well as I think I do, then I'm certain that she won't be able to resist saying something to Marco when she clocks him disembarking right next to me. A remark that will, in all likelihood, make me want to throw myself off the jetty and into the freezing water below.

'Taggie, darling – please tell me this young man is the extra Christmas present you told me was still in the post.'

Sometimes I hate being right.

Elsie is literally clapping her hands together with glee at the sight of Marco – and she's not the only one: Gladys, who clocked my Italian companion as soon as we came back into view from the front of the boat, is in serious danger of tripping over the stalks that are attaching her eyeballs to her face, while poor old bespectacled Will-yum is looking most put out behind her, his moley features all curled up in dismay at finding this handsome new addition to the group.

'Elsie, this is Marco,' I say quickly, deciding that it's best to pretend she didn't say anything about him being her Christmas present. 'He works at a restaurant down in Como – he's Shelley's friend,' I add.

Marco narrows his eyes at me for a split second, but then he's back laying on the charm as thickly as Parmesan over a bowl of pasta, complimenting Elsie on her colourful hat and scarf combo and making a fuss of Bruno, Gino and Nico, who are yapping away like hairy gnats by her feet. I know that all three of the chihuahuas must be secretly thrilled to be meeting so many new people en masse, but you wouldn't think it to look at them. I have to hide a smirk behind my hand when Will-yum, following Marco's self-assured lead, bends down to pet them only to recoil in horror when Gino promptly bares both rows of his pointy teeth and growls like a tiny dinosaur. Meanwhile, their elderly pack leader is still focusing all her attention on Marco.

'Well, aren't you a tonic,' she exclaims, beaming up at him.

'And I'm a measure of gin!' booms Gladys, seemingly oblivious to her husband flapping his arms up and down like a distressed ostrich.

'It is very nice to meet you ladies,' Marco says, kissing both Elsie and Gladys's upturned cheeks and only just swerving his head away in time to avoid a third smacker right on the mouth from the most colourful member of our group.

'Are we still walking up to Punta Spartivento first?' asks Elsie, hushing Gino and Nico as they start barking at a group of passing teenagers. Bruno, the little angel, has stopped yapping now and is scrabbling at my leg. Squatting down, I scoop him up into my arms and plant a kiss on his cold, wet nose.

'That dog is smitten,' remarks Elsie, looking at the two of us fondly, and Marco smiles in agreement.

'Bruno has very good taste,' he remarks, and I hurriedly turn my back on the two of them before Elsie can catch my eye.

'Right then, everyone – are we all ready?'

The group all nod their heads, presumably keen to start moving again and warm up their limbs, and glancing around I realise that we're the only passengers from the boat that are still standing here. I really am being a terrible tour guide today. Sal will not be impressed if I bring his guests back with chilblains. But then Bellagio's main harbour *is* beautiful, with a wide, cobble-covered road snaking its way past the row of cafés and gift shops behind us, a cluster of tangled yet decorative lime trees in a large square courtyard beside us, and a breath-taking view of open lake and distant mountains right in front of us. Bellagio is smaller and sleepier than Como – especially at this quieter time of the year – and there's a hushed stillness in the air that seems to reach right inside you and slow the beating of your heart. The morning sun is sitting low in the sky, bathing the middle portion of the nearby buildings in buttery light, and a gentle breeze tickles at the tendrils of hair on my cheeks.

You don't need to be an artist to be moved by this place, but I can see that the group I have with me are just as captivated as I'd hoped.

I'm surprised when I turn back and find Marco still standing there, his head slightly on one side as he looks at me, almost as if he's trying to work me out. I wish he wouldn't.

'Don't you have a meeting to go to?' I ask, squeezing Bruno's tiny cold paws softly between my fingers.

He shuffles his feet. 'I have some time.'

'Marco has offered to come with us,' interjects Elsie, and I know without looking at her that she's got a mischievous expression on her face.

'I'm sure he's far too busy,' I argue, but my delivery is as weak as my belief that saying the words will make the blindest bit of difference. That's the thing about Elsie – she has a way of always getting what she wants. She would call it 'the benefit of old age', whereas I know better. She simply doesn't take no for an answer. She never has, and I imagine she never will. No wonder she and Marco have hit it off so well.

'Nonsense!' Elsie declares, proving my point. 'He can keep me company while you're working.'

'Are you sure you don't mind?' I ask Marco, and he smiles good-naturedly.

'It would be my pleasure.'

As we all turn our backs on the lake and begin walking away across the cold, damp cobbles, I hear Gladys loudly asking Marco if he's ever considered posing nude for a portrait, and I only just manage to bury my laugh in Bruno's soft, brown fur.

18

Lucy

Bellagio is exactly as I remember it. I don't know what I was expecting, because I knew there wouldn't be a dirty great McDonald's on the harbour and a skyscraper blocking the view of the mountains, but I didn't think I would step off the boat and feel instantly as if I was a teenager again. It's as if someone has reached through the twisted pathways of time, snatched me up, and deposited me here in the past. And, as well as being unnerving, it's oddly comforting at the same time. For a few moments, all I can do is stand still and stare, a wide grin expanding my cold cheeks.

Pete is quiet beside me, subdued by the majesty of Bellagio's timeless beauty – the multi-coloured cobbles decorating the pavement beneath our feet, the butterscotch-coloured buildings bathed in light, the ornate lampposts and contorted branches of the trees. And it's not just the harbour that is splendid enough to render the two of us mute. The view over the lake behind us comprises a glorious sweep of dark-blue molten water, unblemished sky and vast, distant hills. The houses and villas of Varenna, on the opposite shore, look like pieces from a Monopoly board, dwarfed as they are by the bulk of the land. I take a deep breath, and feel Pete slide his gloved hand into mine.

'Now I see why George Clooney bought a place here,' he murmurs, and I nod in agreement. One of the things I love most about Como – and this entire area of Italy, in fact – is how unspoiled it all is. So much of England has been desecrated by greedy construction companies, the land carved up to make way for faster trains, bigger roads, blocks of apartments too expensive to live in, and with every new eyesore that is erected, another piece of Britain's beautiful heritage is lost. They haven't allowed that to happen here, and I'd put good money on the fact that they never will.

'Now you see why this place is known as the pearl of the lake,' I say, turning to look at Pete. 'Come on, let's find out if I can still remember my way around.'

Bellagio is famous not just because a certain silver fox from Hollywood decided to buy a villa nearby, but also because of its unique location. The arms of Lake Como are an inverted 'Y' shape, and Bellagio sits at the base of the triangle, between the two arms. When you reach the most northern part of the town, it's possible to stand on the shore looking out across the section of water where the Como and Lecco sides of the lake come together, and feel as if you're on the tip of the world. Well, that's how I used to feel as a child, anyway, and I can't wait to show Pete and see what he thinks. First, however, I want to take him through the town, so we cross the road and head right past a small collection of shops, cafés and a large hotel, which looks to be closed for the winter.

'I remember it being so busy here when we used to visit,' I tell Pete. 'It feels like a ghost town today.'

Aside from a few groups of tourists and the odd

shopkeeper, there aren't many people around at all, and I take advantage of the deserted streets by making Pete pose for a series of photos. When he insists on taking a selfie of the two of us, it's hard not to combust with pleasure, but then as soon as he shows it to me, I'm reminded yet again of the photo I found. His ex-girlfriend is so striking, with her dark hair and wide eyes, and now that I've seen her, I'm finding it impossible to forget just how perfect they looked together. I hate that my mind does this to me, that it disloyally compares me to others – why can't I just live in the moment, rather than raking up the past all the time?

'Let's go up here,' Pete says, interrupting my self-destructive train of thought. We're at the base of a wide, uphill street, with cobbled steps leading past houses the colour of peaches and honey. Pots of evergreen plants sit outside many of the smart wooden doors, and looking up I can see oak shutters, and balconies with decorative wrought-iron railings. What a dream to have a holiday home in a place like this, I think. Would you eventually become blasé, or would the beauty always remain as intoxicating as it feels today? I like to assume it's the latter, and chide myself for being so critical of London. OK, so the charm of the UK's capital might be trickier to find, but it's still there, in the parks and along the banks of the Thames. I shouldn't blame London for the fact that I work too hard to ever appreciate it; what I should do is make more effort to get out there and enjoy it, and I say as much to Pete as we make our slow way up the hill.

'Sounds good to me,' he agrees happily, but he seems a bit distracted. I need to stop babbling on about a load of old nonsense and let him soak up the atmosphere. The view is getting better the higher we go, and we stop so many times to take photos that my phone battery has drained to twenty per cent by the time we reach the top. It's a strange feeling to be able to see the roof tiles of the houses that a few minutes ago were towering above us, and beyond them the lake is dappled gold by the light from the sun. If it wasn't for the tasteful array of Christmas decorations and fairy lights strung up between the buildings, the pictures we've amassed could just as easily have been taken in the summer.

I'm tickled pink that Pete is enjoying himself – and he is, I can tell from the colour in his cheeks and the way he can't seem to stop grinning – because booking this trip was a bit of a gamble. He could easily have said it was too soon for us to go on holiday together, and if he had, I would have ended up wasting the only time off that I'd ever had over the festive period by sitting on Julia's sofa sobbing. My poor big sister – she's had to put up with a lot of drama from me over the years, and it's almost always been for the same reason. There is more to life than boyfriends, I know, and I always agree with her whenever she makes that exact point, but then I can't deny the truth, which is that I want to be in love and I want to have a family. Those two things are irrefutable.

'Oh, wow – look at that!' Pete exclaims, peering through the window of a gift shop and making an impressed 'oohing' sound as he sees a hand-carved wooden chessboard on the other side of the glass.

'Are you a big chess fan, then?' I reply, and he grins at me, all excited.

'I'm more than a fan – I used to be the school chess champion!'

'You did?' I must have pulled a face as I spoke, because Pete starts laughing.

'It's not that shocking a thought, is it?' he asks. 'I may not look much like a geek now, but that's exactly what I used to be. Honestly, I used to spend every summer holiday playing chess. I'd even play against myself when my family got fed up with me asking.'

'Oh, you poor thing!' I cry, immediately touched by the image of a lonely little Pete shut away with his chessboard.

'We'll have to play one day,' he tells me. 'Although, I warn you – I'm seriously skilled with a queen at my disposal.'

'I wish I'd known about your secret chess obsession,' I say. 'I could've got you a set for Christmas.'

We move away from the shop and Pete wraps an arm around my shoulders.

'You're sweet,' he says, then releases me and looks around. 'I can't believe this is where you came on holiday,' he remarks enviously. 'I had to put up with camping in Wales every single summer, where it rained so much that cowpats would run right under the tent.'

'I've never been to Wales,' I admit, cringing as he stares at me in mock horror.

'Never?'

I shake my head. 'Nope. And I've never been to Scotland or Ireland, either.'

'Whaaat?' He's clearly astonished. 'That's crazy! Well then, we'll have to go.'

My chest expands with joy.

'Really? You'd take me?'

'Of course I would,' he replies. 'I will! You just get a long weekend booked off, and we'll go.'

'Ah . . .' I groan, crestfallen. 'A long weekend might be a bit of a big ask – especially since my boss let me have this week off. Perhaps after Easter . . .' I trail off as I see his smile droop.

'Sorry,' I apologise in a rush. 'My job doesn't have the most sociable hours, does it?'

'That's true,' he agrees, stopping to look at me properly. 'But I think what you do is incredible. Honestly, I admire you so much. Don't ever say sorry for who you are or what you do – it's those things that define you.'

'Oh, don't,' I say shyly, feeling my frozen cheeks heat up. Compliments make me more uncomfortable than tights that have lost their elasticity.

'Did you always want to be a nurse?' he asks now, and I mull over the question for a moment before answering.

'No,' I say slowly. 'When I was nine, I wanted to be a teacher. Then I wanted to be a police officer. Then I considered the army – but only for about ten minutes,' I add, laughing at the look on Pete's face. He must be thinking what anyone else would think if they looked at me – how could a girl like that ever be fit and strong enough to be a soldier?

'So, you always wanted to work with people?' he surmises, and I smile.

'Yes, I suppose I did. I don't really do too well on my own; I never have.'

Pete stares at me for a few seconds, and I wonder if I've been too honest, but then he puts one of his big arms around my shoulders and pulls me towards him.

'You're not on your own, Lulu,' he says, his voice muffled by my woolly hat. 'I'm here now, and I'll look after you if you look after me.'

'I'd like that a lot,' I say into his chest, and his grip grows tighter.

We continue strolling through the back alleys and winding roads, past wine bars with bright red shutters, window boxes full of winter flowers, and *ristoranti* emitting mouth-watering aromas of garlic, lemon and oregano.

There are other tourists milling around, but only in groups of five or six, and it doesn't feel as unbearably hectic as I know it would have if we'd chosen to visit in July or August. We don't see many families with small children, either, and after a while I joke to Pete that we might be the youngest people in Bellagio today.

'You mean you might be,' he laughs back, referring to our five-year age gap.

Pete tells me more about his childhood holidays, building sandcastles and riding donkeys, and admits that his parents didn't have an awful lot of money in those days. They made do, he explains, and came up with creative ways to treat him and his brother so that they never felt as if they were missing out. This must be why he's always so keen to spoil me, I realise – now that he's able to do so, it means more to him than it would for most people.

Of course, this realisation just makes me love him all the more, and to stop myself from tearing up with the emotion of it all, I begin to tell him tales from my own family holidays. Perhaps it's because he already knows that my parents are no longer together, or maybe it's because I've been openly discussing them as they were, but after a while he starts asking a few hesitant questions about what exactly happened to split them up. Usually I would change the subject, but today I feel more comfortable about the idea of sharing a bit of the load that I always haul around with me.

And so, I tell him about my mum's growing coldness towards my dad, which began that summer here in Como and gathered pace over the years, finally building into an unstoppable avalanche of resentment. I try to explain how it felt to get that phone call from him late at night, when he told me through his tears that she had left, and that she would not be coming back. Mum had called Julia first, so I suppose Dad felt obliged to contact me. I hope it wasn't just that, though – I hope he reached out to me because he wanted support. As upset as I was at the time, my priority was, and has been ever since, the welfare of my father.

'As far as I'm concerned, my mother chose to distance herself from me and Julia,' I tell Pete. We're leaning against a wall drinking a takeaway coffee each, and a vibrant patch of purple and yellow pansies is bursting out from between the cracks in the stone. 'She's never once apologised for screwing over my dad – or us, for that matter.'

'It must have been a difficult time,' Pete allows, blinking as he gazes up at the clear sky.

'It was,' I confirm, swallowing a sip of my drink as my voice begins to waver.

'But what would you rather she had done?' he asks, and I turn to him in surprise.

'What do you mean?'

'I mean, do you think she should have stayed with your dad even though she didn't love him any more?'

His question has baffled me so much that for a full minute I don't say anything.

'I think she should have at least tried to make it work!' I say at last, far more aggressively than is totally necessary, and Pete widens his eyes.

'Perhaps she did,' he argues, his expression unreadable. 'Did you ever ask her?'

'I . . .' I pause, my cheeks colouring as I realise that my answer is no, I never did – not really. I simply cut her out of my life until I was ready to forgive, and then I didn't let her talk about it. Her answers were never satisfactory, as far as I was concerned, and so I held up my hand to her whenever she broached the subject. As the years passed, she gave up even trying. She couldn't ever tell me what I wanted to hear, so there was no point.

'Why are you on her side?' I ask Pete, shame and confusion making my voice quiver.

'I'm not on her side,' he says, a deep sigh misting the cold air in front of us. 'I'm on your side – I always will be.'

'But then why . . .' I begin, but he continues talking.

'I just think that things come to an end for a reason, and yes, it might be sad, and yes, the other person might not agree with your reasons, but when something isn't right, then it just isn't. Sometimes things are too broken to fix.'

I fall silent, sobered by his reasoning. He's not just talking about my parents now; he's talking about his own experience – but which of the two has Pete been? Has he had his heart broken, or has he stomped all over someone else's? The photo predictably swims back into view. Why would he keep it hidden away if he didn't still have lingering feelings? Surely if he was the one to end things with that girl – and looking at her I find this very hard to believe – then wouldn't he find it easy to discard any memories that he had?

'My head hurts,' I mutter, rubbing it and sighing irritably.

Pete tips back his cup and then crushes it in his hand. I want him to say that he's sorry, or say anything, really, that will reassure me, but he doesn't. Instead, he grabs my hand and pulls me backwards in the direction of the way we've just come.

'Enough of this depressing talk, Lulu,' he says with stern enthusiasm. 'Let's go and have some lunch, yeah?'

I nod, leaning against him as we walk to show him I'm OK, but inside I'm churning with worry. What if he's not the man I thought he was – what if he's cruel? Or worse, what if he's still in love with somebody else; somebody that hurt him, just like my mum hurt my dad?

I'm so caught up with it all that I forget why I was leading Pete along this particular Bellagio street in the first place.

19

Taggie

'Gino, no! That is not a toy. Gino! Leave it. *Leave it.*'

It's very hard not to laugh as the naughty little dog scuttles away across the stony beach, a selfie stick clamped between his pointy teeth and a definite expression of smug self-congratulation on his furry face.

'Sorry,' Elsie apologises, throwing up her arms in defeat. 'He'll get bored and drop it in a minute, don't worry.'

The young French couple, who inadvisably put their selfie stick down on the ground, don't look entirely convinced by Elsie's assurances, but the girl is enchanted by Bruno at least. He's no longer in my arms, but on the wet, muddy beach, shivering and gazing up at all the assembled females with those huge, dark-brown eyes of his. Nico, meanwhile, has taken a shine to Marco – and he's not the only one. I can hear Gladys's shrill, flirtatious giggle from here, and she and Marco are at least twenty feet away, over by the edge of the water. Poor Will-yum has been instructed to take photos of the two of them together, and Marco only agreed on the proviso that Nico be in the pictures, too. Quite some work of art that's going to be.

We've been at the northernmost tip of Bellagio for half an hour now, the beating sun keeping us warm and the incredible views providing plenty of inspiration to my group of artists. Known as Punta Spartivento – 'the point which divides the wind' – it's an undeniably beautiful yet strangely eerie spot. When you stand right on the edge of the water looking north to where the snow-capped mountains mark the beginning of the Swiss border, it can feel almost overwhelming, as if the lake could swallow you whole.

In the summer months, this semi-circle of beach is packed with visitors, but today we've got the place pretty much to ourselves. Monochrome stones litter the ground between the dead white husks of plants, and part of the stone stairway leading down from the road has crumbled and fallen away. I didn't want Elsie to even attempt them, but she was determined, and before either of us knew what was happening, Marco had lifted her right up into his arms and carried her over the gap. I wish he hadn't, though, because she's been unable to talk about anything else ever since.

'It was as if I weighed barely a thing,' she keeps saying dreamily, clutching my arm and closing her eyes. 'I felt like a young woman again.'

It's a good thing she doesn't know that it was Marco who rescued me when I fell in the lake. I'd had to tell Elsie about it, because she'd been awake when I arrived, dripping wet, back at her house, and she'd been predictably enthralled by the story. If she knew that Marco was, in fact, my Italian knight in shining leather jacket as well as hers, she'd probably cartwheel up the mountainside in a frenzy. I'm surprised he's still here hanging around with us, to be honest. I'm sure he has far more important things to do with his free time than pose for photos with crazed, middle-aged women and carry other, less crazed women across beaches. I'm loath to admit it, even to myself, but I quite enjoyed chatting to him on the boat up here today. I used to have lots of male friends back in London – well, they were more *his* friends – and talking to Marco has made me realise that I do miss the company of men. Shelley is fun and I adore Elsie, but sometimes it's nice to get a man's perspective on things. Sal doesn't count, because he's my boss – and because the two of us only ever seem to discuss things that are directly related to work.

'Oh dear,' Elsie mutters now, pointing discreetly into the middle distance. 'I think Gino may be burying his treasure.'

It's true, he is. All I can see of the little bugger is the tip of his rigid tail – the rest of him is obscured by the edges of a muddy trench.

'Gino,' I say sweetly, tiptoeing across the stones towards him.

A low growl echoes out from the hole.

'Come on, now,' I soothe, crouching down on my haunches. 'That's not yours, is it?'

The tail is vibrating now with excited rage, and I reach across and brave a light touch, only to almost fall over backwards when the tiny ball of indignant fur begins yapping at me in earnest.

'You little . . .' I say between gritted teeth, righting myself with my hands and promptly getting mud all over one of them.

Gino pops his head up out of the hole and regards me with distrust, his beady eyes fixed on my hands. He knows

I want that selfie stick, and there's no way he's going to give in.

'Having some trouble?'

I look up to find Marco staring down at me, his eyes crinkled with amusement and his hair all blown upwards on one side. Nico has followed him over and is now looking with some interest at the tiny crater dug by Gino, his minuscule nose sniffing the air and his tail twitching with the expectation of a treat. Spotting his adopted brother so close to his new, most prized possession, Gino leaps right out of the muddy cavern and starts growling with alarming menace.

'Now, now, boys,' I chide, trying my best to sound stern, even though I find the pair of them utterly ridiculous.

'Here! What's this?' calls Marco, and I look up again to see that he's now brandishing a bit of driftwood. The dogs, recognising that a game is about to begin, immediately stop yapping and stand to quivering attention by his feet.

'Ready?' Marco teases, showing them the stick.

They stare at him, completely transfixed.

'One, two, three . . . FETCH!'

He releases the stick and Gino, Nico and myself watch in silence as it flies off through the air and lands a good distance away among the rocks.

'Well done,' I say, standing up as the dogs go haring off across the beach. I've retrieved the selfie stick from the hole, and now I swivel my bag round so I can find a tissue to wipe off the mud and slime.

'It was nothing.' He shrugs expansively. 'I used to have a dog when I was a boy.'

'Lucky you,' I reply, grimacing as a good deal of the dirt ends up on the leg of my jeans. 'I always wanted one, but my mum and dad weren't keen. They said they'd be the ones who ended up walking it, but I don't think they would have.'

'Did you play outside a lot as a child?' he wants to know, and I look at him in surprise.

'Yes. How did you know?'

Again, that non-committal lift of the shoulders.

'I am the same.'

Gino has brought back Marco's stick, having screamed at Nico for even daring to chase it, and is now dancing around in idiotic but very cute circles by his feet.

'Did you grow up here?' I ask, watching as the stick soars through the air once again.

'Yes and no,' he replies, looking at the distant dogs rather than me. 'I was between two homes.'

'Where was the other one?' I enquire.

'Another place.'

Well, that much is bloody obvious, I think, wondering why he's being so cagey.

'You must have lived in Leeds for quite a long time,' I state.

'Why do you say that?'

He's very good at answering polite enquiries with more questions, this man. But two can play at that charade.

'Why do you think I do?'

He provides me with a wry grin before answering.

'You tell me.'

'Oh, for God's sake,' I say, and he laughs good-naturedly.

'Your English is very good,' I point out, and he coughs

in reply, reaching down to throw the stick for Gino yet again. Nico has given up trying to play the game and is instead digging his own hole right next to Gino's, sending splatters of mud flying in all directions as he does so. I take a large step backwards, and Marco, glancing down, follows suit.

'I did spend some time in England,' he confirms, and I'm just about to open my mouth and ask how much time, when I'm interrupted by an excitable Elsie as she rushes towards us.

'The Frenchies are having a lovers' tiff,' she tells us, her voice hushed but impish.

We all glance over to where the young couple are, indeed, gesticulating at one another. The girl is red in the face and looks close to tears, and the guy is running his hands through his hair, tugging at it with impotent rage.

'Ooh la la,' I remark quietly, dropping my eyes as the girl looks over in our direction.

'They were perfectly lovey-dovey, and then a message came through on the chap's mobile phone and all hell broke loose,' Elsie says, with a certain amount of glee.

'Probably his ex-girlfriend,' I state, and Marco scoffs.

'What?' I demand.

'Women,' he replies, totally deadpan. Elsie chortles, but I immediately feel a prickle of irritation.

'Do you mean, the women who message their ex-boyfriends, or the women who get angry when they do?' I ask.

Marco smiles. 'Both.'

'Well,' I reply, careful not to let my grumpiness leak into my voice, 'I could say the same about men.'

'Now, now, my dears,' Elsie places a placating hand on each of our arms. 'I think it's always best to agree to disagree when it comes to this subject.'

'He started it,' I mutter, before I can stop myself, and Marco laughs out loud, bending down to pick up and throw Gino's stick yet again at the same time. His shirt has untucked itself from his jeans, and as he bends over I catch sight of the waistband of his boxers against smooth, tanned skin.

'Taggie was a very argumentative child,' Elsie says now.

'Elsie!' I protest, frowning as Marco urges her to elaborate.

'I always used to tell your mother not to worry about it,' she puts in cheerily. 'Only people with very high intelligence bother to argue about things.'

'Are you saying that because you enjoy a bicker?' I guess, and she grins.

'I don't know what you mean.'

'Hmmm,' I reply, giving her my best disapproving expression.

Marco throws the stick again. Gino is going to keel over soon from exhaustion. Well, that or sheer pleasure. It's not often that he gets somebody's attention all to himself like this. Bruno has wandered over to join us now, and is doing his usual thing of begging to be picked up. As if I hadn't already got enough mud on these jeans; now I have muddy paw prints all over them, as well. It's a good thing I'm hopelessly besotted with the silly creature.

'So,' Marco says. 'You spent a lot of time outside as a girl, and you were naughty – what else?'

'She used to sneak off all the time,' answers Elsie. 'It drove her mother mad.'

I feel as if I'm being ganged up on here.

'And she had imaginary friends – two of them.'

'OK, that's enough,' I insist. 'I don't think Marco needs to hear about—'

'Froggle and Bella?' finishes Elsie. The soft skin of her cheeks is strawberry pink with pleasure, and her eyes are glinting with mischief.

'Froggle?' asks Marco, scooping a panting Gino up into his arms and kissing the top of his head.

'He had the head of a frog and the body of a man. That's right, isn't it, Taggie?'

I pull my mouth into a thin, hard line.

'That's right.'

'And Bella was a princess?'

'She was.'

'She used to sit at the end of my garden, in the shade of the lemon tree, and chat away to Froggle and Bella for hours,' Elsie tells Marco. 'It was so sweet.'

'Did you not have any real friends?' he jokes.

'Not here, I didn't,' I say, defending myself. 'This is what happens when you're an only child – you develop weird traits and have no choice but to conjure friends out of thin air.'

'What happened to Froggle and Bella?' Marco asks, again with that crooked smile he seems to habitually wear.

'They got married and lived happily ever after,' I say quickly, improvising as I go along. 'It turns out that Froggle was actually a prince who'd had a spell cast over him, so when Bella kissed him, he lost his frog head and got his human one back.'

'I see,' he replies, scrunching up his face as Gino licks his nose. I've never seen that angry little mutt be so affection-ate before – especially not with a man. Marco must have washed with Pedigree Chum shower gel or something.

'Taggie knew at the tender age of five that she'd have to kiss a lot of frogs to find her prince,' Elsie says. She sounds bizarrely proud of the child version of me for coming to that conclusion so early on in life, which is utter madness. There is nothing good about spending time with frog-men, or wasting emotional energy on them, as I know only too well.

'Have you?' Marco wants to know. Gino has gone and fallen asleep in his arms now, his tiny head resting on the sleeve of his new hero's leather jacket and his dirt-streaked paws tucked up underneath his even dirtier tummy.

'Have I what?' I say, deliberately obtuse.

'Kissed many frogs?'

I hesitate before answering, my mood darkening as the inevitable image fills my mind. There was nothing frog-like about *him* when we first met; no transformation was needed, as far as I was concerned. No, in his case, I started off with a prince, and he slowly but surely turned into a frog.

'A few,' I say at last, settling on a half-truth. 'But I don't plan on kissing any more of them ever again.'

Elsie must have finally sensed my discomfort, because the next second she's looped her arm through Marco's and is asking him if he'd walk with her to the shore so she can look across the water.

'I'm not as nimble as I used to be,' she explains, man-aging to flirt and play the helpless old lady simultaneously.

'Come on,' I whisper to Bruno as they walk away. He's still nestled in my arms. 'Let's go and see if anyone's ready to have lunch yet.'

20

Lucy

'Oh my God – is that a shrine to George Clooney?'

I look across to where Pete is pointing and promptly gasp with laughter. There, in an alcove halfway up the restaurant stairs, shut in behind a decorative metal lattice and lit up from behind like a statue in a church, is something that indeed looks an awful lot like a shrine to Mr Clooney. There's a photo of the man himself in an ornate gold frame, which appears as though it's been taken here in Como – he's wearing sunglasses on his head and you can see water behind him. Then, next to that, is another framed photograph of Villa Oleandra, the grand house that he bought in nearby Laglio, plus three bottles of wine. One of the waitresses, who is busy running up and down the steps ferrying trays of drinks and food, sees us looking and hurries over.

'That is Mr Clooney's wine,' she says, pride making her chest swell. 'You can buy it here, if you would like to.'

Flipping open my menu, she points to a list on the final page.

'Seventy euros!' I exclaim, loudly enough to make the departing girl turn her head.

'Sorry, George,' Pete jokes. 'I loved you in *Ocean's Eleven*, but not enough to pay that much for your plonk.'

'As if the cheeky fox needs even more money,' I add, flicking back to the start of the wine list.

'There, look – a carafe of local red only costs twelve euros. That's a bit more like it.'

'I'll treat us to the Clooney wine if you want it,' Pete says, stroking my hand.

'Don't be silly,' I say, looking at him incredulously. 'It's such a rip off!'

'We are on holiday, though,' he reminds me. 'And it's still Christmas. Sort of.'

'I'm not fussed,' I assure him, lacing my fingers through his. 'You don't need to spoil me. Being here with you is treat enough.'

I'm being honest, too. Despite all my own fears and inner voices of torment and insecurity, I am having a mostly amazing time with Pete. The conversation we had about my parents is still lurking in the back of my mind like a relationship Grim Reaper, but I'm determined to ignore it. What I need to be is bubbly and sweet, not grumpy and distrusting.

'Have you ever been on holiday with a boyfriend before?' Pete asks without warning, and I blanch.

'Not really,' I admit, deciding quickly that a flat no will only make me sound naive. I have been away for weekends with significant others before, anyway, just not to places that required a boarding pass.

'What about you?' I say, already dreading his reply.

'Yeah,' he hesitates. 'With my ex-girlfriend. We used to go twice a year at least.'

'Right.'

I feel like he's just punched me in the gut.

'She wouldn't have let me buy the Clooney wine either.'

It shouldn't matter to me what his ex-girlfriend was like, but for some reason I hate the fact that the two of us have anything in common. I want to be the opposite of her. It makes no sense whatsoever, but there it is.

'How long were you together?' I hear myself ask.

'Five years,' he says, his voice non-committal. 'Just over.'

'That's a lot of holidays,' I manage, and find that I've completely lost my appetite. When the same waitress reappears a few moments later to take our order, I choose a tricolore salad instead of the pizza I'd had my eye on. If Pete notices my unusual restraint, he doesn't mention it – and, of course, his appetite is totally fine. I stay silent as I watch him ask for a large portion of taglione with red shrimp and clams.

'We saw a lot of the world,' he says, picking up the thread of conversation exactly where he left it. 'But we argued a lot, too.'

'Oh?' I daren't say anything else.

'Yeah.' He sighs, fiddling with his knife. 'She always wanted to be out seeing something or doing something, while I preferred to spend time sunbathing by the pool, or sampling all the local food and drink. It used to drive her mad.'

'Couldn't you have done both?' I ask, perhaps stating the obvious.

He pulls a face. 'You would think so.'

Privately, I'm thinking that his ex may have had a point, because I enjoy a bit of sightseeing too – but nothing on the planet is going to make me side with her over Pete.

'Is that why you broke up?' I continue, blushing at my

own bravery. I'm straying into very choppy waters here, and I fear that my emotional state is the equivalent of a rowing boat full of holes. I want to know details, but I'm fearful of how they'll make me feel. Thankfully, the wine arrives at that moment, which provides Pete with a pause in which to formulate a careful reply and gives me something to do with my fingers other than use them to tear my paper napkin into very small pieces in my lap.

'It wasn't the only reason,' he reveals, his brow knotted. He looks as if it's painful for him to even recount the details, let alone share them with me, and I feel guilty then to have asked the question. Then again, wasn't it him who started this by volunteering the information?

He picks up the glass of wine I've just poured for him, swills it around, then puts it back down on the table.

'She was . . .' he begins, and I can tell he's genuinely struggling with what to say. It's an odd place for us to be having such an intimate conversation, because many of the tables here in La Lanterna are occupied and a cheerful cacophony of crashing pots, raised voices and laughter is seeping out from the door leading into the kitchen. This feels like the kind of chat that we should be having in bed, perhaps in the dark, so we can hold each other and he can avoid having to look at me as he speaks. Pete's having trouble doing the latter now, and as I watch him, he lifts his head and deliberately fixes his eyes on a shelf full of miniature bottles of limoncello that is fixed to the wall above us.

'I haven't talked about it before,' he admits. 'About her, I mean. My mates aren't really the type for deep and meaningfuls, and my parents were just pissed off with me.'

'Pissed off with *you*?' Now I really am intrigued.

He nods, finally glancing at me before looking quickly away again.

'I was the one who ended it,' he says. 'I think my mum had high hopes for a wedding, and she hasn't forgiven me yet.'

'Does she know about me?' I say, my voice small. I strongly suspect that I know the answer already, so it doesn't come as a surprise when he shakes his head.

'Not yet.'

'I see.'

'Please don't read anything into it,' he implores, fixing me with a big-eyed stare as I gulp down some of the wine. 'It's not because I don't care about you – I do. It's just that I don't want the hassle and all the questions.'

This must be why he hasn't properly introduced me to his friends, either – because I'm still his dirty little secret. The practical side of my brain is busy pointing out the reasonable facts: that Pete was with his ex for a long time, and that of course those close to him would need a period of adjustment following their break-up. My irrational side, however – which has always been the more dominant of the two – is jumping up and down, waving a red flag and screaming at the top of its much louder voice that I've been seeing Pete for months now, so why is he still being so secretive? It also unhelpfully reminds me that there is a lot I don't know about the situation – not to mention who the hell Pete's been ignoring calls from. Is mysterious Manny the ex-girlfriend who can't get over him? Was that her in the photos I found?

'I'm not reading anything into it,' I say at last, the

tremble in my voice making the lie sound far less convincing than I would like. 'I just wish you'd told me all this stuff sooner.'

'There's nothing to tell,' he replies, sounding weary. 'But I am sorry for bringing up the whole subject of my ex. I don't know why I did. It was stupid.'

'It's OK.' I touch his hand. 'I want you to feel like you can talk about it if you need to.'

He considers this, his features set.

'I don't think I need to talk about it,' he sighs, sounding far less convincing than I suspect he would have liked. 'I just want to draw a line under it all, to be honest.'

There's a hint of something in his tone that sounds to me like regret, as if the situation is not how he would have chosen it to be. But then he did say that he was the one to end things, so perhaps his ex-girlfriend reacted in a bad way. Maybe the whole thing is too traumatic to dredge up?

'So, you don't speak to her still, then?' I ask at last, feeling my heart begin to race with anxiety.

He glances up in surprise. 'No, of course not.'

'You don't have to pretend for my sake,' I add, being careful to keep my delivery light. If he thinks I'm not fussed either way, then he's more likely to be honest.

'I'm not pretending,' he assures me, sliding both his hands across the red tablecloth and picking up my wrists. 'To tell you the truth, I don't think I'll ever see or speak to her again.'

I give him a look that I hope conveys sympathy at the same time as mild discombobulation, and lean back in my creaky wooden chair.

'Let's talk about it later, all right?' I suggest gently, and am immediately rewarded with a huge smile of relief.

'Thank you,' he mutters. 'You know, things were never easy with her like they are with you – it's part of the reason I think we work so well together.'

It's ridiculous how happy that comment just made me feel.

'Really?'

'Yeah. I felt like she . . . Well, she didn't ever like to be wrong – not about anything. She didn't have any give, while you're just so . . . Kind, I guess. Kind and reasonable.'

'Comes with the territory when you're a nurse,' I reply, embarrassed to be praised so highly.

'I don't think it's your job that makes you the way you are,' he says, his head cocked to one side and his gaze direct. 'I think you're just made that way.'

'Well, I think you're pretty damn perfect,' I murmur.

Pete screws up his face in disbelief. 'Hardly!'

'Well, perfect for me, then,' I say, quickly adopting a jokey tone. 'You're the lime in my gin and tonic; the Iron Throne to my Cersei Lannister.'

'Who?' he asks, looking confused, and I remember then that he's only seen a few episodes of *Game of Thrones*.

'Just perfect,' I reply. 'That's all you need to worry about.'

'I think we should drink to that,' he declares, raising his half-empty glass. 'To having found each other.'

I smile as I lift my own glass to meet his.

'To us.'

As if by magic, the food arrives as soon as we've toasted, and Pete tucks into his pasta with gusto. To be fair to him, the taglione does look and smell incredible, and my taste buds throb with envy as my nose picks up scents of fresh chilli, tarragon and warm shrimp. The tricolore salad is a worthy runner-up, however, and I almost weep with happiness when I discover that the hollowed-out tomato that I assumed was a fancy garnish has, in fact, been stuffed with a fresh basil pesto. When I dip my knife in and spread it over the creamy slabs of mozzarella, I swear I hear a fanfare start to play in the depths of my stomach.

We barely talk to one other as we eat, which isn't like us, but in a way, I'm grateful. The methodical action of cutting up food, chewing it, then swallowing is giving me time to digest what I've just heard. I find that I can forgive Pete for not telling his mum about me yet, but I can't quite move past the holes he left in the story about him and his ex. I want to know why he ended things, and when it was. And, most importantly of all, I want to know whether he still has any lingering feelings for her. If he has, then I'm honestly not sure how I'll react.

21

Taggie

Marco finally heads off to his meeting when I've rounded up the group ready for lunch, but not before lifting an unashamedly ecstatic Elsie into his arms and gallantly carrying her back over the crumbling steps. I follow closely with the two naughtiest and muddiest dogs, while shy, red-faced Tim gingerly clutches a docile Bruno.

'Must you go?' implores Gladys, wrapping her fingers around Marco's arm and beaming up at him.

He smiles at her. 'I must.'

'Agatha, tell him he simply *must* stay,' she instructs, her voice all shrill and babyish.

'You'll see him again on the boat back to Como,' I tell her, before directing my attention towards Marco. 'Won't she?'

He nods.

'There's only one boat back at this time of year,' I explain, not just to Gladys but to everyone assembled around me. 'If you miss it, you end up stranded.'

From the look on Gladys's face as she gazes after a departing Marco, she would quite happily volunteer herself to be stranded in Bellagio for the night, so long as he was trapped here with her. I bet Gladys was one of the popular girls at school, who always had to have a boyfriend – or at the very least a stonking great crush on someone completely unattainable. I had friends like that, and they used to frustrate me so much. I never saw the appeal in mooching around after boys, playing kiss chase or writing love notes in class. The lads I knew growing up were simply my mates, who I rode my bike with or played tag, the very same boys who later became my drinking buddies, or my mosh-pit wingmen at local gigs. It was a long time before my hormones finally caught up with me and made me see any of them differently, and even then, I was extremely picky. I've never indulged in a one-night stand, can count the number of flings I've had on my thumbs, and even a random snog with a stranger is an extremely rare occurrence. It's not because I'm frigid or boring, it's just because I don't fancy that many guys. When I do meet someone that turns my head, I tend to keep hold of them. Well, I do until they decide that they don't want me any more.

We've all been walking as I've been thinking, and I feel a wave of gratitude towards Elsie for assuming the role of group leader. I can see her at the head of the pack now, the three chihuahuas trotting along beside her and her multi-coloured woolly hat at a jaunty angle atop her soft white curls. The sun has risen as far as it's going to, and the surrounding landscape is dappled with soft amber light. We're following the lake back round towards the main harbour, and cypress trees stand tall and proud on the other side of a high, cream-stone wall, which is separating the road from the undergrowth beyond.

Every now and then, the warm façade of a villa will emerge from between the thick foliage, their outside walls painted red, yellow or blue. Many of the wooden shutters here in Bellagio are painted bottle-green, and as I stare up at them I'm reminded of Marco's eyes. He has such strange colouring for a native Italian, because even though he has the dark hair and that self-assured swagger, his eyes aren't the brown that I'm accustomed to seeing over here.

'Miss Torres?'

I swing around to find Tim a few feet behind me, his arms crossed against the biting cold and his face aflame.

'Hello, Tim,' I say, happy of the distraction. 'What can I help you with?'

He stares at me with big eyes.

'Is your mum OK?' I ask, looking around until I locate Sue ahead of us.

'Yeah,' he says, jogging slightly to keep up with my fast pace. I'm often told that I cover a lot of ground quickly for such a small person, which of course just encourages me to walk all the faster.

'Has that man gone?' he asks then, flushing almost purple.

He can only mean Marco.

'Yes,' I reply cautiously, wondering where this could be going. I've always been aware that flirting is not my forte, but I'm practically gold-medal level compared to poor Tim. That is, if flirting is what he's attempting to do now.

'Is he your boyfriend?'

I stop walking, and he comes to a clumsy halt next to me.

'Why do you want to know?' I ask, folding my own arms and pulling what I hope is a kind expression. I have no intention of anything romantic happening with Tim, but I must be careful not to be rude. My mouth has got me into trouble so many times.

'I thought we could . . . Maybe have a . . .'

He hesitates as I shake my head.

'I'm sorry,' I tell him. 'But I'm not allowed to go on dates with hotel guests – it's against the rules.'

'Oh.' Tim looks sadder than a week-old teabag.

'Sorry,' I say again, silently thanking Sal and his strictness for giving me the perfect excuse to turn Tim down. He might not be my type – and far too young – but I can tell that he's a sweet guy. It's nice to be reminded that there are still some out there. And I admire him, in a way, for having the balls to make such an obvious approach. I'm not sure I'd ever do it.

Rather than allow the awkward silence to drag on, I start telling Tim more about Bellagio, and why so many people are enchanted by it. He's a sculptor by trade, he tells me, and only really came along so his mum wouldn't have to travel here alone, but even he has found himself inspired by the sheer breadth of the landscape here. Talking about Como is one of my favourite pastimes, and I'm nattering away to Tim so happily that the trudge back into town seems to speed by.

I suggested the famous La Lanterna as a lunch venue earlier, but Elsie disagreed, pointing out quite rightly that it would most likely be busy. I rather like the cosy, hectic restaurant, with its cluttered shelves of limoncello and its bright red tablecloths, but I'm happy to go along with what Elsie decides. She is the Bellagio local, after all.

Our route to her chosen venue takes us right back through the main road of the town, and when we pass La

Lanterna, I peer through the steamy windows and see that it is, indeed, packed. My wily friend was right – we would never have got a table for all of us in there.

'Just up here,' calls Elsie, her voice slightly breathless from tackling the steep hill. I do worry about her navigating these twisty cobbled passageways, but trying to stop her leaving the house would be as impossible as fitting a horseshoe inside a matchbox – it's not even worth trying. She would argue that all her walking with Gino, Nico and Bruno keeps her fit, but I think she's driven outside more by the social aspect than a desire to be healthy. Elsie knows everyone in Bellagio, and her daily walk around the area means that she collects enough gossip to keep her occupied all evening. I know this, because she'll often impart the lot of it to me during our frequent phone calls. I always make a point of ringing Elsie if I can't make it up here. She would say it's because I like checking up on her, but in truth I love hearing all the news – it makes me feel as if I belong here. I talk to Elsie now more than I do with my own parents, and I do feel slightly guilty about that. I hope they understand that I'm simply trying to put myself back together. They know too much about what happened in the spring, back in London – I could see it in their eyes before I left and I can hear it in their voices when I speak to them now – and it makes the weight of what I'm feeling even harder to bear. My poor dad has been left with the job of untangling the ties of my former life, while my mum took the brunt of my inconsolable misery, as it was for a time. Coming here was as much about giving the two of them a break as it was about me escaping – it's not their job to look after me.

We've finally arrived at our destination, and the group file ravenously under the green and white striped awning and through the glass door of La Grotta, which is tucked away from the rest of the shops and cafés in a small courtyard. I suspect Elsie must have made a call at some stage of the morning, because a large table has already been laid out for us all, and three waiters hurry forwards to take people's coats as soon as we're over the threshold.

'Elsie!' cries a small man with a shiny round face and an even rounder belly, bustling across the room like an excited chicken.

'*Ciao, ciao,*' he says, kissing each of her cheeks and then stepping across to greet me in the same manner. The two of them must be close, because the next second they're chatting away in a rush of Italian far too fast and fluent for me to understand. I hear the word 'Taggie' come from Elsie, and the short man gazes at me in delight.

'I hear so much about you,' he exclaims, transferring his attention from Elsie to me. 'Elsie talk about you ever since you were a little girl.'

Wow, so these two really do know each other well.

'*Salve, signore.* It's very nice to meet you,' I say, charmed by his enthusiasm.

Elsie explains that his name is Giorgio, and that he inherited La Grotto from his father, whose papa before him had opened the place. Elsie had been great friends with Giorgio senior, but the older man had sadly passed away last winter.

'My father,' Giorgio says emotionally, unabashed tears glistening in his eyes. 'He was a great man.'

'I'm sorry for your loss,' I tell him, and he nods in

silence, grasping Elsie's proffered hand as tightly as if it were a life raft.

'Poor, sweet Giorgio,' Elsie whispers, as we take our seats. 'His father was devastated that he never married. I didn't have the heart to tell him that his son was gay.'

'Does he . . .?' I ask, and she smiles conspiratorially.

'Yes, with a landscape gardener called Ernesto. I often see the two of them walking their dog. They've got a Bolognese called Pepe, such an adorable thing, all fluffy and excitable. Gino and Nico hate her, of course, but I think Bruno is rather in love.'

The little brown dog looks up at the sound of his name, a twitch of pleasure in his tail, and Elsie beams like a proud mother.

'Dogs are far better company than men,' she confides, not for the first time. 'I'm far happier with my boys than I ever was with any of my husbands, God rest their souls.'

'Perhaps I should get one,' I suggest, and I see Elsie's blue eyes crinkle with mischief.

'A dog, or a husband?'

'Elsie,' I warn, but I can see she's about to unleash.

'Marco must be worth a date, at the very least,' she says, picking up the menu and squinting at it for a second before tossing it down. If I know Elsie as well as I think I do, she'll let Giorgio choose her lunch. The members of the group at the far end of the table have begun ordering carafes of wine, and baskets of oven-warm bread are being set down between plates. The smell makes me realise how hungry I am, having had my breakfast before the sun was even up this morning, and I tear into my bread before the waiter has even removed his hand.

'Don't be naughty,' I chide Elsie, and she pretends to look wounded.

'It's not naughty of me to want my favourite girl to have a bit of fun,' she protests. 'If I was your age, I'd have been shoving you out of the way to get to him, but as I'm not . . .' She leaves the end of her sentence unsaid, but her meaning is clear.

'I'm not interested,' I say primly, trying not to smirk at the sad expression she pulls.

'I think there's something wrong with your eyes,' she replies, all concern. 'Shall I call my optometrist friend Maria and ask her to book you in for an appointment?'

'There is nothing wrong with my eyes!' I exclaim, half-laughing.

The waiter has made it back down to our end of the table again, and Elsie pulls yet another sad face when I tell her that no, she cannot under any circumstances have a whole carafe of wine to herself.

'Just a glass, then?'

'A *small* glass.'

'Spoilsport!'

As soon as the order is written down, Elsie predictably returns to the subject of Marco.

'I just think it might be nice for you to have a boyfriend here,' she says, trying a slightly different tack. 'I worry about you getting lonely.'

I gesture at the group sitting around us and notice Tim staring at me over the top of Will-yum's shiny bald head. 'I'm hardly lonely, Elsie. I barely get any time to myself, to tell you the truth. I have Shelley to keep me company – and you. And anyway,' I add, raising a hand when she goes to interrupt, 'I'm not looking for a boy-friend.'

This last statement halts her argument momentarily, but I can see those tenacious cogs of hers whirring behind her eyes. Elsie knows about my ex, of course, but she doesn't know all the grisly details of our break-up. I begged my parents not to tell her, because I wanted this place to be free from the tarnishes of that time, and of what happened. Taking that into account, I suppose I should appreciate the fact that she's finding my reluctance to move on frustrating. And she's right – Marco is, un-deniably, a very attractive man, but there's a lot more to a person than just the way they look. I barely know the guy, yet, so how can I know how I feel about him?

'It's been a long time,' Elsie says next, her voice low but kind. 'You are allowed to be happy, you know? That's all I want for you.'

But it hasn't been all that long, I think. Seven months ago, we were still living together. I was balling his socks into pairs for him as I unloaded the tumble drier, picking up the crunchy peanut butter that he liked from the super-market and leaning my head on his shoulder while we watched TV on a Saturday night. When I think about those small, simple gestures, it seems impossible that the two of us have reached the point we're at now, where I cannot bear to see or speak to him, and he is a stranger once again, just as he was the night we met. I remember sitting at my parents' house after everything had come crashing down, my legs curled underneath me on the arm-chair, staring unseeingly at the television. That weird film had been on, the one where Kate Winslet's character has her ex-boyfriend, played by Jim Carrey, erased from her memories, while he tries, and fails, to follow suit. *Eternal Sunshine of the Spotless Mind*, it's called. Such a beautiful title for such a bleak premise. Would I erase my ex from my memories if I had the chance? Some days, yes – but then if I did, would I ever learn from what had happened?

'I'm not unhappy,' I assure Elsie, sipping the glass of orange juice that's just arrived. And it's true, most of the time. If I can just get through this first year, I'll be OK. One day at a time, that's what my mum always says.

Elsie looks sad now, as if she's heard everything I've just been telling myself in my head, and wraps her fingers around the soft part of my arm.

'If I ever meet this ex-boyfriend of yours,' she says, her lip curling at the thought, 'I'll set the dogs on him.'

We both look down to where Gino, Nico and Bruno are fast asleep under Elsie's chair, each one snoring like a tiny lawnmower, and I can't help but shake with laughter.

22

Lucy

The sun begins to droop as Bellagio's many clocks tick on through the afternoon, and the light pours down from rooftops to balconies, creeping across windows and through railings. Long shadows stretch haphazardly across jumbled cobbles, and tiny birds pick through the dust in search of crumbs.

Pete and I walk off our lunch by heading up to Punta Spartivento on the northern tip of Bellagio and clambering over a broken set of steps on to the grubby beach below. I watch while he attempts to skim stones across the surface of the lake, looking in vain for shells to collect and taking endless photos of the distant Alps. Inspired by the view, Pete tells me a story about the last time he and his mates went on a skiing trip, neatly omitting the parts about drinking themselves into a stupor on a regular basis – which I know they most certainly would have – and instead focusing on how many tricks he learnt to do on a snowboard.

'I'm surprised none of you ended up with a broken neck,' I exclaim, as he shows me a video on his phone of himself and his friend Sean, each of them taking it in turns to soar through the air and land in an inelegant heap on the snowy ground.

'Yeah,' Pete agrees, chuckling. 'Sean especially – you know how clumsy he is.'

Clumsy is exactly the word that Sean had used to describe himself when he arrived at A&E that fateful day, having tripped over his own shoelaces while on the escalator at Camden Town underground station and broken his leg in three different places on the way down. He wasn't making all that much sense, thanks to the morphine shot that the paramedics had kindly administered, but he still managed to poke fun at himself. When I asked him if he wanted to call anyone, he said he'd already texted his 'best boy'. I've been grateful to him for sending that message ever since.

Pete turned up a few hours later, by which time Sean had been taken upstairs to a ward. The breaks to his leg were severe enough to warrant surgery, but there wasn't a free slot until the following morning. I was the nurse in charge of looking after him, so it was me who got to bring Pete through from the waiting room, but that day wasn't the first time we met. It happened a whole month beforehand, down in the hospital canteen.

I had been on shift for ten hours at this point, and only an hour before had helped attend to a woman in a terrible state. She was so distraught by what had happened to her that it had left me shaken, and I can remember feeling an overwhelming need for something comforting. In the absence of a hug, chocolate was the next best thing, and so I used my short break to pop down and buy the biggest bar of Dairy Milk that the canteen had on offer. It was standing there, by the shelves of confectionery, that I first saw Pete.

He had that look common to most of the visitors to All Saints who aren't patients: tired, bewildered and a bit lost, and my heart immediately went out to him. I could tell that he'd come in straight from work, because he was dressed in a shirt and tie, the latter pulled away from his throat and lying half-knotted across his chest. There was wax in his ginger hair, but it was sticking up where he'd run his hands through it, and he was staring unseeingly at the packets of pre-prepared sandwiches, chewing on his lip.

'I wouldn't go for the BLT,' I said, making him jump a fraction. 'Plenty of L and T, but barely any B. I got one last week that was purely T, if you can believe that.'

He looked at me, puzzled but friendly enough, and picked up one of the packets.

'How about the tuna mayo?'

I curled up my nose.

'Bread's always soggy.'

He put it back down again with a grimace.

'Cheese and pickle, then? Surely you can't go wrong with that?'

'Better,' I allow, looking up at him just as he glanced down at me. 'But I still say the all-day breakfast is the best they have on offer.'

His eyes searched the jumble of sandwiches until he located the one he was looking for.

'All-day breakfast it is!' he said, holding it up with a flourish.

After that he accompanied me over to the coffee machine, where I showed him how to insert the little pods, and then we found ourselves in the queue together, where he offered to pay for my food.

'Oh no,' I replied, handing over some coins before he could insist. 'It's embarrassing enough that you've caught me buying this humongous bar of chocolate.'

He shrugged, as if seeing my purchase for the first time.

'I'm a big fan of the stuff, too,' he admitted. 'But maybe not for dinner.'

I asked him what he was doing at the hospital as we wandered back towards the lifts, and he muttered something about a friend having an accident, but didn't go into detail.

'Well, it was nice to meet you,' I said, going to walk away, but something in the look he gave me made me hesitate.

'Bye, Lucy,' he said at last, smiling at me as the lift doors closed, and I'd crossed my fingers in the hope that it wouldn't be for the last time.

I thought about Pete for the remainder of my shift, and all through the following one, too.

The weekend came and went, but still there was no sign of him at the hospital. I couldn't find him online, because I didn't know his surname, but that didn't stop me trailing endlessly through hundreds of men called Pete and Peter on Facebook, hoping to spot his face. After a few weeks had passed, I was getting ready to file him along with all the other missed opportunities I'd had in life, when suddenly, just over a month to the day after we'd had our first conversation, there he was, standing in the A&E reception area.

'Pete?' I asked, delight at seeing him again elbowing its way past my usual shyness.

He blinked a few times, bewilderment slowly turning to recognition, and then he grinned.

'It's you,' he stated happily, and my insides started doing the conga.

He was dressed in a dirty rugby kit and there were dried patches of mud all over his legs. We both looked down at the state of him, then back up at each other, and laughed. I couldn't believe that he was back, standing right in front of me, and he couldn't seem to take his eyes off mine. If love at first (or second?) sight is possible, then it's probable that I fell head over heels for Pete at that very moment, and my feet haven't reconnected with the ground since.

Pete is still lobbing stones into the water ahead of me, punching the air triumphantly every time he manages to get one to skim, ignoring the squawking birds that keep flying up from the surface in fright. If Julia were here, she'd already have told him off for scaring them, but I decide to let them fight their own battles. Instead, I take photos of him, using the sport mode on his proper camera to capture the rapid movement of his wrist and the twist of his body. I love his strong arms, and the broadness of his shoulders. He's the biggest and most muscular man I've ever been out with, not to mention the sexiest, and just looking at him is enough to arouse me. Just as I always am when I'm close but not next to Pete, I'm clutched with an urgent need to touch him, and hurry forwards across the mud and gravel.

'Hey there, bird botherer,' I say, sliding my arms around his middle from behind and slipping my hands into the front pockets of his jeans.

'Hey yourself,' he says, dropping the stone he was about

to throw and turning around to face me. 'Are you impressed by my skimming skills?'

'Very,' I reply obediently. 'First the chess secret and now this – you really are a dark horse.'

'My dad taught me,' he explains. 'Probably to stop me playing chess for once in my life.'

My hands are back in his pockets, and I can feel him stirring into life against my stomach.

'What are you trying to do to me?' he murmurs, nibbling my ear until I squirm.

'Nothing,' I say sweetly, inching my forefinger across further.

'How long is it till the boat leaves?' he asks, pressing against me.

'Almost two hours.' I make it clear that this information saddens me as much as it does him. 'There's only one afternoon service at this time of year.'

'Damn it,' he breathes, taking a step back and rearranging his jeans.

I want him to kiss me, but when I move towards him he hops to the side, out of reach.

'Stay away, nympho,' he jokes, batting away my hands when I stumble after him. 'Otherwise I'll be forced to take you right here, right on this beach.'

'You wouldn't dare,' I taunt, grabbing for him but only catching his glove.

'Oh, believe me, Lulu,' he says, his voice a low growl. 'I would.'

As much as the idea excites me, there's no way I would ever let him do such a thing. It's the middle of the afternoon! How would I ever face my dad again?

The horrible voice re-emerges in my mind then, urging me to ask Pete if he ever had sex with his ex-girlfriend on a beach, or in a park, or anywhere more adventurous than the confined interior of a bedroom. Why do I feel the need to know? Why can't I stop goading myself?

'Lulu?'

I swivel my eyes round. 'Yes?'

'Are you OK?'

'Fine.'

He frowns. 'You're doing that thing again, where you disappear into your own head.'

Oh, so he has noticed.

'What thing is that?'

'You know what thing. It's like you're here with me one second, then gone the next.'

I stifle a pretend yawn. 'I'm probably just tired.'

He doesn't look convinced, so I plaster one of my re-assuring nurse's smiles across my face.

'Come on, you sexy thing,' I tell him softly, standing on my tiptoes so I can kiss him on his unmoving mouth. 'Why don't we go and see if Bellagio has any gelato places open?'

He agrees to that, albeit begrudgingly, and I fill the silence with determined chatter about the time Julia and I had an argument when we shared an ice-cream sundae, and my stroppy sister ended up throwing half of it in my face.

'She's mad, your sister,' Pete sighs, endearingly protect-ive of even the six-year-old me, and so, suitably encouraged, I reel off more entertaining tales from my childhood as we walk. Pete begins to cheer up again in no time, his earlier concern forgotten, and I feel the tension start to leave my body. I must try harder to stop doing this to him – and to myself, for that matter. He'll end up getting sick of me, and it's not as if he'd find it hard to replace me with a younger, skinnier and less neurotic model. It wouldn't be the first time, and I'd only have myself to blame. All this new information about his ex-girlfriend has left me feeling off kilter, and I need time alone to digest it all. But against that, I'm also feeling an increasing need to keep Pete within reach at all times. My gut is whispering to me that my relationship has become precarious, and it's impossible to ignore it completely.

A sleepiness has fallen over the village by the time we make it back to the narrow roads lined with gift shops and boutiques. Lake Como's post-lunch calm is a phenomenon I had forgotten about in the years since I was last here, but I remember it well now. In a country where food and, by extension, mealtimes are as vital as a pulse, it's not surprising that the days here are structured around them.

'I can't imagine actually living in a place like this,' Pete comments, just as I was about to declare how much I would love to buy an apartment here. It comes as a bit of a surprise, too, because I had assumed he was a fan of quiet, sleepy places – he moans about London often enough.

'But it's so beautiful,' I point out.

'Yeah, but even that would wear off after a while, wouldn't it? And it's just so quiet. I think I'd get bored after a few days up here.'

Given that I was the one who chose Como as our holiday destination, his words do sting a bit, but it's my love for this place, not concern for my own feelings, that makes me say, 'I think you're mad.'

He stops, rubbing at his nose. Both of us have runny ones, thanks to the icy temperatures.

'Mad?'

'Yes, Mister – mad. As in loop-the-loop loopy. Bellagio is gorgeous – and, trust me, it's anything but quiet in the summer. You'd be lucky to find an empty restaurant seat at all in July, and in August the beer has been known to run out.'

'Bloody hell!' Pete's properly aghast by that last nugget of information.

'That's why I wanted to bring you here now,' I continue, drawing his attention to the beautiful Christmas decorations outside the nearest shop. 'So you could see the place at its best, without hundreds of tourists getting in the way.'

I watch his expression change as my words sink in.

'This is why,' he beams, wrapping his arm around me as we continue to walk.

'Why what?' I ask.

'Why I . . .' He pauses, takes a breath. 'Why you're so damn irresistible.'

'Soppy idiot,' I say with a laugh, but inside my intestines are tangled like wool. He was going to tell me that he loved me then, I know he was. So, what stopped him?

23

Taggie

Once we've settled the bill at La Grotta and downed the shots of limoncello handed around for free by an exuberant Giorgio, I tell the group that they have the next few hours free to roam the streets of Bellagio by themselves. Many of them want to go back to the beach we visited earlier to take more photos, while Gladys is intent on dragging Will-yum around the shops and Sue is keen on visiting the Basilica di San Giacomo with Tim. They all have their bearings now, because I've shown them most of the area anyway. Well, except for one place – but that's for my eyes only.

Elsie and I make our slow way back to her yellow house on the hill, and I make us a cup of tea, sipping it at the kitchen table while she bustles around feeding the dogs and chopping onions and garlic in preparation for a soup for later. She obstinately refuses my offer of assistance.

'I like doing it,' she insists, wiping her streaming eyes on the bottom of her apron. 'You work hard enough without having to wait on me hand and foot.'

I'd argue back, if there was any point whatsoever, but I do rebel a bit by slyly cleaning the toilet and basin when I nip into the bathroom for a wee.

It's nearing four p.m. when I hug Elsie goodbye and

make my way out through the front porch, admiring the multi-coloured glass panels as I go, then almost tripping over the altar broom balanced against the wall of the house. What is it with me and clumsiness lately? I really must try to get a bit more sleep.

This whole area has barely altered since I was a child, which makes me love it all the more. So many of the homes up here are vast and grandiose, but Elsie's single-storey cottage is cosy and charming, and it has character, too. I associate it with so much happiness, and even now it still pains me a little to leave it behind, even though I know I'll be back again within a matter of days. I'm just debating paying a visit to my second favourite location in Bellagio, when my phone rings in my pocket.

'Hello, Mum.'

'She's alive!' she cries, and I grimace into the handset.

'That joke has never been funny.'

'Oh really? Why are you laughing then?'

'I'm not,' I protest, but even as I say the words, I'm giggling. My mum and I go through this same spiel more or less every single time she rings me.

'I'd stop joking if you'd start answering more often,' she tells me, and I grumble incoherently. She's right, of course. I do screen her calls – but it's not because I don't want to talk to her. I just don't want to talk about *that*.

'So,' she says, without preamble. 'About the flat.'

I sigh.

'What about it?'

'Your dad says the work is almost done, and the second valuation is scheduled for the first week of January.'

'Right.'

I don't want to think about the flat, our flat. Which was supposed to be our home.

'We've been over there this morning,' she continues, 'and it's looking good. Your dad thinks you're looking at three hundred thousand at least.'

'Did you see . . .?' I begin, the final word withering and dying on my tongue.

'Him?' Mum guesses, and I swallow rather than reply. 'No, he's away. He texted Dad to let us know, which I suppose was decent of him.'

I tut.

'It will all be over soon enough, my darling. Once the place is sold and you have what is rightfully yours, none of us ever have to mention him again.'

This should cheer me up, but instead it makes me want to cry, and I lean against a low stone wall for support.

'Sorry,' I mutter, only just managing to stop my voice from cracking. 'Sorry that you've both had to deal with all of this crap.'

'Nonsense,' Mum croons, and I picture her familiar, pale-skinned face tilted to one side. I might have my father's eyes, and his thick black hair, but my delicate little shape is all my mum. If only I still had her incredible strength to go with it.

'It's no bother at all. I only wish I could do more to cheer you up.'

'Have you . . .?' I try again, but it's impossible to say his name without giving in to the tears. Luckily, however, my mother is a very shrewd lady.

'The last time I spoke to him was at the beginning of this month,' she says, being careful to remain stoic. 'Your dad was out when he called, so he got me, which I could tell he wasn't thrilled about. We just talked about the flat and he asked how you were – but don't worry,' she adds, hearing my sharp intake of breath. 'I didn't tell him anything at all.'

My shoulders droop in relief.

'Thanks, Mum.'

'There's really no need for thank yous,' she says in earnest, and I want to cry again because she's being so nice. I wasn't fair to either of my parents when I went back and lived with them. All they wanted to do was be there for me and help, and I closed myself off and refused to let them in. I thought it was better to shield them from it, but they have never given up asking if I'm OK.

'I just . . .' I pause, taking a deep breath and deciding to be honest with her for once. 'I just don't know what I would do if I had to face him. I'm scared of how I would react.'

'That doesn't ever have to happen,' she reminds me. 'He can't get to you over there in Italy.'

He can't, it's true. He may know that this place was special to me when I was a child, but I never brought him here. I'm confident that he wouldn't think to look for me here even if he wanted to find me, which I'm sure that he doesn't. I'll never forget the look on his face the last time I saw him, that mixture of pity and guilt and misplaced affection. He'd tried to touch me, and I'd clawed at him and screamed. I was like a wounded animal, and he was my tormentor.

I blink away the memory along with my tears, and ask my mum to tell me what else has been going on. After a few minutes, she hands the phone over to my dad, who asks me hesitantly if I'm eating enough, and what the latest tour group are like. Happily, this gives me the perfect excuse to tell him all about Gladys and Will-yum, and he's soon shouting highlights out to my mum in the background, the two of them chuckling as I explain about the Peach Perfection collection. By the time I hang up, the fingers of my right hand have practically frozen to the phone, and I rub them together vigorously as I make my way back down the hill.

I reach the harbour before any members of the group, and decide to sit for a while watching the sun sink down behind the mountains, choosing a wicker chair outside a café and pulling the complimentary blanket over my knees. Now that the shadows are beginning to lengthen, the temperature is dropping rapidly, and when the waiter strolls across to take my order, I ask for a glass of *vin brulé*, thinking that I can drink it at the same time as checking my emails. There's still so much to organise for the New Year's Eve party, and I'm currently waiting to hear back from two potential DJs, plus a local guy who says he can lay a temporary dance floor in the ballroom. However, just as the waiter returns and puts my drink down on the table, Marco comes into view up ahead, his hands deep in his pockets and his forehead creased into what looks like a scowl. When he walks closer and spots me, however, his expression is immediately transformed by an easy smile.

'*Ciao,*' he says, as soon as he comes into range, bending over to kiss me lightly on either cheek and then gesturing to the chair beside me. 'Can I sit?'

'Of course.'

There's a beat of silence as he arranges himself on the cushion, crossing one long leg over the other and resting his ankle on his knee. Unlike me, he doesn't pull the blanket over himself, but I notice that he, too, opts for a hot drink when the waiter appears. The *vin brulé* here in Bellagio isn't as sweet as the stuff down at the Christmas Market in Como, but rather tangy and tart, and I empty in a sachet of brown sugar and stir it.

'Elsie is a lovely woman,' Marco announces, squinting slightly in the setting sun.

I nod. 'She is, but she's also a troublemaker.'

'How do you know her?' he asks, and so I tell him about Elsie's friendship with my late grandmother, and about how she moved here for love.

'I can tell she is a romantic,' he says, smiling as he sips his coffee.

I laugh out loud at that. 'Maybe in the beginning,' I tell him. 'But I think all that had worn off by the third husband.'

'Third?' Marco widens his eyes. 'Well, now I like her even more than before.'

'I'm sure she'll be happy to hear it,' I say honestly.

'Where are your people?' is his next question, so I reassure him that Gladys isn't currently in the vicinity, and he visibly relaxes.

'How did your meeting go?' I ask politely, remembering how fired up he was about it on the boat up here this morning, but his face immediately darkens.

'It did not go well.'

'Oh, I'm sorry.' I hesitate. He isn't even looking at me now, but staring moodily out over the water. Gulls are dancing on the surface, and the distant houses on the opposite shore are glowing bright like hot coals in a grate.

'I need to make more money,' he sighs, swilling the dregs of his coffee around in his cup. 'The plan I have, it is going to cost me much more than I thought.'

'How much more?' I enquire nosily.

He looks at me, his mouth downturned.

'Many, many thousands of euros.'

'That many?' I say, trying to jolly him. 'It must be quite something, this plan of yours.'

'It is not a plan, it is a dream,' he corrects, picking at the rubber sole of his shoe. 'You cannot put a price on a dream.'

Except this one, clearly, I think, but decide it's best not to say and risk antagonising him.

'How long have you been dreaming about it?' I prompt, and he looks wistful as he replies.

'Since I was a little boy.'

I can't imagine this tall, masculine man ever being a little boy. It's impossible to picture him without his easy confidence and those looks he keeps giving me, so loaded with suggestion. He must have had the same strange green eyes as a child, but he would not have understood the power of them until much later in life. One of the best things about being young is that you never see yourself through anyone's eyes but your own, and you accept yourself, for the most part. It's only when you grow up, and start to rely more and more on the opinions of other people, that the early version of you is lost. For me, it was always my height. Being smaller than most caused others to treat me more delicately, as if I was a fragile ornament that might break if it was touched. As a result, I became tougher, and now one of the things I hate most is people trying to protect me. There is nothing more patronising than a man calling me 'cute'.

Marco, however, has done no such thing – despite having to come to my rescue at the beach two months ago. In fact, now that I think about it, he's never mentioned my height once, or looked at me like I'm a feeble little pixie. Perhaps that's why I'm warming to him so easily.

I extract my phone from my pocket to check the time. It's gone five p.m. now, not long until the boat arrives. I suppose I ought to get up and start searching for the members of my group, but it's so nice and cosy here under the blanket. I don't think Marco is going to elaborate on this dream plan of his. He's fallen into a sullen silence beside me, his eyes fixed resolutely on the water and his foot tapping out his impatience beneath the table. When I drop down some money and start to get up, however, he quickly follows suit.

'Can I walk with you?' he asks, and I smile.

'If you want to.'

We start by looping through the trees in the courtyard next to the water, the two of us trailing our hands across the rough bark as we pass each one. A further stroll leads us along the promenade, where stripped jacaranda trees are casting shadows across the pavement, and the approaching dusk is making the mountains glow blue. The sun is barely visible now, just a twinkle on the horizon, and the water below has turned silver in the dusk.

I take deep breaths of cold air down into my lungs, feeling my senses open to drink in all the sights, sounds and smells, and listen while Marco tells me about his job at the restaurant, and the plans he has for New Year's Eve.

'Do you know where you will be?' he asks.

'I'm organising a big party at the Casa Alta,' I tell him, feeling myself expand with excitement at the mere thought of it, only for nervous energy to creep into all the gaps when I remember the emails that I still haven't found time to answer. 'I had to talk my boss into letting me do it, so I'm hoping it will be a big success. Shelley's been helping me, too. I sent her into Como today to put up posters.'

'But you must watch the fireworks,' he says.

'We will,' I assure him. 'But from up at the hotel.'

'It is better by the water,' he says, and I nod to show him I agree.

'I don't think it would go down too well if I snuck away,' I say lightly. 'Sal would probably fire me.'

'I think you should come to Vista Lago,' he replies. 'Where my friend works. We are having a party also.'

I smile gratefully, but I don't tell him what I'm thinking, which is that the prospect of New Year is a scary one for me – and not just because the party I've been planning is my big chance to prove myself to Sal. Such a lot was lost this year, and I'm not sure how I'll feel when it reaches its end. Perhaps it will be a positive step towards recovery, or maybe it will send me right back to where I started when all this happened – I just don't know. At least overseeing things at the Casa Alta on New Year's Eve will provide me with a brilliant distraction. After Elsie's house, the old hotel is the place that I feel the most safe and secure here in Como, and I'm not sure that going to a party in a bar with Marco and his mates would be a good idea. I must make sure that Shelley doesn't find out it's even happening, or she will drag me all the way down there by my size threes as soon as the clocks have struck midnight.

We make it back to the café having rounded up most of the group, and I see that a small crowd has already started to form next to the jetty. There's no sign of the boat yet, and so Marco and I duck out of the cold underneath a covered archway, where a souvenir shop has set up racks of notebooks, postcards and calendars.

'Oh look, chihuahuas,' I say, reaching down to grab a calendar off the bottom shelf. Unbeknownst to me, however, Marco has spotted another one two shelves higher, and he goes to grab it at the same time as I bend forwards. There's a thud as his hand connects with my nose, and I stumble backwards in surprise, my eyes streaming and my hands clamped over my face.

'*Scusa, scusa!*' Marco cries, rushing towards me. But before he can get there, he's grabbed from behind by a pair of very big hands and roughly yanked off to one side.

'I saw you, mate,' shouts the intruder. 'I saw you hit your girlfriend.'

My eyes are still watering too much to see what's going on, so I flail one of my hands uselessly in front of me.

'Stop it,' I mutter, as loudly as my throbbing nose and mouth will allow. 'It was an accident.'

I can still hear scuffling noises, and then Marco begins shouting at the man in Italian, telling him to let go of him or else. Bloody men.

'STOP IT!' I yell, this time letting go of my bleeding nose and blinking away my tears.

'Fucking hell – Taggie!' exclaims a shocked voice, and everything inside me freezes in place.

It can't be him. It *can't*.

I bring a shaking hand up and use the sleeve of my coat to wipe away the tears and blood covering my face. I almost don't dare open my eyes again, but something deep inside me compels me to do so. And there, standing not more than a few feet away from me, his mouth slack with disbelief and his eyes wide with shock, is my ex-boyfriend, Pete.

24

Lucy

One moment we were walking along, hand in hand, admiring the sunset and discussing where to have dinner, and the next Pete had vanished. I watched in alarm as he bounded across the road and underneath a covered archway, only for sounds of a violent scuffle to follow him out. Too shocked and scared to do anything other than stand still and stare, I heard a flood of Italian followed by the sound of a woman shouting, 'Stop!' It was this, in the end, that unstuck my boots from the ground and propelled me forwards. I don't know what I was expecting to find, but never, not in a million centuries, would I have guessed it would be this.

'Taggie?'

I hear Pete say her name just as I recognise her. She's even more petite than she looked in the photos, and though her face is a mess of blood and tears, she's unmistakably the same woman from the photographs. Pete is gazing at her with an expression of pure horror, while another man, who's tall and looks to be Italian, is rearranging his leather jacket and muttering under his breath.

'What happened?' says a voice, which I only realise is my own when the three of them turn to look at me.

'I hit her,' the Italian says, his voiced tinged with contrition. 'It was by mistake, an accident. The calendars . . .' He trails off as he realises nobody is really listening. Taggie – so that's her name – looks as if she's about to faint, and Pete appears to have lost both the power of movement and speech. As bewildered as I am by all of this, my medical training remarkably still manages to kick me into action, and I hurry across to Taggie and wrap my arm around her shoulders.

'She's shaking,' I tell the two men calmly. 'Can you fetch me a chair, please?'

I direct the second comment towards the Italian, and he does as he's told, coming back less than half a minute later with a wicker café seat looped under one arm.

'Here,' I say gently, lowering Pete's ex-girlfriend on to the cushion and crouching down so I can see her face.

'Napkins, please,' I instruct, and again it's the Italian man who jumps into action. Pete is still staring at the three of us as if he's seen a ghost. There's a rash of colour on his neck and cheeks, and I can see a muscle twitching in his set jaw.

I help Taggie to tilt her head forward and show her how to pinch her nose. The tears have made the blood look more alarming than it really is, and after a few minutes she removes the tissue and opens her eyes, looking at me properly for the first time. I'm struck by a fresh wave of recognition, which I know must be thanks to all the time I spent conjuring up her picture in my mind, and I find myself unable, in that moment, to feel anything other than pity towards her. She may be Pete's ex-girlfriend, the very same person who I have tortured myself by picturing over and over again these past few days, but nobody deserves to be smacked in the face as hard as this – especially not someone so small and delicate.

'*Grazie*.' This has come from the Italian man, and I

accept his offer of a handshake. He doesn't extend the same courtesy to Pete, but then I can't really blame him. My boyfriend looks as if he wants to murder someone. I'm just about to ask him if he's OK, too, when we're all startled by the sound of a horn blasting.

'The boat!' I exclaim, looking at each of them in turn. 'We have to go,' I tell Pete, and clutch his rigid arm. 'There isn't another one.'

Pete, however, seems to be totally incapable of movement or speech.

'Come on,' I urge, before turning to address Taggie. 'Will you be OK?'

She nods, but doesn't smile, and allows her Italian friend to help her up out of the chair. It occurs to me then that they're probably getting the same boat back to Como as we are – why else would they be hanging around this freezing cold harbour?

'Come on,' I say again to Pete, but he only moves once Taggie and her friend have left, and then he refuses to look at me. We make our way towards the queue of people filing aboard, and I dig in my bag for the tickets I bought earlier. My body seems to be on autopilot, but my brain is screaming with unanswered questions. What the hell is Pete's ex-girlfriend doing here? Why won't he speak to me? And why isn't he doing everything in his power to reassure me that everything is going to be OK?

Even as we proceed in silence along the gangway and sit wordlessly down on two seats towards the back of the upper deck, I know that there's nothing he could say even if he did know how. Everything is very much not OK, and nothing will ever be the same again.

25

Taggie

I'm back in the toilet again.

I can feel the vibration of the boat's engine below me as I perch on the downturned seat, a wad of tissue catching the trickle of blood from my nose and the relentless tears from my eyes.

Pete is here in Como. What the actual hell?

I don't know how I managed to hold it together enough to count the heads of my group as they boarded and check that they all had somewhere to sit. I must look a total state – so bad, in fact, that even Gladys was rendered speechless at the sight of me. I was aware of Marco telling her sheepishly that he'd accidentally punched me in the face, but I ran downstairs and locked myself in here shortly afterwards, and nobody has come to find me yet.

I thought it was some sort of cruel joke at first, or that I'd been hit so hard I was seeing things, and had somehow conjured up my own repetitive nightmares of the past six months. But no, it was really him. It was really Pete, the man who I had spent five years of my life with, the same Pete that I hoped I would marry one day, the rugby-loving radio producer I had picked as the future father to my children. That Pete.

A fresh torrent of tears joins the last, the flimsy toilet

paper disintegrating in my fingers, and I muffle a loud sob with my fist while I reach round for a new batch.

How the hell did he find me? Or was it pure bad luck that he'd ended up in the same small corner of Italy that I had, on the very same harbour, on the very same bloody day? He did seem surprised, from what I can recall, but then I didn't dare look at him once I was sure it really was him standing there in front of me. I was too distracted by the shock, and by the pain in my face. That girl who came to help me was so nice, I think fleetingly. Lord knows what she must have thought when she stumbled across the three of us. I hope Marco has explained about the accidental punch.

I brave a sniff, and wince as my nose and top lip throb in protest. Lowering the tissue, I test the movement of my nose with timid fingers, bracing myself for more discomfort but finding the pain manageable. He hasn't broken my nose, then. Thank God for small mercies.

It's chilly here in the toilet cubicle, and I'm shivering as much from the cold as I am from shock. It was only a few hours ago that my mum was promising me I'd never have to see or speak to Pete again, and now he's here, in Como, on this boat. No matter how many times I tell myself that it's happening, I can't quite seem to grasp it, and I can feel my heart rate getting faster and faster beneath my many layers of winter clothing.

'Taggie?'

It's Marco, his thick Italian accent muffled by the door.

'Go away.'

A deep sigh filters through the wood.

'Are you OK? Did I break your nose?'

'I'm fine.' I mutter. 'And no.'

'Can I see it?'

I want to tell him to piss off, but I can't stay in the toilet of this boat all evening. I'll have to come out at some point and take the group back to the Casa Alta. What if Pete waits for me on the shore? What if he follows me?

I sit back down abruptly, but miss the toilet seat and end up sprawled on the floor. Marco must have his ear to the door, because the next second he's hammering on it, telling me with unbridled urgency that I must let him in.

Taking a few deep breaths to calm myself down – all of which are painful – I pull myself up and unfasten the lock. One look at Marco standing there on the other side of the door, however, his eyes shining with worry, and my face collapses once again into tears.

'I'm sorry,' I sob, leaning against him.

It feels oddly comforting to have him hold me like this, so tightly and safely against his silly leather jacket. He smells faintly of coffee and day-old aftershave, and I lean my weight against him feeling pathetic but resigned. For so many months now I've been sneaking off to cry in corners, and now that it's all caught up with me, I feel helpless to stop it. Marco isn't saying anything at all, but the solid bulk of him is helping. The bottom deck of the boat is deserted save for the young French couple from earlier at the beach, who are sitting quietly by the window holding hands. I'm so grateful to them for not being nosy. I'm not sure if I would have managed not to pry.

I let myself be led to a chair and sit down, all the while keeping my eyes trained on the stairs in case Pete re-appears and I'm forced to make a run for it. Marco must be wondering who the hell that man was, who pulled him off me so roughly, but he doesn't say a word about it; he simply keeps one arm around me and scrolls through his phone with the other. It's only when I glance away from the steps that I see he's sent a text message to Shelley, asking her to wait for us at Como harbour with several taxis.

He sees me looking and smiles briefly.

'I thought you would want to get back quickly,' he explains. 'I will stay with you until you are in the taxi.'

I could kiss him.

'Thank you,' I mumble.

'It is the least I can do,' he replies, squeezing my shoulder. 'After I punch you in the face.'

'It's OK,' I reply, wincing again as the movement of my lips hurts my nose.

The sun has set now, and the circular windows on this deck are black with night. I know if I pressed my face up against the glass, I'd be able to see lights coming on all along the east and west shores of the lake, but I don't think I'll be pressing my face up against anything for a while.

'Let me look at you,' Marco murmurs, slipping a finger under my chin and gently raising my face. I wait for him to keep speaking, but when he finally opens his mouth it's merely so he can moisten his lips, and I watch as his tongue rests just behind his bottom row of neat, white teeth. It's been so long since I was this close to a man, to a human, even. It feels better than I thought it would, but there's a huge uneasiness there, too. Pete was the last man to hold me in his arms like this, and what I'd felt then turned out to be nothing but emptiness.

As soon as Marco moves his head a fraction closer, I jerk my own away, and when I turn to face the stairway once again, Pete is standing there. From the look on his face, it's obvious that he's seen everything – and he does not look impressed.

26

Lucy

I tried to stop Pete going down there, but he wouldn't listen. It's like he's turned into a different person in the half-hour since we bumped into Taggie, and I can't get through to him. Whenever I speak, he bats away my words as if they're irritating gnats, and he's refusing to tell me what is going through his head.

'Don't go down there,' I warn, my voice stern but pleading, but Pete is already on his feet.

'I need to,' he says, looking at the floor rather than me. 'I have to make sure she's OK.'

What about ME? I almost yell, but it's clear I'm no longer his first consideration.

I watch in appalled silence as he walks away from me towards the top of the ferry stairs, where the two of us watched Taggie stagger down shortly after we left Bellagio.

'Go after him,' hisses a voice, and I spin round to where a woman wearing a bright red fleece is peering at me with unashamed interest.

'I beg your pardon?' I stutter, unable to quite believe her audacity.

'You can't let your boyfriend run rings around you, isn't that right, Will-yum?'

The balding man beside her in a matching fleece nods with fierce agreement.

'No ring-running.'

My mouth opens and closes like a cat flap in the wind.

'Off you go,' the woman bosses again, using her hand to shoo me.

Who the hell does this woman think she is?

I stand up, tutting and huffing in a most un-Lucy-Dunmore-like manner, then do exactly as she suggested and follow Pete down the stairs. I'm so full of nervous anger that my arms and legs are shaking, and I grip on to the handrail to steady myself. Pete is motionless at the bottom of the carpeted steps, his attention fully focused on Taggie and the Italian, who I notice has his arm around her. He's looking right back at Pete, a sneer on his handsome face, and the tension in the air between them is uncomfortably dense.

'Tag, are you OK?' Pete asks. Hearing him use her name so casually is like taking a bullet.

'She is fine.' This from the man beside her.

Taggie's nose has stopped bleeding, but the skin on her face looks clammy. I take another few steps down and when she sees me, she smiles tentatively, then whispers something into her companion's ear.

'She says thank you,' he tells me. 'For helping with her nose.'

'Do you want me to take another look?' I ask, but before I can venture any further, Pete reaches out an arm to stop me.

'Hey!' I push against his arm. 'What are you doing?'

'Just go back upstairs, Lucy,' he instructs.

'No!' I retort automatically, feeling my face heat up.

Usually I would never argue with him – or with anyone, come to that – but Taggie is my patient in this scenario, and not even Pete can get in the way of me trying to do my job.

Taggie has found her voice at last.

'How do you two know each other?' she asks, and Pete seems to visibly shrink.

'I'm his . . .' I deliberate just for a split second. 'His girlfriend.'

I hear a cough and glance towards the far corner of the deck, where a young couple are staring over in our direction. I wish I was them, watching this madness unfold rather than being stuck in the midst of it.

'How long have you been together?' Taggie wants to know, her voice ice-cold, but Pete replies before I have the chance.

'Not long,' he hurries out. 'We've only just started seeing each other.'

Taggie looks to me for confirmation, and I know she can tell just how hurt I am. She really is quite astoundingly beautiful, with her thick, black hair and her large, dark eyes. No wonder that Italian man is so infatuated.

'You're a liar,' Taggie snarls, and Pete winces.

'It's been five months,' I say, wanting her to know just as much as I want Pete to stop pretending that I'm nothing.

'Is that so?' she replies.

Pete has gone back to being mute, but this only seems to wind her up more. The Italian, meanwhile, looks unsure of what to do, and the two of us lock eyes for a second, both of us beseeching the other to help.

'What are you doing here, Pete?' Taggie says then, her voice sounding about ready to crack.

When he doesn't answer, I reply on his behalf. Apparently, I'm getting good at it.

'It was my idea. I booked it all. Pete had nothing to do with it.'

She looks so stricken and weary that I almost feel compelled to run across and hug her, but I can't do that now. She is the ex and I am the new girlfriend – the two of us may as well be oil and water.

Pete chooses that moment to lurch forwards towards Taggie, but before he can reach her, his path has been blocked by her tall Italian admirer.

'Marco,' Taggie says, her voice weak but stern. 'Don't bother. He's not worth it.'

Marco releases his grip on the front of Pete's coat and pushes him lightly away, only for Pete to take another step forwards. What the hell is he playing at?

This time, however, it isn't Marco who stops him in his tracks; it's Taggie. Before I, or Pete, or even Marco realise what's happening, she's up out of her chair and is pummelling her fists against his chest, screaming at him to leave her alone, to go away, to 'drown yourself in the fucking lake, for all I care'.

For a moment, he just stands there and takes it, and then, in one swift movement, he grasps Taggie by her wrists and pushes her firmly back down into her seat.

'It wasn't my fault,' he cries, the volume of his delivery stunning her into silence. And then he says it again, more quietly but with just as much emotion.

'It wasn't my fault.'

27

Taggie

When the sun rose this morning, slipping its determined fingers through the crack in my curtains to find me already awake, it felt like an imposter. What could possibly be so bright and so beautiful on a day like today? I used to take such comfort from the feel of it warming my bare toes, and such delight from the way it made the frost covering the hotel lawns sparkle like fairy dust, but now all I want to do is chase it back down behind the mountains, so that the landscape might be shrouded in the same darkness as my heart.

If it wasn't for the throbbing in my nose, I'd think that I was unable to feel anything. The shock of bumping into Pete yesterday, coupled with the knowledge that he must have found himself a brand-new girlfriend just weeks after the two of us split up, after *it* happened, has left me numb. Shelley knew something was up as soon as she saw me hurry off the boat with Marco, and her inquisitive eyes were as big as the moon in the sky above us when she realised how attentive he was being. I kept my head averted, not wanting her to see the full glory of my injured face. True to his word, Marco hadn't let me out of his sight until I was safely in the back seat of a taxi, but he needn't have worried in the end. After our altercation on the bottom deck of the boat, Pete had retreated up the stairs and was gone as soon as we docked in Como, his kindly blonde girlfriend presumably not far behind. I'm aware that I should feel sorry for her, but with everything that's going on, I don't think there's room in me for anyone else.

One thing is certain, though – Pete hasn't told her the whole truth. He hasn't even begun to.

I roll over on to my side, my hands wrapped around my middle in a feeble attempt at comfort, and wonder how the hell I'm going to get through the day. I'm supposed to be taking the group up to Cernobbio today, but I'm not sure if I can. I'm not even sure if I can face leaving this room, let alone the hotel. Not even my desire to be noticed by Sal is enough to chivvy me along – my fighting spirit has been entirely zapped.

My phone vibrates with a message. It's Shelley.

Are you awake? xx

I groan. Poor Shelley, she must be absolutely desperate to know what went on. I ditched dinner last night and came straight up here, and the group must have been in the bar all night, because she didn't come and knock, like I assumed she would.

Yes. I text back.

Can I come and see you? is her prompt reply.

Yes.

There's a tap on the door before I even have time to swing my feet out from under the covers, so I shimmy up the bed on my elbows instead and call out for her to come in.

'I was standing outside the door,' Shelley says, proud rather than contrite. 'I didn't want to just barge in.'

'It's OK,' I tell her, and my voice comes out all croaky.

'Bloody hell!' she exclaims, looking at me in horror as she nears the bed.

'What?'

'Your lip!'

I raise my hands to my face. My top lip *is* a little swollen, but from the expression on Shelley's face you'd think I'd grown an extra nose or something.

'It's nothing,' I mutter, shifting as she sits down on the edge of the duvet, trapping me in the bed.

'Did one of the group do this?' she demands. 'Was it that weird little man with the red face and fingers like pencils?'

'No.' I take a deep breath. She'll probably find out eventually, anyway.

'It was Marco.'

That stops her prattling in its tracks. For a moment she says nothing, just stares, then all her questions come out in a whoosh.

'Why did Marco hit you? Did he try it on and you rebuffed him? Did he go to punch a rival suitor and get you instead? Wow, I didn't think he was the violent type. And what was he doing in Bellagio anyway? Did he follow you? Oh my God – he's a stalker, isn't he?'

'Whoa, whoa, whoa!' I silence her with an upward palm. 'It was none of the above. I bent over at the wrong moment, that's all. He was standing next to me and reached for something. It was a total accident.'

Shelley sniggers. 'Sorry, it's not funny, but poor Marco.'

'Poor Marco?' I repeat.

'Yes!' She's still laughing. 'He's mad about you, and now he's gone and done this. You've cursed his lothario charms.'

There is only one man I would curse if I had the choice, but I don't say as much to Shelley. I'm very relieved that she's not asking more questions. The two of us have become close these past few months, but I haven't even mentioned Pete to her, let alone what sent me running out to Como. She seems to think all that happened to upset me yesterday was that I got hit in the face – and that is more than fine with me.

'Does it hurt?' she asks next.

'It's bearable,' I say. 'But I don't feel much like taking a tour out today. Do you think Sal will let me off this once?'

She frowns. 'Have you even *met* Sal?'

'Good point.'

I reach around her for my hairband, which I tossed on to the bedside table last night, and start pulling my unruly locks up into a large bun. Perhaps if I get up, have a shower, and force myself to do normal things and revert to the classic Torres way of bottling everything up, then I'll feel better. But I don't hold out much hope.

'I know!' announces Shelley, making me pause mid-bun wrap. 'I can take the group to Cernobbio for you today.'

'I don't know if—' I begin, but she cuts across me.

'I'd like to. I never get out in the daytime, and I know Cernobbio really well.'

'Do you?' I'm not entirely convinced.

'Yeah.' She waves a hand around. 'There's that hidden garden with the sculptures, the map house, Como Burger . . .'

209

'Como Burger isn't a famous landmark,' I remind her.

She widens her eyes in mock horror. 'Well, it should be. Have you even eaten there?'

'Not yet,' I admit.

'Well, there you go. Trust me – the group and I will have a whale of a time. There's just one catch.'

Dread bubbles in my belly. 'What's that?'

'You'll have to run the bar for the day.'

The pub I worked in at university was rather unimaginatively named the Red Lion. It had a sticky, threadbare carpet, an ancient dart board and a pool table in the back that wobbled whenever you leant over it to take a shot. Our wine list consisted of one red and two whites, and most of the punters I served were hardened ale drinkers.

The bar at the Casa Alta Hotel is a little different.

I waved Shelley and the group off an hour ago, and was touched by the fact that they all seemed sad to have lost me for the day. Gladys, especially, had plenty of questions as to why I was playing barmaid instead of going with them, but Shelley helpfully drew her away with the promise of lunch at Como Burger. I don't know how much they all saw yesterday, or if they heard Pete yell at me. I'm hoping the boat's engine was loud enough to drown him out, but Gladys's expression this morning seemed to hint otherwise. Still, there's nothing I can do about what happened. I'm just focusing on trying to get through this weird day in one piece.

I had planned to get more preparations underway for my New Year's Eve extravaganza, now that Sal has agreed to cough up the cash for my chosen DJ, but Shelley has also left me a to-do list, and I kicked off by restocking all the fridges and deep-cleaning the glass washer. There aren't many guests around, so I've pretty much been left to my own devices. Sal, to his credit, took one look at my injured face and agreed with Shelley that I should stay put. He's gone out for the day, too, so as well as manning the bar, I also need to listen out in case the phone rings in his office.

It doesn't seem to matter how many glasses I polish, all I can think about is the look on Pete's face yesterday as I launched myself at him. I'm still too shaken to know if what I'm feeling is regret or a low, trembling anger. Perhaps it's a bit of both. I'm embarrassed that Marco saw me in such a state, but I don't blame myself for that. I blame Pete. Not for the first time in my life, I wish that I wasn't an only child. I wish I had a sister I could call. Of course, I do have my parents, but telling them would only make them worry even more than I know they do already. My mum would probably get on the next plane over just to put Pete in his place, and I don't want that to happen.

The knowledge that he's here, in Como, walking the same streets as I am and breathing the same cold air, is making me feel nauseous. This is my place, my safe haven – how dare he come and pollute it with his new relationship?

As I work through Shelley's list, I find myself thinking about Lucy, my replacement. I can see why Pete likes her – she couldn't be more different to me. She's got the gorgeous womanly shape I've never had, the perfect English rose complexion and that long, blonde hair. And she's tall, too – she looks right next to him, whereas he and I were always stared at by passers-by. The hulking great rugby lad and his tiny girlfriend. Why did I ever think it would last?

Because you loved him, whispers a small voice in my head.

Yes, because I loved him.

I don't want to think about the day we broke up, but I can't help it. The memory of it is wrapped so tightly around my heart that it feels like barbed wire, and any attempt to dislodge it could be fatal. It still hurts all the time – especially today.

Pete waited until after we'd eaten dinner and were sitting side by side on the sofa. Our sofa. The one we'd picked out together when we first bought the flat. How excited we'd been then, how we'd laughed as we bounced on endless cushions to test their springiness.

'Tags,' he'd said. 'We need to talk.'

The four words that no human ever wants to hear from the person they love.

'What's up?'

I had remained upbeat at that stage, my voice high and uncharacteristically shrill.

He'd taken a deep breath, and that was when I noticed the tears in his eyes.

'Are you OK?' I asked. 'You're not ill, are you?'

He shook his head. 'No, nothing like that.'

'Well then, what?'

I hadn't meant to sound so impatient, but his odd manner was freaking me out.

'I'm scared,' he admitted then, refusing to meet my eyes.

I picked up the TV remote and muted *Come Dine with Me*.

'Scared?' I repeated. 'Scared of what?'

He sighed then, and I could tell how much he was struggling.

'Scared of what I'm about to say.'

For a brief, absurd moment, I thought that maybe he was about to propose. We'd joked about getting married before, but only when we were out drinking. I didn't think it was high up on our list of priorities.

'Pete,' I said, reaching for his hand. It felt limp and heavy. 'You're scaring *me*.'

And then it happened. He opened his mouth, the same mouth that I'd kissed so many times, that I'd seen spread into a happy grin as soon as he saw me, and told me that he didn't love me any more, that he didn't see a future for the two of us. That he thought we should break up.

I wanted to know why, of course. I ranted and shouted and yelled that what he was telling me wasn't fair. Had he even tried to fix things? Why didn't he talk to me before it got to this point? Why couldn't we work on it? How could he just throw away five years? How could he throw me away? Us away?

He had listened to all of it, but his mind was made up. He didn't love me, and that was the bottom line. No amount of raging or begging would change that, and once I'd run out of words I simply curled up into a ball and sobbed. He hadn't even attempted to comfort me.

I'm startled out of my miserable trance by the sound of the phone ringing in the office, and in my hurry to reach it, I accidentally drop the champagne flute I was polishing on to the wooden floor, where it smashes into pieces.

'Shit!' I mutter, stuffing the cloth inside the front pocket of my apron and walking quickly across the hallway.

'*Pronto, l'hotel Casa Alta.*'

'*Buongiorno, posso parlare con Taggie?*'

My stomach plummets to the floor.

'Hello. Who is it?'

'It is me,' comes the reply, and I swear I can hear his smile.

'It is Marco.'

28

Lucy

I feel as if I'm living in the middle of a nightmare.

Everything that I thought was true is now false; nothing is making any sense. It's as if someone burrowed their way deep into my mind until they discovered my absolute worst-case scenario, and then spun it into reality. I could have chosen anywhere in the world for Pete and me to spend our first holiday together, but I chose here – the exact same place that his ex-girlfriend did.

Taggie might be the one who was punched, but I feel as if I've been gored by a charging bull.

Pete was silent during the walk from the boat back to the apartment last night, and shut himself in the bathroom as soon as we got there. Moments later, I heard the shower begin to run and, unsure of what to do next, I simply sat on the edge of the bed and waited for him to re-emerge. When he did, his eyes looked red.

'Are you OK?' I asked. He had yet to extend the same courtesy to me.

'Not really.'

He looked so forlorn standing there, the water from the shower dripping off his chest, his wet hair plastered across his forehead.

'About Taggie—' I began, but he silenced me with a look.

'I can't, Lulu. Not now. Please understand.'

He crossed the room and rifled through his case, extracting clean underwear and a T-shirt, then headed back into the bathroom and shut the door.

I wanted to run after him and bang on the wood with both fists, but of course I didn't. Lucy Dunmore isn't *that* girl. She's the meek one in the corner not making a fuss. The supportive one, the kind one, the one getting walked all over as readily as if she was the living room rug. In that moment, I envied Taggie and her fiery temper. The way she had hit Pete on the boat may have looked crazy, but at least she had done something. I hadn't done a thing save for stand there and stare.

'You hungry?'

Pete had come out of the bathroom fully dressed and was doing a very good impression of a man who hasn't just run into his ex-girlfriend in the middle of Italy and had a horrible confrontation with her on a boat.

I gawped at him, aghast.

'No, not really. Are you?'

'I could eat,' he said, looking apologetic. His enormous appetite is something I have always found lovable about him, but not now. Not after everything that has gone on.

'We should talk about what happened,' I said in reply, but he shook his head.

'Tomorrow. I promise tomorrow.'

My deep sigh told him all he needed to know, but instead of elaborating on why he required an entire twelve hours to get his thoughts in order, he merely reached for his coat and started pulling it on.

'Pete—'

'Just leave it alone, Lulu, I'm begging you.'

I couldn't believe he was being like this, so cold and so stubborn. It was only a few hours ago that he'd been telling me how much I meant to him, and now he had completely shut me out. It wasn't fair, and the injustice I was feeling made me cross my arms and glare at him as he sat down to tie his laces.

'Are you coming with me or not?' he asked, so briskly that tears welled up in my eyes. I wished I had the strength to tell him where to go, but silly little Lucy has never been strong. It's why things like this always happen to me.

'Tomorrow morning then,' I told him, standing up. 'That's when we'll talk about it.'

Dinner was awful. I pushed a salad around my plate in a circle, while Pete steadily drank his way through five bottles of Peroni and several straight whiskies, sticking strictly to the subject of work, and refusing to meet my eyes as he explained at great length how a radio broadcast mixer works. He was drunk enough to be wobbly on his trainers as we stumbled back through the streets, and passed out on the bed fully clothed shortly afterwards, so that's exactly where I've left him this morning.

It takes Julia a while to answer, which isn't surprising really, given that we're an hour ahead here, and the sun has only just come up.

'Hello.' Her voice is suffocated by sleep.

'Ju, it's me.'

That's all it takes to start the tears – hearing my sister's voice and knowing that I can talk to her.

I hear her cough, then the sound of what I assume is the duvet being lifted out of the way.

'Hang on a sec,' she whispers.

I've wandered down to the shore and turned left, following the pathway as it leaves the roadside and cuts through a small park. There's a deserted play area for kids and the kiosk where you buy boat tickets has its shutters down. Save for a few locals walking their dogs and some young men heaving nets into a fishing boat, there isn't a soul around. It's going to be another beautiful day, with a proud sun and a solid blue sky, but the colours may as well be shades of grey as far as I am concerned. This place is sullied now.

'Sorry,' Julia says, her voice now at its usual volume. 'I didn't want to wake Abby.'

'It's OK,' I sniff, coming to a stop by a wooden bench and sitting down. I wish I'd thought to pick up a hot drink on my way through the town. It's not going to take long for the late December chill to work its way right into my bones.

'What's happened?' she asks. 'Why are you crying?'

Two ducks are waddling over from the edge of the lake, their beady eyes shining in the pale morning light and their feathers slick with moisture. I try to focus on them, but everything is sliding into a blur as the tears continue to fall. Julia is doing her best to soothe me, but I can't seem to get my sobbing under control. It all feels as if it's slipping away from me – Pete, our relationship, the future I had let myself daydream about.

'Lucy, listen to me,' Julia instructs. 'Take a deep breath.'

I do as she says.

'Right. Now take another. Right down into the bottom of your lungs.'

I continue breathing deeply until I've stopped crying, and wipe my face angrily with the sleeve of my coat. Julia lets me recover before asking any more questions, instead filling the silence by telling me about her and Abby's plans for New Year. I envy the two of them and their uncomplicated relationship. Does their both being women make it easier? Or is it simply because they are both so honest with each other? Whatever it is, it works. They trust one another and confide in one another, and the result is a loving and stable union – the like of which I have never managed to find.

'So,' she says at last, and I swallow another lump. 'What has that idiot Pete done now?'

And so, I tell her. Julia says nothing at first, save for a few intakes of breath, but when I get to the part where Pete tried to lie about how long we'd been together, she splutters indignantly.

'The bastard!'

I love my big sister.

'What was his excuse for lying?' she demands.

'Well, that's just it – he won't talk about it.'

'What do you mean?'

'I mean, he's so far refused to answer any of my questions. He's promised me that we'll talk this morning, but I don't even know where to start, Ju.'

'You can start by telling him he's a stupid prick,' she rages.

I grimace into the phone.

'Don't pull that face,' Julia says, spookily accurate with her knowledge of my reactions as usual. My poor sister – this isn't the first time she's had to help me pick up the pieces because of a man.

'You should have seen her, Ju – his ex. She was so angry with him.'

'She's not the only one.'

'No, but I mean *really* angry. She looked as if she wanted to kill him.'

Julia pauses as she mulls this over.

'Do you know why they broke up?'

I think back to the conversation Pete and I had at Bellagio yesterday, when he confessed that he was the one to call time on his last relationship.

'No . . . But he told me it was him who ended it.'

'That would explain why she was angry,' Julia surmises, but she didn't see what I saw. The look on Taggie's face as she laid into Pete. It wasn't just anger, it was pain. And something else, too, something that's been haunting me ever since: fear. What could Pete have done to make his ex-girlfriend fearful of him?

'I knew he was a cagey bastard,' Julia is chuntering now. 'There's always been something not quite right about him.'

'You've met him twice,' I point out gently, but once my sister is on the warpath, she's not one to be easily deterred.

'Twice is more than enough,' she argues. 'And just you wait till the third time, if there is one – I'll be giving him a piece of my mind, that's for sure.'

Sometimes my sister can take her loyalty a step too far.

'I don't think that would help,' I groan. 'I just need to know how to handle him today. What shall I say?'

I can hear a kettle boiling now, and the clatter of a spoon against the side of a mug. Julia must be making her morning coffee. She has it black with three sugars. Three!

'There isn't much you can say,' she advises, her tone now more conciliatory. 'He's the one who needs to start talking.'

She's right, I know she's right.

'I'm scared this is it, Ju,' I say then, and immediately start crying again. 'I'm scared he'll finish with me.'

'Oh, Lucy.' Julia sighs with dismay. 'Don't you see? It's not you who should be scared, it's him. You shouldn't be worrying about him dumping you. What you should be doing is thinking about whether you still want to be with him.'

Another long intake of breath follows.

'Promise me you will think about it. I don't like that he's made you this upset. And it's only been a few months, for heaven's sake. What other secrets is he hiding?'

'I promise I will,' I assure her, but I know breaking up with Pete is not an option. Despite everything that happened, I still care about him. Yesterday I was getting ready to tell him I was in love with him. What kind of person would I be if I just turned my back on him as soon as something like this happened? Doesn't he deserve the chance to explain? If it was the other way around, I would want him to listen to me.

'I should go,' I tell Julia. 'I don't want him to wake up and find me gone.'

I stand up from the bench and begin walking back the way I came, scattering a flock of hopeful seagulls as I go. Julia only hangs up when she's reiterated her point about being careful and thinking about what I want, and finishes by telling me to call her later with an update.

'And if you want me to fly over there and break his bloody nose for him, I will.'

I don't doubt her for a second.

29

Taggie

'Hi . . .'

I stop, unsure of what to say next. Marco is silent on the other end of the line, no doubt picturing the shaking, emotional mess that he helped into a taxi the previous evening.

'Are you OK?' he says at last.

'Yes. Well, no. My face is OK, if that's what you mean.'

He sniffs. 'I meant that, and . . .'

He pauses. Perhaps there isn't an Italian word for 'crazy mental breakdown', or maybe he's just avoiding using it.

'Thank you for helping me,' I say quietly, pushing aside a stapler and sitting down on the edge of Sal's desk. 'I'm sorry you had to see that – see me like that.'

'There is nothing to say sorry for,' he replies, and I make a small muttering sound.

'What are you doing tonight?' he asks then, and I frown in confusion at the abrupt change of subject.

'Um, nothing,' I admit, immediately cursing myself. This is what happens when people catch you unawares – you can't help but land yourself in it by being honest.

'Will you come to meet me?'

Can he seriously be talking about a date? Today? After what he witnessed on the boat?

'Where?' I ask warily. There is no way I'm venturing into town, not now I know that Pete and Lucy are *in situ*.

'The lake,' he replies. 'The west shore, by the big wheel.'

I know where he means – it's not quite in the town, but about halfway between there and here. The Ferris wheel has been erected as part of the area's festive celebrations, and I can see its multi-coloured lights from my bedroom window at night.

What I really want to do this evening is climb under my duvet in my big bed upstairs and hide, but I owe Marco this much. He may have done his best to break my nose, but he also defended me and had my back against Pete with no questions asked.

'OK,' I say. 'But it's not a date.'

He laughs at that, and I find myself smiling despite my sour mood.

'Not a date,' he agrees, before adding, 'I will be there at eight o'clock.'

'Eight-thirty,' I reply, for no other reason than because I don't like being told what to do.

'Okay,' he says. '*Ciao*, Taggie.' And then he's gone.

The rest of the day passes without incident, with both the bar and the hotel phone remaining blissfully quiet, and I take advantage of the time to try and get ahead with my party plans. I order in enough fairy lights to put even the snazziest Santa grotto to shame, triple the standard Prosecco haul and sweet-talk one of the sous chefs into making a batch of canapés so I can test them in advance. Unfortunately, despite all the distractions, being alone most of the day does mean that I have far too much time to think — and there's only one subject on my mind.

The more I try to make sense of the way I reacted yesterday, the worse I feel. I've never been demonstrably emotional, and I've always managed to maintain self-control, but when I saw Pete standing there in front of me, I lost it. I know I did, and the ferocity of that rage scared me. What does it mean when you can't even trust yourself? In those few moments on the boat, where I hurled myself at Pete and screamed at him to leave me alone, I genuinely lost myself. That screeching, flailing girl was not me; she was a banshee.

In the days after Pete dumped me, I was muted with shock and resentment. We lived together, so we still had to come home from work every evening and face one another. He kept trying to begin a conversation about when he should move out, but I shut him down every time. I wasn't ready to accept what was happening, and I didn't know what to do. That was how we were for two whole weeks, and then everything changed.

I think I could have forgiven Pete for falling out of love with me, but I can't forgive what he did next.

'It wasn't my fault,' he'd shouted at me on that boat. But it was. It was his fault.

I pass the hours cleaning everything I can lay my hands on in the bar, starting with the glasses, then all the bottles. By the time Shelley and the group arrive back, not long after six, I'm halfway through polishing all the small round tables.

'You know we have a cleaner for that?' is her first comment, as she dumps her bag on the bar top with an exclamation of relief.

I pause mid-scrub.

'I like doing it.'

'If you say so. How's the lip?'

'It's fine, thanks. How was your day?'

Shelley glances over her shoulder to make sure there's nobody else within earshot, then she stage-whispers, 'Gladys and Bill.'

I pull a face and stage-whisper back, 'I know!'

Shelley laughs and makes her way behind the bar, reaching for a glass and filling it with water from the tap. I still can't drink the non-bottled stuff without getting stomach ache, but she's got used to it.

'Honestly, I've never met anyone so blunt in my life,' she continues between gulps. 'And she wouldn't stop going on about some bloke who had a row with his girlfriend on the boat yesterday.'

'Oh?' I enquire, my body tensing up.

'Yeah, according to Gladys, this random guy apparently stormed off and his other half went after him, and then the whole group heard her yelling at him, and then him shouting right back.'

'I see.'

'Did you hear anything?' she asks, mistaking my mortified silence for mere distraction. I've moved over to the window now, my eyes searching out the ripples on the dark surface of the lake. Of course they all heard me, but they wouldn't have been able to see who it was.

'No,' I say, my voice tight. 'I was sitting at the front with Marco, trying to stop my nose bleeding, and you know how loud the engine noise is on that boat.'

'Marco is a very good distraction,' she says then, sounding deliberately dreamy.

I cough.

'I know, I know – you don't fancy him,' Shelley says, and I turn from the window in time to see her rolling her eyes. 'But even you can't deny the fact he's fit.'

'How many tickets have we sold for the New Year's Eve party again?' I ask, firmly changing the subject even though I know more about the sales figures than anyone else does. Luckily, after the subject of Marco, the sacred guest list is Shelley's favourite topic of conversation, and she's soon telling me all about the hordes of people she accosted up in Cernobbio today, and how many of them seemed keen to book.

'I think it's going to be a brilliant night,' she enthuses. 'Even if we do have to put up with Gladys and Bill.'

'Yeah,' I agree, but my delivery is half-hearted at best.

'Cheer up,' Shelley jokes. 'This is your party, remember! Your big chance to prove to Sal just how amazing you are, so that he falls over himself to promote you.'

I imagine Sal's impressed face when he sees all the decorations I've ordered, the murmurs of delight when the carefully selected food appears on tables, and the expressions on the faces of the guests when the fireworks light up the dark sky, and I find my smile again.

'You're right,' I tell her. 'It's going to be the best New Year that Lake Como has ever bloody seen – and the first of many parties that I'm trusted to throw in this hotel!'

'That's more like it!' she declares, holding her hand out for the apron I've just taken off. 'I would never have forgiven you if you'd bailed and left me to get pissed all by myself.'

'Would I do such a thing?' I tease. The truth is, what

I'm feeling most is relieved that I had the idea for this party in the first place. Now I know for certain that Pete is here in the vicinity – and he's bound to still be here for the New Year; it would be odd if the two of them left before – I'm keen to stay well away from the bars in town. The chances of their turning up here at the Casa Alta are minuscule, and that is a huge comfort.

'You not staying for a drink?' Shelley says, pouting at me as I reach the doorway.

I need to wash off the smell of furniture polish and stale wine before I go down to the lake to meet Marco, but I'll never hear the end of it if I confess as much to Shelley.

'My face is really hurting again,' I fib. 'I might go and lie down for a bit.'

She waves me off, telling me that she'll see me after dinner, and I know I should put her straight. By the time she realises I'm not in the hotel, however, I will be long gone. As I take the stairs back up to my room, I'm aware of a feeling in the very depths of my belly. Is it nerves at the prospect of seeing Marco again, or excitement? Either way, it makes a pleasant change from the rumbling rage and fear I've had to endure all day. Perhaps it will do me good not to think about Pete for a few hours. I'm going to do my very best to try.

30

Lucy

Pete is sitting waiting for me when I get back to the apartment, a cup of coffee sitting untouched on the table in front of him and a sheepish expression on his face.

'Hi,' I mumble.

'Hi,' he replies.

I go to unwind my scarf, but Pete stands up.

'Don't. I've booked us a surprise.'

I sigh. 'Pete, we really need to—'

'Talk. I know – and we will. But we need to go right now, or we'll be late.'

My resolve to be tough on him splinters like old driftwood.

'Fine then, whatever you say.'

We're back outside on the street less than a few minutes later, and Pete reaches for my hand. He's acting as if nothing has changed between us, as if I wasn't there to witness his ex-girlfriend lay into him with her fists as she wept. This whole surprise thing has thrown me, but I suspect that's Pete's reason for arranging it.

'Come on,' he says. 'We'll get a taxi.'

'Where are we going?' I ask, utterly mystified as he hurries me through the Piazza del Duomo and past the impressive façade of Como's cathedral.

'If I tell you, it will ruin the surprise,' he replies.

We pass a Christmas tree almost as tall as a house, its blue lights dim in the daylight. Small groups of people are starting to settle in for breakfast at the nearby cafés, and my stomach rumbles in envy as a waiter flounces out with a plate of scrambled eggs and smoked salmon. It's not like Pete to skip a meal, so I can only assume that whatever he has planned will include food. It occurs to me then that a lot of what we do as a couple revolves around food. Most of our dates are either meals out in restaurants or dinner cooked by me, and in the five months we've been together, we've only been to the cinema twice and a museum once. It makes more sense to me now, though. Now that I know he's been keeping me a secret.

It takes only a few more minutes to reach the taxi rank by the edge of the lake, and Pete is careful to whisper our destination into the ear of our driver, so as not to give it away. He seems excited by all this – buoyant, even, although he's doing his best to disguise it – and I'm finding it hard to remain stoic. I don't want him to think that he can sweep all this Taggie business under the carpet – I'm not going to let him off the hook that easily, even if the idea of arguing does make me want to weep. Feeling like the world's most needy girlfriend, I sneak my hand across the back seat of the car and wrap my fingers around Pete's, only for him to immediately return the pressure.

'Here we are,' he announces less than ten minutes later, and I look through the window and gasp. Looming above us, its huge blue-and-white corrugated front blocking out the sun, is the vast steel hangar comprising the Como Aero Club.

I turn to Pete.

'You didn't?'

He smiles sheepishly, and I can't help but think how absurdly handsome he looks.

'I did!'

I looked into how much it would cost to go up in a seaplane when I first booked the trip over here, and decided that it was probably more important that Julia and my dad get a Christmas present.

'Pete, this is too much,' I protest, my resentment evaporating at speed as we clamber out on to the tarmac.

'Please say you've never done it before,' he says, re-arranging his blue woolly hat.

'I haven't,' I confirm. 'But it's so expensive – I can't let you pay for this.'

'Too late,' he replies happily, and leads me over towards the glass reception booth. It soon transpires that Pete booked this treat weeks ago, not this morning as I perhaps rather unfairly suspected, and after a brief safety talk, we're climbing into a seaplane after our grey-haired pilot. It's snug inside, with room for two up front and two behind, and Pete and I buckle in as the propellers splutter into life.

'I used to watch these planes as a child,' I tell him, excitement making me giddy. 'I never dreamed that I'd ever go up in one.'

'Well, then,' Pete says, his hand firmly clasping mine, 'I'm very happy to be the one making your dreams come true.'

He says it without a trace of irony, but I can't quite find it in myself to be angry with him. Not here, not during such a special moment – I don't want any more memories tarnished before they've even begun. And so I say nothing, instead fishing my phone out of my bag and getting the video function ready so I can record the take-off.

Even if I wanted to talk to Pete about Taggie now, he wouldn't be able to hear me over the sound of the sea-plane's engine, which is even louder than the one on the boat. I look down at the water as we begin to move, and my mouth opens with delight as the churning surface swells white and splashes up against the windows. Pete is doing the same, but on the opposite side of the plane, and I feel his fingers tighten their grip on my own.

'Ready?' the pilot asks, turning in his seat. He's so tanned, he looks like he's been painted with wood stain. Perks of being up above the clouds so often.

'Ready!' we chorus.

I experience a thrill as the small aircraft throbs and lifts, its nose propeller a blur as we leave the lake behind and soar upwards into the clean, blue air. It takes us just minutes to reach our cruising altitude, and all the while the surrounding landscape is unfolding around us. From up here, the lake is a pale cashmere blue, and the mountain-sides a rich basil green. The private villas that remain hidden behind high walls at ground level are laid out below for all to see, and my eyes widen as I take in the manicured gardens and covered swimming pools. There is so much colour to behold, and so much light – it's simply impossible to feel anything but alive and enthralled by it all.

Pete seems to be just as enamoured as I am, and each time we turn to one another and our eyes meet, he beams at me. *He did this all for me*, a small voice whispers. Before I even knew that Taggie existed, he had booked and paid for this surprise, and pictured how happy I would be when I found out about it. I can't take away this fact, and I'm glad. I don't want Pete to be that person I saw on the boat last night, the man I couldn't help but see through Taggie's eyes – I want him to be my Pete, the man I'm in love with.

We're further along the lake now, not far from Varenna, and I gaze down at the papaya-coloured buildings hugging the length of the shore. The sheer scale of the mountains is enough to hush me, the purr of the engine a steady vibration in my limbs, and as we round a corner and see a tiny white church come into view, I find myself swallowing down a gulp of emotion. How could I have thought that Lake Como was sullied by my parents and their silly disagreements? I'm ashamed that I ever questioned the power of its beauty, now that I can see it all so clearly. This was what I needed to remind myself of just how extraordinary this place is, and why I will always love it, no matter what happens to my heart while I'm here.

It's only when we're coming back in to land, twenty minutes later, that the morning's trepidation begins to resurface inside me.

As surprises go, I don't think I've ever had a better one, but while this flight was fun, romantic and unforgettable, it can't make up for what's happened, for the dishonesty and Pete's reluctance to talk about things. When he was sitting across from me at dinner last night, barely speaking and hardly able to look me in the eye, it was as if the past few months had never happened – I had felt like I didn't know him at all, and it scared me. No, this little adventure has been a good distraction, but it hasn't fixed what was broken yesterday, and when I look at Pete, I see that he feels it, too.

All I can do now is hope that he's able to be honest with me. Anything less than that, and I don't know what I will do.

31

Taggie

Marco is easy to spot from a distance. I can tell just from the casual way he's lounging against the railings that it's him. There's a sharp wind tonight, and he's pulled a red hat over his black hair and tucked the ends of a matching scarf into the front of his battered leather jacket. He sees me coming and stands up properly, an easy grin on his face and an arm stretched out ready to greet me.

We exchange a *'ciao'*, his far less timid than mine, and then he bends down to kiss my cheeks. I'm not quite as short as normal this evening, because I've opted for my favourite pair of black heels, and when he's done kissing me hello, Marco leans round to inspect them.

'Nice shoes.'

'Thanks,' I reply. 'I thought they might help distract people from my swollen lips.'

I wait for him to laugh, but instead he bends over again until his mouth is almost level with mine.

'They look perfect to me.'

I roll my eyes.

'Listen, about the boat . . .' I begin, but he shakes his head.

'Do you want to talk about it?'

Taken aback by his directness, I stutter out my reply. 'I, er, no. I suppose I don't.'

'Well, then.' He shrugs expansively. 'It is forgotten.'

'OKaaay,' I agree, waiting for the catch. Marco doesn't seem remotely fussed. If anything, he looks bored by the whole subject, which is great, of course, but also puzzling. I don't think I'd be so calm if I'd witnessed him behaving the way I had.

'Shall we walk?' he prompts. 'Unless you want to ride on the wheel?'

We both look up at the flashing lights and the wobbly carriages.

'No, thanks,' I tell him, and I'm sure I detect a flash of something close to amusement in his eyes.

I thought I would feel uncomfortable, being down here by the lake with Marco, but in truth it's fine. He's very easy company, and I like the way he doesn't feel the need to fill every silence with nonsensical babble. I grew up in a quiet house – my dad worked from home quite often and spent a lot of time in his study, and my mum has never been the type to sit in front of daytime TV, or even have the radio on when she's pottering around the house. When I was still living there, we'd all come together in the evenings to eat dinner and perhaps watch a film, but the three of us are all very independent souls, so I'm quite content to pass hours at a time without making a peep. Maybe it was the same for Marco, although it's hard to imagine any traditional Italian family home being anything other than deliriously chaotic and filled with people.

Pete used to say that he felt on edge whenever we went

to stay with my parents. The silence there made him nervous, rather than relaxed. Pete is a big, noisy man. He crashes pans in the kitchen, sings in the shower, turns the TV on in the front room and the radio on in the bedroom. It used to drive me mad when I was trying to read, or work, or even just have what I called 'quiet time'. I used to chase him out of the flat and tell him to go and be loud down the pub instead.

Perhaps that's why he stopped loving me.

I can feel cobbles through the soles of my shoes and look down to see that we've reached the large, stone-laid compass, which sits right next to the gate leading out to the pier. Stretching out into the middle of the lake with a large, mirrored sculpture at its end, this wooden walkway is supposed to be the best vantage point from which to watch the famous New Year's Eve firework display. Bobbing in the water beside this end of the pier and for a good thirty feet in each direction on either side of it are hundreds of boats. They range in size from two-man fishing vessels to swanky super-yachts, and each one has a name proudly emblazoned along the bow. It's hard to see all of them under the orange glow of the park's lampposts, but I do spot several *Maria*s, a *Moon River*, and a scruffy-looking dinghy, humorously called *The Don*.

'You remember what I told you?' Marco prompts. 'About my dream?'

I nod slowly. 'Yes.'

'Here she is.'

I peer through the gloom to where a battered, cracked and rust-covered boat is moored not far from the shore. It looks like it was once used for fishing, because a tangle of nets is covering the rotting boards of the deck, but I doubt it ever goes far these days. I can see that it's predominantly painted blue and white, but most of the paint has flaked off, and there's no sign of a name, either.

'Isn't she beautiful?' Marco murmurs, his voice full of admiration and awe.

I frown, confused yet reluctant to say anything that might spoil his moment.

'I guess so,' I say finally, squinting at the boat. There are two porthole windows on either side of what would have been the captain's cabin, and these, coupled with the smooth, rounded curve of the bow, make the weary vessel look as if she's smiling.

'I have always loved her,' Marco continues. 'Ever since I was a boy, and I first saw her out on the water.'

So this is why he can't commit to going out with any of the local girls around here – he's too in love with this old boat.

'What's her name?' I ask politely, but Marco shakes his head.

'Once upon a time she was *Lario*, but now she has no name.'

'That's sad,' I say, hoping it's the right reaction.

'Yes,' he agrees. 'Very sad.'

'She's the reason you need money!' I exclaim. Wow, that penny took a long time to drop; it must have been tossed off the surface of the moon.

He nods, turning his attention from his floating beloved to me. 'I want to restore her to glory,' he explains. 'But more than that, I want to turn her into a restaurant.'

'That's your dream?' I guess, and he smiles.

'That is my dream.'

'Then you must!' I tell him, feeling enthused. 'She deserves to be great again.'

And it's true, she does. It's tragic that she's been left here to rot and be forgotten, especially when there's a whole lake right here, just waiting to be explored. And what a fabulous idea of his, to have a restaurant that is also a vessel – I can picture the events he could host on her already, and goosebumps rear up on my arms.

Marco is beaming at my obvious enthusiasm, showing off his very white teeth.

'I knew you would love her,' he says. 'I thought it might cheer you up to see her.'

Why he thought that, I have no idea, given the fact that she is, essentially, a floating rust bucket – but he was right. I do feel cheered by her, and even more so by Marco's grand plan to resurrect her.

'You could hire her out for parties once she was done up,' I tell him. 'Or romantic cruises around the lake – or even wedding dinners. Anything, really – there's so much scope for her to make you money. It could be amazing!'

He's clapping his hands as I reel off my list of suggestions, and seeing him so proud and happy makes me feel great. I really shouldn't have condemned him as just another man-whore, because he's clearly much more than that. He gave me the benefit of the doubt after he'd been forced to haul me out of the lake, and I should have extended the same courtesy to him. Marco is focused and driven and passionate – all the things I try to be and hold in such high regard, and tonight, for the first time in a very long while, I feel comfortable alone in a man's company. I had hoped I would manage it again one day, but I never would have guessed that Marco, of all people, would be the one to get me there.

'So, what's the plan of action?' I ask him, leaning over the railings so I can get a better look at the boat. In the past three or so minutes, I have decided that Marco's dream is one that I'm prepared to help him realise. I want to see him succeed, and I'm genuinely fired up.

Marco, however, has gone back to being too cool for school, and kicks at a stone.

'I don't know yet.'

'The meeting you had in Bellagio . . .?' I query, but he shakes his head.

'I offered the man who owns her everything I have, all my savings, but he said it is not enough. He would rather see her sink to the bottom of the lake than sell her to me.'

'That's stupid,' I say needlessly. 'Won't he even consider it?'

Marco grumbles out a no.

'What about a loan?'

He shakes his head. 'The bank does not think it is a worthwhile investment. They say I do not know how to turn a boat into a restaurant.'

'Pah!' I declare, making him jump. 'What the hell do they know?'

Marco laughs through his nose.

'Exactly. That is what I told them.'

The fact that the bank probably has a perfectly valid argument is beside the point. Marco had my back, and now I have his.

'Well, we need to make a new plan,' I say, with far more confidence than I feel. I know even less about turning a boat into a restaurant than I do about the offside rule, but where there is a Taggie Torres will, there is always a way.

'You will help me, then?' he asks. 'With a plan?'

I look up at him, at his silly red hat and those strangely beautiful eyes, which are still so mesmerising even when they've been turned inky black by the night.

'I'll do everything that I can,' I promise him.

We stay for a time by the water's edge, talking and plotting and laughing together as the stars emerge, one by one, high above our heads. When Marco buys a hot dog from a cart in the park and breaks a piece off for me, I don't even mind that the tips of his fingers brush against my lips, and when a splodge of mustard dribbles down his chin, I have no qualms about wiping it away and licking the sauce off my hand. The New Year's Eve party might be a good distraction and the means of showing off my organisational skills to Sal, but the thought of turning something as barren as Marco's boat into a fully functioning business has woken me up more than anything has in years, and I imagine that I can hear the cogs of my brain screeching into motion.

When I let myself into the hotel later, taking extra care to tiptoe past Shelley's bedroom door, it dawns on me that I haven't thought about Pete or what happened for more than a handful of minutes all night. If a broken and neglected old boat can be brought back to life by finding someone to love her again, then maybe, just maybe, I can too.

32

Lucy

'I don't know where to begin,' Pete mutters.

I take a breath, my voice hushed. 'Why don't we start with what happened yesterday?'

The two of us have wandered through the doors of the cathedral that we sped past earlier on our way to the Aero Club. I can remember being bored by the grand Gothic place of worship as a child, but today I'm fascinated. When Pete initially wandered off to take covert photos of the two stone lions supporting the fonts, I found that I was content to simply stand at the midpoint of the altar, gazing up at the intricate stonework above and admiring the vast tapestries hanging down at various points along the wall and from the ceiling. Their musty scent adds an extra layer of antiquity to the setting, and for some reason I find it soothing.

Pete turns to face me.

'I'm so sorry, Lulu. I had no idea Taggie was here.'

'I know you didn't,' I allow, the image of his stunned expression coming back to my mind. 'It must have been a shock.'

'Just a bit,' he agrees, his face grim.

'Why did you lie to her, though?' I whisper, staring at the Nativity scene in front of us and drawing strength from the serene-looking shepherds.

'When did I lie?' he exclaims, loud enough to get the attention of a passing family.

'Shhh,' I say, attempting to calm him with my tone. 'I mean when you told Taggie that we'd only just got together.'

'Oh,' he says, shamefaced. 'That.'

'It was pretty bloody awful,' I point out, my eyes slipping down to the baby Jesus in his straw-lined manger. The doll's eyes are painted the same bright blue as Pete's.

'I'm sorry about that,' he mutters. 'I just panicked in the moment – I didn't want to hurt Taggie any more than I already have. She took the break-up really badly, so I knew she wouldn't appreciate the fact that I'd met you so soon.'

'How soon was it?' I ask, and he sniffs. 'Was it too soon?'

'No, it wasn't too soon, it was more than a month. Me and Taggie, we had been over for a long time, at least in my head.'

'In your *head*?' I repeat, immediately suspicious.

'I knew I didn't love her any more months before I even met you,' he says, his expression one of dismay. The dim lighting in the church is making his face look tired and lined, and it takes all my strength not to reach up and stroke the coarse stubble on his cheeks.

'I tried to ignore it, but it ate away at me. In the end, I didn't feel like I had a choice, so I told her I didn't feel the same and that we should break up.'

'When was this?' I ask him.

'Back in May,' he replies. 'I don't remember the exact date.'

I bet Taggie does.

'And that's really why she hates you so much?' I continue. 'All that drama on the boat was just because you told her you didn't love her any more?'

Frustratingly, he shrugs.

'It must be.'

'What did you mean when you told her it wasn't your fault?' I add, changing tack.

Pete's eyes narrow, and I can tell even in this poor light that he's gone red.

'Just that it wasn't my fault things fell apart. I know I was the one who ended things, but our relationship was rotten to the core – it had been for ages.'

'Did you ever cheat on her?' I say evenly.

'No!' He looks wounded by the mere suggestion.

'Do you know what she's doing here?' I add. 'In Como?'

Pete pulls off his hat and tucks one of his ginger curls behind an ear. Buying himself some time, I think disloyally.

'I honestly don't know,' he says finally, and so adamantly that I believe him. 'I know she used to holiday here when she was a kid, but I had no idea she'd come back. If I did, I would have suggested we went somewhere else, trust me.'

'Perhaps that's why she's so familiar,' I blurt unthinkingly, remembering a second too late about the photo I'd found while snooping through Pete's stuff.

'Is she?' Pete is surprised.

'Maybe I saw her here when we were both little kids.'

'Perhaps,' Pete rubs a hand through his hair.

'Who is Manny?' I enquire, taking off my own woolly hat and rolling it into a sausage shape with my hands.

'Eh?'

'The person who called and you ignored them, said it was nothing.'

He grunts with hard, unamused laughter.

'Manny is Taggie's dad. He's acting on her behalf because she refuses to speak to me. We're selling our flat,' he adds, and it all becomes swiftly and horribly clear. That's why he's been doing the place up, and that must be why the flat has no real charm or character – Taggie must have taken it all with her when she left. There isn't really anything I can say in reply to this piece of the puzzle, so I chew my lip thoughtfully instead.

'Listen,' Pete says, drawing my attention away from the figures of the Nativity and turning me round gently to face him. 'I'm sorry you had to find out about Taggie like this, and I'm sorry I lied to her and shouted the way I did. What you need to understand is that the break-up was traumatic – not just for her, but for both of us. Have you ever had to tell a person that you don't love them any more?'

I think about my mum leaving my dad.

'No,' I admit.

'It's not very nice,' he goes on. 'I didn't want to hurt Taggie, and I still care about her, of course I do, but not in the way that I care about you.'

'Which way is that?' It's barely more than a murmur, but Pete is close enough to have heard.

'You know how much you mean to me,' he says. 'I know it's weird that you haven't met my mates yet, and I hate that I couldn't take you to my cousin's wedding, but it's only because my family need a bit of time to readjust. It doesn't mean that I don't love you.'

Did he just say love?

'Did you just say love?'

He takes my hand, and this time I let him.

'Yes, I did – and I do.'

'Do you mean that?' I ask, forcing my eyes up to meet his. 'I mean, really mean it?'

He kisses the tip of my nose.

'Yes, I really mean it. I don't want to lose you, Lucy Dunmore, not now. Not because of something that was over a long time ago.'

'And you've told me everything?' I half-plead. 'There aren't any more secrets?'

He blinks, his blue eyes earnest.

'No more secrets.'

33

Taggie

After getting up even earlier than the birds this morning to give myself time to put all the finishing touches to my Casa Alta New Year extravaganza, the group went and announced at breakfast that they'd all decided to wander around Como for the day by themselves. I had been planning to take them on a sightseeing tour of nearby Varenna, but a very late night in the bar the previous evening had left even Gladys's energy levels depleted. Better that they have a restful day, she assured me, so they would all be full of beans for the party.

Unable to find much else for me to do at such short notice, and with my event to-do list fully ticked off, Sal graciously agreed that I could take the day off, so long as I'm back at the hotel before it gets dark. We're going to start decorating the main dining hall this evening ready for the party, and afterwards Shelley has insisted that the two of us have our own night out. Obviously, I don't want to go anywhere near the centre of Como for fear of running into Pete, but I can't very well tell Shelley that without going into the entire backstory, and that's something I'm not prepared to do. It's bad enough that Marco has been exposed to it all, although I trust him not to gossip about me. Not only is he disinterested, he's also let me in on his own secret, so in some ways we're in the same boat.

I smile to myself as I think this, knowing that Marco would almost certainly be very happy to be in a boat – even one rocked by scandal and full of emotional holes.

Once I knew I had a good few hours to myself, I resisted the temptation to hide away in my bedroom, and instead hopped on the bus up to Bellagio. The chances of Pete being there again are slim to none, and I'm always looking for an excuse to spend time with Elsie and the boys.

I can't believe how incredible the weather has been this past week. The sun has shone every day, and there have been fewer clouds than you'd find puddles in the Sahara. I take the long route to Elsie's cottage, stopping to smell the wild flowers growing in robust clumps atop the harbour walls, their bright yellow petals as vibrant as a firework against the unblemished backdrop of the lake. On the far shore, the mountains sit as they always do, rooted and unmoving, and the smudgy morning light makes them look as if they've been drawn with pastels. They're not the dark brown you would expect, but a heady riot of blues, pinks and creams, and the white-tipped peaks glow like lamplight.

I climb the cobbled hill, past La Lanterna, which is just opening its doors for the day, and carry on round until I reach the narrow pathway that will take me down to the shore. I can remember so clearly the first time I stumbled across it, and how excited I was to veer off the main road and into the unknown. Of course, now that I'm older and wiser I know I'm not the only one who knows about the hidden little beach at its end, but I still like to think of it as mine. I wonder if Marco feels the same way. After all, it is the place we met.

I glance at the time. It's close to ten a.m. Elsie is expecting me, but I can be half an hour late. The urge to venture down to the isolated stretch of shingle is a strong one, and I set off along the path before I can change my mind, following it first up, then across the ridge of the hill, and then back down again. When I get to the wooden gate and the sign fastened to the wall, telling me in strict Italian that I'm about to trespass on private property, I ignore it and clamber over, wobbling slightly as I scale the top bar. Being small may never have stopped me doing what I want, but occasionally it slows me down.

I can see the water now, as calm as a bath at the base of the slope, and beyond it the outline of sailing boats, each one reflected in the surface of the lake below. A high wall stands guard on each side of the passageway opening, and I relish the feel of my boots sinking into the crunchy earth underfoot. It's impossible to go right without walking straight into the lake, so I hop across to the narrow concrete walkway that follows the wall around to the left, and walk slowly up to the fateful corner. This time, I won't be attempting to jump over to the dilapidated old rowing boat.

Save for the faint sound of lapping water and the odd cry from a passing bird, it's wonderfully quiet, and I lean against the sun-warmed stone and close my eyes. I spent so many hours here as a child, plotting my future, dipping my toes in the clear water and breaking up Elsie's home-made breakfast loaves for the ducks. It was all so easy then, adulthood a tiny speck far away on the horizon, but being back here in the same spot now, with the landscape barely altered from how it was more than twenty years ago, I feel as if I've reached a crux. Now that everything I'd had mapped out has fallen to pieces, I need to decide where to live, what to do and even who I want to be.

I love it here in Como, where the sun shines every day and the views in every direction are enough to make your heart sing, and it's been so much fun spending more time with Elsie. But is working as a tour guide at the Casa Alta really what I want to do indefinitely? And even if I manage to pull off this party tomorrow night with aplomb and persuade Sal to promote me to the position of events manager, is that really going to be enough? A few days ago, I would have answered yes, but now I'm not so sure. Marco's concept of turning a boat into a restaurant kept me awake last night in the best possible way. His passion for the project is wonderfully contagious, and the more I think about it, the more I realise that what I might want is something that I can call my own, too.

In my darker moments, however, I feel torn by the prospect of plotting my own future. I'd been resigned to trundling along the path that I assumed fate had chosen for me, and now that I've been ripped off it and thrown back to a crossroads, I'm not sure I'm equipped to know which way to go.

My phone beeps in my pocket, shattering the shifting silence with its ugly modern sound. I'm expecting it to be Elsie, so when I see Pete's name, I almost drop the handset into the lake in alarm.

I'm sorry I yelled at you, it reads. I hope you're OK.

No, I am very much not bloody well OK. I hate him even more now, for contacting me when I'm standing in my special place, trying my damn hardest not to think about him. It's bad enough that he's here at all, let alone sending me messages.

I told you to leave me alone, I type furiously, pressing the send button as hard as you can on a touchscreen phone without causing it any damage.

I wait for a full ten minutes, my heart racing and my fingers twitching with displeasure, but he doesn't send another one.

34

Lucy

I had thought I would dislike Taggie if I ever met her, and she is everything she seemed from Pete's photographs – petite, beautiful, exotic – but all I really feel towards the poor thing now is pity. She looked so wretched on that boat, so broken down, and I wouldn't wish that level of misery on anyone – not even the person I hold most responsible for damaging me beyond repair. Being a nurse has meant that I've had to develop a thick skin over the years, but I do still get shaken up by the sight of people in pain, and that was exactly the case with poor Taggie on the boat. I hope she has people around who will look after her.

After our chat yesterday, Pete and I agreed to draw a line under everything that happened up in Bellagio. Julia will probably roll her eyes when I tell her that I forgave him for fibbing, but I do understand why his knee-jerk reaction was to lie to Taggie. He didn't do it out of spite to me, but out of regard for her feelings, and both of us have agreed to tell each other nothing but the truth from this point forwards. It feels as if we've reconnected, but more than that – our relationship feels more serious, and more grown-up. I trust Pete not to withhold the truth from me any more, and I haven't been able to say that about a man in a very long time.

Today we've decided to head over to Cernobbio, which I've never been to before, but which the guidebook informs us is 'charming and attractive'. TripAdvisor has also ardently recommended Ristorante Miralago as the ideal place to sample the catch of the day, and that detail was all it took to persuade me and Pete, who are both fish-mad, that the five-kilometre walk was worth the effort.

We head along the western shore of the lake hand in hand, me admiring the reflection of the landscape on the surface of the water, and Pete pointing out the seaplanes that are busy flying low overhead. The frozen air is fresh and smells faintly of pine, and fallen leaves crunch beneath our feet as we reach the lakeside park and stroll past the Ferris wheel.

My phone buzzes in my pocket.

Julia has been trying to reach me all morning. I sent her a message late last night after Pete had fallen asleep, telling her not to worry and that everything was OK, but she's still demanding to speak to me. I know what she'll say if I answer, though – she will tell me I'm being too soft on Pete, and that I need to punish him more for lying. That's her, though – confrontational and begrudging – I'm far more like our dad, and will do anything to avoid being combative. While I understand Julia's need to protect me, I just can't face an ear-bashing. Not on such a beautiful morning.

'Who's that?' Pete asks, after I've opened my bag and shoved my phone to the bottom.

'Julia,' I say. 'I'll call her back later.'

I'm sure Pete will have guessed that I've reported back to my sister, but he wisely chooses not to pull at that particular thread. Instead, he changes the subject by asking me to tell him more stories about some of the bizarre cases we've had at the hospital. Apparently, there's nothing more hilarious than tales about unfortunate men that have got certain parts of their anatomy stuck in various household appliances, and Pete is soon bellowing with laughter loud enough to frighten the birds out of the surrounding trees.

We take the route that leads us through the grounds of the palatial Villa Olmo, with its breath-taking views and manicured gardens that are so unlike the wild tangle that my dad long ago gave up on, and continue along the main road. There isn't much traffic, save for the odd car and convoy of cyclists, and it's nice to simply breathe in the alpine air and savour the warmth from the sun. It's nice being with each other, too, now that all the drama is behind us. Pete is such easy company, and the more time I spend with him, the deeper my feelings go. When we reach a small roundabout, he points ahead of us, to where a large yellow villa is nestled on the upper slopes of a hill.

'Look,' he says. 'That's the Casa Alta Hotel.'

I peer at the sign on the opposite side of the road, then up again at the impressive building.

'Wowee,' I remark. 'It's quite something, isn't it?'

'Are you still happy to see the New Year in there tomorrow?' he checks. Since our talk, he's started running everything past me, seeming more anxious to make sure I'm happy.

'Of course!' I beam at him. 'I can't wait.'

What I don't add is that it will be nice to spend the evening away from the centre of Como, where Taggie could so easily stumble across us. The chances of her choosing the exact same hotel as us to spend New Year are virtually zero. She's far more likely to be out with her Italian friend, or back up in Bellagio. We'll be safely out of the way at the Casa Alta.

Cernobbio turns out to be every bit as charming and attractive as I'd hoped, with its higgledy-piggledy houses thrown against the slopes of Monte Bisbino and its quaint collection of shops, cafés, gelaterias and boutiques. Larger and livelier than Bellagio, but far less hectic than the neighbouring Como, Cernobbio offers a best-of-both experience to foreign visitors, and it isn't long before I've begged Pete for his camera and am persuading him to pose beside twee fountains carved from stone, and elegantly festive shop window displays.

'The Swiss border is on the summit of that mountain,' I tell Pete, using my chin to indicate the vast, snow-topped peak in the middle distance. We're sitting down on a bench beside the water, sipping takeaway cups of *vin brulé* to keep warm and watching a hopeful gang of pigeons strut around in an unwieldy circle by our feet.

'That close?' he exclaims. 'That's pretty crazy, isn't it? You know so much about this place, Lu. You must have been studying the guidebook before we left.'

'Oh, you know,' I begin, then stop as we both look down at the sound of my phone vibrating in my bag yet again.

'You should just answer it,' he says. 'Julia doesn't strike me as the type to give up easily.'

I laugh without humour. 'You're not wrong.'

Leaning over to give him a quick kiss on the lips, I stand up and retrieve my phone, waiting until I've walked a few feet away before sliding my finger across the screen to answer.

'Hello . . .'

'At last!' Julia is not amused. 'I thought you'd thrown yourself in the lake.'

'No, you didn't,' I correct mildly. 'I texted you about two hours ago.'

'I've had a fight with Abby,' she says, her voice high.

'Oh no,' I cry, immediately full of concern. 'What happened?'

'You did.'

I've walked all the way across to a cluster of bare lime trees now, and I lean against the crumbling trunk of one for support.

'What do you me—'

'I told her about you and Pete, and explained what happened, and she took *his* side. Can you believe it?'

I can't. Abby is warm and kind and supportive.

'Why did she do that?' I ask, feeling hurt. I knew I shouldn't have answered the bloody phone.

'She said . . .' Julia pauses, presumably deciding whether to continue.

'*What?*' I persist. In the distance, I see Pete take out his own phone and stare at the screen.

'She said you'd brought this on yourself.'

For a moment, I can't even speak. I feel like I've been winded.

'Erm, ouch. How does she figure that?'

Julia is in full rant mode now, angry with her girlfriend and desperate to unleash her fury.

'Well, she knows about your little . . . problem. You know we tell each other everything. Anyway, she reckons that Pete wasn't honest with you because he knew you'd react badly, and she basically accused you of being unstable, so I told her where to go.'

'My little problem?' I repeat.

'Yeah, you know, the fact that you can be a bit paranoid. And jealous.'

'I didn't know we referred to it as "Lucy's little problem",' I say acidly. 'And I didn't know you were psychoanalysing me with your bloody girlfriend!'

'Oi!' Julia is cross now. 'Don't start on me – I've been the one defending you for the past few hours.'

What is it that people always say? That the truth hurts. They aren't wrong.

I take a deep breath. 'I don't know what to say.'

I hear her sigh. 'I don't, either.'

'I'm sorry you had an argument, and I'm sorry I was the reason.'

'You always do that,' Julia groans, clearly exasperated.

'Do what?'

'Apologise for things that you shouldn't. It's not your fault that a vile toad of an ex-boyfriend treated you like rubbish all those years ago – it's his. And it's not your fault that Abby can be an argumentative cow sometimes – it's hers.'

'I'm sorry for being the way I am,' I say, stupid tears welling. 'I wish I wasn't.'

'This is exactly what I mean,' Julia says, her voice becoming gentler. 'The way you are is fine. It's better than fine – it's great. Your jealousy stems from the fact that you're insecure, and you're insecure because of what you've been through. You don't need to change for a man, you need to change for yourself. You're confident at your job, and you're so great with people – far better than I could ever be – yet you beat yourself up when it comes to men. It makes me so sad, Luce. And when Abby tries to make out that it's a choice rather than an affliction, it makes me bloody mad. That's why I yelled at her.'

I pick at a bit of the tree bark until it flakes apart.

'Do you think I need professional help?' I ask, my voice small.

'Maybe,' Julia replies. 'Or maybe you just need to spend some time on your own, rather than with a man who makes you feel constantly on edge. I know Pete does that, and this latest debacle has proved he can't be trusted.'

'He's told me everything now,' I say loyally. 'We've agreed to draw a line and focus on the future.'

'Hmmm,' she mutters.

'It's different now,' I continue, telling her a half-truth. 'I stood up for myself yesterday, I promise you I did. I asked him outright why he lied, and he told me.'

'Wonders will never cease,' she says drily, but I can tell she's softening.

'Make up with Abby,' I urge. 'Life's too short.'

'I'll think about it,' she replies, and I know that's the best I'm going to get. I'm so lucky to have a sister like Julia, I think, as I say my goodbyes. She may be blunt and feisty, but she's also fiercely loyal – a trait she most certainly gets from Dad. I can't deny that what she told me about Abby didn't hurt, though. I know I'm prone to jealousy and can be a bit possessive, and it's true that I do give myself a hard time, but simply telling me to stop isn't going to work. I've been repeating the same pattern of behaviour since I was nine years old, so it's going to take a hell of a lot of work to change.

I make my slow way back towards Pete, who is looking at his phone instead of me, and as I draw close he stuffs it quickly back into his pocket.

'Anything important?' I ask lightly, returning his kiss of greeting.

'Nah,' he replies, standing up and wrapping an arm around me. 'Nothing you need to worry about.'

35

Taggie

Elsie greets me with her usual enthusiasm, planting a kiss on each of my cheeks and telling me I look more beautiful than a summer's day. She's been saying that to me since I was seven, but it still makes me glow. The dogs fall over themselves to be the first to touch me, and I make a fuss of them in turn before picking Bruno up off the floor and propping him up on my shoulder.

'You're soft on that dog,' Elsie remarks, heading for the kettle. 'Shall we take our tea out into the garden?'

I'm not sure if it's because of the incident on the boat, or because I'm simply weary of facing everything alone, or because tomorrow the year will come to an end, but as soon as Elsie and I are sitting at her little metal table overlooking the lake, a blanket arranged over our knees, I tell her everything. I start on the day that Pete broke up with me, and I finish with the message he sent me today, and all the while she listens without interruption, her pale-blue eyes full of sympathy. When I'm done, and the tears finally fall, she shuffles out of her chair and wraps her thin arms around me. She smells of lavender and, faintly, of dog biscuits, and I sob my heart out against the itchy material of her shawl until I have nothing left.

'You poor, poor darling,' she says, again and again. 'I had no idea what you'd been through. I'm so sorry.'

I nod, unable to speak.

'I know how you feel,' she adds, causing me to sit up in surprise.

'You do?'

She nods, her mouth a tight line and her eyes glassy.

'It was a very long time ago, and I thought my heart would never mend. But if life has taught me anything, it's that a person's heart is very much like an elastic band. Even when it's broken, it will still bounce back. All you have to do is learn to trust someone enough to hand it over again, without worrying about the sting if they let it go.'

'I hope you're right,' I manage, and she grasps my hand.

'Time is a good healer,' she says. 'It's the oldest cliché in the world for a reason.'

I sniff in response.

'No wonder you don't want to start dating again,' she adds, braving a chuckle. 'If I'd known, I would never have gone on about you and Marco so much. Sorry about that, darling.'

'It's OK,' I mumble. 'You meant well.'

'I should have guessed something else was going on. Obviously, I've asked your parents many times, but they always brush me off.'

'I asked them not to tell you,' I admit. 'I just wanted to try and forget about it when I got here, and I was doing OK, I really was – but then bloody Pete showed up out of the blue and I just . . .'

I stop as I realise my voice is getting louder.

'I'm just still so angry,' I finish. 'I can't help but blame him.'

'Oh, darling girl,' Elsie reaches across and wipes a tear off my cheek. 'If you need to blame him, then go right ahead – but it's nobody's fault. Something like that never is, it's just damn bad luck.'

'Why is it so easy for him to move on, though?' I groan. 'Why doesn't he feel the same way as me? Why does he get to be happy and I have to feel like shit?'

Elsie puts her head on one side, her white curls illuminated by the sun, which makes her look as if she's wearing a halo.

'Because he's weak,' she says with a sad little sigh. 'It sounds to me as if he's pushed all his emotions to one side, like a lot of men do. Feeling guilty isn't very nice, and so he's chosen not to deal with it. Whereas you, my darling girl, you are dealing with it – even if you think you're not. You always have been strong.'

'I don't feel very strong,' I mutter, and she grins at me with encouragement.

'You don't have to feel it,' she says. 'You just have to believe it.'

Bruno has zonked out in a patch of sunlight on my lap, and Elsie and I both glance down, the two of us instantly enchanted by the twitching of his little legs and his sleepy snuffling noises.

'Bad dream,' Elsie whispers, putting a finger across her lips.

Bruno and I have even more in common than I thought.

'Come on,' I reply, being careful not to wake the tiny

mutt as I get to my feet. 'If I'm cold, then you must be freezing – let's go inside and I'll fix us some lunch.'

For once she doesn't battle with me, leaving me alone to potter around in her kitchen while she takes a watering can around the garden. This constant sunshine is all well and good, she informs me, but the lack of rain is wreaking havoc on her peach trees.

I make a tomato and onion salad, tearing up fresh basil from the pot on the windowsill to sprinkle on top, then cook off some mushrooms and lardons with a splash of white wine, and bring a pan of water to the boil for pasta. Cooking is one of the things I miss most about my life back in London. Living in a hotel sounds idyllic to many people, but the novelty of having someone else cook all your meals for you soon wears off. I love the process of preparing a meal and setting the table, deliberating over which bottle of wine in the rack will go best with whatever it is I've prepared. The only time I get to stretch my aspirational chef legs in Como is here, but Elsie will only let me take over her kitchen occasionally. She's just as keen on cookery as I am.

I'm just stirring cream into the sauce when my phone beeps again.

Can you talk?

It's Pete.

No, I reply, putting down the wooden spoon I'm holding on to the draining board.

Later?

I chew the inside of my cheek, my fingers hovering above the screen.

There is nothing to say, I tap out, swearing in earnest as the pasta water bursts its lid.

When are you back in London? he replies.

He must think I'm here on holiday like him, so he really does have no idea. I wonder then if he's even asked my mum and dad where I am, or if he's been content to bury his stupid big face in the dirt like an earthworm, just as Elsie said. I don't want him to know that I'm living here. I don't want him to know anything about me.

That is none of your business, I message back, picking the spoon up again and stirring my sauce. Some of the mushrooms have adhered themselves to the bottom of the pan, so I pour in another glug of wine.

Pete's next response renders me mute with anger.

Please say that you'll forgive me.

When Elsie comes in through the back door a few minutes later, she finds the sauce burning, the pasta a stuck-together lump, and me sitting on the floor, crying yet again.

36

Lucy

We make it back from Cernobbio just as the sun is beginning to set, and the sky has turned from blue to mauve to pink. Pete was quiet this afternoon, and seemed subdued – even when I treated us both to a gelato for the walk back along the lake. Despite our promise to each other to be unflinchingly honest, I haven't told him exactly what Julia and I discussed when she called, and he hasn't told me what's causing him to be so out of sorts. I keep alternating between feeling worried and being annoyed, and I've been replaying what Julia said about being on edge around Pete over and over on a loop in my head.

'Shall we go back to the apartment for a bit?' he asks.

Perhaps that's what we need, some time alone in which to reconnect physically. When we cross the threshold, however, Pete removes his coat and shoes, murmurs something apologetic about not feeling very well, and promptly lies down on the bed, facing the wall instead of me. So much for make-up sex. I wait until I can hear his gentle snores, then creep out into the stairwell and close the door gently behind me. I don't know where I'm planning to go, but I do know that I don't want to be cooped up in there.

For the first time since we arrived in Como, I realise

that I'm missing work. Being a nurse is relentless, draining and poorly paid, but it's also dynamic, uplifting and often miraculous. I like feeling useful and being helpful, and I love my team, too. We all support each other as closely and loyally as if we were one big family, and I miss that feeling of being a vital cog in the big machine of the hospital. I know who I am at work, but with Pete I'm never sure who to be. He tells me that he loves my caring side, but then goes cold on me whenever I start to relax into myself. It's confusing.

I stroll aimlessly around the Piazza del Duomo, tossing a two-euro coin at the feet of a living statue dressed from head to toe in silver, and with a spray-painted face and hands. He may have a very annoying squeak, but any fella who stands outside in the cold all day deserves a little bit of a reward. Dusk is the time of day when the streets are busiest, and the two main squares are full of families and groups of young Italians. Every other person seems to have a dog with them – and some even have a whole pack of the things, many of them dressed up in tiny coats.

Crossing the road opposite the ice rink, I walk all the way along the road hugging the lake, only stopping when I reach the entrance to the *funicolare*. I had thought vaguely about going up to Brunate and admiring the evening view, but now that I'm here it feels too far away. I don't want to experience new things by myself, anyway – I'd rather do it with Pete by my side. I'm just contemplating turning back, when I spot him on the other side of the road. His leather jacket is zipped right up against the cold and his chin is pressed down against the top of his chest, but it's definitely him – the man from the boat.

'Excuse me,' I call out, running after him before I have time to chicken out.

He turns and looks at me in confusion.

'*Si?*'

'I . . . Hello, we met on the boat. I mean, well, in Bellagio actually. I helped your friend with her nose.'

'Ah,' he says, his features relaxing a fraction as he makes the connection. 'Yes.'

'Is she OK?' I ask, and see him narrow his eyes. They're an extraordinary bright green colour.

'I think so, yes,' he says, but he doesn't return my smile.

'Oh, well, that's good.'

He looks over my shoulder. 'Where is your . . .'

'You mean Pete?' I guess, and he nods.

'Sleeping.' I smile yet again with what I hope is sheepish humour.

'Are you and Taggie—' I begin, but stop abruptly when he frowns at me.

'No.'

'Oh, I'm sorry. I just thought that you were, you know. You seem close.'

'We are friends,' he states, glaring at me with an expression that I can't quite read. He could be pissed off, or bemused, or neither – it's impossible to tell.

'I see.'

He's not very chatty, this man. His name comes back to me then, and I point across the road to a sign that I spotted on the walk down.

'Is that your place?' I ask.

He glances up, and the ghost of a smirk passes across his face.

'No.'

The Hotel Marco sign is made from huge, illuminated red letters, but the 'E' and the 'L' are broken. I would wager that it's possible to see 'Hot Marco' from right over the other side of the lake, but don't go as far as pointing that out to him. He doesn't seem to have any trouble understanding me, but his Italian accent is thick, and he's not giving me an awful lot in the way of conversation. Just when I think he's going to make an excuse and leave, however, he steps towards me.

'What did he do, your boyfriend?'

I'm momentarily taken aback by the question.

'What do you mean?'

'Pete. What did he do to Taggie?'

'He broke her heart,' I say in a small voice, feeling horribly disloyal.

Marco stands up a bit taller.

'And?'

'And nothing,' I reply, becoming flustered.

'You believe him?' Marco asks, not unkindly.

'Yes,' I say, cursing the wobble in my voice. Coughing to stabilise it, I repeat myself, this time with far more authority.

'I think he has done something very bad,' Marco states, clearly unconvinced by what I've just said. 'I have known many women,' he adds, which doesn't surprise me in the slightest. 'And I have never known a woman to be upset in this way.'

'You must care about her very much,' I say, uncomfortable with where the conversation is going.

'Of course,' he agrees. 'She is . . .' He searches for the word. 'Extraordinary.'

I can't agree, so instead I say nothing. I just stand there feeling absurdly like I'm about to cry. Marco reaches across and touches the top of my arm.

'I have to go to work,' he says regretfully. 'Look after yourself.'

By the time I've got my emotions back under control and regained the power of speech, Marco has gone, and I'm left alone by the side of the road.

Pete is predictably less than impressed.

'Who the hell is he to make assumptions about me?' he mutters, banging his bottle of beer down on the table. We're sitting under a heat lamp at a café facing the Duomo, and Pete is having to raise his voice over the jangling Christmas music that's blasting out from the speakers. It's even busier now than it was at sundown, and I wince as a harassed-looking mother hurries past with a screaming baby in her arms.

'It doesn't matter what he thinks,' I soothe. 'I believe you, and that's all that matters.'

'I don't want him filling Taggie's head with nonsense, either,' he adds, immediately looking apologetic. 'Sorry, Lulu, I know I said we wouldn't talk about her, but it just pisses me off when people that I don't know make assumptions about me.'

'You don't even know him,' I point out, my heart hammering. 'You'll probably never see him again.'

'Hmmph,' comes the reply.

Pete takes another miserable swig from his bottle.

'Who he is, anyway?' he rants. 'A fucking dickhead waiter with too-tight jeans and gel in his fucking stupid hair.'

I decide not to point out that Pete wears gel in his hair, too.

'He said he's Taggie's friend,' I correct gently. I've never seen Pete this angry before, and it's horrible to witness. I've dealt with injured toddlers that have thrown smaller tantrums, but so far, I haven't dared say so.

'How can he be such a good friend of hers, anyway?' he mumbles miserably. 'She's known him what – two weeks at the most?'

'How do you know how long she's known him?'

'Well, she can't have been in Como that long,' he states, taking another swig. 'She's only here on holiday.'

'Didn't you say she'd been coming here since she was a child?' I remind him.

'Yeah, so?'

'So, maybe she isn't here on holiday. Maybe she moved here.'

That shuts him up.

I use the excuse of needing the toilet to get away from him for five minutes, hoping that by the time I return he's had a word with himself. Perhaps I shouldn't have told him about my encounter with Marco, but I wanted him to know that Taggie was OK. And, if I'm being honest, the still-paranoid part of me wanted to gauge his reaction at the same time. Now I wish I'd kept schtum. Jealousy is a trait I know all too well, and I recognise it in the way Pete's behaving. He may say that he's not in love with Taggie any more, but clearly that doesn't mean he's ready to let another man take his place as the most important person in her life. It's ugly and unreasonable, but I do understand it. I was horribly jealous of Taggie when I didn't know anything about her, but now that I do, I don't feel envious. What I do feel is a need to protect her, and to help – and yet again I'm struck with a strange sense of déjà vu. One which is refusing to go away.

37

Taggie

Shelley insists on getting a taxi down to Como after dinner, because for once she's wearing heels. Unlike me, she's not used to her toes being crushed and her arches aching, and she's started limping before we're even out the front door of the hotel.

'How do you deal with this agony on a daily basis?' she asks, grimacing as we reach a portion of the pavement that's cobbled.

'Years of practice,' I reply, taking her arm and guiding her to safety.

I took a very long, hot bath when I got back from Elsie's earlier, and I conditioned and curled my hair. I might feel crap on the inside, but that's no reason to look rubbish on the outside. I've made a good start on all the party decorations for tomorrow, and I'm starting to feel mildly nervous about the event now, which is always a good sign. This dinner and disco extravaganza is just too important to go wrong – my future job satisfaction depends on it.

'Shall we go to the Duomo?' Shelley suggests, coming to a halt beside the pedestrian crossing. 'I haven't been to see the Nativity scene in there yet, and I've heard it's beautiful.'

'No,' I say abruptly, and she turns to me in surprise.

'I'd rather have a drink!' I add, and she grins wickedly.

'Now you're talking.'

The Christmas Market is absolutely heaving tonight, as Sal warned us it would be. This is the day that many Italians arrive in the area ready for New Year, and every bar and restaurant gets booked up within hours. I don't mention Marco's friend's bar, because I know Shelley will lead us there anyway, but I do experience a small pang of disappointment when we get there and find no sign of him. He's probably working, of course, making as many tips as he can to add to his boat fund, but I can't help hoping that he passes by Vista Lago later, once his shift comes to an end.

Shelley, who is never one to mess about when it comes to a night on the tiles, orders us a round of tequilas to go with our beers. I knock mine back, for once relishing the slightly sick-making rush that immediately follows, and head to the bathroom to check my face. I should write Bobbi Brown a letter of thanks for helping me disguise my tear-stained cheeks and puffy eyes, I think, peering at myself in the mirror above the sink. When my phone buzzes inside my bag, I know it's him, and it's all I can do not to hurl it at the wall.

Tell your boyfriend to mind his own business, it reads.

The subject matter and stroppy tone are both so unexpected that I laugh out loud. Did Pete even mean to send me this text?

I put my phone down on the edge of the sink and extract my lipstick. I've gone for a scarlet shade tonight called Lady in Red, which I hardly ever wear, but I like how it makes me feel. Sassy and strong women wear red lipstick, and that's the persona I'm channelling tonight.

Another message comes through.

Where are you? I need to speak to you!

Is he for real? I switch the phone off with shaking fingers and head back out in search of more tequila.

'You can drink a lot for a hobbit,' Shelley remarks, putting down her empty bottle of beer only to miss the edge of the table and send it spinning on to the floor.

'Oops!' she giggles, reaching down a hand only to fall on the floor right after it.

'What are you doing on the flooooooor?' I cry, pulling her arm uselessly. I'm laughing so much that I've lost all my strength, and I didn't have that much of it to begin with.

'Help meeee!' she wails, grabbing my knee and trying to stand up. It doesn't work, though, and soon I'm lying under the table on top of her, both of us in hysterics.

'*Ciao*, ladies.'

I recognise that deep, Italian accent.

'Marco!' I sing in delight, wriggling off Shelley until I'm propped up with one knee on either side of her waist. 'Help me up!'

He looks at me with amusement, unzipping his jacket and tossing it over a nearby chair.

'Come here,' he says, taking my hand in his own, slightly colder one. 'Up you come.'

'Thanks!' I trill happily, almost careering right into him as he pulls me up from the ground. This is the third time he's discovered me on my bottom instead of my feet – it's becoming a habit. Shelley makes no effort to move, instead waving at Marco from her spot beneath the table.

'She dropped her bottle,' I explain, collapsing into the chair next to him. And then, more by way of an explanation, 'We love tequila.'

'I wonder if you will say the same thing in the morning,' he replies.

'Pardon?' I shout, and he gives me a look.

'I'm glad you're here,' I tell him boldly, for once not caring that Shelley can hear me. 'I had an epiphany today,' I add, and he frowns in confusion.

'An epiphany is like a——' I begin, but he interrupts.

'I understand epiphany.'

'Clever clogs,' I say, tapping his nose with my finger.

For a second he just stares right at me, and our faces are so close together that I can smell the toothpaste on his breath.

'Drink?' he asks.

'Beer, please!' I tell him, and hear Shelley say something that sounds the same. While Marco's over at the bar, I grab both her hands and pull her back up into her chair.

'He's so gorgeous,' she says dreamily. 'I want to kiss him.'

'You should,' I whisper back, wondering why the words feel like razor blades in my mouth.

'He likes you, though,' she whispers back, pouting sadly.

'He likes boats,' I giggle. 'Show him your sails and maybe he'll drop his anchor.'

Shelley salutes Marco when he returns with three bottles of beer, then blows him a kiss when he goes back to collect two pints of water.

'Drink this,' he instructs gently, putting one down in front of each of us.

'Boooooo!' complains Shelley, curling up her nose. 'More tequila!'

'No more tequila,' Marco says firmly, but it's obvious he finds the two of us hilarious. I feel bad now for making fun of his boat obsession, and decide to make it up to him by reading his palm.

'This is your life line,' I slur, running my finger along one of the creases in his hand. 'And this, right here, this is your love line.'

He closes his fingers around mine.

'What does it say?'

I'm aware of a pulse beating insistently from somewhere deep inside my body.

'That you will make many women fall in love with you,' I declare, trying and failing to release my hand from his grasp. Shelley is at the bar trying to order more tequila, but the barman is pretending she isn't there.

'What if I only want one woman?' he asks, his voice playful.

'You can't argue with the lines,' I say regretfully, then add as an afterthought, 'Your hair looks nice today.'

He mutters something in Italian.

'It does!' I insist. 'Did you run out of gel?'

'Your hair is curlier today,' he remarks, picking up one of my ringlets and running his fingers through it.

'Do you like it?' I ask, my voice sounding weird and husky.

'I like it,' he confirms.

Shelley has given up badgering the barman now and has transferred her attention to the DJ, who is beckoning for Marco to join him.

'*Scusami,*' he says, letting go of my hair and standing up. I watch him stroll across the room, admiring his long, lean legs and the broadness of his shoulders inside his shirt. Shelley's right, Marco is gorgeous. I don't know why it's taken me this long to realise just how gorgeous. That inexplicable pull I experienced the very first night we came to this bar has never felt stronger than it does now, and it dawns on me that I feel perfectly comfortable around Marco. I don't mind him touching me any more. More than that, I quite like it.

I reach for my beer and take a gulp, enjoying the feeling of being out, and being tipsy, and not feeling angry or tearful or anything other than blearily at peace. I don't have the energy to be sad tonight. I just want to go back to being me again – the Taggie Torres who hadn't had her heart broken, not once, but twice. I miss her.

Marco returns to the table with Shelley trailing behind him.

'Where are your shoes?' I gasp, laughing as she points under the table.

'I took them off. They're bad shoes that hurt my feet.'

'Naughty shoes!' I cry in support, kicking out a leg and sending one of Shelley's stilettos skidding across the floor of the bar.

'My shooooe!' she slurs, scurrying after it. And then, 'I love this song!'

The DJ, presumably after much begging from my brilliant friend, has put on 'Never Forget' by Take That.

'I love it, too!' I squeal, clambering across Marco to reach Shelley and throwing my arms around her with glee just as the chorus kicks in.

When I look back towards the table, Marco has cheekily stuck a finger in each ear and is laughing at the two of us, his green eyes shining as he watches us jumping up and down.

As Shelley swings me round and I stumble over her discarded shoe, I look again at Marco. There's a brief, profound second where he simply stares back, and then he brings a hand up to his mouth and blows a kiss at me.

38

Lucy

The last day of the year begins with clouds. Thick and grey and forbidding, they drift in front of the sun and dull the colours of the landscape, turning the lake from brilliant blue to sludgy green.

I've ventured out on my own again, having left Pete to sleep off his half of the many bottles of beer we consumed last night, and come down to the edge of the water. I'm not sure what it is that draws me down here time and time again, but the need I feel to stare out across the lake is the same one I had as a child. It was even more difficult to sneak off alone back then, because Julia was never more than a foot away from me when we came on holiday. Back in Suffolk, she had her own friends and would boss me out of her bedroom whenever they came over, but in Como she needed an ally, someone to keep her entertained. I can remember well the day I took her down to the secret beach I'd discovered in Bellagio, and how proud I was of myself. I forever wanted to impress my big sister, who always seemed so much stronger and more together than me, and that desire has never wavered since.

Being back in Como again after so many years has reminded me of who I was as a kid, so much stronger and more independent than I am as an adult. Perhaps my reluctance to spend time alone has all been in my head, because this is the second time now that I've felt compelled to slip away from Pete and venture out by myself. Am I less of a wimp than I think I am, or is it being back in Como that's brought out this braver version of me?

It's not even nine a.m. yet, but the harbour is buzzing with activity. Waist-height metal railings are being erected all along the shore, and in the distance, I can see a group of men in high-visibility jackets milling around a large stage. There is going to be quite some party down here tonight, and now that I'm witnessing the preparations, I'm almost sad that Pete and I will miss most of it. When we first agreed on dinner and dancing at the Casa Alta Hotel, I was content with the thought of spending the night sitting opposite him – I imagined that it would be romantic. But since last night there's this new tension between us, and now I fear that it may be more of an awkward affair. The old Lucy would have done anything to make things better; she would have held her tongue and been supportive of Pete no matter what, but I don't feel like that Lucy this morning – and it's not just because I'm hungover. I don't want to keep sidelining myself – especially not when the person I'm doing it for is acting so unreasonable.

I make my way through the park that has become so familiar over the past few days, and carry on past the Ferris wheel, thinking to myself that I'll sit for a while on the wall by the big war memorial. When I get there, however, the need to keep moving spurs me on, and I follow the lip of the lake round until the Aero Club comes into view. I like this part of the lake, where one park trails off and another begins, and I get a tingle as I look at the seaplanes bobbing in the water. That surprise flight Pete booked for us was an amazing experience, and I must make sure that I never forget how wonderful it felt to be up there with him, making an amazing memory for both of us to treasure.

The sun is winning the battle against the clouds now, and the wind is chasing torch beams of light across the surface of the water. Every time I look up and outwards, the scenery changes, as browns become golds and greys become blues. I could stand for hours in the same spot and see so many things differently, just as I'm starting to see my relationship with Pete in a less clear-cut way now. Ever since I met him, all I've wanted is to be with him – I've never stopped to question whether or not it's the right thing for me. I keep coming back to the suggestion that Julia made, about me spending some time by myself, and wondering if she's on to something. But am I having these thoughts because I really want to be alone, or just because I'm scared that Pete will do to me what he did to his last girlfriend?

I've drawn level with a seaplane now, which is anchored just offshore, and beyond it there's a girl wearing a brown duffle coat, feeding bread to an excitable congregation of ducks, swans, seagulls and pigeons. I realise that it's Taggie a fraction too late, and there's nowhere for me to hide. Before I can turn back the way I came, she looks up and sees me.

'Oh,' she says, with barely a flicker. 'It's you.'

39

Taggie

My first thought when I see Lucy standing there in front of me is how pretty she looks. Her blonde hair is fanned out over her shoulders, and she's wearing a dark-green coat that perfectly complements her pale skin. While I shuffled down here in trainers and last night's make-up, she's painted her lips rosebud pink and added a hint of blush to her cheeks. She looks healthy and well rested, unlike me. Last night's tequila, coupled with my ongoing inability to sleep for more than a few hours at a time, has left circles under my eyes that are darker than treacle, and my hair is a matted nest.

'I didn't mean to sneak up on you,' she says, glancing at me nervously. One of the swans has waddled over to her hoping for more bread, and she takes a deliberate step away.

'I'm just glad you're alone,' I tell her. 'What have you done with Pete?'

'He's asleep,' Lucy mutters, daring to meet my eyes. 'He had quite a big night – we both did.'

I remember the messages I got from him, the warning about my supposed boyfriend minding his own business, and frown with renewed confusion.

'Pete's a terrible drunk,' I say, squinting slightly as the sun emerges from behind a cloud. The two aspirin tablets I swallowed before I left the hotel haven't kicked in yet, and this unsettled weather is doing little to ease my headache.

Lucy is looking out across the water rather than at me, but she doesn't seem defensive or even uncomfortable – in fact, she's oddly calm.

'I'm finding out lots about him on this trip,' she admits. 'I thought I knew him quite well, but I guess I don't. Not really.'

So, he's told her then. I'm surprised, but strangely not upset. Talking about it with Elsie must have helped me even more than I thought. There I was thinking that the answer was to bury it all, but that was just me being a coward, which is not a Taggie way to behave. However, I don't want to talk about it with Lucy. She is still Pete's girlfriend – the woman he replaced me with.

'Do you live here?' she asks me then, and I'm so relieved she's changed the subject that I answer her truthfully, explaining about Elsie but not letting on where I work. She would be bound to tell Pete, and I don't want him turning up at the Casa Alta.

'You're so lucky,' Lucy enthuses. 'This place is so incredible – I've loved it ever since I was a child.'

'You came here as a kid, too?' I reply, and she nods.

'Yes. Every year until I was fourteen.'

Perhaps that's why she seems so familiar to me. Could it be that we encountered one another as children? The chances are slim, but then it would explain the nagging feeling I have that she and I have met before. I think about mentioning it, but then change my mind. She probably refers to me as 'that crazy Taggie woman' already, given what she witnessed on the boat. And anyway, I remind myself, she's friends with the enemy.

'Are you OK?' Lucy says then, at last turning to face me properly. The birds have given up on us now and wandered away, and I stare hard at a pigeon that's flown up on to the bench nearby.

I take a deep breath. 'I will be.'

'I really do think Pete's sorry, you know,' she mumbles. 'He feels so bad for hurting you.'

'He turned his back on me,' I tell her, failing to keep the hostility I feel from slipping into my voice. 'I don't know if I can forgive him for . . . Well, you know.'

Lucy seems to agree, but there's a hint of enquiry in her expression, as if she wants to ask me a question but is too scared.

'Do you think he's a good man?' she says, which strikes me as weird. It feels like a trick question – especially in light of what I know he must have confessed to her.

'I used to.'

'Do you still love him?'

'I don't really think that's . . .' I pause, not wanting to be rude but feeling stung by her directness.

'It's OK.' Lucy braves a small smile. 'I shouldn't have asked. I'm doing this new thing where I try to be brave and stand up for myself more, but it's not really me.'

Folding my arms across my chest, I dip my chin until it's hidden inside the top of my coat. I don't want to cry in front of her; I want to prove that I'm strong.

'I can't believe it's the last day of the year,' she says then, her hands deep in her pockets. 'Time seems to go so fast these days.'

'Mmm-hmm,' I reply, still unable to speak for fear of a sob escaping.

'We leave on the second,' Lucy adds, tucking a strand

282

of hair behind her ear. There's a diamond stud in her lobe, which keeps sparkling in the light from the sun, and an intricate floral brooch pinned to the front of her coat. The sky above us is almost completely blue now, and I gaze up at it in the hope of absorbing some of its reassuring beauty.

'I thought you'd want to know.'

'Thanks,' I manage.

'Back to work for me,' Lucy groans good-naturedly, adding an eye roll for effect.

'What do you do?' I ask, wondering if she's someone from Pete's radio office.

'I'm a nurse,' she says, smiling properly for the first time since she walked over. 'I work in the A&E department at All Saints Hospital in London, which is pretty mental, but I love it.'

I open my mouth to reply, but nothing comes out except a hoarse sort of gurgle. My cheeks are burning and I feel my heart flutter inside my chest. I need to get away. I don't want to be here any more.

Lucy is peering at me now in concern, and I stumble backwards away from her.

'Are you feeling all right?' I hear her ask as I turn, so I wave a feeble hand in response.

'Taggie!' she calls, more loudly this time, but I shake my head, slipping now as I hurry away from her across the slimy cobbles.

'Leave me alone,' I shout. 'Both of you, just leave me alone.'

The next time I look back she's still standing there, a green and blonde smudge against the grey of the pavement. I watch as she shakes her head, with pity or confusion I don't know, and then she walks away.

40

Lucy

I'm not sure what just happened.

One minute Taggie seemed to be warming to me, and the next she seemed to turn to stone right in front of me, as if she'd seen a ghost or something. I tried to follow her, to check she was OK, but she waved me away as if I was contagious.

I shouldn't have asked her if she was still in love with Pete, but it just came out. I selfishly wanted her to let me off the hook and tell me that she's over him, but what the hell was I really expecting? That she'd give the two of us her blessing? Even I know that's utterly absurd. Now I've upset her so much that I've caused her to get ill. I should have kept my stupid mouth shut. This is what happens when I try to channel Julia and ignore who I really am – I end up hurting people. If I wasn't so insecure and paranoid all the time, then I wouldn't have said anything to Taggie at all. But I am, and so I made a pathetic attempt to forge an alliance between us. Taggie isn't the bloody enemy here, though – I am.

I hurry back along the promenade, too distracted to enjoy the crunch of the dry leaves underfoot or the flawless vista of water and mountain and sky. Pete will be awake by now, but I have no idea what to say to him, or even if I should mention seeing Taggie at all. Didn't we promise to be honest? I insisted on it. But I know that this will only wind him up, and perhaps even make him angry. I can't face another outburst like the one he had over Marco yesterday.

My mind is made up for me when I reach the apartment and find Pete still in bed. As soon as I close the door, he holds his arms out to me, and I rush gratefully into them. Taggie seemed so fragile this morning, her dark, beautiful eyes ringed with fatigue and her fingernails bitten down to the quick. I don't want to be lonely and broken like she is, I want to be loved and cherished, and Pete is offering me those things. If I give up on him now, won't I just become the architect of my own misery?

'Sorry I wasn't here when you woke up,' I rush out, kissing his neck, his chest, the warm hollow of his throat.

'You've got nothing to be sorry for,' he croons, taking my face in his hands. 'You're perfect. I'm the one who should be apologising.'

I love it when he holds me like this, his big arms pressing me tightly against his chest. I feel safe in the nook of his affection, as if nothing can touch me.

'It's OK,' I assure him. 'I just want to forget it.'

'I should have told you sooner about Taggie,' he says slowly, and I tense up at the mention of her name. It's impossible not to picture her stumbling away from me, her face ashen. 'Bumping into her after so long has knocked me off kilter, but that's no excuse, I know. I didn't talk about her before because I wanted to leave it in the past. It was all so . . .' He pauses, squeezing me harder. 'Messy and upsetting and horrible. I know it was my decision to end things, but that doesn't mean it was easy.'

I think about Taggie's face when I asked her if she was still in love with him. How she'd had to fight to stop herself from crying.

'I understand,' I tell him, and he kisses the top of my head.

'I just want to focus on you now,' he says. 'On us. I want to leave the past in the past and move on.'

'Look,' he adds, letting go of me to pick up his phone from the bedside cabinet. 'I'll delete her number now, and all the messages. I'll never mention her again.'

'Stop.' I place a hand over his. 'You don't have to do that. I trust you.'

'I will do it,' he says. 'For you.'

I shake my head. 'Don't.'

He sighs and replaces the phone, pulling me down until I'm lying next to him. He's still under the duvet, while I'm on top of it, and I reach across to stroke the red hair on his chest.

'You can talk about her, if you need to,' I tell him. 'You can talk about her with me.'

'I don't want to talk about her,' he states, slowly beginning to unbutton my coat. 'I want to talk about you.'

'You do?' I murmur, playing along.

'I want to talk about your face,' he whispers, running a finger along my cheek. 'And your neck,' he says, again stroking. I prop myself up and he helps me wriggle out of my coat. I'm wearing a black polo-neck tucked into jeans, and he tugs at the waistband, his eyes never leaving mine. He still hasn't kissed me, but I can feel the warmth of his breath on my lips, and I shiver with pleasure as he slips a hand under my jumper and walks his fingers up towards my bra.

'I definitely want to talk about these,' he whispers, extracting one breast from the satin cup and circling my nipple with his thumb. It's the first time he's touched me in such an intense way since we bumped into Taggie, and my body responds instantly with a hunger I didn't know I was feeling. I want him to tear my clothes off me, but he's intent on taking his time, first removing my top and bra, then moving across the bed to inch down my jeans. Once I'm laid bare save for my knickers, he works his way up my body with his tongue, tasting and tickling and nibbling until I'm practically begging him to let me join in.

When he's satisfied that he's teased me enough, Pete takes my hand and guides it into my underwear, his low voice husky with arousal as he tells me gently what to do, where to touch, when to stop. Usually I would blush and squirm and roll to one side, but today I feel fearless, and I find I can meet his gaze with equal intensity. This is what we needed, to reconnect with each other and, more than that, venture into new and more intimate territory. Despite everything that's happened, I feel closer to Pete in this moment than I ever have before, and when he finally, blissfully, kneels between my legs before pulling me forwards on to him, I look right at him and utter the three words I've been wanting to say for so long – the statement I wasn't sure until this moment that I truly meant.

'I love you.'

41

Taggie

I knew I'd seen Lucy somewhere before. I knew it, but I still can't believe it. I'm not even sure how I've made it through the past few hours in one, sane piece, and if it wasn't for this evening's party, which I've spent so long planning, I think I would have fallen apart. As it is, there's so much on my to-do list that I haven't had any choice but to put this morning's encounter by the lake firmly under lock and key in my mind, and pretend it never happened.

'Agatha!'

'Piss off,' I curse under my breath, before turning around. 'Yes, Gladys?' I say sweetly, my fake smile making my jaw ache.

'Can you tell Will-yum that he must wear a proper suit tonight? He's trying to get away with jeans.'

'Bill, you should wear a suit,' I parrot obediently, even though he's welcome to turn up dressed in a rainbow-patterned thong and nothing else for all I care.

Gladys's husband looks miffed.

'It's too tight,' he whimpers, looking at his wife be-seechingly. 'I've put on weight since we've been here.'

'Nonsense!' she booms, playfully pinching his cheek. 'Oh, you do say the silliest things.' She turns back to me. 'And Agatha,' she adds.

Now what?

'Yes?'

'Is your friend Marco going to join us at the party tonight? I should so like to pinch him for a dance.'

'No,' I say, in my best apologetic voice. 'He has to work.'

'Oh, what a shame,' she cries, stepping closer so she can whisper in my ear. 'I was rather hoping to pinch him for a New Year's kiss, too.'

I laugh, only realising a fraction too late that she wasn't joking. She can't seriously think that Marco would be willing to slip her the tongue under the mistletoe – can she?

'We shared a moment,' she confides now. Bill has wandered off to talk to another member of the group, no doubt still sulking because he didn't get his own way with the suit, and Gladys is now telling me in a hushed tone all about how her and Marco's eyes had met and she'd felt it 'in her bones'.

'Felt what?' I reply.

'Lust!' she declares, before bursting into noisy snorts of laughter.

Shelley finds me banging my head slowly against the wall in the office.

'Hungover?' she asks, and I nod wearily.

'Me too. Bloody tequila has a lot to answer for.'

The two of us were so drunk last night that Marco had to walk us to the taxi rank and sweet-talk the unimpressed driver into taking us home. He was worried that we'd throw up all over his seats, but what he should have been worried about was our singing. Unfortunately for him, 'Never Forget' by Take That contains some extremely high notes.

'Do you know what you're wearing yet?' Shelley adds, slipping into Sal's chair so she can check Facebook on his computer. I haven't even looked at my account since I left London – there are too many people on there that I want to avoid.

I shrug, my mind still soup.

'A dress.'

'Well, obviously,' she retorts. 'But which one?'

'A black one.'

'Why, are you in mourning?'

'Ha ha,' I retort, feeling wounded. I leave her to it, letting the office door bang shut behind me, only to collide with Sal, who is coming the other way with a large wreath of holly in his hands.

'Ouch!' I cry, as the sharp edges of the leaves come into contact with my bare arms.

'*Attento!*' snaps Sal, clearly irritated. I've been giving him tasks all day, as diplomatically as I can, but it's become increasingly plain with each passing hour that he is not a man who likes being told what to do. He's now ranting away about napkins, and I hold up my hand to silence him, quickly suggesting that he leave the finer details to me, and help set out the canapés on their silver trays instead. However, from the expression on his face, you'd think I'd just asked him to walk barefoot across hot coals.

Bloody men.

By the time the sky outside the windows has turned black and the lights on the opposite shore begin twinkling like fireflies, everything is in its place. The waiting staff stand poised in the grand dining room, ready to offer flutes of

Prosecco to the guests as they arrive, and a wonderful aroma of slow-cooked beef and garlic is wafting up the stairs from the kitchen. Sal has allowed me to totally outdo myself with the decorations, and strings of fairy lights in various colours are arranged around pictures and door frames. Each table has been set with the hotel's finest silver, and on my suggestion, Shelley has designed song request cards to be handed over to the DJ while everyone's eating. She seems completely oblivious to my strung-out mood, and pulled me to one side as soon as I came back downstairs in my dress to tell me how much she fancies the local guy I hired to lay the temporary dance floor. This wouldn't usually surprise me, except that the man in question isn't all that much taller than me – basically a good six inches below Shelley's normal height threshold. Then again, he has spent most of the afternoon down on all fours working, so perhaps she hasn't realised.

The disco part of the evening is taking place in the ballroom, and from there the guests will be able to slip out through the old-fashioned French windows and across the manicured lawn in time to watch the fireworks at midnight. There's a vast Christmas tree dominating one corner, and mistletoe hangs in the doorways leading through to the dining room and reception. It all feels festive and fun, exactly as I painstakingly planned it to, but I disloyally can't wait for the whole night to be over. Ever since I realised earlier exactly where I knew Lucy from, a horrible thought has been creeping its way through my insides, closing like a fist whenever I allow myself to dwell on it. I don't want to believe that it can be true, but, if the past few months have illustrated anything at all, it's that extremely horrible things can and do happen.

Gladys must have heard about the complimentary bubbly, because she's the first one from the group to come down from the guest bedrooms upstairs. Bill follows in her wake, red in the face and wearing a plum-coloured suit jacket that's straining dangerously at the button. For once, they haven't dressed in co-ordinating colours, and I have to admit that Gladys has never looked better. She's opted for black, just like me, but unlike me she's clad in a jumpsuit rather than a dress, and has gone to the trouble of setting her hair in curls and applying surprisingly tasteful make-up. I felt too dazed to bother with all that in the end, settling instead for a super-high ponytail, a slick of dark-red lipstick and a simple gold chain around my neck, which was a Christmas gift from Elsie.

Not in the mood to hang out in the bar area with a newly enamoured Shelley, but reluctant to get trapped with a lurking and even more red-faced than usual Tim, I go instead to the kitchen, on the pretext of helping Luka the chef with the final preparations.

'Taggie,' he declares, his red cheeks shining. 'You know I love you, but get the blooming heck out of my kitchen, yes? I have twenty-eight covers tonight.'

'But I can help,' I begin.

Luka shakes his lovely head and points over my shoulder towards the door.

'Out, *tesoro*.'

'I am not your darling,' I grumble to myself as I jog back up the stairs. I know he's only shooing me out because he knows full well that my job is to greet the guests, not carve the meat, but I still feel as if I've been told off. And I hate being scolded – I always have. It's up there with people trying to look after me all the time, which is my behavioural kryptonite.

I've just re-emerged in the entrance hallway when Sal comes out of his office, frowning as soon as he sees me.

'Agatha, stop running away and bloody hiding.'

He never calls me Agatha.

'I'm not,' I lie.

He narrows his eyes and thrusts a clipboard at me.

'*Silenzio*. It is your party, so you must tick off the guests as they arrive – and Taggie.'

'*Che cosa?*'

'Smile, for God's sake – it is a party.'

He's right, of course he is – I need to stop feeling sorry for myself and suck up all this impotent anger, if only for a few hours. There's a lot riding on this party, and if anything goes catastrophically wrong, I can bid my hopes of a promotion farewell. However, I decide grumpily, taking the list and standing in place just inside the big front doors, the only thing that would make me smile right now is the ground cracking open below Sal's feet and swallowing him whole.

42

Lucy

I'm the one who sees her first.

Pete is busy counting out euros for the taxi driver, while trying and failing to thank him in Italian, so his back is still turned when I look up and spot her gawping at us in horror from the open doorway of the hotel.

'Taggie's here,' I say, without preamble.

'What? Where?' Pete sounds as alarmed as his ex-girlfriend looks, and I glance at the two of them in turn, trying to decide what to do.

'Oh, shit,' he groans, rubbing his forehead in agitation.

Taggie has disappeared, but Pete is still staring at the spot where she was just standing, a muscle twitching in his jaw.

'Do you want to leave?' I ask gently, taking his rigid hand.

'I don't know,' he says, sounding harassed. 'What do you want to do?'

'I think we should stay,' I say honestly, and when he looks at me I smile encouragingly. 'It's New Year's Eve, Pete. Some might say it's the perfect time to make amends. You don't really want to go back to London and have that horrible shouting match on the boat be the last time you spoke to her, do you?'

He screws up his face.

'I suppose not.'

'It's a big place,' I add, looking up at the vast yellow building in awe. 'It's not as if we'll be sitting next to her at dinner.'

'At this point, nothing would surprise me,' Pete mutters, but at least he's squeezing my hand now.

'Let's go in and see what happens,' I suggest. 'If it's awful, or if you find it too weird, then we'll just leave, OK?'

He smiles grimly.

'OK.'

We both take a deep breath and head up the wide stone steps, me wobbling a bit in my high heels and Pete looking as sheepish as a dog that's been caught with its nose in the fridge. A smart plaque on the wall next to the entrance is engraved with the words 'Casa Alta Hotel' and warm light spills out to greet us from a large, square-shaped reception hall. The polished wooden floor gleams, and there's more wood panelling on sage walls. A reception desk is set back to the left, complete with a vase full of winter blooms and a brass call bell, and a faint murmur of voices is filtering out from an open door opposite the bottom of the stairs.

'I guess we just go in,' I say quietly, when nobody appears.

Pete grasps my hand a little tighter.

'Come on then.'

We walk through the doorway into a long, rectangular dining room festooned with fairy lights. The walls are painted in a soft cream colour, while claret curtains tied back with a twisted length of gold rope hang by ornate windows even taller than Pete. Two vast chandeliers are casting a pleasant glow over the tables, all of which are topped with gold and white striped cloths. Silver cutlery glints, and the polite chatter from the twenty or so other guests competes with the soft sound of classical music. Taggie is nowhere to be seen.

'Well, this is a bit fancy,' Pete says into my ear, trying to lighten the mood, but it isn't enough to dampen the flame of foreboding that is burning away ferociously in my gut. My instinct out on the steps was to face the music, but now that we've crossed the threshold, I feel nervous. The Taggie that I saw on the boat and the version I met feeding the birds were very different, and I have no idea which version of her will come out tonight. She told me she worked in a hotel, but hadn't given me the name, and it feels wrong that Pete and I have come here to the Casa Alta. It's her turf, and we're invading it.

A waiter wearing a bow tie to match the curtains hurries forwards and offers us a glass of Prosecco. Pete, I notice with unease, knocks his back almost in one. We're just heading to the makeshift bar to get him another, when our path is blocked by a middle-aged woman looking extremely glamorous in a black jumpsuit. Behind her, looking slightly less self-satisfied, is a man that I assume must be her husband, who is wearing a suit jacket at least two sizes too small.

'It is you!' the woman declares, loud enough to alert the attention of several nearby guests.

'I'm sorry,' I say politely. 'Do I know you?'

'Will-yum and I,' she gestures to the uncomfortable man at her side, 'were on the boat with you a few days ago. You had a row with your boyfriend.' As she says this last part, she stares pointedly at Pete, who glares right back at her.

I recognise her then, remember the red fleece jacket and the bossiness, and brace myself for what I know is going to be an excruciating exchange.

'I'm glad to see the two of you have made up,' she titters, seemingly oblivious to Pete's intense hostility. 'I told her to go after you, didn't I, Will-yum?'

'You did, Gladys,' her husband agrees.

Pete is glowering so hard that I fear his look of fury will burn a hole right through the fabric of this woman's outfit.

'Right, well,' I begin, turning to walk away, but the woman puts a cold hand on my arm.

'You mustn't let it worry you,' she says, looking at me with gentle reproach. 'Will-yum and I used to bicker all the time, but it's only because he cares about me so much.'

Shouldn't that be we *care about* each other? I think, but instead I just smile.

'I'll be at the bar,' mutters Pete, and hurries away before I can protest.

'I'm Gladys, by the way,' the woman adds, ignoring my proffered hand and going in for a kiss on each cheek instead.

'Lucy,' I reply, looking over her shoulder to locate Pete.

'The food here is very good,' she's telling me now. 'Will-yum has been enjoying it a bit too much, haven't you Will-yum?'

'A bit too much, yes.'

'Sorry, excuse me,' I say, turning my back and leaving them mid-sentence. Taggie has just appeared through a second door at the far end of the dining room, and is scanning everyone's faces. She's pulled her hair back into a very high ponytail tonight, which makes her look far more severe than usual, and I can see the deep berry red of her lipstick from here. She looks devastating, but dangerous, too, and I shudder involuntarily. The two of us locate Pete at the same time – he's leaning against the wall staring into space, and he looks utterly miserable – so I hurry over to reach him before Taggie does.

'Everyone's sitting down for food,' I say brightly, when I'm still a few metres away. Pete looks up, his eyes narrowing a fraction as he's dragged back into the present moment.

'Right.' He flashes a flat smile. 'Come on, then.'

I glance around fearfully, trying to see where Taggie went, but she must have scarpered again. The way she was looking at Pete, I wouldn't be surprised if she's gone to fetch an axe to chop off his head.

'What's up?' Pete asks, as we take our seats and he notices my jumpy demeanour.

'What?' I say, distracted. 'Oh, nothing. I was just . . . Taggie.'

'Relax,' he says, smiling at me reassuringly as he holds up his glass to be filled by a passing waiter. 'I know Taggie, remember. She's an ice queen when she needs to be. There's no way she'd cause a scene in a place like this.'

I think about the tears Taggie had to fight to contain in front of me, and experience an unexpected stab of irritation towards Pete. She doesn't seem like an ice queen to me, but I suppose it suits him to label her as one – it must help him to feel less guilty for breaking her heart.

The first course of antipasto arrives, and I watch in a daze as Pete tears apart strips of prosciutto and dips warm bread in the tapenade. He's drinking red wine at an alarming speed, and seems incapable of sitting still. For all his assurances that everything will be fine, he's clearly extremely jittery, and this makes me feel even more unsettled than I did before. I can barely eat a thing, and twice I crash my own wine glass against the one full of water when I set it down. I think I'd feel better if Taggie simply came and sat at the table with us – at least then I wouldn't have to keep checking over my shoulder.

'So,' Pete says, when the attentive waiter has removed our plates. 'Got any New Year's resolutions?'

Is he being serious?

'Um . . .' I reply, baffled that he would ask such an inane question in these circumstances.

'Mine is to travel more,' he barrels on. 'We should pick our next holiday destination tonight. Right now! I vote for somewhere sunny. How about Easter?'

'I don't think I'd get the time off,' I remind him, which is the truth, but I see my response has disappointed him.

'You could ask, though.'

'I will,' I concur. 'But I don't think it's fair on everyone else, to be honest with you. I got Christmas off.'

'Doesn't it ever get to you?' he wants to know. 'Being so overworked and underpaid?'

'I love my job,' I say, perhaps with more impatience than I meant to. Pete's always been so supportive of my crazy hours in the past. I had no idea that he thought I was being taken advantage of – and my defences go up automatically.

'Have you ever looked into working in private health-care?' he asks, finishing another glass of wine.

I fiddle with my fork. 'No.'

'But wouldn't it mean earning more?'

'It's not really about the money, though,' I counter. 'Being a nurse isn't just a job to me – it's who I am. If I did anything else, I'd be miserable.'

I want him to respond by applauding my dedication, but instead he just smiles sadly and stares down at his place setting. It is hard for people to understand how much my job means to me sometimes – especially those who work in the private sector – but I'd always thought Pete was one hundred per cent supportive. Tonight, it feels as if he almost pities me, and I don't like it one bit. Then again, perhaps he's just being defensive because he's so on edge. I know he must be, because I am, too. There's a crackling unease in the air between us, and I get the feeling that anything either of us says or does is going to irritate the other.

'Nature calls,' Pete announces then, pushing out his chair so that it scrapes across the wooden floor and walking stiffly back out towards the reception. Why, oh why, did we decide to stay here? I think despairingly. Only a few hours ago we were wrapped naked around each other, and I felt as if he was an extension of me – but now he feels distant again, like a stranger.

I sip my glass of wine morosely, studiously ignoring the solicitous waves coming from Gladys and her husband, who are seated a few tables away. The candle flickers as I breathe through the flame, and I listen in silence to the laughter and hushed conversation emanating from each corner of the room. When the main course arrives and there's still no sign of Pete, I toss down my napkin and go in search of him.

I wait by the toilets at first, feeling ridiculous, and ask another male guest to check inside for a tall, ginger-haired man in a blue shirt. When he comes out and assures me the bathroom is deserted, I wander through into a large ballroom, then discover an empty bar area. Aside from various waiting staff and a buoyantly courteous middle-aged Italian man with salt-and-pepper hair, I don't see anyone, and I'm just heading back through the entrance lounge when I hear it, the sound of angry voices coming through a door behind the reception desk. Ignoring the lump of apprehension that's wedged tight in my throat, I tiptoe forwards and press my ear to the wood.

43

Taggie

I was waiting for him when he came out of the toilet.

I know Pete well enough to predict exactly how he will behave when faced with a situation he finds deeply uncomfortable, so I knew he would proceed to drink too much and would therefore need to empty his bladder. Staying carefully out of sight until I hear the sound of the water running followed by the hand dryer, I ready myself, then take a step forwards to block his path.

When he sees me, he says nothing at first, just looks at me in that resigned way that I remember. He knows I have him cornered, but he's not going down without a fight.

'So, this is where you work now, then?' he remarks, looking around. 'Bit nicer than your old office in Farringdon.'

I ignore him.

'You need to stop messaging me, Pete,' I say, making myself look at him.

'I thought we should talk,' he argues. I can't fathom that this is the same man I used to share bubble baths with on a Sunday evening, each of us taking it in turns to read out sections of the paper and then laughing when the pages inevitably ended up in the water. Some weekend mornings, he would sneak out to the bakery on the corner of our road, then bring a platter of my favourite pastries to the bedroom. I used to tell him off for dropping flakes of buttery pastry on the sheets, and he would shut me up by kissing me. What happened to that man?

'There's nothing to talk about.'

He sighs. 'There is, Tags—'

'Don't call me that.'

He pulls himself up a little taller, which strikes me as classically stupid, given that I barely reach his chest, even in these four-inch heels.

'We should talk about the b—'

'DON'T!' I almost shout, bringing up my hand. Tears are threatening now, but I'll be damned if I'll let myself cry in front of him – not again.

'I just wanted to tell you to leave me alone,' I say again, ironing out the tremble in my voice through sheer force of will. 'You have a new girlfriend now, so focus on her.'

I wonder if Lucy told him that we ran into each other. For some reason, I don't think she did – but then she presumably hasn't realised what I have. She hasn't remembered the place we met.

'Will it help you to know why?' Pete asks then, his voice now more conciliatory.

'Why what?' I demand, crossing my arms defensively across my chest. The tears are still there, I can feel them, and it's taking every ounce of self-control I have not to let them fall.

'Why all of it,' he exclaims. 'Why I ended things in the first place, why I didn't come back after you told me, and why I wasn't there after it happened.'

'I don't want to talk about what happened,' I say, hating

how fearful I sound. 'Just leave me alone, Pete – I'm warning you.'

'What will you do?' he says childishly. 'Set your Italian boyfriend on me?'

He must mean Marco, I realise, and it's so bloody typical of him that I find myself laughing. Trust Pete to be jealous, even after everything he's done, after everything he left me to go through alone.

'He's not my boyfriend,' I spit. 'But if he was, he'd be a massive upgrade on you.'

He opens his mouth to retort, but I turn on my high heels and walk quickly away, heading resolutely for Sal's office, and the lock it has on the door. Before I can barricade myself inside, however, Pete has run after me and shouldered open the door, sending me staggering backwards across the carpet.

'GET OUT!' I yell, reaching for the phone. 'I mean it, Pete. I'll call the police.'

'No, you won't,' he replies, but there's no menace in his voice. He sounds beaten down and exhausted. Despite my better judgement, I replace the receiver in the cradle and push the spare wheelie chair towards him with my foot.

'Sit down,' I instruct, pulling out Sal's chair and lowering myself on to it with a sigh.

He does as he's told, his eyes heavy with sadness, and the two of us stare at each other.

'What happened to us?' I say quietly. 'When did we become these people?'

'All I ever wanted,' he says, his big hands resting on his thighs, 'was for us to look after each other – but you would never let me.'

I'm about to argue back, but then realise there's nothing I can say. I know that what he's accusing me of is true.

'You had to be the one in charge of everything,' he goes on. 'You hated it when I surprised you, or when I tried to help you. You shut me out so many times that eventually I stopped trying – and I thought I loved you enough not to mind, but . . .'

'But you didn't,' I finish sadly.

'I realised that I wasn't being myself with you. I felt like I couldn't be,' he admits, and I look at him in surprise.

'Of course you could.'

'No, Tags, I couldn't. I felt like there was no balance with you, with us, and it ate away at me until there was nothing left. It wasn't that I didn't love you; it was that I couldn't.'

I close my eyes briefly, and tears snake out across my cheeks.

I did always want to be the one in charge, he's right about that. And I did struggle to let my guard down in front of him, but that was only because I've never known how to be vulnerable. I was brought up to be tough, to stand on my own size threes and not allow anyone to make assumptions about me, or look down on me as if I was helpless. But then, when something happened that I couldn't control, something that tore through me with a ferocious misery from which I had no escape, and I needed Pete to be there to catch me, he was already gone.

Pete has his head in his hands now, and he doesn't look at me as he continues.

'When you told me about the baby, I was just so scared. We had only just split up, and we'd been arguing so much.

I didn't see how we could bring a child into that, and I was worried that you wouldn't let me into its life, that you would do it all by yourself, like you do everything.'

'You told me you didn't want it,' I remind him, the memory of his words even now cutting through me with such agony. 'You said I should get rid of it.'

'I never said that,' he protests. 'I wished it hadn't happened, but I would never have told you to do that. When you told me about it that day, you felt like a stranger. You were so, I dunno, smug about it all, like you'd won or something. It was as if you thought you could wave that baby under my nose and I'd come running back to you.'

'Was that so wrong?' I ask, raising my voice. 'We had been together for five years, Pete. We lived together. You were my best friend – I assumed that would count for something.'

He shrugs dejectedly, unable even now to give me the answer I needed to hear then. I want him to say that he was wrong, but even if he did, it wouldn't change what happened next.

'When I got that call saying you'd lost it,' he says, and I have to dig my fingernails into my arm to stop myself from screaming, 'it absolutely destroyed me, Tags, it really did.'

'It destroyed *you*?' I cry. 'You didn't even want it!'

'It's not that simple, though, is it?' he says. 'It was still my baby, just as much as it was yours. I'm devastated, too.'

'You didn't even come to the hospital,' I snap, wiping the tears off my cheeks with both hands. 'My dad told me that he called you, but you never even bothered to show up.'

'I did,' he mutters, and I stare at him in shock.

'No, you didn't.'

'I was there,' he says, and looks right at me so I can see the blues of his eyes. I used to love staring into those eyes so much. The first thing I thought of when I found out I was pregnant was that I wanted our baby to inherit them.

'I just couldn't come in. I couldn't face it. You'd never let me be there for you before, and I didn't know how to even begin to do it then.'

'I needed you,' I say then, and immediately I'm sobbing again. Pete shifts in his seat, still immobilised by his stupid dread of doing or saying the wrong thing. What he doesn't seem to understand, and which I can't find the strength to tell him through my tears, is that I was still in love with him back then. He was the one I wanted to be there – not my parents, not the doctors and nurses – but him. That's why I can't forgive him. I thought that he wasn't even there – the fact that he was is new information, and I begin to process it as I dab at my eyes with a tissue from the box on Sal's desk.

'I'm sorry, Tag,' he says, and it's the first time I've heard him sound properly sincere since before we broke up. 'I'm sorry for all of it.'

'You were there at the hospital?' I ask, to be certain that I've understood this right, and he nods.

'Pete,' I say, knotting my fingers together to stop them shaking, 'where did you meet Lucy?'

I can tell I've caught him off guard with the question, and his cheeks flame red with distress.

'Out,' he mutters. 'In a bar.'

'Liar,' I say, standing up so I'm almost the same height

307

as him. 'I saw her that day. She looked after me when the ambulance brought me in. I remember her face.'

Pete opens and closes his mouth.

'Did you pick her up there, at the hospital?' I demand. 'While your ex-girlfriend of five years was lying bleeding and crying in a cubicle, wondering where you were. Did you chat up the fucking nurse that had just mopped me up?'

'No.' He shakes his head. 'It wasn't like that.'

'Tell me, then. What was it like?'

Another shake of the head.

We both start as the office door opens to reveal Lucy. It's obvious straight away that she's been crying, but they aren't tears of pity for me or for her, they're tears of anger. I know, because I have shed so many of the same.

'Taggie,' she says, her eyes flickering over her boyfriend before finding mine. 'It's true, I did meet Pete that day. I'm so sorry.'

There's a short and mutually horrified silence, and then I'm up on my feet and pushing past both of them. I hesitate for no more than a split second in the deserted hallway, then turn and run blindly out into the night.

44

Lucy

I have never forgotten what it felt like to be cheated on by Johnny when I was nine, but he wasn't the only boy to trample all over my feelings. When I was fourteen, a boy named Toby wrote me a note in class, asking me to be his girlfriend. I had been harbouring a secret crush on him for over a year at the time, so I immediately replied with the word 'YES', written in pink highlighter, only for him to announce to the entire room that he'd only been joking. That one stayed with me for a while.

It took me years to risk acting on another secret infatuation, but when I did, it was with Spencer. I met him while I was studying, and he was the epitome of charming. Everyone loved Spenny – he was the life and laughter of every party, the ultimate gentleman who held open doors, picked up the tab on dates and, best of all, he was hopelessly devoted to me. At least, I thought he was.

It started with small comments, here and there. Casual questions about what I'd eaten for lunch that day, and reactions of disbelief when I told him honestly that it had been a salad. 'Don't worry, juicy Lucy,' he would say, patting me on the bottom. 'I'll still love you no matter what.'

The months passed, and slowly but surely the little confidence that I had started to fall away. I stopped seeing friends, stopped eating carbs, and stopped being able to look at myself in the mirror. Spencer made sure that he was always the one comforting me if I was feeling bad about the way I looked, but he was manipulating me in such a clever way that I wasn't even aware of it. Even Julia, whose distrusting dial is permanently switched round to the highest setting, was taken in by Spencer's charm offensive. When we would visit my dad and her, the two of them would grin along when he referred to me as 'squishy', and neither seemed fazed when he playfully tutted over how many slices of toast I had for breakfast.

It was after a full year of small but devastating put-downs that I discovered Spencer had been cheating on me with a girl he'd met online. I stumbled across their Facebook messages to each other, but instead of confronting him like any normal, self-respecting woman would, I blamed myself. This girl was slimmer than me, and prettier, and I honestly believed then that I had forced my own boyfriend into the arms of another woman because I couldn't resist the odd chocolate biscuit. The stupid thing was that the sadder I was, the more junk I consumed, and so I was the heaviest I had ever been. This, coupled with the knowledge that the man who I thought loved me was fooling around behind my back, led me deep into a dark depression.

It was Julia who worked it out eventually, of course, and who went to Spencer's posh city office and called him out in front of his colleagues. It's no wonder that she's so hyper-protective now, but it still doesn't seem to matter how many times she tells me that I look perfect, and that Spencer is no better than a sociopath. When I'm at my lowest ebb, I still find myself summoning back that poor, sad and slightly-too-heavy version of myself, and I let her get inside my head again.

Over the years, I've seen friends of both sexes treated appallingly by the people claiming to love them, and I've witnessed first-hand the scars that their behaviour can leave behind. My dad has never got over the hurt inflicted on him by my mum – he carries it with him like a rucksack full of rocks, and I know I have been doing the same. It's all very well people urging you to leave the past behind you – the reality is, it's not that easy.

All this is going through my head as I study Pete's rigid profile. After Taggie ran out of the office in tears, he simply put his head in his hands and I couldn't get more than a few words out of him. Eventually I suggested we come back to our table. I needed time to make sense of what I'd heard, and I assumed he would get straight back on the wine – but he hasn't. I can't face any more alcohol, either, just like I can't face food. This latest revelation has made me feel as if I'm tied into literal knots.

I knew I had seen Taggie somewhere before, and now that I know exactly where, I can't believe I didn't recognise her sooner. But then, why would I ever make that connection? She had been in such a state when she was brought in, near hysterical as she begged and pleaded for the doctor to tell her that her baby was OK. I could see it in her eyes, though – she knew just as well as the assembled team of medical professionals that the baby was lost. There was blood already drying on her legs, and she had it all over her hands. Her father, who I now know to be the mysterious Manny, had arrived not long after

Taggie did, and I remember that he wept silently as he stared down at her.

Pete should have been there, too, but he wasn't.

I was probably only in Taggie's hospital cubicle for a few minutes, but seeing her so distraught had shaken me up. It was the main reason I went down for a chocolate bar in the first place – I needed something to comfort me. It feels abhorrent to me now that what I actually ended up finding was Pete.

Everything I heard him say to Taggie, about his reasons for breaking things off, and even his initial reluctance towards the pregnancy, makes sense to me, but what I don't understand is how he could start another relationship so soon after such a loss. I need to ask him if I'm going to stand any chance of muddling my way through all this mess, but I'm also terrified of what he'll say. I don't want to believe that Pete – my kind, thoughtful, protective and loving Pete – could be the sort of man who not only refuses to support a woman he used to love through something so traumatic, but also replaces her with the next girl he meets. It's unfathomable.

People are starting to get up from their tables and drift through to the ballroom. The DJ has kicked off his eclectic playlist of song requests, and the guests look giddy with the promise of a party. Pete glances towards the doorway, then looks at me.

'I don't really feel like dancing, do you?'

I shake my head. 'No.'

'Come on,' he says, taking my hand as he stands up, leading me, not towards the flickering disco lights, but the hotel exit. As we reach the hallway, I wonder vaguely if I should tell one of the staff that Taggie's upset, but I don't want to enrage her even more. She must have friends she can turn to here; it is her home, after all.

No, I decide, glancing up at Pete's pale features. The best thing either of us can do for Taggie tonight is respect her wishes that we leave her alone.

45

Taggie

The cold hits me like an errant wave, causing me to gasp as I half-run, half-stagger down the driveway of the hotel. For the first time in my life, I curse my high heels, which were not designed with gravel in mind. All I can think is that I need to get away. I can't look at Pete, or Lucy – I can't look at either of them.

Wrapping my arms tightly around my shoulders, I hurry through the side gate and along the path leading down to the lake, tripping every so often in my haste, and looking regularly over my shoulder to make sure nobody is following me. Lucy must have heard everything. I know she did – I could tell from the look on her face. At least she had the grace to be honest with me, unlike Pete. I don't even know who he is any more.

By the time I reach the park, I'm far enough away to stop running, but my heart is still racing with anxiety. Looking back the way I came, I see the Casa Alta sitting on top of the hill, so beautiful and striking against the dark backdrop of the surrounding landscape. Golden light leaks out of the windows, making the night air glow, and I can just about make out the silhouettes of party guests on the ground floor. The disco will have started by now; people will be wondering where I am. I know it's my party, my big night, my chance to show Sal what I'm made of – but I can't be there, I can't do it.

Every time my mind takes me back to that day, I want to scratch the memory away. Sometimes when it wakes me in the night, it feels so real that I pull aside the covers and check for blood on the sheets. I imagine that I can feel the pain of it again, clutching at my stomach like the talons of some hell-sent creature, and without warning I'm bent double, clawing at the wall.

I lost my baby. My heart, my soul, my unplanned but so welcome reason for getting up in the morning, for breathing in and back out again, for keeping myself safe and cared for, the very purpose for existing and the best single thing I had ever done.

How can all that have come to nothing? Where is my baby? I ache for it.

I sit down abruptly on the cold, hard earth and raise my hands until they're in my hair, yanking out my ponytail with a sob and clenching my fists until I can feel my scalp burning. Lifting my chin, I see stars, way up above me, and I curse them. And then I'm screaming, and it feels as if my chest will burst, and my hands are on the earth, the dirt under my nails, my throat burning with misery and my guttural howls like that of a wild animal.

I'm so sorry, I think helplessly. *I'm so sorry that I lost you.*

When I come back to myself, I'm sprawled sideways beside the path. Ahead of me at the base of the lake, Como town is throbbing with colour, noise and activity. Revellers are spilling out on to the streets in anticipation of the fireworks, and I can hear music coming from the live band that is playing on the temporary stage near the war memorial. As I draw closer and am enveloped by small groups of excited people, the temperature rises enough for me to loosen the grip on my arms. I know my face must be a mess of cried-off mascara, but nobody seems to notice. Everyone is too busy dancing, or cheering, or sipping their cups of sweet *vin brulé* as they snuggle against their significant other.

Stalls selling hot dogs, burgers, candy floss and over-priced bottles of bubbly are set up along the promenade, and bins overflow with takeaway plates and dirty napkins. A group of young Italian men attempt to block my path, jokingly holding out their hands for me to dance with them and offering me a sip of whatever they have decanted into their plastic water bottles. I dodge around them, shaking my head, refusing to meet their eyes, and carry on through the crowds until I can see the ice rink in the distance. At no point have I thought about where I'm going, but now that I'm here, I find that my legs seem to have their own purpose, and I'm carried by them through the crowds, along to the crossing, and towards where I know he'll be.

La Vita é Bella restaurant is a hive of activity, with every table occupied both inside and out in the little greenhouse area, and it's a few minutes before I see him. He's just emerged from the kitchen carrying two pizzas, an easy smile on his face and a burnt-orange shirt making his green eyes glow even brighter than usual. I stay back, under the shadow of a nearby doorway, but somehow he still sees me. A few seconds pass where he simply frowns in confusion, and then, before I can gather myself together enough to turn and run away for the second time tonight, he's deposited the pizzas and is hurrying over.

'What is the matter?' he asks at once, taking in my lack of coat, my wild hair, my mud-covered hands, my tear-stained face.

When I don't answer, he takes a breath and then gently pulls me forwards against his chest, wrapping his arms around me.

'You are freezing,' he exclaims, running his hands briskly up and down my arms. 'Where is your coat?'

'At the hotel,' I mumble. 'I had to . . . I couldn't . . .'

'It's OK,' he says, interrupting me before I start crying again. 'It will be OK.'

'Marco!' yells a short man with a stern expression, who's just emerged from the outdoor seating area. He takes one look at me, before launching into a volley of Italian. I realise then how this must look, some girl turning up here in the middle of Marco's shift, covered in tears and falling into his arms. I would make the same assumption as his boss – that I'm just another random tourist that Marco's messed around.

'I should go,' I say, extracting myself, but Marco looks uncertain.

'No,' he tells me, his hands on my shoulders. 'Wait here.'

The short man and I watch – he with irritation and I with numbness – as Marco pushes open a door inside the restaurant and disappears, only to return less than a minute later with his battered leather jacket in his hands.

'Here.' He thrusts it at me. 'Put this on and go to the bar. I will meet you there.'

I usually hate being told what to do, but for some reason Marco's measured instructions are comforting, and I accept the jacket with gratitude, pulling it on as I turn to go and hugging it close to my body. Vista Lago is only a few streets away, and I inhale Marco's scent as I make my way there. It's faintly peppery, with an undertone of citrus, and the jacket feels warm and soft. For the first time since I ran out of the office back at the Casa Alta, I feel safe.

The bar is predictably heaving, but I'm glad of the anonymity all the merry bodies provide. I don't have any money on me, having fled the hotel without my bag, but Marco must have let his friend know that I was coming, because as soon as I find an empty stool in the corner and sit down, a large glass of red wine appears in front of me.

Alcohol feels like a bad idea, but I'm craving something to balance me out a bit and stop my heart from hammering against my chest. I still feel cold all over, despite the heat of the bar and Marco's jacket, and my teeth continue to chatter as I bring the glass up to my lips. I don't have any idea what I'm doing, but I know I can't go back. I don't even want to see Elsie, or speak to my family. I need to make sense of all this by myself.

The clock behind the bar informs me that there's only two hours of this year to go, and good riddance to it as well, I mutter internally, taking another swig. The DJ is playing some sort of U2 mega mix, and I watch through hazy eyes as people begin to dance and sing along. Only twenty-four hours ago, Shelley and I were doing the exact same thing, but now I could no more face dancing than I could fly a seaplane over the lake. I knew that talking to Pete about the baby, our baby, would make everything come flooding back. Now I feel as if I've lost it all over again, and the pain is unbearable.

'*Ciao, bella.*'

I look up from where I've been staring glassy-eyed into my drink. Marco's expression is all concern, his jet-black hair windswept as if he ran all the way here.

'What happened to work?' I ask, my voice croaky.

He shrugs. 'I quit.'

'What?' I'm appalled. 'Why?'

He touches my cheek, just briefly, to reassure me. 'My boss would not let me come, so I told him he had no choice in the matter. He didn't like that very much.'

'I'm so sorry,' I wail, making to cover my face with my hands, then recoiling when I see how muddy they are. 'I'll talk to him for you.'

'*Dai*,' he says, gently lowering my arms. 'It's OK. I hate that job anyway.'

U2 have been replaced by Justin Bieber, and an elderly Italian couple are now trying to waltz along to lyrics about it being too late to say sorry.

'I will get us a drink,' he says, and I watch him move towards the bar. He hasn't even asked me what happened, or why I'm upset. He didn't ask in Bellagio, either, after I bumped into Pete, or on the night he showed me the boat. But it's not because he doesn't care – clearly, he does – it's just not his way. I guess that I knew subconsciously he wouldn't pry when I decided to head straight to the restaurant and find him. He seems to know instinctively the right thing to do and say to make me feel protected, and I can't deny that's exactly how I feel right now. I remember again the pull I felt towards him that night we properly met, and how familiar he seemed despite being merely some stranger who'd rescued me from the lake. It's still there – but now I feel more able to accept it.

'I brought you amaretto,' he says on his return. 'You need something sweet, you're shaking.'

'*Grazie*,' I say, taking it out of his hand, his fingers brushing against mine. 'I'll pay you back.'

He scoffs.

'Be quiet.'

There's a pause, and I watch him sip his beer in silent contemplation.

'I'm sorry,' I say again, and this time he looks exasperated.

'Taggie,' he says, his voice low. Putting his drink down on the wooden ledge next to us, he cradles my upturned face in both his hands and stares at me. 'You have nothing to be sorry for, OK?'

'OK,' I murmur, blinking rapidly.

'Good,' he replies, and for a second I think he might kiss me, but instead he lets go of my face.

'I am happy,' he tells me, clinking his bottle against the side of my glass.

'Oh?'

'That you are here with me,' he confides. 'Now we can spend New Year together.'

His straightforward positivity is endearing, but there's no energy inside me to take it in.

'I'm glad I'm here,' I say honestly, getting up on unsteady feet and giving him the best attempt at a smile that I can muster. 'One day I'll explain everything, I promise.'

As I turn away towards the bathroom, I catch a flicker of something pass across his eyes – the echo of a feeling, perhaps, a silent wish – and just like that, I'm warm again.

46

Lucy

Pete is crying.

The two of us left the warm cocoon of the Casa Alta Hotel a few minutes ago and made our way outside on to the front lawn. There's still over half an hour until the firework display is due to start, so when he roused himself from a long, self-imposed silence and suggested coming out here, I initially assumed it was to bag ourselves a good spot from which to watch. I was wrong about that.

'Oh, Pete,' I console, grasping his arm as he goes to cover his face with his hands. He's sobbing so hard that his shoulders are heaving, and his muffled howl of anguish makes me feel as if my heart is shattering into pieces.

'Sorry,' he splutters, fiercely wiping his eyes and cheeks. His face is collapsed with grief. It's awful to see him like this, and I'm reminded uncomfortably of the first time I saw Taggie, so desperate and hopeless in the hospital.

'Taggie?' I guess, but he shakes his head.

'No.'

'The baby?'

He can't bring himself to answer, but nods his head up and down, giving in to more angry tears as he takes in my stricken expression. Stepping forwards, I pull him into my arms as best I can, my spiky high heels sinking into the mud, and rub his back until he gets himself under control.

'Sorry,' he keeps muttering, and I hush him. I don't have to be a nurse to know that he needs to let it all out, and so I let him, saying nothing more than a few encouraging and sympathetic words. It's freezing out here, with a biting wind that seems intent on cutting right through me, and I squeeze Pete a fraction tighter in an attempt to warm up.

Eventually, after much sniffing and snuffling, he pulls back and fixes me with puffy blue eyes, his expression conveying everything I know he must be feeling – humiliation, wretchedness and guilt. As slapped sideways as I've been by the evening's events thus far, and the revelation that he's been anything but honest with me, I can't help but feel sorry for him. Yes, he acted badly and he lied, but there's no denying how terrible he feels now that he's been forced to face it. He needs me to be there for him, and at the moment, I'm glad that I can be. This is about more than our relationship; it's about loss and grief.

'I'm a fucking mess,' he grunts, attempting a laugh.

'Don't do that,' I chide gently. 'Don't take on more than you need to. I'm still here, aren't I?'

He nods, fighting back more tears.

'I don't understand why you are.'

'Did you not hear me this morning?' I ask. 'When I told you that I loved you, Pete, I meant it. I'm not going to abandon you when you're so upset.'

'I don't deserve you,' he sniffs. No man has ever said that to me before except my dad in the aftermath of my mum leaving, when I nursed him back from debilitating heartbreak. He was grieving the loss of his marriage, of the person he loved, while Pete is grieving the loss of his child. A baby he never knew he wanted until it was gone.

'I've been such an idiot,' he groans now, looking at me again. 'I thought I could just ignore what I was feeling and carry on as normal, but when I saw Taggie tonight, I just . . .'

Pete trails off, unable to put into words exactly what he felt, and I glance back up towards the hotel. I can hear strains of Abba playing in the ballroom, and the shrieks of dancing guests as they swing each other around, no doubt giddy at the thought of the year ending, another beginning.

'Talk to me,' I urge Pete, taking his hand and leading him slowly across the grass. There's a flower bed full of white winter roses ahead of us, glowing mutely in the darkness.

He takes a deep breath.

'What do you want to know?'

'Everything,' I say. 'Start at the beginning.'

We're far enough down the curve of the hill now to see the lake. At this time of night, with just the moon for company, it looks like a vast swathe of ebony satin. The iconic mountains that sit so boldly on the horizon during daylight hours are shrouded now under the cloak of night, and the dark sweep of sky feels limitless.

'Taggie was always vigilant when it came to taking her pill,' Pete says at last, sounding regretful. 'When she first told me that she was pregnant, I thought she was lying – I accused her of making it up to win me back.'

'Oh,' I say, unable to disguise my dismay.

'I know,' he replies, his expression grim. 'All we'd done

for two weeks was snipe at each other and throw accusations around. I know that's not an excuse, but that's how it was.'

'And then?' I press gently.

'She showed me the test, then made me sit in the bathroom with her while she did another one, just to prove that she was telling the truth.'

He screws his face up. 'I should never have let her do that.'

I wait for him to gather himself again before giving him another soft, verbal nudge to continue the story.

'She was really happy, and so sure that the baby would change everything,' he tells me. 'We had talked about having a family one day, you know, before – so she knew I wanted children. But all I could think in the moment was that it was wrong. Her face when I told her . . .' He stops, fresh anguish distorting his features.

'It was horrible,' he finishes.

Turning from the view to face Pete, I take hold of his rigid hands and start to rub his fingers. I made sure I put on my coat before we came out here, but my gloves are back in the apartment in Como, and my fingers are stinging with cold.

'She was doing what she always did, which was tell me how things were going to be,' he recalls. 'She told me that we were having the baby, and that we would be doing it together. I just saw red.'

'Did you really try to persuade her to consider an abortion?' I ask, needing to know the answer. Taggie had intimated as much when I was listening through the door of the office.

'No.' Pete shakes his head, the hurt back in his eyes. 'All I said was that having the baby wouldn't change anything between us, and she got so angry with me then. She was yelling at me that we had to at least try to make things work, for the baby's sake, but she wasn't asking – she was telling. I'd had five years of her telling me what to do, and I just snapped. I couldn't do it any more.'

He lets out a long, deep sigh and stares out across the lake.

'I told her I didn't want to raise a child with her,' he mutters. 'That I didn't want this.'

'Oh, Pete,' I sigh, with sympathy rather than distaste.

'I don't even know why I said it,' he says, shaking his head. He looks as if he might cry again, and I'm aware that I should wrap a comforting arm around him again, but something stops me.

'It was the whole horrible situation we'd found ourselves in that I didn't want, and all the hurt and pain – I didn't mean the baby.'

'But then she lost it,' I finish, closing my eyes as an image of the Taggie I saw in the hospital floats unheeded into my mind, her poor face split in two with the pain of what was happening to her, what had already happened. It upsets me now even more than it did then. Whatever picture Pete has painted of Taggie, I have met her myself now, and I have my own view. I feel nothing but sorrow for her – for both of them.

'Yes,' he mutters, wiping his eyes. 'She lost it. And she blames me for that.'

'It's not your fault,' I tell him quickly. 'It's nobody's fault.'

'I know what she thinks,' he says, his breath pooling in the cold air in front of us. 'She thinks that because I didn't jump for joy when I found out, that I somehow jinxed the whole pregnancy. Do you think she's right?'

I can't bear the sadness in his eyes.

'No,' I say, finally stepping forwards and sliding my arms around his back so I can hug him. 'She's not right about that. I suppose blaming you helps her not to blame herself as much, which I bet she still does, regardless. That's the thing, though – neither of you could have done anything that would have made any difference either way. There is no blame, because there is no one at fault.'

'She moved out the morning after she told me she was pregnant,' he goes on, holding me tightly against him. 'Told me she was going to stay with her folks for a while. I must have messaged and called hundreds of times, but she never responded. I didn't hear anything from her for three weeks – not a text or anything – then Manny called and told me she'd been taken to hospital, and . . .'

He didn't need to finish the end of that sentence, because I knew what had happened next. I'd been in the team who tended to her first.

'And me?' I ask tentatively, and feel him relax beneath my arms.

'You were like an angel.'

'Don't be silly,' I scold, but there's a grain of happiness behind it.

'I mean it,' he insists. 'You were the first person to be nice to me in what felt like forever. My friends were all pissed off with me about Taggie; my mum was on the phone daily, telling me to man up and beg for forgiveness;

and that day in the hospital, Manny looked at me with such . . .' He pauses, struggling to say the word. 'Well, contempt,' he adds sadly. 'I know he had every right to be angry with me, but he knew me, Lulu, just like they all did. I wasn't a monster, I was still the same old me. I just happened to have fallen out of love with my girlfriend.'

I cast my mind back to all the conversations I've had with friends whose ex-partners did the same thing, and how we vilified them. Hell, I condemned my own mother for falling out of love. But there is truth in what Pete is saying, and it feels like an injustice purely because I'm the one standing here with him, months after it all happened – the one on his side of the emotional crater. But I know how agonising it must have been for Taggie, and when your emotions are as fragile as hers must have been, it's impossible to be logical and fair. Her heart was broken, and so irrationality was winning over everything else.

'She made it all sound so callous and grubby earlier tonight, this thing between you and me,' Pete says then, his sniff turning into a sigh. 'But it wasn't like that. I know I met you at the worst possible time, but we just got on, didn't we? For that ten minutes in the canteen, it was like a light had gone on after months of darkness. That sounds really cheesy, doesn't it?'

'Yes,' I agree. 'But I understand what you mean. I didn't forget you for a moment, you know. I kept hoping that I would somehow bump into you again.'

'All I did for weeks was work, and mope around at the flat. I didn't see anyone, I barely spoke to anyone I didn't have to. All the stuff with Taggie and the baby left me feeling so numb, and she point blank refused to see or speak to me. But through that whole time, at the edges of it all, you were there in my head. I don't think I even realised it until Sean broke his leg and I saw you again, then as soon as I did, I just knew.'

'I remember thinking it was fate,' I say, smiling up at him as I remember how thrilled I was to see him.

'Thank God Sean broke his leg,' Pete adds, the hint of humour in his eyes again. 'Remind me to buy him a pint sometime.'

I smile in response, but I'm not ready to draw another of our lines and move forwards quite yet. I still have a few questions that I need answers to. It must be nearing midnight now, because I can hear the other guests crunching over the gravel and heading down the hill towards us. There's a buzz of excited anticipation in the air, and I edge closer to Pete so that my voice will be muffled.

'Did you really never speak to Taggie again?' I say, and Pete sighs.

'I tried to,' he replies. 'But her parents screened all my calls. After a while, Manny got in touch and told me that Taggie wanted to sell the flat, and that I should contact him from now on. That's how it's been until now – until I saw her standing there by the harbour in Bellagio. I had no idea she'd even left London, let alone the UK. After we lost the baby, she cut herself off from all our mutual friends, and I may as well have been dead to her most loyal crew. None of them would give me the time of day.'

'Have you spoken to anyone about the miscarriage?' I want to know, and he takes a deep breath that's laced with discomfort.

'I told my mum, but apart from that, just you,' he admits.

'Has it helped?' I say, already knowing the answer.

'It has,' he confirms, kissing me lightly on the lips. 'You have.'

'One minute!' someone calls from behind us, and I peer round Pete's bulk to see a large crowd of people standing a little way away on the grass. Everyone's faces are turned upward in preparation, and the charged atmosphere is making the air feel warmer somehow. By rights, tonight ought to have been the final crack in my already shattered relationship with Pete, but there are too many pieces I still need to make sense of in my head. I need to lay them out, like a broken-up jigsaw on a table, and work out if there's a way of fitting them back together again. It can wait, though. There is still time.

As I turn back around and feel Pete's arms tighten around me, I see the distorted reflection of the first New Year firework explode across the surface of the lake.

47

Taggie

I had thought it would be hard to watch as this year ended and another began. I assumed that I would think only of all the things I had lost, and the mistakes I had made that I could not undo. I was afraid that the clock would strike twelve and I would desperately try to claw the hands back around, force them to rotate unnaturally until I could take back what I wanted from the past. But when the crowds around us cheer and the fireworks begin to explode overhead, I feel nothing but relief. I have survived this year, I am still here, and I'm not alone.

Marco and I left the bar just before midnight to come down here to the lake. It's so busy tonight that it could be the middle of summer, except that it's still absolutely freezing.

'Aren't you cold?' I ask after a time. Marco refused to have his leather jacket back, and is standing next to me now in just shirtsleeves.

'I am fine.'

I peer closely at the tiny bumps all over his bare arm.

'You look cold to me.'

He stops watching the fireworks and turns to me.

'I will live.'

My stomach rumbles, and I try to remember if I had any dinner, or any lunch, for that matter, and find that I can't. It feels like hours ago that I was up at the Casa Alta setting everything up for the party. Sal is not going to be happy with me when I eventually go back.

'I think I'm going to get sacked,' I tell Marco.

'Maybe you should quit first,' he replies. 'Like me.'

'Maybe,' I agree. 'I still can't believe you did that.'

Marco puts his head on one side, and I can see the reflections of the fireworks in his eyes.

'Sometimes the right thing to do is obvious,' he explains pragmatically.

'I feel like it was all my fault,' I reply sheepishly, jumping as an extra loud bang sends a shudder through the air.

'It was not,' he says gently. 'Maybe it is fate that is to blame.'

'I hate fate,' I groan. 'I'd much prefer it if we got to make all the rules.'

'But you cannot control everything,' he argues, clearly amused by me.

'Why not?' I demand.

'Because,' he murmurs, steering me gently out of the way of a passing group of girls wearing glow-in-the-dark bunny ears, 'it is much more fun not knowing what is going to happen.'

I consider this in silence, waiting until the last firework has crashed across the sky before replying. Infuriatingly, I must concede that he has a point. After all, I had no idea that I would end up down here with him tonight and, despite the circumstances and the constant ache in my heart, I'm not having a terrible time. Far from it. But I don't want to let him win the argument, and so I say, 'What about bad things?'

He raises his shoulders, flinching slightly as the icy wind finds us.

'Bad things happen.'

'But if you knew they were coming, then perhaps you'd have time to prepare,' I point out. 'You wouldn't get caught unawares.'

'Did a bad thing happen to you tonight?' he asks then.

I close my mouth.

'Taggie?'

I don't know how to even begin to tell him, so I just shake my head.

'OK,' he says, seemingly nonplussed. 'Shall we go and watch the band?'

I follow him through the cluster of people peeling away from the fence set up around the lake. Now that the display has come to an end, the families with younger children are heading to bed, and I'm forced to run a veritable gauntlet of pushchairs and prams. If it wasn't for the cruel meddling of fate, I'd still be pregnant. Well on my way to becoming a mother for the first time. The fact that I'm not still feels like a sick joke, and I'm forced to take a few deep breaths to stem my tears.

Marco, who has reached instinctively to take my hand, as the two of us are jostled from side to side by human traffic, doesn't appear to be aware of my turmoil, and once again I feel gratitude towards him for understanding when not to pry. By asking me that one simple question just now, he's letting me know that the door to the conversation is open, but that he has no intention of making me walk through it. Whenever something was bothering me with Pete, he would prod and poke and badger at me until I gave in, and we would inevitably end up arguing. No matter how many times it happened, he never seemed to learn not to behave that way, and it was so bloody exasperating. Then again, I think guiltily, perhaps my need to control everything was just as annoying for him.

'Look.' Marco has stopped walking and is pointing at the sky. Grateful for the interruption to my depressing train of thought, I glance up and feel my eyes widen with pleasure. There are hundreds of Chinese paper lanterns in the air, each one glowing bright gold against the blackness, and I watch as they soar upwards away from the earth.

'Each one is a wish,' he tells me, taking a step closer until he's standing right behind me. I can feel the heat of his breath on the back of my neck. 'You whisper what you want into the lantern before you set it free, and then it searches the universe to find it.'

Predictable tears well in my eyes.

The lanterns are merging with the stars high above us now, and it's becoming difficult to tell them apart. After I miscarried, my mum tried to comfort me by telling me to think of the soul I had lost as a star, something that will never dim in beauty or vitality, and at the time I'd dismissed her with scorn, just as I'd cursed the stars earlier tonight. Standing here now with Marco, though, looking up at this twinkling tapestry of hope and wishes, I finally understand why she said it. And not only that, I find that the idea comforts me, too.

'We should get one,' I say, unable to tear my eyes away from the spectacle. 'You could wish for your boat.'

Marco lets out a laugh, before placing a hand on my shoulder.

'You are sweet,' he tells me, sounding genuinely touched. 'But I have already had one wish granted tonight.'

There's a pause as I wonder whether or not to ask him what he means. The amaretto-induced tipsiness I felt immediately after leaving the bar has lessened now, and my nerve has gone with it. I can't assume he's referring to me, but then I also don't see how it could be anything else. His delivery is so often matter-of-fact – it makes him very difficult to read. I'm not sure if I prefer this more serious version of Marco, or the playful one who flicks my ponytail – but I know that I like both more with every passing hour.

Before I can formulate any of my thoughts into words, however, Marco has taken hold of my hand again and is leading me on through the melee of tourists and locals towards the stage. There's a vigorous Italian folk band called Circo Abusivo playing live, each member dressed in an array of colours and a funny hat, and the mood in the audience is one of exuberant joy. It's impossible not to feel cheered by the bouncy beat and the cheeky lyrics, and soon even the perpetually cool Marco is bopping along with abandon, his cheeks pink with effort and a wide smile making him look even more handsome than usual. Groups of Italian teens are dancing together in circles, their shrieks of pleasure making me laugh, and I look up at Marco to see that he's chuckling, too.

It feels like my big showdown with Pete up at the Casa Alta happened days ago, let alone hours. Finding out that he'd been at the hospital after all, but not come in to see me, was upsetting. But then to discover he'd met and presumably fallen for Lucy on the very same day . . . That had felt unforgivable. But is it really? I've spent so many months now dwelling on what happened, so many hours have been wasted just going over and over the events of those few weeks, when what I should have been doing is trying my best to move on. Being here now, in one of my favourite places with – yes, I can't deny it any longer – one of my favourite people, has reminded me that life does go on, and that it's OK to not be sad all the time, or angry. I'm tired of all that. For the rest of tonight, at least, I'm going to shut Pete and what happened away in a closed area of my mind, and try to leave it there.

Marco and I continue dancing together until the band has played their third encore, then we traipse slowly back towards the city centre with the rest of the New Year stragglers. The stars are still there, pinpricks of light decorating the heavy curtain of night, and strains of music drift across the lake from the opposite shore. There is rubbish all over the pavements, but I know that by dawn it will be gone. The people of Como are very serious when it comes to taking care of their beautiful town, and I love them for it.

'Do you want another drink?' Marco asks, slowing down as we pass a small stand selling *vin brulé*. I shake my head.

'I think I'm OK, *grazie*.'

'Shall we go to Vista Lago?' he suggests, stepping over a half-eaten hot dog. 'The bar will be open until the morning, I think.'

'You should go,' I urge, feeling suddenly guilty. 'I've taken up enough of your night as it is.'

'Taggie,' he warns. 'Do not start this silliness again.'

'Sorry,' I mutter, amused by his mock-stern tone. 'I'm just exhausted.'

And I am. Now that I've articulated it, I find that I'm so tired I could curl up under one of the trees and fall straight to sleep.

'Are you going back to the hotel?' he says, putting a hand in the small of my back as we cross the road beside the ice rink. It's closed for the night now, and the shutters have been pulled down on all the wooden stalls in the Christmas Market.

'I . . .' There's a pause as my words wither and die on the end of my tongue. I don't want to go back to the Casa Alta yet. I can't face it – can't face all the questions and rebukes. It doesn't feel like a safe place any more.

'You do not want to go,' Marco guesses, and I nod, feeling pathetic.

'You can stay with me,' he offers, quickly holding up a hand when he sees my shocked expression. 'I mean, sleep over. I have a couch.'

'OK,' I say, before I have time to change my mind, and he smiles with relief.

Marco lives in a small apartment about fifteen minutes' walk away from the lake, not far from Como's central railway station, situated above a grocery store. The air in the stairway up to the front door smells mildly of garlic and lemons, but that scent is replaced by a peppery one that I recognise as his, as soon as we cross the threshold. I'm pleasantly surprised to discover that my Italian friend is fastidiously tidy, and everything in his compact, four-room home appears to have its place.

Ignoring a rather beaten-up green sofa and a low

336

wooden coffee table with a gleaming glass top, I walk across the front room and pick up the photo frame on the mantelpiece.

'Are these your parents?' I ask.

The dark-haired couple in the black and white photo are both smiling, and if I was to guess, I'd say it had been taken up in Bellagio. I recognise the snow-topped mountains in the background.

Marco takes it from me, his expression unreadable.

'Yes,' he says at last. 'It was taken a year before I was born.'

'Are your parents still together?' I ask, even though I have a feeling from his manner that they aren't.

He shakes his head. 'No.'

Apparently, that's as much information as he's willing to share, because before I can reply he's turned his back and is heading into a small kitchen.

'Coffee?'

'No, thank you,' I call. 'Just some mineral water, if you have it?'

The fridge door opens and closes, and I hear a kettle begin to boil.

'Can I borrow your bathroom?' I ask, and he sticks his head around the open door.

'Only if you bring it back.'

'Funny,' I grin, taking off his leather jacket as I leave the room.

I hardly dare look in the mirror, but when I do, I find that I don't look all that bad. The dancing has given me a glow, and the ponytail that I casually scraped back together in the toilet of Vista Lago so many hours ago now has stayed in place all night. That's one of the benefits of having this ridiculously thick hair, I think to myself, going to pull out the bobble and then changing my mind. I don't want to scare Marco by reappearing as a wildebeest, not when he's been so kind to me.

He's sitting on the sofa when I get back and has taken off his shoes. A cup of coffee sits on a coaster on the table, my water beside it, and I pick the glass up gratefully as I lower myself down next to him.

'Thank you,' I say, but he pulls a face.

'It is only water.'

'I mean for letting me stay here,' I explain. 'And for tonight, for looking after me and not asking questions.'

'I think we are friends?' he says, and I nod.

'Of course.'

'Well, then, you do not have to thank me.'

'But I want to,' I argue, poking him, and he grins.

'Then I must let you.'

It's so refreshing, I think to myself, to be able to sit and talk to a man without the conversation descending into an argument. Towards the end of our relationship, all Pete and I ever did was disagree on things. But no, I promised myself that I wouldn't think about him.

'You are tired,' Marco states, raising an eyebrow as I yawn widely.

'Sorry,' I say again, covering my open mouth with my hand. 'It's been a very long day.'

'I can sleep here.' He points to the couch. 'If you would prefer the bed?' But I laugh.

'On *here*?'

We both look down at the snug two-seater sofa we're

sitting on. Marco is a six-foot man – there is no way he'd even fit half of himself on this thing.

'I would make it work,' he assures me, but he's fooling nobody.

'You have the bed,' I order him, copying his mock-stern voice of earlier. 'I insist!'

'Fine,' he says, taking a nonchalant sip of his coffee. 'You are the boss.'

There's a short beat of silence as we look at one another, and I'm aware of a tingling sensation in my hands and along my arms. I'm still only wearing my black party dress, and I shiver involuntarily. Marco, seeing this, leaps to his feet.

'You are cold,' he says, vanishing from the room and returning less than a minute later with a large grey T-shirt and a thick red blanket, which he arranges around my shoulders. He's doing what I have always hated people doing – fussing – but for some reason it doesn't seem to irk me as it usually would. Could it be that I enjoy being looked after by Marco?

'I will leave you alone now,' he says, picking up his coffee. 'Try to get some sleep.'

'OK, boss,' I say, saluting him lamely, and he considers me for a second before crouching down so we're practically nose to nose.

'Goodnight, Taggie,' he breathes. 'Happy New Year, *felice anno nuovo.*'

I go to reply, but no sound comes out. I can't seem to stop gazing at his green eyes, which are so full of warmth as they look at me. The next thing I know, I've leant forward and pressed my mouth up to his, closing my eyes as

I feel his tongue move forwards and brush against mine. My body throbs as he kisses me tenderly and with care, his fingers trailing across one cheek, making me shiver with desire. I can feel a hunger for him building inside me, a passion that I had forgotten could possess me, and press myself harder against him. Marco dips his chin away from my lips and rubs his nose along my cheek. I want him to kiss me again – more than that, I want him to devour me. Help me to forget. But he doesn't.

Instead, he stands up and takes my hand, lacing his long fingers between mine, and smiles.

I watch as he turns and leaves the room in silence, and hear the click as he closes the door behind him.

If anyone had asked me less than twelve hours ago if I thought this fresh, new year would be a happy one, then I would probably have scoffed at them with derision. But now, as I settle down underneath Marco's warm blanket, his T-shirt smelling so deliciously of him against my skin, I'm starting to believe that it really could be.

48

Lucy

I'm still awake when the sun comes up on the first day of the new year.

Pete and I stayed up talking for most of the night, not just about Taggie and the lost baby, but about the future of our relationship. I opened up to him about my struggle to trust people, and he listened as I told him all about my ex, Spencer, and how his barbaric treatment of me had left such deep welts of insecurity.

Pete made it very clear to me that what he wants is for us to look after each other. He wants to be the one to erase all my self-doubt and make me feel like the incredible person he claims I am. It's what I've always wanted, and I should be cartwheeling with joy this morning – but I'm not.

After he fell asleep a few hours ago, I lay here for ages feeling unsettled. Despite all my protestations to Pete about the importance of honesty, there is one thing I still haven't been completely truthful about – and now it's all I can think about. The sad fact is, I haven't been myself with Pete, not consistently. I worry that he loves me because I've been letting him take control and make decisions; I've carefully played the part of the perfect, unswerving girlfriend so well that he's fallen for it completely. I've sold him an image of myself rather than the real thing, made him believe that I'm the cream on his apple pie, and now I'm scared that he won't like who I really am. But more than that, I'm not sure if I even know who the real me is any more.

The desire to call Julia and beg for advice is a strong one, but I manage to resist. She deserves a day off from my neuroses, and she's bound to be fast asleep now, anyway. It's high time I stopped presuming that my big sister has all the answers. She's the stronger one, that much is undeniable, but the only person who can really see inside my head and know what I'm thinking and feeling is me. I need to decide not only who I am, but also who I want to be – and I need to do it by myself.

My phone buzzes with a 'Happy New Year' message from Dad, and a wave of emotion sweeps over me as I picture him waking up alone, yet again, in a house that by rights should be bursting with the chaotic colour of family life. Whatever self-disparaging traits I inherited from little Johnny's betrayal that day in the playground were exacerbated a thousandfold when my mum left. It was as if the bogeyman had come to life and crawled out from under the bed, as I'd always known he would. I had feared for so long that people were capable of cruelty, and my own mother had proved me right, which I guess was why I was too angry to hear her out when it happened, and have been too proud to broach the subject since. Maybe it's not pride, though – perhaps it's fear.

I know that Julia demanded answers, because she gave me a blow-by-blow, embittered account of the entire exchange, so I also know that my mum simply reiterated the facts, which were that she no longer loved our dad, and that she could not stay with him. Why is it that I'm able to understand and sympathise with Pete's actions concerning Taggie, but still find it impossible to forgive my mum? I'm aware of how hypocritical it makes me, but I can't seem to separate sense from sensibility. Pete hasn't said as much, but I can tell that what he desperately wants is for Taggie to forgive him. Knowing what I know, however, I'm doubtful that she ever will, and he is going to have to accept that, even if he doesn't like it very much.

It's impossible to be a nurse and not learn about people. I'm in a unique position, because many of the men, women and children I meet are going through something traumatic or frightening. I've seen people break down when they learn that the father they didn't speak to for ten years has been killed in a car accident. I've held the hands of grandmothers whose grown-up children have moved abroad and can't make it over in time to say goodbye, and I've seen doctors shut themselves into empty offices to weep over the baby they failed to save from meningitis. I have seen the best, the worst and everything in between, and still I haven't learnt to let go of my grudges. It's not just my mum and my ex-boyfriend that I refuse to forgive – it's myself. Today is the start of a brand-new year, and I'm determined to stop this endless cycle of self-destructive behaviour I've been pedalling out, and embrace the very real chance of a happy future.

Pete stirs just before midday, pulling me against him and nuzzling his face into my neck. He's predictably ravenous, so as soon as we're both up, showered and dressed, we wander down to the eastern side of the lake for some breakfast. There's a café with outdoor tables facing the water, and we choose one without shade to make the most of the sunshine. It can't be more than a few degrees above freezing, because I can see my breath in the air, but the sun makes it feel much warmer. By the time our hot chocolates arrive, I've taken off my hat and gloves and put on my sunglasses.

'I can't believe we fly home tomorrow,' Pete says, squinting as he takes in the view. 'It's going to be horrible going back to work.'

I had just been thinking the opposite, so instead of agreeing I simply smile in sympathy. I'm going to miss Lake Como, of course I am, but I'm also eager to get started on the plan I came up with in bed this morning – and I have missed being at the hospital, too, even though I didn't think I would.

'Shame we can't take the sunshine with us,' I say. 'If winters in England were as gorgeous as this, everyone would be in much better moods.'

'We should look at holidays next week,' he says then, fiddling with his paper napkin. 'Get something in the diary so we've got it to look forward to.'

I smile. 'Yeah, maybe.'

Breakfast arrives – a crostata pastry oozing with wild berry jam for me and a bacon baguette dripping grease for Pete – and after we've eaten we order two coffees to take with us and stroll along the path beside the water. While the pavements have been cleared of any party detritus, the water is still playing host to a collection of rubbish, and we see everything from empty wine bottles to polystyrene food containers floating on the surface. The Chinese paper lanterns that we saw lighting up the sky on our walk back from the Casa Alta last night have long since gone out, and many are now bobbing around in the shallows. Pete waits until we've wandered halfway along a narrow, curved pier before raising the subject of Taggie, and when he does it's with reluctance.

'I suppose I should go back to the hotel later,' he says, looking at me sideways. 'You know, to see Taggie again, to explain.'

There's a seagull on the wall ahead of us, and it cocks its head to one side, deciding whether to take flight. As soon as I lift the camera to take a photo, it's gone.

'If you want to,' I reply, carefully non-committal.

'You don't think I should,' he states, turning his face towards the sun.

'I'm not sure it will make you feel any better,' I say. 'That's not the same thing.'

'I need to explain,' he pauses. 'About you.'

'Do you?' I ask. 'Do you really? Because it might just hurt her more. She probably needs time to digest it all.'

He considers this for a minute as we continue along the pier, and I stare down to where the light is casting shadows across the concrete walkway.

'Maybe I'll just send her a message,' he says, looking down at the boats moored below us. 'Tell her that I'm here if she wants to see me, and . . . Well, tell her that I'm sorry. For all of it.'

I take his proffered hand as we reach a small wooden bench decorated with graffiti. It's funny how these scribblings feel so romantic in a setting like this, whereas in

London the same spray-painted words would look so grubby. There are padlocks attached to sections of the railings here, too, just like those that people leave in Paris and parts of London. They're supposed to signify enduring love. The coming together of two halves.

'I think that's a good idea,' I tell him, and smile encouragingly as he takes out his phone. Now even if Taggie doesn't respond, as I suspect she won't, then he will know that he did something. That he tried.

And that's all that any of us can ever really do, isn't it?

49

Taggie

Shelley is waiting for me in reception when I come out of Sal's office, her cherubic face the picture of concern.

'Well?' she asks, holding out her arms ready for a hug if I need one.

'A warning,' I say, holding up a piece of paper. 'Two more strikes and I'm out.'

'Tchuh!' Shelley mutters as I step into her embrace, and I smile. To be fair to Sal, he wasn't as angry as I probably would have been in his position – he was more disappointed than anything, which is of course far worse. I explained about Pete, leaving out the more morbid details, and he did seem to forgive me for running out on him and the party I'd spent so long planning. However, as he kindly but firmly explained afterwards, I had broken the rules, and there were consequences. Given that he only let me organise the party because I was so insistent, taking a bit of a gamble at the same time, I can't be that cross with him. In fact, I'm the one who feels guilty now for making everyone worry.

'I'm sorry I ran off,' I say to Shelley now, following her into the bar, and she turns to me sheepishly.

'I didn't actually realise you had until we went out to watch the fireworks,' she says. 'And then, when I went to get my phone and call you, I found a message on it from Marco, telling me that you were OK.'

'Really?' I'm surprised. 'He never told me he'd sent it.'

'Did anything happen?' she asks immediately, but I quickly shake my head.

'I told you, we're just friends.'

'If you say so,' she replies, but I can tell that she doesn't believe me.

'Honestly,' I say. 'Nothing exciting happened. We had a few drinks and danced, and then I crashed on his sofa.'

The memory of Marco's lips pressed hard against my own assaults me.

'You went to his house?' Shelley is practically foaming at the mouth with glee. 'What's it like? Where does he live? Does he have any hot, single flatmates?'

'Whoa!' I interrupt, laughing at her sudden burst of excitement. 'One thing at a time.'

Once she's satisfied that she has every detail about my time spent in Marco's apartment – excluding the part about the kiss, which I can't share until I make sense of it in my own head – Shelley hands me a mug of tea.

'So,' she begins, frowning when she sees my reaction. 'Don't pull that face. I'm worried about you.'

I shake my head. 'Don't be.'

'Taggie, I know you think I walk around with my head in the clouds most of the time, but there aren't many clouds in Como.'

She's not wrong there.

'I know you've been sneaking off to cry in the toilets,' she continues. 'And I didn't say anything before because I didn't want to push you. But after last night . . .' She lifts her shoulders in a gesture of helplessness. 'I can't pretend not to notice any more. I wouldn't be a proper friend unless I asked you what was the matter.'

'I need to go and have a shower,' I reply, putting the tea down on the bar. I'm still wearing last night's little black dress, with Marco's borrowed clothes over the top, and I feel like I smell.

'Taggie,' she argues, but I shake my head.

'It's a long story, but I will tell you.'

'When, then?'

I've reached the door before I reply.

'Later, I promise.'

It's not that I don't trust Shelley, I think guiltily, jogging up the stairs just as the guests start making their way down for breakfast. It's simply that there's such a lot to tell – and I'm too worn out to face it. Marco's sofa turned out to be surprisingly comfortable, but when the sunlight streamed in through the curtainless window just after six a.m. I found it impossible to fall back to sleep. Pinching a dark-red jumper that he'd left over the back of a chair, I'd scribbled a thank-you note and let myself out, heading straight through town and back along the western shore of the lake.

Thankfully there are no tours set up for today, so once I've caught up on emails in the office and checked that my group is occupied, I'm free to do whatever I want. Rather than feel deflated by the events of the previous evening, I feel oddly energised. Perhaps it's the fact that a new year has begun, or maybe it's simply that Marco's kiss healed some of the hurt and chased away the very real fear I had that there was no going forwards for me – but whatever the reason, I'm determined to make the most of it. For the past few months, I've been unable to see my situation clearly, but now that I can, I know it's time to make some changes. I've spent enough time hiding myself away and licking my wounds. Bottling everything up hasn't helped me at all, it left me screaming in the mud, and I don't want to feel like this any more. I'm willing to do whatever it takes to get better, no matter how hard it might be.

I had a relationship, I lost it. I had a baby, and I lost that, too. But what I have never lost is myself. One thing I can be sure of is who I am, because I've always been her. Agatha Ruby Torres: strong-willed, stubborn, bossy and controlling, but also loyal, loving, protective and brave. I know what my flaws are, and I embrace them, but I appreciate how they can be infuriating to others. Pete could not move past the fact that I was entirely self-sufficient, that I didn't need him to look after me all the time in the same way that he needed me, and I know now without even a smidgeon of doubt that the two of us were wrong for each other. I loved him because he loved me, but also because he was so much like me, with his stubbornness and his need to protect. In order to stay true to who we are as people, one of us would have had to change, and that is never the right path for a person to take. Nobody can pretend all the time – it would drive you mad.

This morning, for the very first time since that horrible day when Pete confessed that he didn't love me any more, I feel grateful to him. He was brave enough to recognise just how broken we were, when I refused to see it, and I've given him so much grief about it ever since. The fact that he met Lucy at the hospital still feels like the very cruellest twist of fate, but then that's life sometimes, isn't it? Last night I couldn't even bear to look at him – at either of them – but the feeling has dimmed since the initial shock wore off. I always have been the type to react before I act, and that's exactly what I did. What is really telling is who I ran to in that moment, the person I wanted to be near after I fled, but dissecting that right now is a step too far for my frazzled brain.

I call my mum and dad once I'm clean and re-dressed in jeans and a jumper, wishing them both a happy new year before filling them in on what's been going on. They're both understandably concerned, and downright appalled when they learn that Pete turned up with a new girlfriend in tow, but that soon changes to pride when I assure them that I'm OK, and that I think I may even finally be on the road to recovery. When I add that I'm planning a trip home very soon, my mum starts to cry, and I'm hit with a fresh punch of guilt at the turmoil I must have put them both through. It must be unbearable to watch your child in so much pain, yet be unable to take it away.

I hang up feeling tearful and quickly fire up my laptop. Como is quite a small place, but if there are any English-speaking counsellors living in the area, then I'm determined to find them. It was foolish of me to think I could get over losing my baby alone, without help from anyone, and I wonder now if it would have been any easier if Pete and I had been together and in a good place when it happened. It was unfair of me to blame him – I've always known deep down that it was – but I needed to lash out at someone, and in the midst of my turmoil, it did feel as if he had wished our baby away somehow. What was it Elsie said to me the day I told her? That I should do whatever it takes to feel better. That must be what Pete was doing when he started seeing Lucy. I had chosen Como as my sanctuary, while he had stretched himself out in the warm hammock of her adoration. It makes perfect sense.

There's a knock at the door.

'Who is it?' I call, just as Shelley walks in.

'I could have been naked,' I point out, and she grins.

'That would have made your visitor pretty happy.'

'My visitor?' I ask, my hands going clammy as I immediately think of Pete.

'I'll give you three clues,' she replies, her eyes gleaming. 'He's tall, dark, gorgeous, Italian and really good at ice-skating.'

'That's five,' I inform her, but I can't stop smiling.

50

Lucy

The park on the eastern shore of the lake is even prettier than its larger neighbour in the west, with neat, well-tended flower beds bursting with colour and immaculately trim patches of lawn. A vast and proud Scots pine tree overlooks the water by the pathway, and fine gravel crunches pleasantly underfoot. There's barely even a breeze today, and the sky is a dense, concentrated blue. The lake is covered with a thin layer of ripples, its surface broken only by the occasional inquisitive bird, and the air is cool and odourless.

Having exhausted Como, Pete and I are attempting to follow the curve of the lake round to Torno, a small commune about five kilometres away, which boasts several grand waterside villas and a small, attractive town centre. I've never been there before, so I'm relying on the guidebook, but the map inside is rudimentary at best.

We haven't seen many people so far but, as I keep having to remind myself, it's New Year's Day. If I was in England right now, I'd either be on a shift or in bed, recovering from the previous night's excesses. Pete hasn't mentioned Taggie for hours now, and as far as I know, he hasn't heard back from her since sending his message. Instead, he keeps talking about all the places he wants to take me when we get home, and how he's determined to introduce me to his parents and friends. I'm making all the right noises, but I think he can tell something's up.

'What were you like as a child?' he says, putting his arm around my shoulders as we stop to admire the view for about the twentieth time.

'Shy,' I confess. 'But inquisitive. What about you?'

'A bloody nightmare,' he admits, running his free hand through his ginger hair. 'I'm amazed my parents didn't drive me to a densely wooded area and leave me there.'

'Pete, that's horrible!' I admonish. 'I bet you weren't as bad as you think you were.'

He shakes his head. 'I was a belligerent little shit when I was a teenager, too. It makes me feel so bad when I think back to it now.'

'The worst thing I ever did was pinch Julia's clothes,' I tell him, smiling at the memory of my sister's angry face appearing in my bedroom doorway. 'The stupid thing was, she would have said yes if only I'd asked her permission. She always was better at sharing than I was, but for some reason I chose to sneak in behind her back.'

'That's because she's a control freak,' Pete says. 'Trust me, I lived with one for over four years. When I met Julia, I knew straight away.'

'She did used to be very protective,' I allow. 'Well, she still is. I remember once when we were here on holiday and I snuck off to the beach by myself. She was so mad that I'd left her out, but I just wanted some time by myself.'

'By yourself?' Pete repeats, clearly surprised. 'How old were you?'

'Oh, about nine or ten,' I reply, moving away from the

wall and continuing to walk through the park. 'I found this little place in Bellagio that was completely deserted, and I pretended that I was the only one who knew about it.'

'Did you ever take Julia there?' he wants to know.

'I had no choice,' I tell him with a chuckle. 'She threatened to drown my Rainbow Bright doll if I didn't.'

'Harsh,' he comments.

'It was a bit,' I agree. 'But in the end, it was a good thing I did, because we had so much fun playing down there. My mum and dad never knew about it – they thought we were hanging out with some local kids we'd met, but in reality, we were at this beach the whole time.'

'Why didn't we go there?' he asks, and I feel the heat rush into my cheeks.

'I couldn't remember the way.'

It's a lie, of course, but it feels like so long ago now. So much has changed since our day out in Bellagio.

'Maybe it's a good thing we didn't find it,' Pete says, and I turn to look at him.

'How so?'

'Well, often when you go back to a place you loved as a kid, it's not the same. The magic has gone, you know? I used to build dens and all sorts in Epping Forest when I was about ten. I felt like I had my own private kingdom, but going back as an adult, it all seemed to have shrunk somehow.'

'Maybe you're right,' I agree. 'The beach is probably not even there any more, or it could be on private property.'

'Exactly,' he says, squeezing my shoulder. 'It's in the past. But I tell you what, the next holiday we go on, we'll find our own secret beach, yeah?'

I smile as encouragingly as I can, but I can't quite bring myself to agree.

The two of us continue walking until we reach the entrance to a closed lido, its faded blue shutters pulled forlornly down for the winter, and Pete puts a hand up to the front window and peers through the glass.

'It's massive,' he remarks, turning to me. 'I bet it's full every day in the summer.'

'There's one in Bellagio, too,' I tell him, remembering. 'Me and Julia used to go. She always thought that she could think herself tanned, and refused point blank to use the sun cream my mum gave us. Of course, she ended up getting horrible sunburn one year, and my mum was so cross that she grounded her.'

'On holiday?' Pete is understandably aghast.

'I know. Not much logic went into that decision,' I reply. 'As if the poor crispy duck wasn't suffering enough. It was the pain and the peeling that taught her never to use a factor-four oil again, not my mum's silly ranting.'

'What did you do without her to keep you company?' he wants to know.

'I stayed in with her most of the time,' I say. 'We watched loads of Italian soap operas in the hotel games room – it's where I picked up most of the language I know.'

I don't remember that holiday in a bad way at all, in fact. Julia and I created our own little world within the four walls of that Bellagio hotel – one that our parents were unable to penetrate. The world of make-believe is far more fun than reality, or it certainly was for us.

'There's no way through here,' Pete says then, coming

to a halt in the deserted lido car park. The pavement disappears under the bolted-shut metal gates in front of us, and there doesn't appear to be an alternative route.

'We'll have to go up,' I tell him, pointing towards the wooded base of the hill on our right. There's the beginnings of what looks to be a path snaking up through the trees.

'Great,' he deadpans. 'You know how good I am with hills.'

'This isn't the same as Brunate,' I tease. 'It probably just rejoins the road a few metres up.'

Shaking his head, Pete follows me across the tarmac, and before long we're gazing back down at the lido from way up the hill. The pathway is nowhere near as steep as the one we tried and failed to scale on our first day here, but it does zig-zag high enough to offer some incredible views.

With the sun beaming relentlessly through the branches of the trees and fallen leaves crackling underfoot, it feels like we're strolling through the glorious autumn landscape of a painting. No wonder so many artists and writers have been inspired by this area of Italy.

Just as Brunate proved impossible to reach on foot, so Torno remains stubbornly elusive. After clambering all the way up to where the path does, indeed, rejoin the road, Pete and I discover that there are no pavements to walk along, leaving us no choice but to risk death or go back the way we came. We wisely choose the latter, eventually coming out on a residential road not far from the funicular.

'We've come around in a massive circle,' states Pete, clearly amused.

'Oh, look at that,' I exclaim, pointing down towards his

feet. The ground is covered with multi-coloured confetti – another remnant from last night's festivities.

'Pretty,' he agrees, bending down and scooping up a handful.

'Here comes the bride!' he cries, showering me with it.

'Big, fat and wide,' I sing back, just as I used to as a chubby kid in the playground.

'Lucy!' Pete scolds. 'Those aren't the words.'

'Well, I am, aren't I?' I reply, my tone challenging.

He looks confused.

'No, of course you're not.'

'I'm not exactly skinny,' I point out, and he pulls a face.

'Neither am I.'

'So, you admit it?'

I'm only triumphant for a split second, though, because I can see in his eyes that he really does agree with me. I am big, fat and wide.

'What's brought all this on?' he asks, reaching for me.

'Nothing.' I step backwards so he grabs air.

'Lulu, what's the matter?' he pushes, and stupid tears well up in my eyes.

'Just be honest with me, Pete,' I mutter. 'I know what I look like. I know what Taggie looks like – there's quite a big difference.'

He sighs deeply.

'I knew it,' he says sadly. 'I knew you were still thinking about her.'

'Not in the way you think,' I tell him honestly, kicking up a pile of confetti. 'It's just what girls do. We compare ourselves to each other – and we especially compare ourselves to ex-girlfriends.'

'But why?' Pete looks genuinely mystified.

'We just do!' I mutter, which I'm aware makes me sound like a petulant child.

'Lulu, look at me,' he says, gently taking my rigid hands in his. 'This is going to sound like a line, but it's not. I think you're perfect, just the way you are.'

'I'm not Bridget Jones,' I reply sulkily.

'No, I know that. You're far sexier,' he says with a grin.

I know he fancies me. I know it, so why can't I feel it? Why do I keep being so hard on myself?

'Yes, OK, Taggie is tiny,' he goes on. 'But that's not why I was with her. There's more to a person than the way they look, you know.'

'I know that,' I say, my voice small.

'And the thing is, which I've only really worked out since being here with you, is that I was with Taggie in spite of who she is,' he says, dropping my hands so he can use his own to gesture in the air.

'I overlooked the things that made us incompatible, because I thought I should, but deep down I knew it was wrong. Taggie deserves someone to love her *because* of all the things she is – not in spite of. That's the way I feel about you, Lulu. I love you because of who you are.'

'But that's just it,' I interrupt, taking a deep breath and looking at the ground. 'You don't know the real me – not really.'

Pete abruptly starts laughing, and I glance up at him in surprise.

'Oh Lucy,' he exclaims, beaming at me. 'Do you really think you're that good an actress? I do know you – I see you. You might think you're hiding yourself, but I see how kind you are, how tolerant, how warm and how caring. I see the way you rushed to Taggie's aid when she was hurt, and how you let me cry on your shoulder when by rights you should have been punching me in the chops. I see how much you love your family, and your friends, and I see when you use your one tea break at work to go out and buy coffee for the homeless men who beg on the corner of the street. I see all of it – I see you. And I see the way you beat yourself up. That's the only thing I would change about you, Lulu, and I want to help you overcome whatever demons you're holding on to. I want you to love yourself as much as I do.'

'I don't know what to say,' I mumble, my face burning with a mixture of love and humiliation. This is too much to take in, and my words are a jumbled mess in my head.

'Trust me, Lulu, if this was real wedding confetti,' he adds, picking up another handful from the ground, 'I'd drag you to the nearest church and make you marry me, right here in Como. I would, Lulu, I mean it. I want to be with you more than anyone I've ever known.'

I look up at his bright blue eyes, at the marmalade freckles across the tip of his nose, at the fullness of his lips, which are stretched into a beseeching half-smile, and I know in that moment exactly what it is I must do.

51

Taggie

I find Marco standing in front of one of the Casa Alta's grand, tall windows, staring out across the dark-green sweep of hillside beyond the glass. The view from here in the bar is one of my favourites in the hotel, because you can see grounds, lake and mountains without even having to tilt your head. Marco must find it just as mesmerising as I do, because I'm only about two feet away when he turns.

Seeing me there behind him, he smiles.

'*Ciao.*'

His voice sounds deeper today, as if he's yet to shrug off the layers of slumber.

'*Ciao,*' I reply, feeling absurdly shy. Reaching across, I lightly brush my fingers against his elbow. 'Thank you for last night.'

'You ran away,' he states, eyeing me with typical bemusement. The sunlight beaming in through the window is making his eyes look the same colour as an infinity pool in a glossy holiday brochure. They really are remarkable.

'I thought you'd be glad to get rid of me,' I joke, and he puts his head on one side.

'I like your hair like this,' he says, idly picking up a section and rubbing it between his thumb and forefinger.

'You mean washed?' I reply light-heartedly, and he smiles again.

'Undone. And yes, washed is nice. You smell like . . .' He bends to sniff, sending about three thousand volts of unexpected desire around my body at the same time. 'You.'

I don't have the heart to tell him it's my almond-blossom anti-dandruff shampoo.

'Sorry for stealing your jumper,' I say then, lifting the item up in my arms to show him that I've brought it back, along with the T-shirt he lent me to sleep in.

He shrugs. 'Keep them.'

'Don't be silly,' I chide, firmly hanging both the jumper and T-shirt over his leather-clad arm. 'I always meant to return them; I was just really cold this morning.'

'What are you doing today?' he asks then, abruptly changing the subject in the strange yet endlessly entertaining way he always seems to.

'I, er . . .' I falter, tripping over the lie as I'm about to say it. Why am I trying to send this man away, when I know what I want is to see him, to spend time with him? It was only a few hours ago that I left his apartment, and in the time since then I feel as if I've missed him, which is of course ridiculous.

'I was supposed to be working, but . . .' He holds his flat palms out to either side.

'Oh God, the bloody restaurant! I'm sorry. Again.'

He laughs magnanimously.

'Hush. I told you, I hate that job. I was happy this morning when I woke up and realised that I never have to go back there again. Then I got up to make you coffee, but you had gone.'

I think about saying sorry for that, too, but remember in time how much it wound him up last night when I kept apologising.

'I have the afternoon off,' I say, gratified to see his eyes light up. 'I was going to visit Elsie, but you'd be welcome to come with me. I think,' I begin, grinning as I correct myself, 'I mean, I *know* she would love to see you.'

'And I would love to see her,' he replies. 'And the dogs, too, of course.'

'Well, of course,' I agree, feeling all of a sudden light enough to float away like a balloon. 'Are you OK to wait for half an hour or so, just while I finish off what I need to do?'

'I'll look after him!' Shelley calls out. Marco and I wheel around to discover that she has, of course, tiptoed in and set herself up within earshot behind the bar.

'Have fun,' I whisper, sneaking one final look up at his eyes. 'I'll be as quick as I can.'

I'm halfway back up the stairs to my room when I feel my phone vibrate in the pocket of my jeans. It's a message from Pete.

I'm sorry, he's written. I'm here if you want to talk.

I pause, waiting for the inevitable pain to assault me, but it doesn't come. In fact, I feel OK to have heard from him. There's no anger there, or grief – there's just a twinge of something like sadness. Pete may not have had his heart broken by me, but he's suffered in other ways, just as I have. It's not fair of me to keep torturing him now, not any more.

Taking a deep breath, I tap out a reply and press send before I can change my mind.

*

As soon as Marco and I leave a gleeful Shelley and an intrigued Sal behind in the bar and stroll out on to the sunny driveway of the Casa Alta, he seems to perk up. Bouncing over to the driver's door of a very beaten-up old Fiat, he turns to me and gestures to the passenger side.

'Your chariot, my lady.'

I can't help it, I start laughing, and his face immediately falls.

'What? What is so funny?'

'Your car!' I exclaim. 'I thought that boat was in bad shape, but this is something else.'

Marco runs a protective hand over the faded blue bonnet.

'She is my pride and joy,' he says with a sniff.

I take in the rust-covered panels, the cracked bumper and the large dent in one of the doors, and fold my arms.

'She certainly has . . . character.'

'Enough!' he says, pretending to tell me off by wagging a finger. 'Get in before she hears you and refuses to start.'

'Has she done that before?' I ask, clambering in. Just like Marco's apartment, the inside of his car is immaculately clean, even if she is a bit shabby. An image of Pete's old Peugeot comes to me, with its footwell full of empty crisp packets and muddy rugby boots on the back seat.

'Only with people she really does not like,' he says, slipping the key into the ignition. There's a splutter and a growl, then the decrepit Fiat grumbles restlessly to life.

'Ah,' he says, patting the steering wheel with fondness. 'She likes you. I thought she would.'

'I like her, too,' I assure him, my words loaded with

more meaning than I intended, and again he gives me one of those sideways looks.

'*Bene,*' he murmurs. *Good.*

It's the first time I've been in a car that wasn't a taxi since I've been here, and the novelty of sitting in the front is going to take a while to wear off. Usually when I'm in the Casa Alta van with a tour group, I'm either turning around answering a flurry of questions, or have my nose down studying the day's itinerary, but today I have the freedom to simply sit back and enjoy the view.

The sun is lounging lazily in the sky like a holidaymaker on a recliner, casting its bright, winter light across the surface of the lake below us. As we pass the Aero Club, a seaplane comes in to land, scattering ducks, geese and swans in its wake. Some of the wealthier guests that stay at the Casa Alta go on aerial tours over Como, but it's never appealed to me much. What I love so much about this area is how reassuringly large and protective the surrounding mountains feel, and how vast the expanse of water. To see it all reduced to a toy town from the air might diminish it somehow, and I'm not willing to take that risk. Well, that and I don't have a spare three hundred euros burning a hole in my pocket.

Marco drives with ease and admirable grace, given his vehicle of choice, and I can't help but be aware of how close his hand is to my thigh whenever he reaches down to change gear. The car rattles along quite happily, almost as if it's enjoying the feel of the New Year's Day sunshine as much as its passengers are, and we're through the centre of Como and on the other side of the lake in no time.

I take out my phone and send a quick message to

Elsie — she'll string me up by my ankles if I turn up with a man in tow without giving her the time to do her face — and see that Pete has yet to reply to the text I sent him. Perhaps he's been shocked into staying mute.

'I saw that girl,' Marco says, not taking his eyes off the road. We've just passed the point where the wooded park on the eastern shore comes to an end, and there's rainbow confetti all over the tarmac.

'Which girl?' I ask, the hairs on my arms prickling.

'From the boat,' he says. 'The one who helped you with your nose.'

'Thanks again for *that*,' I quip, and he narrows his eyes at me cheekily.

'She asked me if you were OK,' he adds. 'I told her yes.'

I smile. 'Thank you.'

'But are you?' he asks, glancing at me when I don't immediately reply. 'Are you OK?'

'I am,' I say honestly. 'I really think I am.'

We don't talk much more because Marco needs to focus all his attention on the road. It becomes pretty hair-raising as we cruise further along the coastline, and I try not to wince whenever another car whizzes past on one of the many blind corners. To distract myself, I start looking out for the signs so I can keep track of where we are, mouthing each of the beautiful place names as I read them. There's Torno, Lario, Careno, Nesso and, after a mercifully straight stretch of open road, Lezzeno, all unique and beautiful, all steeped in history and all with spectacular views. Why would anyone choose to live anywhere else in the world?

While the scenery is sublime, I still find my eyes slipping constantly towards Marco. I take in the faint trace of freckles across his nose, the lines on his brow where it's knotted in concentration, and the fingernails bitten down and clean. He's less bulky and muscular than Pete, but in a way Marco is even more masculine. I know from inspecting the contents of his bathroom cabinet that he's not averse to moisturising, flossing and tweezing, but there's nothing girlish about him. He's straightforwardly male, and I find that simple fact hugely comforting for some reason. I've never been the type of woman to crave a man to look after me – in fact, I've been anti the whole concept for as long as I can remember – but with Marco I feel safe. And it's not a bad feeling, actually; it's a nice one.

'Darlings!' Elsie holds her arms out to either side in greeting, pulling first me, then Marco down against her bosom. She smells sweetly of rose water today, and has gone to the trouble of applying lipstick for our arrival.

The dogs are even happier to see Marco than their mistress is, and all three of them pirouette round in tiny circles by his feet, barking excitedly. Even Bruno, who I thought liked me best of all, has transferred his affections, and when I go to pick him up, he tries to nip my finger.

'Happy New Year to you, too,' I retort, putting him down. 'Bloody charming!'

'Typical man,' Elsie says drily, with the ghost of a wink. 'Come on – the kettle's on.'

The two of us follow her, Gino, Nico and Bruno through the front porch and into the hallway, where Marco excuses himself and heads into the bathroom. As soon as the door closes, it takes Elsie approximately five seconds to start firing questions at me.

'Shhh,' I hiss laughingly, lowering my voice to a whisper. 'He'll hear you.'

She sits down at the kitchen table and looks at me appraisingly. Her hair is covered with a gold and turquoise scarf today, and she's swapped her habitual bright-green wellies for a pair of fluffy pink slippers.

'You don't have to tell me anything,' she says, her eyes full of mischief. 'But can I just say that you look better. Happier.'

'Really?' I'm touched, and turn away to start readying mugs for coffee.

'Really,' she confirms. 'You have your light back. I haven't seen it since you came here all those months ago, but today it's as bright as that sunshine out there.'

'It's probably just exhaustion,' I tell her, but there's no discounting my smile.

'Busy night, was it?' she asks coyly, and I look round in time to see her impish grin.

'Not in that way!' I exclaim, unable to stop myself laughing at her bluntness. 'Get your head out of the gutter, young lady!'

'Oh, but it's far more fun down there than up here,' she giggles, holding her hand up above her head. 'And nobody would judge you. I mean, you only have to look at him . . .'

'Look at who?' asks Marco. He's just appeared in the kitchen doorway and is looking at each of us in that casually amused way he has.

'You, dear,' says Elsie sweetly, at exactly the same time as I chirp, 'Nobody.'

Thankfully, Marco has the grace to simply raise an eyebrow. I go back to making the hot drinks, wondering how

I got to this point. Less than twenty-four hours ago I was bereft, then last night I felt as if I'd been slammed into a wall of misery. All the revelations about Pete and Lucy and then all my feelings about the baby erupting like messy, emotional lava should have rendered me bed-bound at the very least. Yet here I am, standing in Elsie's kitchen with a man I've only really known a few weeks, smiling with legitimate happiness and basking in the warmth of our shared moment. It's all the more special, because it's the first day of a brand-new year. I feel ready to put the past behind me and move forwards, and there's no better time than right here and right now.

Marco is sitting down now, ignoring the three dogs, who are all scrabbling to climb on his knee. I open a cupboard and take out their tin of snacks, shaking it to get their attention.

'Treats!' I call. 'Come and get them.'

Bruno's ears twitch, but the other two don't even seem to register my existence.

'Well,' I say, picking up two mugs of coffee and putting them on the table. 'That's put me in my place.'

The three of us pass an easy hour chatting about anything and everything, and I tell Elsie about my plans to head back to the UK in the coming weeks. Marco doesn't say anything, but I feel him stiffen a fraction on the chair beside me, and I quickly reassure them that I will be back. I don't share the real reason behind my trip, however – that's not a lid I want to unscrew today. After a while, Elsie offers to make us some lunch, but Marco insists that he is more than capable. He's not wrong, either, and Elsie isn't the only one watching with pleased curiosity as he rifles through her fridge and begins making a rich pasta sauce from scratch. But of course, he can cook – it's his dream to have a restaurant on a boat – and the thought makes me gaze at him with satisfied indulgence. He's clearly far more passionate about food than he's let on, and watching him scoot happily around the kitchen now, whistling softly under his breath as he works, makes me feel inspired. Everything that's been happening over the past few days has gobbled up any time I would have had to plot, but now I'm becoming excited about Marco's dream boat all over again. Next on my list after my visit back to England will be a business plan – and just thinking about it now is making my heart race with anticipation.

Lunch is, of course, divine, and for once I let Elsie get away with opening a bottle of red wine so we can toast the New Year, not to mention the talents of our Italian chef. However, given the fact that Marco still has to drive us back into Como and I'm trying to be good, Elsie drinks far more of it than we do, and soon announces that she's off for a siesta.

'Don't behave yourselves, will you?' she says as a parting shot, and I stare down at my scraped-clean plate until my blushes have subsided.

'She is a brilliant woman,' Marco comments, helping me clear the table and then leaning against the worktop as I wash up. He did offer to do that, too, but there are limits to how much sitting around and doing nothing I can endure.

I like how we can be together in a space like this and not fill every moment with chatter. Even though I'm feeling hyper-aware around him, I don't have those awful nerves that make you babble absolute rubbish. I used to be like that with Pete in the beginning, and he was the same, so half the time we ended up talking over each other. With Marco, everything is more measured and relaxed, and I don't worry what he's thinking the whole time. I'm confident that if he had something on his mind, he would just say it. He's far less complicated than any man I've ever met before, but then he has so much depth to him, too. Take today, for example. I had no idea he was such a talented cook. He'd never boasted about it or talked himself up. Instead, he's letting me discover new things about him in a more organic way, and our friendship has developed as it should, gradually over time, rather than with the pair of us barking attributes at one another like we're on an audition. I realise there's still lots that I don't know about him, but it doesn't worry me. I trust him, and that is more important to me than anything else.

I wait until the last fork is dried and back in the drawer, then I turn to him.

'Do you feel like a walk?'

He nods. 'Of course.'

'I know just the place,' I smile, reaching for my coat. 'And I think you'll definitely approve.'

52

Taggie

The beach is deserted, as I somehow knew it would be. It's always been my special place, the place I come to think, to feel, to just be. It's the secret I have kept since I was nine years old, the one I never shared with anybody else. Until I met Marco.

The lake is as flat as a mirror, the boats reflected in almost perfect detail in the water, and in the distance the mountains seem to throb, as if a heart was beating within them. I bend down and unclip the leads from three tiny collars, watching as Nico, Gino and Bruno step carefully across the sand and stone until they reach the gently lapping shore, sniffing the cold air as they go. There are no clouds in the sky, and barely a sound save for the wind. It stirs the leaves in the surrounding trees, slipping amongst the branches like a whisper, and somewhere I hear a bird begin to sing.

'I first found this place when I was a little girl,' I say, looking up at Marco as he glances down at me. His dark hair is free of gel today and his floppy fringe almost reaches his eyes.

'I used to pretend that it was mine.'

He smiles, lifting his gaze from me to the horizon. He must have left his sunglasses back at the house, because he's squinting now against the glare of the sun. In this spot, right here on the sloping beach, it could almost be a midsummer afternoon, save for the chill that's working its way through me. I shiver involuntarily as we begin to make our slow way along the narrow concrete pathway, and Marco slides a hesitant arm around my shoulder.

'You are always cold,' he says. 'Let me keep you warm.'

I let myself be pulled against him gratefully, for once simply enjoying the sensation of his body against my own. I wait to feel uncomfortable, but the jitters never arrive. Instead I just feel calm and at peace. When we reach the corner where the walkway curls back down into the water, Marco clutches me even tighter.

'Don't jump!' he cries, laughing as I go to hit him. 'There is so much to live for!'

'Idiot,' I chide, but I'm laughing along with him.

There's just enough room for us to sit down at this spot and lean back against the wall, but Marco is so much taller than me that he's forced to bend his knees to stop his feet from trailing in the lake, whereas the heels of my boots dangle just over the edge.

Gino and Nico are busy digging holes in the soft earth of the shore a few feet away, but Bruno has predictably followed Marco and me, and is now curled up in a ball on my lap. I know that if I lift my chin and turn my head, then my lips will be level with Marco's, and a thrill scampers through me. I want to ask him what he's feeling, but it seems cheap somehow. I don't want to shatter the strange ambience of the moment, so I entertain myself by stroking Bruno until he falls asleep, his gentle snores making both of us quiver with laughter.

'Taggie,' Marco says, his arm still around my shoulder.

'Yes?'

'What is the best piece of advice you have ever been given?'

It's a good question, but one I hadn't been expecting him to ask, so I take my time formulating an answer while he waits, patiently, right beside me.

'Well,' I begin, shuffling forwards a fraction so I can face him without our noses touching. 'When I was still very young, I can clearly remember being set this piece of homework, which was to write a few sentences about what we wanted to be when we grew up, and then draw a picture of ourselves above it.'

He nods, understanding.

'All my friends came back with pictures they'd drawn of themselves as nurses or doctors, firemen or teachers or football players – but I just drew a picture of myself, albeit older and taller – always taller.'

'You didn't know what you wanted to be?' he guesses, but I shake my head.

'Not exactly. I didn't know which job I wanted to do, but my dad had always said to me that the most important person you can grow up to be is yourself. He told me that as long as you stay true to who you are, and what makes you happy, then the rest will work itself out.'

'And did it?' he asks, fixing me with a look I can't decipher.

I smile sheepishly. 'Any day now.'

'But you are still you,' he states, and I nod.

'Yes. I always have been. I guess I always will be. I'm thirty-two now, so I don't imagine I'll change much.'

'You are lucky,' he murmurs.

'To be thirty-two?' I joke, even though his expression hints at something far more serious.

His eyelids seem to be heavier today, or maybe it's just the sun causing them to droop.

'I wish I had known you when I was a little boy,' he continues, his face more intense than before. 'I was not a happy child.'

'Why not?' I ask, ready to be sad for him.

'I was bullied.'

'You?' I exclaim, unable to believe that the tall, proud and self-assured man next to me was ever anything less than super-confident.

'Yes,' he confirms, meeting my eyes. 'I wanted to be someone else for a long time. I did not like being me.'

'But you're amazing,' I blurt, slapping a mortified hand over my mouth and waking Bruno up in the process.

Marco grins. '*Grazie.*'

'Tell me what happened,' I urge, shifting until my knee is touching his thigh. I want to know this man, to drink in every detail and learn him off by heart, to see inside his mind and figure out the way he feels. I want it all.

'Please,' I add.

And so, Marco takes a breath, picks up my cold hands, and begins his story. He tells me that he was born and brought up in Como by his Italian father and English mother, both of whom doted on him. When he was just six, however, their marriage collapsed and his mother moved back home to Yorkshire to be close to her family, with her son spending half his time with her, and the other half back in Como. Teased at the schools in both countries due to his strange Anglo-Italian accent, and unable to build any proper friendships due to his constant back-and-forth lifestyle, Marco began to struggle. He felt especially miserable in Leeds, where there were no lakes and mountains to soothe him, and tried to run away from home on more than one occasion. When his mother remarried, Marco, who was only fifteen at the time, begged his parents to let him move to Italy permanently, and an agreement was reached.

'I used to come to this beach when I was a child,' he explains. 'Just the same as you. I came to drink it all in before I had to go back to Leeds, and I would sit here for hours, trying to memorise every little detail, so I could take it all with me. It was what I did to feel brave,' he adds, and I feel my heart go out to the poor, isolated Marco of so many years ago.

'A few kids tried to bully me at school,' I confide, grinning wickedly. 'They soon regretted it.'

He chuckles with pleasure and holds my hands a smidgeon tighter.

'I can believe that,' he says. 'I almost feel sorry for them.'

'Oi!' I laugh. 'I'm not a monster – I'm just a bit feisty, that's all.'

'You are extraordinary,' he proclaims, talking over me as I go to disagree. 'You know it is the truth. If I'd had a friend like you when I was a boy, someone so strong and so true to themselves, then maybe I would have been happy.'

'But maybe you would not be the same you,' I argue gently. 'And I like this you.'

He lifts his eyes, hopeful. 'You like me?'

I nod, my smile communicating what I cannot put into words. So much of what Marco and I say to one another seems to be through looks alone, as if we're communicating on a different wave length to everyone else. I like the idea of us having that connection, and I'm suddenly overcome with a need to touch him, to feel the solidness of him and know that he's real, even though he's right here. Right here in the very same spot that we found each other.

'It's nice to be here with you,' I say, gazing round at the still water, the proud boats, the blue mountains.

'Yes.' He squeezes my fingers. 'The place we met.'

'Friends?' I ask, leaning back so that Marco can put his arm around me again.

'Of course,' he replies, pulling me close. 'I think now we will be friends forever.'

As the wind picks up and rustles the trees, Marco brings his hand up and strokes first my cheek, then my jaw, then my hair off my face. A moment passes where all I see are those mesmerising green eyes of his, gazing down at me intently. Then he bends his head slowly, so very slowly, and presses his lips against mine.

53

Lucy

I haven't seen my mum since October. She insisted on coming down to London to take Julia out for a birthday dinner, and I was invited along to join them. Stubbornly, though, I deliberately didn't book the day off, and so of course ended up working late at the hospital and only made it to the restaurant after the two of them had sunk a couple of bottles of Prosecco. My mum, tipsy and shrill, had accused me of being judgemental when I told her to keep her voice down, and I'd stormed out soon afterwards. Most un-Lucy-like behaviour, but then she always did bring out the grumpy teenager in me – even before I was one.

As soon as Pete and I landed at Heathrow Airport yesterday afternoon, however, I felt an overwhelming urge to talk to her – and not just over the phone or via email, but sitting down opposite her. I wanted to take in her expressions, hear the tone of her voice, watch her body language. For this to be an honest conversation. And it feels important to me that we do it in person.

I didn't even bother dropping my case off at the flat in Finsbury Park. I just caught the tube to Liverpool Street station and got a train straight out here to Suffolk, where my dad was waiting to collect me. I spent last night at the family home, taking comfort from the familiar surroundings and Dad's home cooking, and now it's the third morning of the year and I'm standing here, on David the pig farmer's gravel drive, watching the shape of my mum grow bigger through the frosted glass panels beside the front door.

'Lucy!'

She's understandably surprised to see me.

'Hi, Mum.'

She bends forward to give me a quick hug, leaning over rather than taking a step out of the house. It's been raining all night and she's not wearing any shoes. From the look of her outfit, my guess is that I've just interrupted her in the middle of one of her many home workout DVDs.

'I hope it's not a bad time?' I say, walking boldly over the threshold and wiping my boots on the mat.

'Not at all,' she replies, a hand patting absent-mindedly at her blonde beehive. She always wears her hair up in some sort of elaborate pile, my mum. Heaven knows how long it must be by now.

'David not here?' I enquire politely, following her into the kitchen. It's achingly modern in here, with granite worktops, polished chrome fittings, and one of those truck-sized fridges with an ice dispenser on the front.

'He's gone to have a look at some pigs that are for sale,' she says. 'Tea?'

'That'd be nice, thanks,' I reply, shaking my head when she thrusts a basket at me containing a range of fruit and herbal teabags in little packets. 'Builder's is fine.'

'Just like your dad,' she quips without thinking, but we both ignore the comment as if she'd never said it.

'Happy New Year, by the way,' I say after a few seconds, and she turns from where she's been resolutely staring at the kettle.

'Thanks.' She smiles. 'You were in Italy, weren't you?'

I nod, swallowing down the lump that's formed in my throat.

'Lake Como.'

'You always did love it there,' she says, stirring in the milk. 'Is it still just as beautiful?'

I think for a moment.

'It's unforgettable, that's for sure.'

If she notices a strange tone to my voice, she doesn't react, instead beckoning for me to follow her through into the living room, where I perch awkwardly on the edge of one of the white leather sofas. There's a yoga mat unrolled not far from a huge, flat screen TV, and a woman with waist-length dreadlocks has been paused in an uncomfortable pose on the screen, one of her feet almost touching the back of her head.

My mum notices me looking.

'Yoga,' she explains. 'Dave got it for me for Christmas.'

I try to smile, but it comes out all lopsided and insincere. It's not that Dave is particularly a bad person, he's just not my dad. The two of us have done a splendid job of basically ignoring each other for the past eight years, and it's a practice that suits us just fine. And anyway, it's not Dave that I'm here to talk to; it's my mum. Now that I'm sitting here, though, with nobody else to steal her attention away from me, I'm finding it hard to get the words out.

'Are you OK, Lu?'

The tears are on my cheeks before I can stop them, and

my mum immediately gets up from her armchair and hurries across her expensive cream carpet to wrap her arms around me. I can't remember the last time she hugged me, and this makes me cry even more.

'What's happened?' she asks. 'Have you and Julia had a row?'

I shake my head.

'Is your dad OK? He's not ill or anything, is he?'

She sounds genuinely fearful for a second, and I shake my head again.

'No, it's not that, but . . .'

I take a deep, shuddering breath.

'Mum, why did you really leave Dad?'

She peels herself away and looks at me.

'You know why, Lucy.' As she says it, she sighs, presumably as fed up of answering the question as I am of getting an unsatisfactory answer. I know that she fell out of love with him, just like Pete fell out of love with Taggie, and my ex, Spencer, did with me – but what I need to know is why. It's no longer enough for her to claim she has no idea; I want her to try harder than that. It scares me so much, this idea of waking up one day to find that you don't love your partner any more – or vice versa. I want to know that it won't happen, not to me.

'I broke up with Pete,' I say then, and watch her wince in sympathy. Her grey eyes are so like mine that sometimes when I look at her, it's as if I'm staring at a future version of myself.

'Oh, you poor, poor darling,' she says, brushing the hair away from my damp cheeks. 'He must be an idiot if he can't see how wonderful you are.'

Of course, she assumes that he broke up with me. It's not as if I don't have experience of being dumped and cheated on and trodden into the dirt – but she could at least have checked first.

'It was me who ended things actually,' I say, sniffing and moving my head away. 'Everything changed in Italy, and I told him I needed some time alone.'

She glances round to where her tea is sitting abandoned, beside mine, on the glass-topped coffee table. There's a coaster under each mug, and a ring of condensation has formed around them both.

'Aren't you going to ask what happened?' I say then, my voice dry, although where would I even start if she did? With the miscarriage? With Taggie? With my own insecurities?

'It doesn't matter,' she replies, staring down at her socks. 'All that matters to me is that you're happy.'

I let out a hard laugh.

'Really, Mum? That's *all* you care about?'

'Lucy,' she begins, but I don't let her finish.

'It didn't seem to bother you how happy I was when you ran off and left us,' I mutter. 'It didn't faze you in the slightest when I told you I'd been cheated on by Spencer.'

She tried to interrupt, but I barrel on and talk over her protestations.

'I used to be just like Dad, you know. I let Spencer walk all over me like you walked all over him – but this time I haven't let it happen. This time I chose to go.'

'I didn't walk all over your father,' she says quietly. 'We talked everything through and he told me I should go. He

382

wanted me to be happy, and I didn't want to lie to him any more.'

'But he was so sad,' I argue, tears threatening again. 'He still is!'

She shakes her head. 'I'm sorry for that, I really am, but there isn't anything else I can do. The truth is, your father has behaved like a bit of a martyr throughout all this. I bet he refuses to even try to meet someone else, doesn't he? Because that would feel like giving in – and I think he enjoys the attention you and Julia give him.'

'Don't say that!' I snap, angry with her partly because I suspect there may be a grain or two of truth in what she's saying.

'Lucy, listen to me,' she says, her voice infuriatingly calm. 'Sometimes being sad isn't a choice – especially when emotions are still raw. But other times you do have a choice. You can either let what you're feeling engulf you, or you can do your best to overcome it. People can learn to cope with awful, horrible things when they put their mind to it – but your dad has never even tried.'

I think about Pete, allowing himself to try for a happy ending with me so soon after losing a girl he once loved and the child they would have had together; and I picture Taggie, so broken but still so strong, and that message she sent to Pete on our last day in Lake Como. It's OK, she had written. I forgive you. All I want is for both of us to be happy.

She lost so much more than I ever have, and yet she's been able to crawl through to the other side of her misery and come back fighting. I know what Taggie would say if she was here right now – she would tell me to cheer up, to wipe my eyes, to stop being such a drip and to woman the hell up. When I told Pete in Como that I needed a break, he looked crushed, but I think he understood where I was coming from. He listened while I explained how confused I felt, and was patient and kind. Once we'd talked it all through, it was him who suggested that I should come here and talk to my mum. He told me that it was important to forgive her, because, he added, 'She's your mum, Lulu.' And he was right, too. But this still didn't take away from the fact that Pete and I had been through more than some couples do in a lifetime in the space of a few days, and it had all just got too much for me. I needed to take a step back to think about what had happened, but also to spend some time with myself for once. I need to be enough for me, but it's not easy.

'I love him,' I say, the last words crumbling into a sob, and again my mum wraps me up in her arms, telling me over and over that it will be OK, that I'm beautiful, that she loves me. It's exactly what I needed, and what I've been missing for so many years – just a cuddle from my mum.

She's saying all the same things that Pete said to me, but I wasn't ready to listen. I wanted to know that the love we had was infallible and untouchable; I wanted to know beyond any shadow of a doubt that he was the one, and that we would never hurt one another – but of course, no such assurance exists. All you can do is be brave and take a chance. Jump in with both feet and hope for the best, just as Julia and I once did on the shores of that beautiful Italian lake, so young and so free to take on everything the world had to offer. And it's all still there, that same world; it's all still there for the taking.

'You know, Lucy, you're not your dad and you're not

me, either,' Mum says then. 'You are you – and nobody can be a better version of you than you can. Just because I left your dad doesn't mean that Pete will leave you, and nothing that anyone else has done can change who you are – only you can do that.'

It sounds so bloody simple, but she's right. Why is it that hearing something from your mum makes you believe it more?

'I have to go,' I say, standing up so fast that my mum almost falls off the sofa. 'I need to . . . I have to go.'

'Please don't go yet,' she says, holding on tightly to my hand. 'Just stay, please. Just for a few hours. I've missed you so much.'

I look down at her, at her ridiculous multi-coloured leggings and soft grey cardigan, at the lines around her eyes and the dark patch of skin on her chest where she's been burnt by the sun one time too many, and I realise that I've missed her, too.

'OK, Mum,' I say, smiling at her. 'But only because it's you.'

54

Taggie

The third week of January is always a tough one. Pay day feels like a distant memory, the mornings are dark and damp, and night time seems to arrive just after you've eaten your lunch. Of all the weeks that I could have chosen to come back to London, this one is probably the dreariest. But then again, I remind myself cheerfully, it's not as if I'm staying for very long.

The walk from the Overground station to the flat feels strange yet familiar. The faces I pass are the same mix of friendly, grumpy and downright hostile that I remember, and the pavements are grey and littered with stains where people have spat out their chewing gum, only for it to be trodden underfoot. I used to walk along this same route at least twice every single day, sometimes more, but those days feel like a lifetime ago. I keep my eyes wide open, taking it all in, comparing it to the stroll I take along the lake in Como every morning to feed the birds, and laughing inwardly at the contrast. London is a vibrant and dynamic city full of incredible people, but it's not my true home. I know that now.

My dad gave me the spare set of keys before I left this morning, so I'm able to let myself in, but I pause for a second by the front door, waiting to make sure that I'm not going to get all emotional. Once satisfied, I venture inside.

Pete is standing in the kitchen, and there's a cardboard box on the worktop in front of him, my name written on the side in felt-tip pen.

'Oh,' he says, his cheeks reddening as I make my way towards him. 'I was expecting Manny.'

'I thought you might bail if you knew it was me coming,' I admit, smiling sheepishly. 'And I wanted to see you.'

'You did?' He sounds hopeful, and again I'm hit with a small slap of guilt for what I've put him through. He behaved pretty badly, but in the end so did I. When I should have tried to understand, I merely raged and ranted and tried to boss him into loving me again. No wonder he was too scared to face me in the hospital. I would have been, too.

'So, this is weird,' I say lightly, putting my keys in my bag. 'Us, being back here, and not screaming at each other.'

'Tag . . .' he begins, but I shake my head.

'Don't say sorry. There's been enough of that, Pete.'

He nods, understanding.

'Do you want a beer?'

'You bought beers in?' I exclaim, laughing as he opens the fridge to reveal a six-pack of tinnies.

He grins, amused with himself. 'You know me.'

'That's true, I do,' I say, accepting a cold can and opening the ring pull with a finger.

'What shall we drink to?' he asks, poised to toast me.

'The London property market, obviously,' I reply, grinning at him. 'I can't believe how much more this place is worth now.'

'I know,' he agrees, taking a large slurp of beer. 'Those

shelves I put up in the front room must have added at least thirty grand to the value.'

'You mean the wonky shelves?' I remark drily. 'The ones you can't put anything of value on in case it falls off?'

'All right, all right!' Pete exclaims. 'So, DIY isn't my greatest skill – but I did manage to fix the toilet flush that time.'

'Give the man a medal,' I retort, but we're both smiling. Pete looks as if he's lost a bit of weight since I saw him last, and there are dark circles under his bright blue eyes. He's wearing a butterscotch-coloured shirt today that by rights should clash with his ginger hair, but somehow it works. He always was good at picking clothes, and not just for himself, either. Some of my favourite dresses are gifts from him, including the one I have on today, which is made from soft grey wool.

'Remember when we first moved in here?' Pete says then, leaning against the edge of the worktop. 'How disgusting this place was.'

'The pink wallpaper!' I remember with a shudder. 'And that yellow carpet in the bathroom.'

'I don't think it was yellow when the previous owners first laid it,' he says, and I pull a face.

'Urgh!'

'I still love it, though,' he continues wistfully. 'It's been really bloody weird living here alone, but I'm going to miss the place.'

'Did you never consider just buying me out?' I ask, but he shakes his head.

'No. This was our place, Tag. It would feel wrong staying.'

'Are you and Lucy . . .' I begin, but stop when I see the look on his face.

'She dumped me,' he says, quickly taking another sip of beer. 'You'll probably say it's karma.'

'No,' I assure him. 'I'm not that bitter – and I'm sorry things didn't work out between you two.'

He looks as if he doesn't believe me.

'I mean it,' I insist. 'Lucy seems lovely, and she was so nice to me in the hospital when . . . You know. There were all these doctors standing over me and talking away like I wasn't even in the room, but she held my hand and made sure I knew what was happening. It made all the difference.'

'She is lovely,' he agrees. 'She deserves far better than me.'

'Is there no hope for the two of you?' I ask, slightly taken aback to discover that I do genuinely want there to be. I wasn't lying to Pete when I said Lucy was a great person – she is. And I could tell how much she loved him.

Pete stares down at his can. 'I'm not sure. She told me she needed some time to think, to be by herself, so that's what I'm giving her.'

'Time alone can be good,' I tell him. 'It sounds to me like she's trying to do the smart thing.'

'What about you?' he asks, and I glance up.

'What about me what?'

'You and that guy,' he says, shifting uncomfortably. 'What was his name again – Marco?'

'Marco is just a friend,' I say, unable to stop myself from smiling as an image of my tall Anglo-Italian comes to mind. 'A very good friend.'

'He's crazy about you, though,' Pete says then, so matter-of-factly that I try to laugh his comment away.

'What?' he says. 'He is! I know I only met him that one time, but it was obvious even then. The way he looked at me was the same way a tiger might look at a passing herd of buffalo. He wanted to murder me.'

'He's just very loyal,' I protest.

'Or very besotted,' Pete points out.

What I don't share with Pete is the fact that Marco is more than just loyal. He's also wise, funny and warm, and rapidly becoming the most important person in my life. We are still just friends, it's true, but I know that what's developing between us is more than that. It's deeper and more urgent. I'm just in no hurry to rush into something new quite yet; I need a bit more time to heal.

'What's in the box?' I ask, firmly changing the subject, and Pete opens the lid to show me.

'Shoes, of course.'

I laugh as I look down at the patent red high heels.

'I left those on purpose! They cripple me.'

'Well, they're hardly going to fit me,' he replies, lifting one out. The heels are a size three, whereas Pete's feet are a gigantic size twelve.

'And they're not really your style, either,' I joke. 'Perhaps thigh-high boots would suit you better. Some of those ones that lace all the way up the front.'

'Sexy,' he deadpans, and we both laugh as he reaches into the fridge for a second beer. I had worried that it would feel sad to be back in the flat with Pete, but I couldn't have been more wrong. It's nice to be reminded of the positive memories, and to be able to laugh together again over little things. When we broke up, there was so much animosity and mutual mud-slinging – the two of us ending up buried so far underneath it all that we lost sight of who we were, of what we had once shared. We forgot that we were friends.

'It's nice to see you,' I say then, voicing what I'm thinking, and his eyes seem to light up as he looks at me.

'It's nice to see you, too, Tag.'

We share the rest of the beers sitting cross-legged on the living room floor, reminiscing about the parties we had here and all the terrible meals he attempted to cook. Pete asks me about the Casa Alta, and I enquire into his job at the radio station, then we talk about our mutual friends, and our families. It's amazing how much can happen in just over half a year, and we find that we have plenty to catch up on. We don't talk about the baby, but that's OK. I'm dealing with it on my own terms, and raking back over the subject with Pete now feels unnecessary. I know that neither of us will ever forget the little life that we created together, and it will always be with us, but what today is about is the future. It's about moving forwards with our lives.

'What are you going to spend your half of the money on?' Pete asks, as we prepare to leave, and I glance around once again at the bare walls of what was, until a few hours ago, our flat.

'I'm thinking of investing in a new business,' I tell him, zipping up my coat.

'Oh yeah?' he replies, turning off the hallway light as I open the front door.

'I've always wanted to help build up something from scratch,' I tell him. 'I just never knew what it was until recently.'

'And now you do?' he asks, closing our door for the final time.

I'm just about to reply when we're both distracted by the sound of his phone ringing. As he takes it out and looks at the name flashing up on the screen, a smile spreads across his face.

'Good news?' I guess, and he nods, holding the phone out so I can see. It's Lucy.

'Answer it, you idiot!' I tell him, touching his arm one final time.

Pete smiles and mouths a thank you, then hurriedly answers his call with a tentative hello.

I pull my handbag further up on my shoulder and re-arrange my arms around the edges of my cardboard box. It's time for me to go, back to where I know there are people waiting for me. As I turn away from the door of the flat and get ready to walk away, I hear Pete take a breath, followed by four little words that make my heart sing for him.

'I miss you, too.'

Epilogue

The path down to the beach is damp from an earlier shower, and the moon is making the stones gleam a whitish grey in the darkness. Stars are scattered like a dusting of glitter across the vast black sky, and the lake below them ripples and stirs.

When I reach the shore, I unfold the blanket I've been clutching to my chest and lay it out flat across the sand. It feels like only yesterday that I was nine years old, and sitting in this very spot for the first time, my future stretching enticingly ahead of me. So much has happened since then to bring me back here, but it feels right that this is the place I keep returning to.

I hear the boat approaching before I see it, a smile of delight tugging up the corners of my mouth. I never fail to feel moved when I see what the two of us have created, our little dream, the one that started with him and grew like a sapling inside me. We have worked so hard and so tirelessly for so long, but it has all been worthwhile. Every blister caused from sanding, every nail broken, every splinter and every chunk of paint-covered hair cut out with scissors. I would do it all over again in a heartbeat.

We named her Speranza — *the Italian word for 'hope' — because in the beginning that was all we had. Hope that she would transform into Como's best and boldest floating restaurant, hope that my business plan wouldn't fail, hope that Marco and I would be able to work together without him being driven mad, and hope that everyone would fall as much in love with our beautiful boat as we had.*

She did, we do, and oh how they have.

Just last week, we hosted our tenth big wedding party of the season, and our dinner cruises are already in TripAdvisor's top ten list of things to do around Lake Como. I've learned more about social media marketing in the past year than I ever thought possible, and barely a day goes by where I don't wake up feeling impatient to get to work – a novelty that I don't imagine will wear off.

Today is our official one-year anniversary, having bought her last February and spent six months getting her ready, so Marco and I drew a line through our bulging diary of bookings and promised each other that we would celebrate. Now that I can see him coming into view, his smile wide and those mesmeric eyes bright, I feel overwhelmed with love, just as I always am. Love for him, for us, and for the life we have together.

Unable to wait for him to make it as far as the shore, I hoist up my dress, kick off my sandals, and wade out through the water towards him, admiring the flex of his arms as he fastens Speranza's ropes firmly into place.

'Ciao, bella,' he murmurs, cupping my upturned face in his hands and kissing me gently and with a tenderness that makes my knees tremble. He's grown his hair longer, and I love the way his rich, dark curls complement his eyes. I could gaze at him all night, and sometimes I do just that. I watch him in his sleep, warmed by contentment, and wonder how I ever got lucky enough to find him.

We spread our makeshift picnic out on the blanket, taking advantage of the solitude to behave even more soppily than we usually do. I feed him olives by hand and he breaks up the soft rolls that are still warm from Speranza's oven, posting the delicious doughy morsels into my mouth and chasing them down with a kiss. If Shelley was here she'd slap a hand over her eyes and tell us to 'get a room, for God's sake', but I imagine Elsie would simply cheer me on. I think, if it's possible, she and the dogs love my boyfriend even more than I do.

We've finished eating and are staring up at the stars when Marco turns to me.

'I have a surprise,' he says, looking mischievous.

'Oooh.'

Picking up the bag that contained all the food, he reaches into the bottom and extracts something large, white and flat.

'What is tha— Oh!' I cry, enchanted. 'A Chinese lantern!'

'I thought we could light it and make a wish,' he explains, folding up the sides and readying a lighter.

'Have I ever told you how much I love you?' I ask, and he kisses me again as we clamber to our feet. I take the lantern and Marco stands behind me, so tall that he can reach both arms around to light it up.

'Ready?' he asks.

I lean back against him, my heart beating hard with emotion.

'Ready.'

We let go, and the lantern soars upwards into the dark, a luminous throb of colour against the night sky, and we watch in silence as it dips and twirls, higher and higher, eventually becoming just a faint glimmer of golden light amongst the stars.

'Did you make a wish?' Marco asks, his breath hot against my ear.

'I didn't need to,' I say softly, taking his hand and moving it down until it's resting against the small but firm swell of my belly.

'My wish has already come true.'

Acknowledgements

It doesn't seem possible that I now have FOUR novels out in the world, but here it is – all shiny and beautiful and very happy to be in your hands. As always, dearest reader, my first thanks must go to you. Thank you for picking up this book and coming on this adventure with me. Please do come and chat to me about it on Twitter @Isabelle_ Broom – I'd love to hear from you.

To my agent extraordinaire Hannah Ferguson – thank you for being so wise, warm and wonderful. None of this would be happening if you hadn't taken a chance on me in the first place, and I will never ever stop being grateful. Thanks also to the amazing team at Hardman & Swainson and The Marsh Agency – you are all legends.

To my brand-new editor, Eve Hall, thank you for taking over the reins and steering me and this book so expertly over the many hurdles we encountered along the way. You always knew that this novel had the potential to be special – even when I seriously doubted it! – and you helped me more than you will ever know. I'm so excited for all the future books we'll now get to work on together. To the rest of the Penguins – Maxine, Claire, Sarah H, Maddy, Tilda, Sarah B, Emma and Jess, not to mention the epic Kimberley Atkins – you are the greatest. Thank you for every single thing you do, and for your continued support and enthusiasm.

I'm beginning to sound like a broken record when I say

that authors are the best people in the world, but they really are. There are genuinely too many of you to list here, but I do want to say a very special thanks to a few. First of all, to the Book Camp crew – aka Cesca, Katie, Cathy, Katy, Jo, Holly, Kirsty, Gemma, Emily and, of course, Barnaby – whether it was sharing wisdom over wine, sharing bubbly in the hot tub or sharing high-fives when we hit our daily word targets, you all helped me fall back in love with my craft during our week away, and I love you all for it. To Kate Eberlen, Fanny Blake, Cathy Kelly, Victoria Fox, Milly Johnson, Giovanna Fletcher, Miranda Dickinson, Gilly McAllister, Adele Parks, Tasmina Perry, Paige Toon, Rosie Walsh, Claire Frost, Cressida McLaughlin, Amy Rowland, Deirdre O'Brien, Sophie Ransom, Fran Gough, Sara-Jade Virtue, Nina Potell and all the many incredible bloggers who have taken the time to read my books, thank you for your kindness and amazing generosity.

Thanks to my nearest and weirdest (you know it's true) friends – Sadie, Ian, Tamsin, Ranjit, Gemma, Sarah, Chad, Carrie, Corrie, Jamie, Molly and Vicky Z. I'd be a far sadder and more boring person without you all in my life. Sorry for cancelling plans when I'm on deadline and going into a note-making trance after dragging you to Sri Lanka, and thank you for coming along to watch me get drunk at my launches, making me laugh pretty much daily, and being there with a sympathetic ear when I'm in need of one. Thanks to the *heat* crew, too, who have never been anything but 100 per cent supportive of my writing career – you are all totes spiffing, yah!

I must also thank my brother, Lysander, who gamely

agreed to accompany me to chilly Lake Como on a New Year fact-finding mission. If he hadn't accidentally punched me in the face and talked me into traipsing up the side of a mountain, then this book would never have gained two of its best scenes! Nobody supports me more than my family, and it's them that I look to continually for inspiration when I'm plotting. Thank you to all of you, but especially to you, Mum. I don't know how you keep loving us all so relentlessly, but I hope you know that we all love you back just as much.

Also by
Isabelle Broom

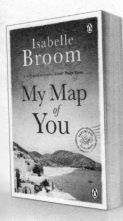

MY MAP OF YOU

Holly Wright is an expert at keeping people at a distance - including her boyfriend, Rupert. But when she is unexpectedly left a house on the Greek island of Zakynthos, the walls she has built begin to crumble.

A YEAR AND A DAY

Megan, Hope and Sophie. Three very different women. Three intertwining love stories. One unforgettable, timeless place. It's a white winter in magical Prague, the perfect place for a romantic getaway. But in this city steeped in history can you ever escape your past?

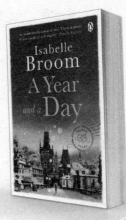

THEN. NOW. ALWAYS

Hannah and her colleagues are in Andalusia, Spain for a month to film a documentary, and it's a dream come true. Not least because Hannah will get to spend long summer days with Theo, her gorgeous boss. It couldn't be a more perfect setting to fall in love...

AVAILABLE NOW

Isabelle
Broom

Follow Izzy on

@isabellebroomauthor

Follow Izzy on

@Isabelle_Broom

Follow Izzy on

@isabelle_broom

Sign up to Izzy's newsletter!

Visit www.penguin.co.uk/authors/isabelle-broom/126001/

He just wanted a decent book to read ...

Not too much to ask, is it? It was in 1935 when Allen Lane, Managing Director of Bodley Head Publishers, stood on a platform at Exeter railway station looking for something good to read on his journey back to London. His choice was limited to popular magazines and poor-quality paperbacks – the same choice faced every day by the vast majority of readers, few of whom could afford hardbacks. Lane's disappointment and subsequent anger at the range of books generally available led him to found a company – and change the world.

'We believed in the existence in this country of a vast reading public for intelligent books at a low price, and staked everything on it'
Sir Allen Lane, 1902–1970, founder of Penguin Books

The quality paperback had arrived – and not just in bookshops. Lane was adamant that his Penguins should appear in chain stores and tobacconists, and should cost no more than a packet of cigarettes.

Reading habits (and cigarette prices) have changed since 1935, but Penguin still believes in publishing the best books for everybody to enjoy. We still believe that good design costs no more than bad design, and we still believe that quality books published passionately and responsibly make the world a better place.

So wherever you see the little bird – whether it's on a piece of prize-winning literary fiction or a celebrity autobiography, political tour de force or historical masterpiece, a serial-killer thriller, reference book, world classic or a piece of pure escapism – you can bet that it represents the very best that the genre has to offer.

Whatever you like to read – trust Penguin.